EACH MUST FACE HIS OWN NIGHT SEASON

This particular inmate didn't behave the way everybody else did; he didn't settle for merely standing with his arms at his sides, doing as little as possible to cooperate while the little spiky thing that resembled a mixture of lower intestines and pale barbed wire came spewing from between his lips. This kid was on his feet, racing around in ever narrowing circles. He was like an exhausted ice skater who knew he was losing the competition anyway and allowed himself to get careless . . .

People were staring at him the way they always watch others who have entered into the process of death: With absorption. Fascination. Crap, dying's great theatre . . .

I thought the toughest part to watch was when he started striking his head on the cement floor and went on doing it for a surprisingly long while . . .

THE
NIGHT SEASONS

J.N. Williamson

ZEBRA BOOKS
KENSINGTON PUBLISHING CORP.

For irreplaceable Mary and with thanks to Ed Gorman, James Kisner, and Michael Seidman, who also believe in me and are bold enough to share some of the same professional values; for Alan Rodgers, who believed in this project from the start; with an affectionate and proud nod to my son Eric William Welhoelter.

ZEBRA BOOKS

are published by

Kensington Publishing Corp.
475 Park Avenue South
New York, NY 10016

First printing: November, 1991

Printed in the United States of America

And I lie here warm, and I lie here dry,
And watch the worms slip by, slip by.
> —Dorothy Parker
> "Epitaph"

I'll stay here among the bacilli.
I'm no fool.
> —Dorothy Parker
> "Letter from a Goddamn Alp"

Prologue

Mind sleeps in stone, dreams in the plant, awakes in the animal, and becomes conscious in man.
— Friedrich von Schelling

What I've never been able to stand are the kind of folks who see something positively horrifying with their very own eyes and then say they "can't believe it." Usually, in those circumstances, a really terrible thing has gone wrong, just the way it did here in the jail. Or it may be something coming down that nobody in this world ever had the guts to imagine before, or even to expect.

So people like that watch a truck filled with suicidal looney tunes — right there on the ol' tube — piling ass into a U.S. Marine base and blowing a bunch of our guys away. And, even as brown and gray smoke twists up over their heads like so many snakes slithering into the sky, those folks say "I just can't *believe* it!"

Well, what they really mean is: They *won't* believe it.

And I'm almost ready to bet you won't either once you've heard this story with all the gory details intact, and even with the mess—this tragedy, this all-too-god-damn obvious human *calamity*—standing right there before your eyes.

Not that I blame you, exactly. I'd refuse to believe the story, too—if I had any choice in the matter; if I hadn't seen what one egotistical son of a bitch with a new scientific idea and no conscience could do to an institution jam-packed with people who couldn't escape even when their lives depended on it.

It reminds me a lot of my mom a thousand or so years ago and all of us watching TV the night those first two astronauts hopped bravely around on the face of the moon. I had fallen asleep in my favorite Snoopy pj's under the card table. On top of it, Mom had spread out a ton or two of varied cold cuts and Chesty potato chips and even onion dip from over at the neighborhood Kroger's. "Dip for the little dip," my big sister Karen had called it. Well, up to the second I'd conked out, I'd continually been reaching up over the edge of the card table to snatch additional fuel for the long voyage, and I got pretty wasted. I mean, for a little kid, it was late as hell. I'd stayed up almost to the middle of the night for the very first time, feeding my face, and that had been sufficient excitement for little Rich.

Then Mom yelled the name she always called me, *"Richie!"*—it came with italics and an exclamation mark—and awakened me to see the magic moment.

There were a lot of those moments back then, courtesy of the coaxial cable. Magic moments. TV was something of a miracle to folks my parents' ages, probably like voodoo to *their* parents. I was in the first generation that grew up with the tube and regarded the television set as belonging in the same category as the vacuum cleaner. We needed both of them and that was that. I guess my own favorite miracle invention, the VCR, will someday seem just about as magical to my son as a black and white TV was to me—if we all survive that which was started here at the jail.

I banged my head on the underside of the card table, reacting to Mom's shout. Then I wriggled out onto the rug and sat up expectantly and she had this *look* on her face. One I had seen often and would see again as I grew up.

"You do know," she stated to her audience, "that this is all a show." Her gaze defiantly swept the room and settled on my face. "It was staged somewhere on the Hollywood back lots."

The news came as a surprise to me, so I ate more potato chips. Some onion dip dripped on the carpet, but no one noticed. Karen didn't do or say anything. Our father turned his head carefully in *his* father's direction. Pop's eyes were open maybe a sixteenth of an inch wider than usual, and I do remember that his mustache twitched.

Grandpa Franklin shook his enormous, sparsely-covered head, then caught my own surprised eyes with a broad, man-to-man wink. "Really?" he asked Mom. Then the realization came to me that he'd actually been on the planet Earth a very much longer while than either my parents, or the two spacemen on the moon, and that what was going on that night probably meant even more to him than it did to the astronauts. But in a different way.

Grandpa's "Really?" egged my mother on. She got

those flaming-red splotches high on her round cheeks and had to gulp down the chips in her mouth so quickly it made her lovely, luminescent eyes water. "Obviously," she informed her father-in-law, "this is more pap for the masses nursing at the public tit."

I risked a glance and a fast smirk at Karen. But she didn't dare give me a return grin even though Mom had used one of the words we weren't allowed to utter.

"It's to keep our minds off the *secret things* going on," Mom continued. She was doing her best to keep one foot planted in a century that was ending thirty years early. She lowered her head to me, partly to check out any possibility that Grandpa was somehow continuing to "warp" his grandson—whatever Mom meant by that—and said firmly, "Richie, you must not believe any of the nonsense you ever see on that screen." Her shoulders fluttered just the way her eyelids always did. "It's . . . it's all bread and circuses." Intrigue flashed in the gaze she swept over her menfolk. "It's to prevent us from learning what *really* goes on, nowadays."

I didn't know what she meant, but I hated being yelled at, so I nodded. And listened to Pop, Grandpa Franklin, and even Karen—once she saw that others were on her side—who were trying goodhumoredly to tease Mom into accepting a chunk of new reality. Fact.

They might as well have saved their breath. It didn't do any good, and I could have told them that, even then.

Actually, Mom was so persuasive and so stubborn about continuing to live in our good, old 20th century that she succeeded in convincing *me* . . . For awhile, at least. Because it sort-of seemed to my juvenile eyes that everybody else in the family, the neighborhood, on the planet Earth, and even on worlds that moonward star-seekers never dreamed of, were aligned against her . . . and I didn't care much for that. It was only what Mom wanted me to believe, sure, but back then I figured mothers were always right. Due to the sheer importance of their roles in life, that is. I wasn't old enough to dope it out that they have many roles, and sometimes might be wrong in one of the realms of unmomlike concerns.

See, my mom invented the concept that conspiracies explain every single weird, inexplicable thing that's happened. And when people who think like Mom don't positively have to accept what they see with their own eyes, they won't.

So it was the reality of that understanding that became one of the few explanations I could cling to when hell seemed literally to break loose in the jail. When folks, not as different from my mother as they might liked to have believed, began dying. Zapped. Destroyed.

I'd have done anything within my power just to stay halfway rational while all the inmates were dying. And I recalled that Mom's idea of two men taking giant steps for mankind being a *conspiracy* had simply been her personal P. S. to President Kennedy's ambush killing in Dallas a few years earlier. Mom had been certain "they" wanted him out of the way — sure about it from practically the instant "they" shot his head to pieces; sure in a fashion that broached no doubt and didn't even seek explanations.

Now I know this theory of Mom's sprang from her

11

inability to come to grips with the notion of our country's president being shot down like a dog in one of its big cities, by a man who wasn't the least bit more imposing than a neighbor, or Dad. Neither of my parents had ever gone to Dallas or any part of Texas, neither one of them knew a thing about political climates or wackos who cared more about blowing out the brains of a complete stranger than they cared about their own families or themselves. So even when lumpy Jack Ruby offed the nerd Oswald, right on goddamn network television, all that meant to Mom was that her instant reaction had just been verified. It seems Oswald "had to be silenced" and that the whole unpalatable sequence of events was not to be believed the way it had been presented or even, for that matter, the way it was perceived by one's own eyes!

If the whole Kennedy tragedy were merely Hollywood, if it *wasn't* believed, then one's horrified focus could blur, shift, then *re*focus on the possibility of conspiracy. Of secrets.

Then Hollywood produced the first, the great moon walk—as a boost to United States PR or something—and Mom started fretting that "they" might be coming for her, too. The fear wasn't constant, it didn't preoccupy all her thoughts; but the fear was there. *They* were coming because she'd been stubborn about "refusing to be sold a bill of goods," and she'd never been hesitant to express her views "like every American has the right to."

Well, I didn't know what to think, as a boy or later. Since moms don't lie, and mine died in her sleep one stark and unforgivably stunning winter's night with absolutely no goddamn warning, without *any* major illness or even a hint that she was sick, I had to wonder about everything she'd told Karen and me.

For a while, at least.

What's the point of this? Frankly I do not see the general public as being a hell of a lot more inclined than Mom once was to accept obvious facts in an incredible situation. And I'm not overjoyed to be interviewed, in depth or in any other fucking way, by TV and newspaper people. Sorry about that, but I was compelled to explain things to the authorities; I'm not compelled to explain them to the press. I'm a literate lush, the kind who says too much—okay? But from everything I've read in the press, the sort of people I have been *trying* to describe for you aren't exactly anxious to accept the word of a drunk! Or to think of the tragedy that occurred here as ranking up there with Chernobyl.

Look, I don't kid myself. If it wasn't for the sheer number of human beings that died here, and the mystery behind it, this story wouldn't see print! It wouldn't be *mentioned*, even once, on network television! And some unknown bird like me, a would-be writer working as a goddamn custodian, would be the last person you'd bust your collective buns to interview. If there was any other option. If anybody else who'd been directly on the scene was still alive to explain . . .

Yes, I'm getting to it—but *my* way. What you can tell your viewers or readers upfront is that this place *wasn't a prison*. Got that? It was a *jail*. Same kind you'd see in any city or town. So don't make it sound as if all the guys who died in this nightmare were Ted Bundy or Diane Downs, all right? Bear in mind that many of us

13

were just awaiting an appearance before the judge. Some of us hadn't been found guilty of a fucking thing and would've been set free. Remember that there's a presumption of innocence for every American, as my mother would have reminded you. Even drunks.

Try to understand. The reason I can't just lay it all out for you — begin by directly describing the individual atrocities that happened here — is because you would either imagine I was behaving like Mom or you'd *over-stress* the ghastly deaths and what all the corpses *look* like, now. You'd find your senses were so overloaded, so swamped by horror, that you'd forget to seek out the *reasons* behind it.

And then that damn monster who caused everything might well go down in history as some sort of fucking misunderstood scientific savior!

I know you don't think that could happen — but if you ever see the coroner's photos of those bloated bodies, their faces swollen with growths worse than the Elephant Man's, you would lose complete sight of the truth about that evil son of a bitch. And about the lost humanity. Folks, *whatever* you think now, you'd just wind up focusing on the gross-outs. That's the way we are. Trust me.

So, it's up to me. Maybe I won't be able to stand it, but I have to try. To live it again in detail. Just like it went down and from my viewpoint . . . knowing most of you can't believe it. Or won't. I have to persuade *some* media types to accept what is entirely unacceptable according to all you have learned in your lifetimes. Because it *isn't me* who will convince some human, *caring* scientists, wearing gas masks and protective suits, to go

14

find the inmates who were released before this happened. *You* have to shout out the news that they're infected — *you* have to become the voices of the dead.

And if I don't do my job and you don't do yours, there's no way on God's green earth anybody can calculate how far this thing will spread.

Now: I was talking of how some folks "can't believe" things that are too hideous or seem impossible — things that can not be anticipated. Right? Okay. I know for a fact that most of us expect the bomb to annihilate everyone someday; in a weird, crazy way, we accept that. If anything must wipe us out, that is how humanity is expected to go. Am I right?

We may all be wrong.

As of the past few weeks, I'm afraid there's another way.

Part One

The Century That Ended Early

Slow's the blood that was quick and stormy,
  Smooth and cold is the bridal bed;

I must wait 'til he whistles for me—
  Proud young Death would not turn his head.

—Dorothy Parker
"The Trifler"

One

1. Rich

The best place to begin the story, probably, is by saying that I got into this awful orgy of death because, very honestly, I've always been able to put away more Budweiser beer and sit up nice and straight doing it than almost anyone else I've ever met.

But I was cold-ass sober, straight as a goddamn arrow, every hour I spent in jail this time, and I'm *not* shooting the bull. Jesus knows I haven't been *that* freaking sober since I was twelve years old, maybe. So at no time are you going to hear my friend Bud speaking instead of Rich Stenvall. Considering the precious little time any of us may have left for me to disseminate the news, I am deeply and truly concerned that those missing inmates be rounded up, quarantined in their homes, and properly examined. I've already passed a couple of psychological tests, but this story simply *won't* be credible to you unless you know me and the details.

God, having a hollow leg is some wonderful claim to fame, isn't it? Well, I wish there could be a more dignified beginning of this for Ronnie's sake, and the kids'—but the truth of the matter seems to be that I am the sole survivor of the county jail disaster because of some ridiculous immunity I've built up over the years with booze. And the only part of it that seems any good at all is that it's about time keeping Bud in business did something for *me* instead of *to* me!

But by the same token, you'll need to accept it as the truth that there's more to Rich Stenvall than being a goddamn alky. Otherwise, there's a very scary possibility that you'll chalk up what I have to tell you to hallucination.

And the truth is, nothing I saw happen could ever be part of *any* man's D.T.s . . .

Presumably, Andre felt those growths coming out the moment they began to force their way through the mass of his big, bulky brown body like a gang plundering a tenement building. He had thrown his massive arms out from his body as far as they'd go, and now—afoot, part great scarecrow and part black Christ—he was evidently hypnotized by the sight of what was squeezing *from his enlarged pores and from the needle tracks running like some weird coded message from his broad shoulders to his wrists.*

What was happening to his ears, poor Andre didn't seem to notice just then. Maybe, what with everything else devouring the man and then pursuing the rest of us, Andre just didn't care. But he managed to turn his head toward me, and that was when—

20

But let's back up a bit and begin with my wife—my second wife, Veronica—for openers. And our two children. Let's leap to the fact that it was pretty damn good for us for awhile. At least, now and then. Till that goddamned heat wave began. The one that made it possible for the germination to start.

Specifically, it was the second of June. Yeah, I know the exact date. Not a lot of time has passed after all. As the calendar flies, anyway; it's been plenty for me. See, June second was when the season and the temperature changed, overnight. Doesn't that generally occur in a great portion of the contiguous United States? (Christ, I love words that say *exactly* what you mean—because they're the only really reliable things now.)

We'd been having drizzling and often freezing rain of late; the nip in the air seemed to chill everyone down to his privates, and the only sign of spring anybody had seen was a shivering robin with a befuddled expression.

Markie, our youngest, put it best, and with a straight face. He's four and has no other expression under full control yet, you see. "Mr. Robin musn't have no calendar where he lives," the boy opined about the cold weather that had been hanging on. Apropos of nothing, I'll mention that Markie has trouble with his G's. About a year ago he took a swig of purple, watery Kool Aid, wiped his mouth on his shirttail—that drove Ronnie nuts—and murmured contentedly, "Rape makes me happy." Since

21

then, Ron has been watching ol' Markie like a hawk.

It'd been so chilly lately that I was wearing a pajama top and sweat pants to bed only the night before Hell came to the surface. The complex furnace was doing its sell-out best to keep the gas company thrilled about its progress with the annual consumer gangbang, and I had trouble falling asleep. When I did, I was shivering.

Then I was awakened abruptly with mucho sweat and the slippery traces of a lousy nightmare pouring over me as though I'd fallen asleep in the shower (which I have done a few odd and decidedly moist times in ye olde past).

But nothing stronger than ginger ale had passed my dry mouth in a few weeks and that onslaught of the first combination of peculiarities frankly disturbed the shit out of me.

Feeling weird and glancing around the room's near darkness, I saw that my wife had kicked the blankets down and off the foot of the bed, and a voyeuristic impulse seized me for a few seconds. Ronnie was lying on her back, and the way her nightie was pasted to her body suggested an interesting sort of face. It was kind of popeyed considering the way her small nipples rose from the sockets of her flattened breasts; tiny-nosed, due to the navel. Above the tightly-curled beard, a smile-face existed as a consequence of stretch marks and wrinkles — after all, it was a thirty-three-year-old mother's tummy.

Six years ago, seeing Ronnie that way would have

me horny as a goat. My wife may no longer be the most gorgeous woman in the galaxy—and maybe she never really was—yet I love her to pieces. She turns me on. But half a brewery had been gulped down my throat during the years *before* Ronnie and I had met, and beer busting is *ball*-busting. That's a fact.

So, as a consequence of that, and the way I burned to take a whiz, and the way the sweat suit pants were stuck to my ass—and even the way I was distracted by how goddamn *hot* and *humid* it had suddenly become on that new June morning—I didn't rise to the occasion. Ol' Sleeping Bear of Grouchiness, as Ronnie and her seven-year-old daughter Bett sometimes like calling me, stayed put. I lay there sensing how crummy and putrid every-thing—or *I*—was and tried to think of some new way of making it—or *me*—better. My eyes browsed through the bedroom of our familiar apartment like someone shopping for a fresh vision of a stale life.

I gazed at the clutter of work clothes I'd be wear-ing that day, left atop my dresser; then I looked at Ronnie's old high school vanity table—the one with the leg I'd partly repaired before wandering off in quest of refreshment. Its surface was stocked by sil-very tubes of mysterious female crap, cosmetic bot-tles, heady sweet-smelling powder boxes aggressively restating their promise that Ronnie would remain forever youthful. It always wiped me out how those dusty, oval boxes and the exquisite French-style tiny bottles appeared to gather up Ronnie's very own dis-tinctive, personal scents and save them for her to ap-

23

ply all over again the next morning. For me to inhale and enjoy.

In some ways, I see now, I was a lucky guy. Before everything became real.

You understand irony? It's *now* that I can see and
understand that. Now . . .

*He was on his feet and racing around in ever narrowing
circles. He was like an exhausted ice skater who knew he
was losing the competition anyway and allowed himself to
get careless. People were staring at him the way they always
watch others who have entered into the process of death:
With absorption. Fascination. Crap, dying's great theatre.
This kind of death, shown on the tube with solid advance
promos, would wean every little Neilsen family from either
soaps or supper.*

*When watching the dying in person, of course, it's not
regarded as good form to enjoy it too openly — the way our
bunch of onlookers were gazing at the kid.*

*I was taught a lesson in the different kinds of pain, and
the way they strike people. This particular inmate didn't behave the way everybody else did; he didn't settle for standing
quietly, arms at his sides, doing as little as possible in order
to cooperate while the little spiky thing that resembled a mixture of lower intestines and pale barbed wire came spewing
from between his lips. This time, whatever the substance
was, it was apparently razor sharp or prickly enough to tear
the lips and make them bleed. Then when it came out bigger,
it was all a moot point. Because the growth spread, then
split the corners of the kid's mouth like a birthing monstrosity.*

I thought the toughest part to watch was when he started

24

striking his head on the cement floor and went on doing it for a surprisingly long while.

On Ronnie's dresser top there wasn't a damned thing. Not after six years of marriage. I groaned inside with that old, guilty, castrating feeling because I knew for a fact that inside the dresser there was precious little as well. And I lay there thinking how my wife was definitely entitled to expensive, imported lingerie, and how she would look so damn *great* in it! Beer isn't the only ball-buster. Poverty is right up there, too.

I gazed elsewhere, saw my smokes, a Bic lighter that was part of a two-for-a-dollar sale at Osco, and an ashtray with the imprint of some bar concealed beneath the burnt ash. On my bedside stand were paperback copies of a western called *Powell's Army,* Martin James' *Zombie House* and an Ed Gorman mystery, an issue of *Science Digest* that was several years old—I knew, because it was once a nine-by-twelve mag full of beautiful illos and it wasn't any more—and a last-month's issue of *Writer's Digest,* which I had never finished reading and never would. On the wall above them was a three-by-five framed snapshot of my mother. Her huge brown eyes seemed to follow me wherever I went like the eyes in that old painting of Jesus she once had. (I think Karen owns it now, I'm not really sure.) I recalled that Mom's photo had been taken a year after her discovery of NASA's relatively insidious space plot and about three years before our family doctor—the only man Mom had ever fully trusted—failed to detect

25

either her bad ticker or the Big C. We swear allegiance to euphemisms, I thought, in the United States of America; and to the conspiracies for which—I blinked and focused on my functionally colorless G.E. windup alarm fairly bursting with passion to raise either the dead, or the Sleeping Bear of Grouchiness. But it was short of its appointed hour and so, by God, was I.

I felt strange, fucking odd. Off my feed. While it wasn't caused by drinking, I recall thinking that while women sometimes have piercing premenstrual cramps, alkies suffer from *pre*-hangover spasms. I was honest-to-God sober and stuck with figuring out what was wrong—with divining any omens and portents for clear prophesy of Ugly Things to Come.

Then I recognized the signals going off all over my nervous system like fat little turds studded with sticks of dynamite and dipped in neon. Recognized, and knew 'em well! Because they were the exact, same, mean mothers I had never found the courage to come to grips with, and the same ones that'd screwed up the majority of my thirty-five years of life—with the exception of the bright, sequined snatches of moments Ronnie and the children had glued together for me to make maybe one full year of respectable human existence.

God, I wanted a drink then *so badly!*

Automatically I glanced at my sleeping wife, now turned on her side, and wondered if she dreamt any more at all. Or if she was pretending to sleep, and maybe hoping to God Almighty she might drift off

26

again and remember how to dream . . .

2. Ronnie

Why does he keep staring at me that way?

Do men really enjoy getting all worked up, even when they know nothing's going to happen? Mother told me once it's a compliment, sort of, being stared at. I think it depends on what it is they want and what it is they mean to do with it. Not that Richard ever wanted anything terrible, ever wanted to hurt me. From him, it's probably a compliment.

Sometimes I think I could tolerate anything the world can possibly hurl at me except anything happening to Markie, Bett, or Rich. And other times I think I could handle something happening to Rich if it happened when he was starting to drink again, sneaking his booze like he was a common alcoholic. I mean, if he had to have a bad coronary at just that instant, and he was still sober as they rested him carefully on a hospital stretcher, I think I could cope with that. Because he wouldn't be embarrassing me and the kids, and he'd come home to me sober, too—and be flat on his back for awhile, and I'd absolutely kill anyone who tried to smuggle him so much as a single Bud Lite! I'd nurse him back to health, and he would be so grateful for that and for having been sober so long that he'd never pop open even one can of beer.

Then there are times I could stand it if a heart attack just . . . took him away, without any ambulance, before he lifted the can to his mouth. Not that I'd know the moment, of course, not that anyone would even know he was drinking until Bett or Markie or I found his body. Alive or dead.

But the strangers with the stretchers, they'd find out; and I don't think I could tolerate the sight of even one more blank-faced polite uniformed man averting his eyes or looking sympathetically at my children while they did what they had to do with my husband. I mean, if I even saw Rich talking to a soldier or sailor, I know I'd feel the freezing-up inside again—along with the shame.

Again he's looking at me. Oh, I know I'm just awful for being this way. And for being a hypocrite. Because I'm not what Rich thinks I am. Back when Pete and I were married and even for awhile after that, I drank like a fish. Why, I've done things I couldn't tell Richie about, even if I lived to be a thousand years old—bad stuff that makes me sick, especially when I think about Markie and Bett growing up. I mean, I have a really good *husband now. A husband who deserves a wife who can get him truly better someday, one who excites him the way he likes to be excited, one who brings out the best of his writing and everything. A real, good,* helpmate.

But I'm me. Me, knowing the time might come this spring or summer when my Richard needs so damn much more than I can possibly give him. I know he feels there's something awful going on around us, but I lie to him when he asks if I feel it too; otherwise, he'd be getting those crazy ideas and start trying to solve everybody's problems.

I think I could tolerate anything the world could throw at me except anything bad happening to Rich or to the kids. To my family. I don't know why, but I think something is *going to happen. Any day now. And I mustn't let him know I feel that way too.*

28

3. Rich

Those signals going off in my head — collectively, they were Rich Stenvall's "dis-ease." That's the way I learned to think of it, anyway, as a "dis-ease." Not that I was the only dumb S.O.B. who ever suffered from that particular ailment. I can't believe that. Besides, in other times, they were called premonitions. They were like little personal omens, historically, and I think they mostly visited old ladies and your basic oddball monk who'd spent too much time in dank monasteries and suffered dry-rot of the brain.

I read up on them years ago when I was still trying to get through college. Which was when they began, by the way, usually when I was trying to really *listen* to some droning professor. My temples would begin to spasm and the dis-ease would kick in seconds after that. The books I researched said that folks were dreaming when they had premonitions, but I questioned that simply because I've always been conscious when they started. Experts of old also claimed that these omens came from post-hypnotic suggestion and sometimes as a product of auto-suggestion — meaning, I guess, people *tried* to bring them into the conscious mind or out of the ether, people who actually *wanted* some clue about the future.

Drunks very seldom have much interest in learning what lies ahead for them or their families and friends. Believe me.

The experts also said that a lot of premonitions were nothing more than vague forebodings and a combination of coincidence and imagination made the payoff of a dream *appear* to be real. Well, my vague forebodings had never paid off at all because I never followed through with them. You see, it's partly mental and partly physical. It comes with odd pulsations, it comes in waves. In the past, I was fool enough to believe I didn't want to do anything but block it out with booze. So, pretty soon the arrival of these eerie waves meant that I was within one cross look or lousy memory of going off on another toot! *That's* the part of it that became a self-fulfilling prophecy for *me!*

Early one morning, after I'd been suspended from school, it came to me like lightning that the dis-ease was something inside me announcing that dreadful things were about to occur, and that I was *needed*. Now I'm pretty sure that most real alcoholics arrive in the same state or condition due to some chemical readjustments, and that running with the ball—figuring out what we're picking up through premonition—could mean we're the fundamentally kind and worthwhile people we usually seem to be when we're sober.

Shit, I *knew* you'd all do that! Jesus, I *knew* you'd smirk and grin! Turn your ignorant faces and pretend you're hiding your real reactions.

And that's one of the main reasons I couldn't find the balls to do anything about the early warnings for so long: I didn't want to watch a bunch of people who wouldn't know an omen from an oven look at me like I'm fucking crazy! Well, there was a time when I'd been holding down a bunch of white collar jobs—trying to be something I was not—and I reached the conclusion that my dis-ease is very similar to two *other* phenomena no one on earth truly understands to this day: The enormous, kick-in-the-pants feeling you have when brilliant, creative ideas are bubbling up inside until you think you might literally burst if you don't *act* on them; and the internal vibes that a genuine psychic has all the time.

For guys like me, who haven't done a fucking thing with either the signals coming in *or* the urge to create, your goddamn overstressed nerves have this gigantic need to sing sweet harmony—but you don't know how. Maybe your nerves can't read the music. But it keeps getting louder, and louder, until you simply don't have any choice but to escape.

Some make out. Or have the dough to go on vacation. But for a lot of individuals like me, it just means trying to *squeeeeze* our trembly bodies inside a can or bottle until we fucking ferment! And that, overstressed media types of the world, that is when one's dis-ease echoes mockingly up from the reeking bottom of the bottle: "Rich, you ignorant sumbitch—you silly flop of a useless scumbag—you blew the big chance to be a hero all over again!"

That's what we're after, you know—the psychics who warn presidents to stay away from cities, the people who create music, the ones who yearn to start trends in art, even some of the people who teach. To be heroes. Because all of us — even most of the alkies like Rich Stenvall — are linked up with time and can't get free of it, even while we sense it's phony — there's a way to get *on top* of every wasted hour and day and year. Even while we're certain there's a way to prove we're important, the way God meant for us to be, by helping *other* people, and finally seizing *control* of our own destinies!

Well, at that nanosecond when it's too late again, I become completely aware that I could have written a smash best seller, one that would *enlighten* humankind. Or painted the next Mona Lisa, created a hot Broadway musical, or clairvoyantly identified the latest crazed serial killer on the West Coast — except that I didn't listen, I chickened out one more time, I got *bombed* again.

Okay, dammit, okay. Here's one of those hairy facts you've been waiting for: Never once did I pay any close attention to that early warning system that God or nature (or maybe my late mother's upbringing) kept piping into my scrambled brain — not until the night of that hot and sticky, utterly pivotal day in early June. And by then it was too late for me to do anything that might possibly have helped God knows how many of my fellow human beings.

4. Crock

It got hot as hell during the middle of that night so Crock got out of bed and headed straight for the bus station to conduct some business. The kind of business he conducted could be done at any hour of the day or night, but kids who arrived in town in the late night hours would more likely prove to be vulnerable — especially if there was nobody else there to meet them.

Within ten minutes after Crock got there he saw her, entering the station like someone walking on glass. She had her hair all frizzed up the way she figured it should be for a teenager running off from home, and it reminded me of something torn from a jagged corner of the sun. Her cheap drugstore bag was pressed to her chest as if it might protect her. Under that, cut-off jeans made her seem, at a glance, naked from the waist down. Crock took that glance and headed for her, exercising those long-lashed eyes of his and commanding those thin, barracuda lips to turn up at the corners. The smile that never let him down.

I knew that the little blond gave Crock the impression she still had hayseed in her underwear and that inside the flat red purse tucked under her elbow he sensed a wallet with a high school logo stamped under the snap; and inside the wallet would be a snapshot of two smiling, middle-aged people called something like Ed, or Ned, and Eunice Marie — and he believed that the blond was destined to weep tears all over the images of her abandoned parents. Just like she was someday destined to return home in torment and shame.

And Crock grooved on, lived on, all that stuff. If someone came loose from the family moorings and had any value at all in the marketplace, Crock collected and called that person his own. Because he knew just how to market them for

33

the highest possible profit. His.

Now he didn't notice Bud or me. Every night for eight or nine days, we'd waited for Crock over by the lockers in the bus station because we knew the bastard would be coming back. We had busted most of the talent in his stable—girls and boys—and ol' Crockie had to be hurting. Besides, the son of a bitch was a business type; he put in the time and didn't mess around much with anything else. He was so dedicated he didn't even see Bud in his tanktop and jeans or me in my dirty-old-man coat at all. We were working hard to give the impression that a minor drug deal was going down, our usual act because of the kind of town it is and the fact that Bud is white. Nobody gave a fuck about that except for the dudes who tried to horn in, and score.

I'd already thought a lot about what made Crock tick, and I've given a lot more thought to it since that night, and what happened at county lockup. Studying a cat like Crock can be fascinating as hell. Like studying herpetology. I know he hated his name his entire life. I think he learned to hate all women and become a successful pimp partly to punish himself for that. The hate. A hooker who knew him pretty well told me Crock's biggest secret was that he regarded himself as a man with extremely high standards, even real scruples—a code he lived by.

According to our informant, Crock described "no-goods" as people who did whatever they felt like doing. Since Crock detested women, he figured that he rarely did what he wanted to do at all! Just yesterday Bud pointed out to me that Crock had "a quantitative outlook on good and bad." Meaning, I guess, that he judged a man—never a woman, because they were automatically evil to him—by how often

34

he indulged in pleasuring himself. Logically, then, he also judged them by how often men forced themselves to do what they hated. Follow this closely now: Since Crock kidnaped, hit on, raped, hooked, generally tortured, and sold a woman at least once every day of his life, and he hated every minute of it, he was therefore punishing himself for hating his old lady . . . So in Crock's weird brain, he was always on the road doing well, being good! He was under control, he was disciplining himself. If a woman liked it, that pissed him off so much he'd force her to make it with the worst damn scuzzballs he could find. I think his ladies must have wished he'd found another way to work off his guilt.

I wanted, of course, to tell Bud that was so much psychological horseshit. But I remembered the other times we busted the son of a bitch and one occasion especially when he told me to be careful how I put the cuffs on him, that it didn't hurt to be gentle when arresting a gentleman! At first, I laughed in his horsey face with its soft, feminine eyes, and then I realized he meant it. The most sadistic pimp in the city — the one every cop in vice knew but couldn't legally prove had killed at least two of his women because they held out on him — thought of himself as sensitive. Sweet. A real pussycat!

I remember what big, rangy ol' Crock said the night we busted him for the last time: "You really think you're punishing me, right?" I didn't know how to answer that. The truth, of course, was that I sure as shit meant to punish the bastard. Crock saw my expression, and that was when he laughed at me, out loud!

We didn't approach Crock till he was through charming the little blond, batting his long lashes and feeding her his highly effective line. I'm aware now that Crock preferred to hit on teenagers who were both young and maybe virgins. He especially went for long, skinny flanks, no ass to mention—if you get my drift—girls who hadn't yet matured and still had boyish *figures. I don't mean that they were necessarily Crockie's preference for sex, but he wanted chicks who looked like they'd be . . . easier for him. A drag queen named Lester Piercey who we rounded up now and then claimed that "Mr. Crock," really craved an athletic black man named Andre. So Lester imagined, anyway. And Crock had threatened to kill soft little Lester, then cram his dick down his own throat if Lester told anybody on the street. Go figure. Whatever "Mr. Crock's" scruples and ideals actually were, it must've been difficult maintaining them where he hung out. Where society really sucks.*

When pretty, blond Officer Randles gave us the high sign, we sidled up on either side of Crock. Randles told us that he managed to find out she was fresh off the farm, with cherry, and he was already offering to show her around after about three fast questions. He would have "shown her around" to a sleazy motel where a lady who worked for him would have "taken care of her"—meaning, Bud and I knew, turning Randles on to heroin. But she wouldn't have met the "nice lady" until Crock had broken her in—and down.

The moment I stuck my service automatic against his right temple, Crock understood that he wasn't going to be doing what he hated and get to punish himself further. He nearly grinned.

"Well, nice bust, boys," Crock said right before he asked if we thought we were punishing him. "I always admire a good, clean collar."

Bud answered. "You aren't going to like it so much down-town, Crock." I remember the pimp glanced at me when I cuffed him — with a more careful touch than in the past. "You're not going to be back on the streets quite as fast this time."

Then Crock made his remark to me, and laughed in my face, and even gave Officer Randles a wink as we took him out to the curb. "Every now and then, Brownie, we should all have a chance to do what we like best." The way he said it chilled me more than anything else Crock had ever said to me. I almost suggested we let the prick go.

Two

1. Rich

I was up and around and living life, going through the motions, without surprise and without any road blocks. That's the way life is. You can have all the hunches and omens you want, but you can never quite dope out the exact *moment* when the weird shit starts to happen.

Old Mrs. Silverberg, she went out to the front of the apartment building, spread out a blanket, and lay there in the blazing sun from 9:05 A.M. in the morning until 3:00 P.M. *sharp* in the afternoon. I was concerned about her and checked on her every now and then until she stood up precisely as the big hand on my watch clicked straight up with the little hand on three.

The thing is, I'd seen Mrs. Silverberg around the building for over two years and never once had she tried to coax a tan onto her funny, fleshy little bod. What's more, the lady generally wore clothing even older than her age properly demanded, and now she had on this skimpy striped bikini. When I'd tried to point out to her that she was probably getting too much sun, old Mrs. Silverberg told me to go get screwed! Sometimes you can't even tell when the exact moment of change begins.

Zeb Hannah worked nights. I didn't know what he did, but I figured he hated his job, or maybe the hours. Hannah was one of those smirking ex-southern guys—if there's such a thing as "ex-southern" anything—who went on looking twenty-eight years old until he turned sixty and got tight-faced and sort of crisp looking. Earl Washington was on welfare, he was black, not really young anymore, and I believe he would've loved to have a good job. So I was in apartment 218, working on the McCoys' air conditioner, and I heard Earl and Zeb—privately, I thought of the southerner as "Hard Hearted Hannah" because his nocturnal hours might mean he's a *vamp* from Savannah or somewhere—talking in the hallway. *More trouble,* I thought, and I peeked out of 218 to see what was happening.

The white guy was just getting home from work. He was tired, and he mentioned that he heard on the television that this might have been the hottest day in June, locally, since 1939. Earl's graying chin went up, and *he* said he heard on the radio that it was merely the hottest June *second* since then. Only

40

it was '33, not 1939. *Oh, shit,* I thought. But Zeb Hannah paused to reflect for a second and then he nodded, "You're right." *Agreeing* with the black Earl Washington! "That *is* what they said, isn't it?" Then Washington wished Hannah a good day. A *miracle!*

Around 11:00 A.M. — out on the sidewalk, right in front of aging Mrs. Silverberg — two dogs got it on. Immediately I considered going to get a hose, you know? There must have been another six or eight male dogs watching the first two, stiff-legged as hell, bouncing up and down in place. Eager to rip off a piece for themselves, if you follow me. But when the fortunate mutt who was first got through, all eight or nine pooches merely trotted amiably up the street — including the female! They wagged their tails and made those muttery-growly sounds that pass for canine conversation. And Mrs. S. — who up until that morning reminded me of a Jewish Mother Teresa — didn't utter a word of complaint, or even bat an eye!

The strange stuff kept up as the hours passed. Around a quarter to five when working guys began to get home, I was over in C building putting new bulbs in the third floor fixtures when this Karl Ryder, age twenty-something, got into a terrific fight with his wife at the door of their apartment. Well, Stephanie — Ryder usually called her "Stef," but he called her other things that night — was one of those young wives who liked wearing next to

41

nothing around her apartment. She was also fucking gorgeous. Once, I had to repair the thermostat in her place during a cold winter day, and Mrs. Ryder had nothing on but panties. But Stef, she just crossed her arms over her fine young titties and said, "Oh, it's *you*, Rich," then let me right inside!

Now, Karl, her husband, absolutely adored that girl. He sent her greeting cards for every conceivable occasion—from Thinking of You At 10:30 Today to Thanks For Giving Me Head Last Night—he brought her flowers on the frigging Fourth of July, and like that. So I was positively frozen in place on that steaming June second when Karl was inside his apartment maybe three minutes, and the door was standing wide open, and he hauled off and *belted* his precious naked little Stef right in the chops! I made a move to defend her, but *Mrs*. Karl Ryder slammed the door in my face. Two seconds later I heard unmistakable sounds indicating that they were making up. And out!

So all day long there were these signs that supported my gut feeling that something bad was going to happen, either in town generally or at the complex or—

I am sure you can tell that, like many longtime, grave-serious drinkers, I'm a guy with many theories. Maybe if I'd taken the right courses in college and actually graduated, you would be calling me a philosopher. But I suppose the best I can hope is that you will regard me as a man with many ideas. Ideas that might somehow explain what happened in the jail. The truth is that whether I had gotten drunk that strange and extremely humid night or not, Noble Ellair's goddamned good-will gifts were *already* distributed and ready to germinate — and all those poor people would have died whether I was locked up among them, or not.

However, it was just as true that my dis-ease, my early warning system, was triggered on that second day of June to give me a clear but terrible choice. I could either attempt to figure out what was going on and try to convince others who shared my special sensitivity to furnish feedback and possibly move to some higher internal level of human perception; or I could get drunk, arrested, and stand by helplessly while people no better or worse than I died quite horribly.

Society, you see doesn't put out a friendly hand toward "strangers" — folks we haven't met yet, that's *all* strangers *are!* We're told that we are a nation under God, that we are caring, curious, compassionate, that we're *eager* to take chances in order to create peace or true progress in the world. We're supposed to welcome new ideas. We're *supposed* to be *modern*. Yet if it's a matter nobody has had the common sense or the guts to recognize, test, collect expert opinion on, or even to imagine, we really can't believe it, we sure as shit don't accept it, and we really can't be bothered.

Sure, shift around in your chair, wait with tremendous GODDAMN IMPATIENCE for me to get to the gore, the dying, the messed-up bodies with the fungus growing out of their pores! But this is all part of the wider story, and you're going to hear it.

Without even hinting about it to anybody but Ronnie, I believed for years that the major events of my life—the best and the worst things alike—should somehow be sensed by many others. Just as I *should* know it whenever life truly turned shitty or wonderful in the lives of others. I took Shakespeare's idea of people-as-actors-on-a-great-stage seriously, and thought that we really *were* immersed in "life" together—not merely isolated and non-feeling machines with arms and legs and genitals. For me, it wasn't quite that highfalutin' Eastern notion that *all* human beings are one, but more that *many* of us *could be*.

And if a potbellied, beer-guzzling flop of a man felt that way, I told myself, surely the Quality People knew and also *practiced* it. I mean, you didn't have to watch the Evening News report on Hurricane Flatulent or read about an earthquake ripping up churches to "sense" that human beings were hurting—and that, when it got *really* bad, nature furnished us with obvious signs that reminded us we were immersed in life together, and that we should turn to one another with real caring and a healthy respect for the God who made the whole, weird batch of us!

What signs? *What* signs? Shit like rain falling in certain areas for record numbers of days, and drought burning up crops. Knee-deep snowdrifts where there was generally sunshine. Basically unexplainable shifts of temperature, the crap about the ozone layer and greenhouse effect. Haunted, hollow looks in the eyes of little bitty children left alone too much, and their tense mothers trying to fit into a world that has new expectations of them. Man, *you* saw statistics about a rise in suicide among teenagers, and *everybody* during holiday seasons—about kids under four feet in height making two-thousand bucks a week selling dope to other kids. Wasn't that a sign of anything to you? Didn't it dawn on you that there was no guarantee that you or your people were going to be left out?

And how did I sense that it was all part of the *same* picture, even before the tragedies in the jail began? I sensed it faster because I'm a drunk. Hell, everyone knows that a man at the neighborhood bar who is drinking slow and steady never met a *stranger,* right? Why, whoever plunks his ass down on the next stool is his pal, his good buddy. Even if you fight him, you *know* him! The question is why a guy has to get drunk to be able to understand all of this . . .

Anyway, small and bizarre things went on hap-

45

pening all day. And each one filled me to the brim with panic and made the sweat turn to ice on my temples. Outside, the weather kept going through countless, subtle changes. Bursts of thunder rumbled like human beings muttering curses at one another, the sounds darting from one portion of the sky to another. Mrs. Patricia Ann Reilly, one of our oldest tenants in age and residency alike, complained to me that an old Swedish thermometer she'd owned for years read 130° Fahrenheit. I went to take a look. When I read it, the thermometer showed the temperature in her apartment was only 30°! Since both of us were perspiring buckets, I felt pretty sure the real reading was somewhere in between. An hour later, Mrs. Reilly was hobbling off to St. Aloysius and casting very wary glances at the sky.

A gay couple named Swanson and Cunningham got me into their apartment to halt an unexplained invasion of ants. They hated killing things, Cunningham confided in me. Sure enough, they had been visited by escapees from maybe half a dozen ant villages and, while I sprayed and stomped, the little black shits ran around in miniature circles instead of just attempting to duck out of sight. What amazed me was that several ants attacked my foot, clawed their way up onto my shoe, and tried to *bite* me through the leather!

More and more, what was going on registered inside me in a disturbing way. I came up with a

thought that I could not have confided then to another living soul. I sensed that *latent knowledge* was
available to me. That I could quite probably dredge
up arcane insights to fight against a bleak evil that
was only *beginning* to happen. An evil that had begun by hiding behind something as awesome and
all-encompassing as earth's weather itself. Terrible
things were starting; and, if I finally *gave in* and
began working out the puzzle I might save lives.

Yet I might also endanger those who mattered
greatly to me.

2. Andrew

*Propped against the headboard of his bed, the mushy
pillow that came with the rented room long since slipped
to one side, he ignored the ache in his neck and looked
down the brief length of his body at things that were not
present in the room.*

*He saw a covey of Cong soldiers with rifles and maybe
two machine guns firing at D Company with no greater
marksmanship than a pack of angry street children, but
with abundantly more ferocity and an eagerness to kill.
That last was what bothered him more than anything else.
Now, he was much more disturbed by the fact that he did
not really see the Cong because of the way they were
cleverly positioned behind the trees and plants of the Martian jungle, and by the impression he had that they were
not shooting at his company as much as sort of slinging*

bullets at them. Everything about them was so other-worldly, so alien to everything the medic and the men around him had experienced in the past, that it was easy to imagine that the slugs slicing up the bodies he'd already treated repeatedly were not machine-propelled but hurled. Loopingly and piercingly slung by arms that magically extruded from their anonymous little bodies and threw the bullets maniacally, willy-nilly, at the highest arc. Then — sssthutter-thutter — the magic limbs collapsed back into their customary human form and the Cong slid into the oily forest, careless death growing where their projectiles had landed.

He saw the faces of the slaughtered men, the maimed and moaning men, and they all had the faces of Andrew Kizner, Jr., at all the stages of Doc's son's growth. Except that he recognized a few of them only by fair conjecture since he hadn't seen Andy at certain periods of his growing up. You see, the mind of the middle-aged pharmacist insisted on honesty. He'd wanted, yearned for, life to be that way — accurately-viewed, honest, fair and just — since he was sent home from Vietnam and into his career as a pharmacist and drunk.

People who hadn't known him before the war had begun calling him "Doc," and it had stuck. He had grievously mixed feelings about the nickname. "Doc" had a nice, friendly sound to it; but it forever reminded him that he'd meant to go on to medical school before serving in Vietnam, and now the irony of the appellation was inescapable. Most things were, to Andrew. Bright, acerbic of wit, well-read, he had acquired in Nam an obsessive affection for both facts and the truth. And he knew the two were not always the same.

For example, it was the truth that he'd wanted to become a physician largely to please his parents and to give his bride Liz everything she wanted. But it was a fact that he was not quite the same person after his tour of duty as a medical corpsman; a fact that his parents died during the same period; a fact that he'd used up a lifetime tolerance for ghastly wounds with blood geysering from them . . . and for looking into trusting eyes at the moment they closed in death.

So he'd become a pharmacist, and a drunk, not quite in that order. And it was the truth that Liz had put up with his struggling against memory and himself for a long enough period of time to give him two kids. A girl and a boy, in that order. It was the truth that sufficient time had passed that their daughter was married now and "Doc" was a grandfather, but that passage of time did not entirely register on him as a fact. Sometimes the intriguing possibility of comprehending how that could be, how there could actually be two or more orders of time, had been enough to keep Kizner seated on a barstool until the joint closed.

And enough time had passed for young Andy to become a man—that was true too—but he wasn't. For a fact, Doc's son was not a man; at least, that was Doc's belief. And the difficulty of trying to differentiate between the fact of Andy's immaturity, on the one hand, and the truth that Andrew, Sr., wanted his son to be and to have so very much more than his father, was what had caused Liz finally to hand Kizner his hat and show him the door.

49

The irony of that was that the now-aging Doc had very frequently needed someone to steer him in the right direction. Nevertheless, he'd been sober for nearly a year now, a rare juxtaposition of truth and fact: because he knew, now, that he would be a drunk for all the time remaining to him whether he was literally drunk or not! And Liz had simply refused to recognize the fact [truth] that their son was following in the only footsteps Doc had provided—an alcoholic's . . .

"And I genuinely thought the boy should at least have the excuse of a war to blame for it," he said aloud. But he also supposed the fact that there was no war being fought with American involvement was not, in fairness, Andy's fault.

This was the day when the junior Kizner had finally asked for Doc's help. A time Doc had longed for, an event he had envisioned through drunken tears as the moment of father/son bonding—belated but ultimately accessible to the two of them. But the only kind of help Doc could possibly give this son whom he scarcely knew was the only kind of help he did not want to provide. The yearned-for moment happened that afternoon at Frank's Drugstore when young Andy reeled up to the red-cheeked, pudgy man working behind the counter who was his biological father. Averting his eyes, Andy sniffled. He sniffled so much that he couldn't stop the snot from wending its way down his chin, which reminded Doc that his was another generation. With a different generation's drugs of preference.

The day stamped in black on the calendar hanging on Frank Gianetti's wall was the second of June. The elder

50

Kizner thought immediately that he should have recognized the signs in Andy; he'd seen them frequently during his tour of duty. The transition from beer to whiskey to drugs was entirely natural. Awful and to be cursed, but natural. It was the truth that he should have gotten his boy help and a fact that he had not. Kizner, Sr., had been far too busy dealing with his own habit.

Doc called his boss, Frank, at home and told him he was locking up and leaving, and he did. But not before stopping off to stock up. Doc brought home enough booze to kill himself if he could get it all down, and something special from one of Frank's locked cabinets for a fail-safe, fall-back need.

Andrew continued staring down the short length of his body and between his bare sausage toes at the range of bottles on his cheap dresser across the room. His landlady, Mrs. Duncan, had seen the telltale brown sacks in his arms and heard the bottles clink against one another as he entered the house, but Andrew didn't care about that, even though he was breaking her cardinal rule. Lying next to the Cong-like army of squat brown bottles was a much smaller, plastic bottle. So far, he'd opened nothing. He'd just lain on the squeaky bed with the mattress that reminded him of an army cot and let the entire range of his sight play over the entire range of a life that seemed then to have been more thoroughly squandered than any he knew.

Accepting the obviously phony prescription (ripped from some doctor's pad when said doctor wasn't looking in Andy's direction) and filling it for his son—or merely stealing the drugs from his boss Frank—weren't considerations that

51

even occurred to Kizner until now. Five minutes from the drugstore, by foot — fifteen years too late for Andy.

He saw the faces of the people whose prescriptions he had filled, of his wife Liz and his daughter Marge, those of his two grandchildren, and the faces of the people he had met at A.A., and he saw in his mind's eye the faces of the Cong. He saw how drenched he was in sweat, even in his old-fashioned undershirt and with his socks and shoes off, and mentally identified the day. June second. No spring again this year, just the damp plunge into summer. There weren't any springs any more. There wouldn't even be fall.

Doc got up and walked barefoot across the room.

3. Jinx Jonah, the Hoodoo Man

By lunchtime at the complex, the total picture hadn't become much clearer to me. I headed back to the Stenvall apartment for lunch and carried the same feeling of malaise along with me. I was eager to get back, partly to be with the people who'd furnished my only contentment as an adult, and partly to find out if they'd heard the rumor being whispered all over the complex. That somebody in the governor's office — well, Mr. Swanson said the mayor's — had confirmed a report privately that Libyan terrorists might have done something to our weather.

On the surface at my place, everything appeared

pretty sanguine. The weather looked like rain would soon come to relieve the man-eating humidity, but it hadn't arrived yet so we ate Ronnie's Sloppy Joes on the tiny balcony, a luxury that cost renters at the Beaumont Estates some extra dough. Part of my arrangement as Number Two maintenance man—up from groundkeeper but still under Rudy Loomis—was a gratis apartment with the works. It was cooler outside; a breeze was picking up suddenly. We figured we could make it back inside, fast, if the downpour finally came.

Markie, at age four, moved like greased lightning. I liked telling him he was "smarter than the average bear, and faster, too!" By the time we had used half a roll of paper towels catching the greasy burger juice dripping from his sandwich, we were all pretty certain it would rain.

I remember that Ronnie's daughter Bett appeared fascinated by the glowering sky that noon, and more so as the clouds became thickset—ominous and leering like a lewd old man. Ordinarily, Bett had little to say to me directly. She was seven, and she remembered her original daddy in that oblique, favoring manner in which I viewed the army ten years after the fact. So I remained the outsider who had lured her Mama away from her real Daddy. The fact that I hadn't even met Veronica Chance Walburg when Pete was still beating up on Ronnie was not allowed to play a vital role in the child's appraisal of me. Bett was still a damn good kid, but part of her had moved with Pete to Hartford, Connecticut.

"I wish . . ." Bett began. She was staring at the darkening sky low above the balcony while she unconsciously wound a silken strand of auburn hair around one finger, tighter and tighter.

When she hesitated, I told her gently, "You wish on stars, angel. They aren't out yet." Aware of Ronnie's always watchful, discreet gaze, I added, "What do you wish, Bett?"

She pondered it as if her thought was hard to put into words. "Everything's supposed to be new at spring. Right? Well, I wish it'd be *really* new this time! I wish it'd change everybody." Her tone of voice was wistful, but I thought a wild glint appeared in her eyes. "I wish you or Mom would get the really neat jobs you both want and Daddy would write to me, and that Markie'd stay out of my things!" Carefully, she avoided turning her face toward me, but I flushed anyway when I heard her final wish: "I wish you'd stop drinking for all the springs in the world and not 'mbarrass me any more."

I had no idea what to say. But I thought the speech was deep for a seven year old, and I figured she'd overheard one of her mother's remarks to me during one of my moments of alcoholic deafness. I also wished a wishingstar would fall on my head.

Ronnie said reprovingly, "Elizabeth Ann Walburg!"—but not till she had waited a long second.

Markie wasn't to be left out. "I wish things, too." The kid was twisting the knife without knowing there was one in me. "But not the stuff 'bout getting in her things." His eyes shot fire at Bett. "You're the one who gets in *my* things."

"Children," Ronnie said. "That is quite enough." She stared firmly from one to the other of them. That kept her from needing to look over at me.

"It's okay." But I was lying. Disturbed, I poured another glass of the powdered, heavily sugared lemonade that Ronnie'd made for lunch—my fourth, I think—of which I'd had the most. Shit, I was Ronnie's *oldest* child! "Bett is right, and you're right too. It definitely *is* quite enough—what I've done to this family." I sensed my Jesus-I'm-treated-without-any-appreciation outrage bubbling toward the surface and the pulses in each temple plus the one I always forget I have in my belly throbbed. From under lowered lids I checked out the thunder clouds rising and falling above the nearby shopping center. It was like some big, black, breathing thing.

"If we have to have a damn storm," Ronnie said to change the subject, "I wish it'd just begin." A lot of wishing going on that day. She was wearing shorts for the first time this year; and when her bare knee grazed mine under the table, it stayed. In sympathy if not passion, I thought. I felt her hot, moist palm burning through the cloth of my workpants' worn knee. "Did you hear the rumors?" She asked that *sotto voce,* which instantly got the attention of both children of course.

"About the governor's office?" I asked.

"I heard the National Guard was placed on alert," Ron answered. It occurred to me that Ronnie hadn't once gazed skyward so far. I guess she was avoiding the sight. "It feels like the clouds are pregnant. What they deliver will be enormous. Or monstrous." She nibbled her lip, smiled embarrassment. "Sorry."

"Daddy." Bett had understood none of that. Jumping up, she came around the tiny table to stand at my side. Her M&M eyes appeared wet. "I *want* to love you," she said under her breath, sounding as if she felt guilty about it. In other words, she might succeed in loving me *if* I'd quit hitting the sauce. I could count the times she'd called me "Daddy" on my thumb and index finger, and she'd never said the other before. It touched the hell out of me. I pulled the kid close, hid my own moist eyes in the hollow of her shoulder while Markie began tugging at my blue shirt sleeve and simultaneously on Bett's skirt.

"Hey, Bett," he explained, "it ain't hard." His grin at his half-sister and me was optimistic as dawn. "He's just Daddy."

I thought automatically *"isn't* hard," but I had this lump in my throat and didn't say it. I just made room for ol' Mark in the bend of my other

56

arm and tickled both children so I wouldn't make any alcoholic crying noises.

Omens. Portents. They didn't have to be evil, dark, openly menacing. Not just as long as they were simply and entirely unexpected . . .

I hadn't dared to hold the flashlight beam on him for any length of time. My nerves could not have tolerated the sight, not in the case of someone I genuinely liked.

So while I was checking out the havoc raised in the rest of the cell, I had no way of telling that he wasn't actually dead yet. There was every reason to believe he was, from the glance I'd had. I'd gone on playing the beam into corners of the uncommon darkness and eventually discovered the other one — the one I hadn't liked at all — and experienced a wholly new horror.

Because this son of a bitch obviously wasn't dead. He was just unconscious, passed out. I didn't even think he'd been germinated yet, and it went through my mind to turn the heavy flashlight around in my hand and send him to join the others.

Then there was the voice of the dead man. Behind me. Calling my name.

"Look," Ronnie said softly. Too softly. I realized she was looking up, finally, and that she was pointing.

The children and I looked up too and saw that the sky was unexpectedly, remarkably *clearing* — but with an abruptness that was uncanny. Distantly, I heard Ron slap a bare thigh and growl something like, "There goes any hope of cooler temperatures."

I told her Earl Washington had heard it was the hottest June second since 1933. Then I noticed that the dark clouds were not scudding across the vast skirt of the sky, but scattering.

Fleeing.

From what? I wondered, and imagined they were flying from this steaming city, from the Beaumont Estates, and from some secret evil that was being hatched somewhere in town.

Then Ronnie was sending Bett inside to wash her hands and face before scooting back to school, and Markie was close at her heels, yapping like a terrier. And that was when I saw love in my wife's eyes. And I saw an expression, too, that was there only briefly before she blanked it out. But I know apprehension when I see it. It's been in my own mirror frequently enough, looking back from my reflection.

Then tears came into my eyes instead of dread, and I couldn't say why; maybe it was because Ronnie usually projected composure, self-control, and the atmospheric whatever-it-was enveloping us had clearly invaded her. With strange intensity I listened to the sounds of Markie and Bett messing around in the bathroom. I detected some unfocused excitement in the way the kids' young voices grew shrill, rising marginally higher than the natural octave of childhood, and I found it inexplicable.

And I silently watched my pretty Ronnie clear

off our frail outdoor table. I knew she was wired too; I saw my composed and rational Ron turn suddenly brittle—like something she'd made herself with a cookie cutter. And out of the glaring, terrible blue, I wondered if this would be the final time I'd ever see any of them and the last time they would see me. Or it might be the final time we would see each other as we were then, unscarred by what was to happen. I strove to rise to the occasion and invent some special, really memorable remark to call out to my busy, partly-frightened children and my distantly disturbed wife, something to be remembered for good, for always. But I drew a blank. Came up dry—which, all things considered, was definitely a novelty in their lives.

"Bread and circuses," I'd whispered to my casketed mother's still and pasty form. I saw that we were all so damn little and kind-of hollowed-out looking in our deaths. With nothing left to fight for or to fight with, our abysmal hatreds and deep-seated dreads and our unique views of our enemies were siphoned off along with our life's blood. I wanted Mom's bright Jesus eyes to open one more time; I wanted her to scare me with a remark that I might forget a day or so later. Karen heard me whisper, "Do you finally know what is really going on now, Mom?", and her big-sister eyes looked just like Mom's for an instant.

I think I knew before I went back to work for the rest of that particular day that I was either going to make the effort to decipher the message from my early warning system or get drunk and make my magical change into Jinx Jonah, the Hoodoo Man.

Maybe both.

4. Lakens of the Lakers

He looks right, drops his shoulder as if making his move — and Jordan lunges out of bounds! McHale steps in close to fill the gap, but Lakens of the Lakers is plainly too much for Kevin to handle in the pivot. Dee Dee already left Ewing tangled up in his own feet back at midcourt. The clock is ticking down; the most exciting All-Star game in NBA history will go into yet another overtime if Dee doesn't make this one count.

Now the great Laker star is making his move. A head fake — the long arm sweeps out like the wing of a huge condor — and Lakens lets his shot fly! The capacity crowd goes wild while the famous, high-arcing hooker rises . . . rises above the outstretched fingertips of the more experienced Boston Celtic star — and it catches nothing but net! The shot is goooood!

Well, it isn't going to take a long time for us to name the MVP in this finest of All-Star games! It has to be the kid from nowhere, the kid whose lifetime of bad breaks even denied him a chance of playing college basketball — the kid who is swiftly replacing most of the great names in the all-time NBA record book.

Dwight "Dee Dee" Lakens — Jerry West's most amazing find since A. C. Green! And West said it would take another twenty years to discover another Kareem! Why, they even said that Lakens of the Lakers wasn't tall enough at six-eight to play the pivot on a junior college team! This is a story to bring tears of gladness to your eyes . . .

Dee Dee pounded the scuffed basketball against the gym floor twice, thrice, then palmed it with enormous nonchalance. Glancing with dewy-eyed modesty toward the sidelines, he saw the six rows of empty spectator benches on either side of the floor. Dee Dee was the only person in the gym of the local Y that afternoon. That was why he'd gone there on a Wednesday—people who had jobs were busy with them, and most other former players wouldn't be there till the weekend—Friday night if, like Dee Dee, they had the same memories that smarted like burning tears inside their heads.

With his glance, the screams of excited spectators were silenced. Pat Ewing was not sprawled on the center stripe, embarrassed and befuddled. The fouled-out Dominique Wilkens who'd said to Dwight in self-disgust that he should not be expected to deal with double D was actually in Atlanta, or maybe vacationing in the Bahamas. No unlikely combination of Dick Enberg, Al McGuire, Billy Packer, Rick Barry, Bill Russell, and ol' Howard Co-selll had told an enthralled audience the way it was.

Because it wasn't that way.

Then Dwight Lakens of Nothing was not alone any longer in the gym because two men who were shorter than he—one black and one white—were striding toward the court. He knew who they were right off. The black dude, he'd been a big fan of hoops around the time Dee Dee *made the high school all-star team. He had wanted Dwight to get more involved with the kids and some "program" he'd worked out for keeping them off the streets. It occurred to Dee Dee that maybe the dude had cared about keeping him off them, too, but that was some time back.*

The white cat, he'd busted Dee Dee two times before. For petty theft. For just getting some walking-around money. He didn't know shit about hoops or even how fiiiine Dwight Alfonso Lakens had been once, just a few years back. He had no programs, this white cat, he was just cop. The man.

"I sure wish you'd help me out, Dee," the brother said as they drew nearer.

"Nice and easy, Mr. Lakens." The man who wasn't a bro. His suit jacket was open, his hand was still empty. His brown holster wasn't.

"You got it." Dwight wanted to keep things that way. His own hand, like his head, was filled with basketball. He hated putting it down. "It's cool." Sighing, he executed a brief and casual fingertip roll, then let the rough-skinned ball glide across the floor in the general direction of a basketball rack. But he'd put English on it with the tips of his fingers and it rolled back, part way. Not far enough. "Stay there, all right?"

Releasing the basketball felt like removing his wide, long-fingered hand from the breast of a beautiful woman.

Didn't those cats know you should never go out on the floor wearing your street shoes?

5. Rich

The rest of the weird stuff that afternoon came at me in sort of a rush; part of it, I've already discussed. There was more, right up to and including—well, when I turned into Jinx Jonah and the world came tumbling down.

Not one, but *two* children in the complex, from different families, were carted off to the hospital with injuries after such unlikely accidents that you wouldn't believe me if I described them. No, I don't think either of them was fatal or even especially serious. Mostly . . . weird.

Three times I was called by tenants to help put out small kitchen fires. Ordinarily I don't get one in six weeks. There was also a *genuine* fire in the woods not far from Beaumont Estates and the fire department got the wrong address. I had to redirect them, and there was considerable damage.

On Channel 59, when I looked at a TV for a second after dousing one of the kitchen fires, the anchorman and his pretty backup were both ill and a talk show host had to sit in. He just read stuff that was coming off the wires or over the phone so I heard about a UFO sighted on the southeastern part of the city. There were supposedly a dozen independent witnesses; one man who looked as normal as I used to look came into the studio and claimed he'd talked with a space woman. The talk show host joked about *someone* being in space around there. Overall, it was a lot more interesting a news show than we usually get.

I also heard the report that two famous, if not beloved, actors out in L. A. had just died, and that made me wonder who the third was going to be. Morbid, I suppose. Sorry.

But if people besides me thought anything as truly bizarre or that it carried some meaning, they must have kept it to themselves. For a while, I was ready to believe that the heat was frying human brains. And I didn't even wonder why mine wasn't on fire too! Then it was night on June second and darker even earlier than it had become in March or April. At first, I didn't mind that in the slightest. At least the peculiar premature sights, sounds, and scents of summer were muffled by evening shadows. Maybe people were happy to stay home, safe for a change.

Then I realized that this stifling, unnatural silence was hanging over the whole apartment complex like something dripping wet. Dirty, and clinging; seeping into the apartments. I wasn't on call that night, Rudy Loomis was, but I decided to phone Ronnie from the work shack and tell her I was working late. I had to try to dope out what was actually happening.

My plan was to take the dis-ease inside of me by surprise and face up to it. Do my damndest to heed the warning signals screaming in my ears. Apart from the fact that I just did not desire to be around them that night, my plan appeared impossible to develop with Ronnie's fretting, wary eyes on me and that alert way kids have of sort of *preparing* themselves for a lush's psychological jump backward. Back across the line of sobriety. It's a kind of intuition children work up when they're exposed to a drunk's ways over a period of time, so that they know before he—or she—does that they're about to get stewed. I'd seen Markie and Bett before, girding themselves, *staring* at me at those times; and sooner or later, I'd lose my temper. I'd get mad at them and use that as an excuse.

Since I really imagined I was going to fight the good fight this time, I decided the battle ought to be waged on my own. By myself. I mean, a drunk is still an independent, reasoning human being. Isn't he? Well, I thought so then.

But while I was unlocking the vacant apartment where my old pal Bud waited for me in his nice new twelve-pack aluminum suit, I abruptly became conscious of two facts: *One*—I had totally forgotten that I'd stashed my brew inside that empty apartment! Do you *believe* that—isn't that *something?*

Two—I realized for the first time that Bett and Markie had truly behaved differently at lunch—that my own children had acted in ways that were hard to fathom. Bett, for example, had never been remotely confrontational. The child had never dared to face me before with what she was thinking and feeling. Yet both kids had been a fraction of an emotional inch away from some kind of indescribable panic.

I also remembered the way my wife Ronnie had seemed . . . well, different. During lunch. And I decided that if what appeared to be disturbing my customarily ballsy wife decided to get its hooks into *me*, then I really shouldn't put myself in the company of my old pal Bud. Under that name or in any of his other guises, he was more persuasive than any other force I'd encountered. Even when he showed up in another form of booze, the son of a bitch was able to convince me I could deal with anything.

I wanted to go somewhere other than that vacated apartment, honest to God I did. The small voice of my dis-ease was whispering urgently in my ear, *Rich, you pitiful souse, you will blow your big chance to become a man if you don't find some courage* now. *It's gut-check time, baby, it's all yours! Just use Bud for a focus, like a goddamn mystic or a fucking Buddhist—a* Bud-*hist!—staring at his belly button. You can* do *it!* Dripping sweat, I threw the door wide—and now I can *prove* I forgot I'd left any beer in there. I switched on the floor lamp left behind by a family on its rent-dodging escape from Beaumont Estates and I stood shaking for a count of three. The lamp provided the only light, but there was a 150 watt bulb in it and it was pooling illumination like a waterfall, and the twelve-pack was *its* focus.

Pristine, unopened, every warm can—I'd forgotten to put them in the refrigerator!—was as aesthetically satisfying and geometrically perfect to look at as a naked woman.

And then I understood why I was there and not at home in my own apartment. I had not wanted the Hoodoo Man to take his failures out on his family again. They didn't deserve it—and I couldn't afford it. Not when I believed, even while the sharp blade of my conviction seemed to become dull and blunted, that the turning point—to virtually everything there *was*—was finally at hand.

Three

1. *Ambling Circuitously Down the Road of Life*

It really *should not* be assumed that I was afraid of hurting Ronnie or the kids if I happened to get smashed again. Not by my own hand, at least. I suppose I might have *fallen* on somebody sometime. No, like my long-suffering daddy before me, I am the most peace-loving and harmless of drunks. I might add that I can be more boring than most lushes. If I'm not in the mood to make speeches, I just fall asleep, even more or less standing up. I'm no threat to man, woman, or child.

But passing out wasn't something that happened easily. I don't think that I've made the picture quite clear enough that I, Rich Stenvall, am the reigning champion of beer drinkers today and hold the unofficial title of The Human Sponge. I have never seen anybody of my sex, age, or size who could put away so many brews and stay erect, even to the operation of a motor vehicle. As a matter of fact, *that's* one of the primary reasons I got into this mess.

What I said about boozing might sound as if I'm boasting. Shooting off my big mouth. Well, damn it, I probably am. Because guys like the reigning Human Sponge—Jinx Jonah Stenvall the First— aren't overburdened by self-respect or regard, but everybody must have *some* bragging rights. Also, we beer-swigging champions are inclined to think we deserve a better break from life, even though we're pretty goddamn sure we'd blow it if opportunity ever knocked.

Please forgive the mixed clichés. You see, I call myself a Hoodoo Man because I'm generally incapable of reaching out for the wellspring of my family's love and have this God-awful tendency to doubt it and shove it away whenever love is offered me. Oh, once in a great while I can imagine for a moment or two that they love me and that I am capable of properly loving them. Once in a long while. Then, I sober up. And I read the scorn in their faces over morning coffee instead of the morning newspaper . . . While I privately wonder with deep-down terror what in the name of God I might have said or done to them the night before.

It was during that late night of the second of June when I realized I had become a carrier. Let me explain.

Back in prehistoric times when I was a kid, I'd enjoyed reading a cartoon drawn by a controversial one-legged guy with a big smile and a big belly, named Al Capp. The cartoon was more famous than you kids could conceive and it was called "Li'l

70

Abner." Well, one of Al's time-to-time characters was a well-intentioned little guy with a name no one could pronounce and which *I* can no longer spell. It was a bunch of consonants with no vowels, like "Joe Mxtzyplyx"; something like that. And the way little Pigpen in the "Peanuts" cartoons later hauled a dark dirt-cloud around with him and Linus had a security blanket, Al Capp's woeful bad-luck character toted dark tidings. Bad news, the way I do. And worse.

Joe Mxtzyplyx was a jinx. He didn't know how he'd gotten that way, and he didn't *want* to be a jinx, but terrible things happened to people whenever Joe just walked by. He grinned, and shrugged, and apologized, forced another ghastly smirk, and left devastation in his wake.

That night of June Two—even before I left Beaumont Estates and made the unforgivably lousy decision to go out Driving Under The Influence—I came to believe that everybody *I* drew near would discover terrible things befalling them.

Way I see it, that's exactly what happened at the jail.

2. *Deadlock*

No one I knew personally had ever been put in Deadlock and left to rot. In fact, around the drunk tank, the consensus was that the old, special cell probably wasn't even used any more—except for its immense and obscene value to the guards at the jail as a sheer threat. I remember it was both Doc Kinsey's viewpoint and mine that holding Deadlock over the inmates' heads was probably as effective as the image of the guillotine would have been, and that's why they kept the damned thing.

A part of me that throbs with acutely painful memory wants to tell these media types every single thing I know about that beat-up jail building, the drunk tank, the Deadlock cell, too—because so very many people perished there. But unless the story is related in context—not just how individual prisoners reacted to the greatest horror since the holocaust—I'm afraid I won't really have done my task.

Now that the whole frigging place is locked up, Deadlock should not be bothering me so much. Part of it is that I have this bleak sense of shame about appearing to readers and viewers as nothing more than a shellshocked lush; the only one who survived. It's perfectly clear to me that considering I saw so much worse at the end of the terror, I shouldn't be so badly disturbed by a memory of that one, lightless, windowless, cramped-up isolation cell. Hell, I wasn't locked up in it! But I am disturbed. After my first glimpse of it, I had nightmares—God, that was even before my more recent arrests for drunk driving—and I still have nightmares about it.

Possibly it's still in my mind because, writer or not, Rich Stenvall never remotely possessed the imagination to foresee the torture that many guys I came to know pretty well would have to endure on their way to hell—but I had let myself believe all the guards' threats about Deadlock. I had promised myself a hundred times not only that I'd live a sober life and never be "detained" again, but that, if I did get arrested, I'd tolerate anything that the guards said or did to me just to keep from being tossed into isolation. I would never, ever resist arrest and risk being sent straight to Deadlock after being booked. Christ, rumor had it—and sometimes that was the only interesting thing going on in the jail—that there was this process an inmate in Deadlock went through. First, a sort of psychic awareness came from not being able to see so much as a shadow, or your own fingers in front of your face. Next, a dismal loneliness that sooner or later made you long even to be bullied by Crock— that do-anything-to-me-only-let-me-out tune hung on—and third, a suffocating sensation that made you believe the air was running low. That stayed too, that got worse. Because you realized it was possible to bang on that two-foot-thick steel door from inside the fucking Deadlock cell until your knuckles oozed blood, and nobody would hear you. Fourth, well, that was personal. Depended on who you were, how you were. But it boiled down to going just a little crazy and, after Gargan or one of the other guards let you out in eighteen or twenty years, you never got entirely well again.

So maybe I can tell you about the lesser but still frightening features of the jail, and gradually kind of build up to Deadlock. Important facts in the men's favor—for example, on average 76 percent of inmates in the lockup consisted of men who were just awaiting trial—guilty of zilch at that point. Thirty-seven percent were charged with mere misdemeanors. And maybe I could leave out the fact that around 70 percent of us had been there before and were paying a return visit . . .

I'd studied this statistical crap soon after I first paid the price for my dedication to Bud and was freed, and I proba-

73

bly studied it to buttress my determination not to go back. I suppose I've always been the kind of guy who reads damn near everything, or anything; copyright pages, labels on bottles, bar napkins — whatever. Well, I found that the data held up for most jails in cities of basically metropolitan proportions. Around 60 percent — not the 85 to 100 percent that pricks like banker Stephen Blackledge wanted to imagine — were black and dirt-poor, dropouts from the sixth grade or before. Twenty-five to thirty of every nine hundred prisoners in cells at peak periods were segregated for psychological reasons; two hundred were there on charges of violent felonies; and around thirty juveniles were usually locked up with the older men. That last fact made me fret a great deal. Twelve to fifteen inmates were there as witnesses or informers whose lives were threatened, and another fifteen to twenty were considered logical candidates for suicide. The men's average ages worked out to between twenty-five and thirty-five.

Not a nice place to visit and too many people did live there, more or less, or soon were dispatched to far worse institutions. Prisons. Not jails.

The problem with overcrowding that was starting to alarm the whole country often was true of, well, "my" jail. Sometimes they ran out of cots and very temporary inmates were told to sleep on mattresses on the floor, otherwise known as Bug Haven, U.S.A. — I've never seen the women's wing.

How could I get anybody to grasp what it felt like after you were booked, led into the cell area, and got your first stark look at the small size of the cells — or the height of the ceilings? Not every institution conveys that particular va-

74

riety of fright at a mere glance . . . the cold fear that has as much to do with the nightmarish antiquity and the perpetuality of "my" jail or "my" drunk tank.

I'll never be able to forget how it felt hearing the door clang shut on a space smaller and closer than your living room and staring up, and up—through shadows that looked like charred, stuffed Thanksgiving turkeys—at a ceiling you couldn't touch if you stood on a tall man's shoulders. Even if you did, you could only turn your head and look across a claustrophobic area without windows or sunlight or real furniture at bars casting shadows.

And Deadlock. If you ever found yourself crouched in that cell, watching the pale institutional light being pinched off by the closing, creaking door; if you waited in darkness, alone, while the seconds became bloated hours and you reached the point where you literally did not know if you were even hungry any more—that was infinitely worse.

How could I make the media or the folks out in TV or newspaper land begin to understand how it felt—unless I explain it all and include every detail concerning the way Lew and Jimmie died there in Deadlock, very possibly experiencing a worse death than anyone else. Because it was so utterly BLACK.

And they thought *they were* alone.

3. Joe Mxtzyplyx

Take your average lower middle-class, ordinary proletariat apartment of median size, don't put any furniture in it, wait for nightfall. Then sit there by yourself the way I did on June second, propped against the frigging wall and sitting on my thirty-five-year-old ass — forgetting just then that I was at the outer limits of our local hoosegow's masculine age range. Maybe most men matured by then; maybe they managed to get themselves better lawyers than mine, Craig Silverman, or maybe they were dead. At the time, I would probably have just said *"good!"* if anyone had reminded me of the standard age grouping, and added, "then they won't want to hassle me anymore — right?"

But I was fighting demons that night, ones I couldn't see and sure as hell did not wish to even glimpse. Not to come on to you like an old temperance lady with a hatchet or anything, but some of those evil creatures seemed to be hovering just above the tops of my unopened twelvepack and pointing their goddamn *fingers* at the easy-open tabs! Add to that moronic image the single source of light in the empty apartment — the floor lamp with the 150 watt bulb. It was like a sun-going nova, a distant sun so fucking flung out into the universe that no man was going to go boldly near the sucker, with or without split infinitives.

The other tenants of the building also seemed to have kicked *their* neuroses into overdrive since it was usually very noisy at night, but *that* night the whole building was quiet as a cemetery. From where I sat against the wall I could make out through the window a billion or so stars coming out to watch whatever was going down. I quietly eyeballed a kitchen chair and a beat-up, discarded card table in the corner, a couple of light years away—

On top of it I saw my typewriter. Topless. I left it that way because a clasp was busted and it was just a pisser to change the ribbon on that baby. The Olympia squatted there on the table like a goddamn ancient mound with talking bones that occasionally conversed with me. This was where I'd gone lately to commit what I laughingly called "writing." Sometimes I produced as much as a half-a-hundred comprehensible words—in, around, and through the whispered congent counsel of my good friend Mr. Bud.

The card table, the chair and the floor lamp were left in the apartment by that family who'd split maybe an hour and a half before the dawn of Rent Day. The stack of decently typed pages belonged to Bud and me and represented the fits and starts work on two novels and four or five short stories that had, well, started giving me fits.

The typewriter was mine. And Ronnie, at least, believed I'd *do* it eventually—succeed as a wordsmith, a literary craftsman, an author. I was thinking about that with a certain feeling of gratitude to my wife when suddenly *I found an open can of Bud,* right there in my *hand!* Astounding sight it was, perfectly *amazing* little wonderment, if not miracle! How did beer get into my hand? I'll never know—but waste not, want not, that is the maxim by which we live.

Now was reflection time. Reflection on times past

77

that are never, in any alcoholic's lifespan, truly gone. My first wife, old what's-her-face, she had watched me go straight down the Yuppie tubes without a syllable of encouragement—unless by encouragement you mean in effect, *"Die*, sucker!" And for her I had never gotten a decent raise, never earned a promotion, and always gotten fucking *strafed* at office parties. Well, right before she offered her ultimate "Get lost" suggestion in a tone of voice that instructed me she was finally *serious,* my ex asserted that it was obvious I would never make it in a "business environment," that I really should "settle for being just a janitor—or whatever proves closer to your capabilities, and *capacity."* So I did. Her advice was all she left me after the divorce came through, and she'd always been miles smarter than me.

I could no longer trust myself much around people. To stay sober. See, the things people expected of me got to be too much, and I don't know whether I just couldn't deliver or I didn't *want* to any more. Then, when my marriage was all over except the screaming—and crying—I recalled one bright day what I'd wanted to do with my life back when I was in high school.

I'd wanted to be a writer.

When I met Ronnie, she'd been through the mill and could hack even that idea. My ambition. What *she* wanted was a husband who could make an earnest effort at making a marriage work. Who didn't punch other people, especially women. Who remembered that he *was* married, and who might manage to croak out the words "You're okay, honey" now and then when the dreaded "I love you" got tangled up in the larynx.

We were both on the rebound, but everything had always been tough as shit for each of us so getting married immediately fitted right into the consistency pattern. I knew that writers had to keep to themselves a lot — *translation:* away from most people — and could use up their ire and wisecracks and resentment and sadness on paper instead of on people; wives. And the family, which soon consisted of Ron's daughter Bett and *our* son Markie wasn't all hung up on financial accomplishment, so that gave us every right in the goddamn world to drop straight out of Yuppyville.

We'd have made it work from the start, really, except for my ongoing love affair with drinking. At the turn of the last century, they called it demon rum. Who can afford rum?

The thing is, Ron was worse than ol' What's-her-face was, in a way. Because Ronnie genuinely believed I had talent. And she actually *hoped* I could do whatever brought me delight — except booze, of course, or beating up on her and the kids.

But I'd never learned any writing discipline; I'd run practically dry by then, and I imagined that the bridge over writer's block ran straight through a beer bottle. That's why I worked out this arrangement with my supervisor, Rudy Loomis, in which we'd keep the fact that the apartment was unoccupied off the manager's books as long as possible. I could use it now and then as a place to write, and Rudy would keep a key for those less and less rare occasions when he succeeded in persuading some unhappy female cave dweller to try the Loomis brand of charm.

I lofted my first empty can toward the corner and simultaneously told myself I was there that night of June Two neither to write nor drink, and capped off this display of versatility by popping the top of another brew. I was present in order to face down the dis-ease and bail out the millions of human beings I discovered in distress. It was up to me. As for the full beer cans I continued to discover in the palm of my hand, I suppose I'd never quite fully accepted the notion that beer drinking gets you as dangerously, out-of-control, stupid drunk as the hard stuff. Which I know now isn't a notion. It's a fact.

Now. When it is much, much too late. For so many.

. . . When I asked Doctor Noble Ellair himself why I believed I had not proved to be susceptible to that which was killing all those other guys, the son of a bitch told me straight out that it must have been because I consumed so damned much beer in my thirty-five years that my crazy body chemistry resisted germination.

That's a real monster of a mother to carry around on one's conscience. Especially whenever I think of some of the stuff the good doctor based his entire career on . . .

"I have a sound philosophical basis for every move I make, Stenvall. I always know precisely what I'm doing."

"Oh? Who's your idol, Doctor? Adolf Hitler?"

"Scarcely." But Ellair didn't bristle when he replied. *"The answer to your question is Gustav Fechner, a 19th century physics professor, at Leipzig."*

"I was pretty sure it would be a Nazi."

Ellair kept his cool, I'll give him that. "Dr. Fechner was the father of experimental psychology, Mr. Stenvall. True, he was German. He was born at Gross-Särchen, in Lower Lusatia, April 19th of 1801. Von Schelling, who said what he did about mind asleep in stone but becoming aware in man, based his observations on Herr Professor Fechner's germinal work in developing psychological laboratory methods."

His germinal work, *I thought at the time.* "I'm afraid I don't see the connection between your idol and . . . what you've done at the jail, Doc."

Ellair gave me his smile, the way some people gave out cold viruses. "Then permit me to clarify it for you, Richard. Gustav Theodor Fechner asserted that there was a variety of psychic life — rudimentary though it might be — both in plants and the beasts of the field."

"Bullshit," I told him plainly.

"With that, Mr. Stenvall, you would at least be among the majority. Permit me to finish." He scrubbed his palms together, but it'd never come off. "My interest became engaged when it occurred to me that man often seems to be losing consciousness, sleeping as if he were entombed in stone. Drugs can do that. If so, I reasoned, it would not be illogical to wonder if the lower or earlier elements of the life

81

chain were beginning to move up . . ." That was very possibly when my eyes opened wider and I sort of gawked at the shrink. "And again, if so, if humankind is beginning to slip back in the chain—it must certainly be the fault of the nervous system. Do you start to see . . . Richie?"

I saw. Oh God, I saw. I didn't, however, want to shut Ellair off from telling me more of it, so I said nothing.

And he kept talking, because he hated being ignored. "Fechner's Law is tied to the nature of stimulus and sensation, does that help your understanding?" Asperity had slipped into Ellair's tone of voice. "With scientific experimentation, Herr Professor Fechner showed that certain forms and proportions effect a natural and pleasing reaction on one's senses. Surely, you follow me now, Stenvall?"

My frown gave me away. I did. Fundamentally, given the horrors I was seeing, I understood. But I had to stay cool, keep in his good graces. Everyone's lives might depend on that. "Is that it?" My own audacity amazed me. "Is that it for your Nazi idol, Doc?"

"By no means," Ellair smirked. Perhaps he was saving the best for last—from his standpoint that is. "Fechner also wrote a tome that he entitled The Little Book of Life After Death."

He made me shiver and I hated that, but I said nothing.

"Stenvall, it dealt with eschatalogy."

"People who show off their educations remind me of my ex-wife."

Ellair wasn't provoked. "Eschatalogy," he said, gliding smoothly on with his condescending explanation, "is the study . . . of last things." He beamed on me. "An underrated science. You may agree?"

"I don't know," I answered. "Clarify it for me."

"Of course. It's a universal concern in religion. It involves the meaning of history as it links up with the very destiny of the world. In the Old Testament, it is expressed through the anticipation of the coming of the Messiah. In the New, its theme pertains to the doctrines of death and resurrection, heaven and hell, the second coming . . ." He let his voice fade to a whisper that moved like a Slinky toy.

"And," I prodded him. I was eager to get it over. "And?"

"And the Last Judgment, Mr. Stenvall. The very Last!"

4. Rich Redux, Reeking

It was maybe ninety minutes after I had first sat down alone on the apartment floor that I felt *sure* I was now tuned in to what was happening that day and night. I had the impression that nature would have warned anybody who was willing and able to listen. And I believed that my fingers were ten conduits to the truth, and that I'd be able to get it all down on paper.

But it took me awhile to get to the card table. The beer can I was toting—one of the final two or three in my twelve-pack—had grown 'specially heavy, and it sloshed . . . at least I think it was the can that was sloshing. "No problem," I reassured myself aloud. I dragged the kitchen chair back from the table and dropped to the seat with a painful thump. "No problem." Neatly resting the Bud can beside the typewriter, I inserted a guilt-free sheet of white bond into its avid guts, cleared my throat, and raised my all-knowing ten fingers above the keys to attack that sucker.

Then I cleared my throat a second time, and waggled my fingers. All there. Ready to let 'er rip.

After an undetermined segment of time passed I took a long draught of phlegm-clearing brew, smiled with remote favor at the stars watching me through the window, and decided firmly that *this* was the time to write. *The* time. *Now!*

Well, my dedicated and concerted energy expenditure clearly warranted my return to the dwindling twelve-pack, for a compound of elixir inspiration and sustenance. Followed eventually by a rather slower and sloppier return journey to card table and to typer. "Type*writer,*" I criticized myself judiciously, aloud, very distinctly, and sat.

Somewhat to my dimly conscious surprise, something actually *happened*, and I started writing. For a long time.

But there was no clock in the empty apartment, my watch battery had opted out; and I wondered dimly, as the seconds passed, if it might have been days since I arrived. I was working *that* hard, *that* well, sweating like a son of a bitch over the words I was Getting Down. Yet I had not heard my beeper emit the smallest summoning sound and a frown began to positively furrow my forehead. I didn't actually think a whole night had disappeared while I toiled at letting my early warning signal through, but an enormous need to be sure Ronnie and the kids were all right abruptly replaced the signs of dis-ease. Tugging my typed sheet of the new *Revelations* out of the Olympia and creasing it with careful precision, I held a corner of it between my teeth while I secured my secret place and then wended one more circuitous path through the apartment building labyrinth of corridors. Toward my own apartment.

I carried along an impression that I'd made a brilliant beginning toward saving Civilization As We Know It — and me too, of course. The humidity and the beer made perspiration pour out of me like I'd become an ambulatory oil derrick, but I was *doing* it at last, I was *answering* the signals! And now I was even behaving like a proper father, interrupting the flow of genius to check on my kids and my wife — I was getting everything *together!*

And the children, sound asleep, looked fine. Wonder of wonders, they were even in their own beds, and my son had managed to put his head at the head of the bed, his feet at the foot. My smile was benign, and alcoholically askew. I remembered how Markie was seized occasionally by a powerful need to sleep in somebody's dresser drawer. Or tucked into the corner of a closet like a puppy being punished. Once, we lost him in there completely, there was an all-out panic alert and we were ready to send out an APB when Markie, scrubbing at his sleep-filled eyes with his tiny knuckles, merely opened the closet door and stepped out. I used to wonder if he might be hiding from the Things lurking under every growing boy's bed. I'd wondered that so I wouldn't have to imagine for a moment that he was hiding from me, and didn't really want me to find him.

Ronnie's Bett had the bad habit of imbibing Diet Pepsi before turning in for the night, and then, unfailingly, she awakened after about an hour. When it thundered, she tended to wander over to her half-brother's bed. Even when he was asleep in the closet, it seemed to offer some soothing qualities she required. My wife's watchful eyes argued without words that Bett should never sleep with a half-brother. I'd look back at her and try to make her see that Markie, at four, was only into pandas, Batman, or periodically one of his half-sister's dolls. Not the opposite sex. Markie didn't know there was one.

I found my own favorite edition of the opposite gender sprawled out on our bed, zonked. There was a time when the way the sleeping Ronnie turned into a plundering conqueror and devoured entire beds had irritated me, particularly when I came back late from being on call. But I'd come to understand, as our marriage showed signs of making it, that it certainly beat the hell out of the old alternative—sleeping alone. And also that, in her sleep, my calm, collected, and well-adjusted wife unconsciously reached out for me. Only me.

The lights were off, and Ron's light-brown hair looked dark, tumbled, and enticingly mysterious again. She slept with her left leg bent and resting on the outthrust right one, and her nightie rode her sweet ascensions like someone who adored exploring hillocks. The flat of her fleshy thigh was a straight line above the slenderness of the almost child-like calf, and I yearned then for a camera to take snapshots that no one else would ever see but me. And I wanted to climb in beside her and pretend somehow to be the same guy she married. But I had a full bladder, an empty Bud can in one hand, and my typed apperceptions of the meaning latent in the early warning system in my other hand.

Suddenly, I was just eager as the devil to read what I'd written! Bumping against the wall, I exited the bedroom, I murmured an automatic "Pardon me," and made a beeline for the bathroom. I peed as fast as I could, forgetting to flip the light switch and remotely aware that my accuracy in reaching the targeted toilet bowl left something to be desired. It took fucking *forever* — it was the Johnstown Flood all over again — and when I finished I barked my shin on something shadowy as I hurried to turn on the lights over the medicine cabinet.

This is what my beerborne muse had come up with:

"Certain people need so badly to be different in a markedly meaningful way that some of the brain cells are attuned to a ceaseless search for ideas that match or agree and harmonize with the changing tides of the sea, all nature, and society. The ancient knowledge was right about natural influences even if they lacked the knowledge available today to figure it out precisely." Precisely was underscored by

...ne above the 6 on my Olympia, and ...key so often I'd ripped a small hole in ...per. *"If such people's imaginations are in reality bar- ...n of any true inspiration,"* the collaboration of Rich and Bud continued, *"all they dare hope is emulation or perhaps enhancement of present trends in climate, weather, and mankind. Sensing failure, the unconscious mind opts either for the drugged state, and oblivion, or achieves such perspicacity that really **prophetic** insights"* — the uppercase 6 was once more put to work here — *"may arise spon- taneously, randomly, formlessly."*

"Huh?" I asked. I suppose the invisible Bud was who I was checking with.

Then there was a string of typed marks — ##### — and a spooky postscript that was far plainer and simpler: *"**Something's growing out there, and it's EVIL,**"* I'd written, overworking the bloody *hell* out of the uppercase 6!

My hand trembled, and the words blurred. I steadied the hand and stared hard at the page.

The last sentence had definitely surfaced from my unconscious. As if *I actually did break through* — make contact with the "dis-ease," and face it on its own ground. Except that I didn't have the foggiest god- damn notion what I meant! *Growing* out *there?*

I let my whole weight fall forward to lean against the wash basin for a very long count. I was not looking into the mirror. I was fearful of being badly embarrassed if I gazed into my own eyes. I might see a disappointment in my face that I could not cope with. The least of what I'd see was a set of features that looked forty-plus going on infinity. Christ, was *that* what I'd tried so hard for years to make myself just *grope* for? This paragraph and a line of occultish mumbo-jumbo was the tool with which I intended to make myself into a responsible adult, a successful, creative, or possibly psychic, mature man?

An inner voice enunciated clearly the term "scumbag flop," but I shook it off with an effort, then gradually raised my head. Attempted rational thought.

"Out there" *did have meaning*, damn it! Someone "out there" *needed me*—not in the customary way, but for *important* reasons. Someone needed Rich Stenvall in ways that would make him stretch, make him *grow*, bring him *out* of himself into a world that had *purpose!*

With a cockeyed sense of elation and drunken mission, I stumbled down the apartment steps and lurched out the front door of the building. Perspiration clouded my vision along with alcohol, and the slanting parking space lines in the parking lot were making me dizzy. I located my '79 Omni (so undesirable it could be safely left anywhere—nobody even seemed to want its parts) in the late-night darkness that was like thick, malefic, homemade jelly.

Right at that moment, there appeared to be a wacked-out rightness in being drunk, going off on a great adventure; the menacing midnight humidity and the silence were peculiarly appropriate, and I

. . . . u to look up at the sky. Already,
. . . . was poking my brazen head and shoul-
. . . . p among the stars. Even the kind of junker I
. . as driving seemed suitable.

On the second floor of the building behind me, a
wife and two children slept, having no inkling of
what I was doing. That should have made me feel
the familiar guilt, but it never even occurred to me
to leave a note. I was like some ridiculous kid, willing to run up debts to *new* people, but unwilling to
see the obligations I already owed to those in my
wasted past.

Still . . . there was a fleeting second when I
hoped the Omni wouldn't start. Sometimes it didn't.
That jalopy would squint at rain or at winter then
shudder mutely and give up. The damn thing ex-
erted will-power — or *won't* power — that reminded me
of a stubborn old man . . . or Mom.

But there were no showers that night, it wasn't
winter, and the engine turned over so quickly I
thought maybe I'd infected it with my own enthusiasm. It took just seconds before I was peeling out
of the complex and turning right, heading north on
38th Street, almost like I had some clearcut plan to
follow.

I didn't. Not geographically. I believed I was attempting to leave every step to God, or Nature. I
was trying hard to go with the flow, with destiny.
And not trying to find a store open somewhere and
buy more beers.

But I *wasn't* speeding. Not enough for any *gen-*

darme to stop me. I never wanted to endanger others when I got snockered, I championed Mothers Against Drunk Driving, and my old set of wheels was cooperating wheezingly—but it was never going to break any land speed marks.

It is pure fact that I wasn't charged with speeding when, twenty minutes later, I was pulled over. Stopped by a black-and-white. Actually, the cars aren't black and white in my town. But I was sure as shooting willing to *believe* that joy-killer's wheels were b&w when the fuzz sounded their siren briefly and flashed their grounded-UFO lights at me.

In another perfect emulation of its stupid fucking operator, the Omni had wandered all over the road, crossing the white line down the middle like the damn thing was floating. One more proof that European shrinks may be right when they smirkingly inform American men that our cherished automobiles, more than anything else, are long, hard dicks. Extensions of us—except that *they're* always ready for action!

Politely, a uniformed officer proposed that I get out and walk said line in the street, and I obliged. The meandering Omni proved to be a prelude to the performance which I rendered. Had the white line been a tight-rope above the floor of a circus, I would have been swept up with the sawdust. I felt so bad and so fuzzy-witted that I took the Breathalyzer test without considering what Judge Neblake would probably say if I appeared before him again.

They read me my rights and chauffeured me all

the way downtown. But it doesn't seem much like the uniform at the steering wheel is a chauffeur when your wrists are held together behind your back by handcuffs. It *hurts* actually, it pinches flesh, pride, and soul. Houdini must've been dying of fucking arthritis or something by the time he let that young jerk hit him in the gut. But then he'd probably never had to ride in the backseat of a car without door handles, or feel mildly grateful for the darkness that kept the people you knew from staring at you as your own parade somehow passed you by.

I had two fuzzy hopes: That Judge Neblake might have the next day off. And that Doc Kinsey might once more have fallen afoul of the law. That is not a nice thing to hope for a person you like, but I never saw the old guy anywhere but in the drunk tank, before or after the horrors.

They read me my rights again while they booked me. I pretended not to understand what they wanted from me — to relax my fingers so they could rol-l-l the tips just so, for prints — and surrendered four one-dollar bills plus some change. If they could reactivate *those* memories in an alcoholic's mind at the exact instant we started to have the next first drink, society might not need AA. I felt as sober as Judge Neblake by then. My ears were ringing and clogging, as if I were on a descending jet. The matter-of-fact atmosphere of the jail is conveyed by the commonplace boredom of all the uniforms who work there and at least half the guys waiting to be booked; and if you really don't think of yourself as a professional hoodlum—one of the Bad Guys—then a jail quickly turns into a cross between a crisis center and a funeral parlor. Society says it's the victim while you feel like *you're* the corpse!

The silly little shield of braggadocio I'd managed to raise had utterly disintegrated when they led me up one flight and down a dimly-lit corridor, methodically, one more scumbag flop walking the last mile. After a dozen paces, I remembered the route and could have walked it in my sleep, which was the condition I craved—that, or just *dying* in the drunk tank. I had no way in heaven or hell of knowing how very close I would be coming to *that*.

My thoughts were beginning to clear by then, and I saw from the almost completely darkened entrance that there were more men present in the tank than during my prior visits. At first, that didn't even strike me as strange. Then I remembered when I was last here. It was Thanksgiving night two years ago, and I had been the dumb turkey carved up—holidays and weekends have a terrific knack for bringing out the best in psychos, suicides, and beer drinkers going for world records. Yet this was mid-week and there was no holiday to encourage the besodden or dishonest of heart toward either misery or malfeasance. Past the tank, those cells I could see, as my eyes adjusted to the gloom, looked crammed from the high ceilings to the body-littered concrete floors. Into those cells went all fourteen legal varieties of criminal activity, and they definitely appeared to be fully occupied. Instantly, my dis-ease spasmed, twisted, but I wanted to ignore the warning. It was Victor Hugo—Charles Dickens—Alexander Dumas time.

The next thing I saw made me break my stride toward the drunk tank, intently *listening* until the yawning guard behind me shoved me forward once more. And until the cell door slammed shut behind me, and I was squeezed in among the male forms sprawled every which way but loose, I had no chance to check out my observation and rush of insight. Then for a time I had to deal with the reek of many varieties of stale booze, vomit, and collective regret. It was—offputting, reminding me of what Doc Kinsey said about a night in the drunk tank being like checking into a cut-rate hotel in Venice recommended by the brother-in-law who didn't want you to marry his sister.

But this wasn't supposed to be a busy evening, according to any events of the country, calendar, or climate I knew about—*unless* what I'd been trying to figure out all day on June second and written down in my drunken inspiration was *right*.

Anyone who's been there will tell you: Inmates of the jail *don't sleep well*. Some have just lost access to cocaine or crack; others are surely drunks starting to come down. And when the joint was crowded as it was tonight, probably one hundred of us had been booked in that day.

Certainly, most of these inmates should have been weeping, hitting on somebody else, muttering and talking, or just gazing off into the circumscribed goddamn sweltering space.

But they weren't. The jail was the *quietest* place filled with hundreds of men that I'd ever seen in my life, including college frat houses and a couple of military barracks. It was as if each man had fallen face-first into a truly dynamic dream, or was sharing someone else's. Or passed out, or knocked out. Or—drugged. I had never *seen* such total sleep.

Two additional facts gave me the willies. First: Nobody was snoring. Not one person.

Second: a tall, almost skeletal figure I saw apparently hiding, stooped and motionless, midway down the corridor between the facing rows of cells. Maybe it was because he was awake, but, for an instant there, among the shadows—

Seeing him was like looking at the living incarnation of *death*.

Part Two

One More in Their Number

Roam with young Persephone,
  Plucking poppies for your slumber . . .
With the morrow, there shall be—
  One more wraith among your number.

—Dorothy Parker
    "Rainy Night"

Four

1. Old Home Week

The Grim Reaper—or whatever the hell I'd been looking at—vanished when I blinked. At least, that's the way it seemed and that was okay by me. If I had wanted to do something about the unidentified observer eyeballing the guys in their cells—something like booking *out* of there—I had no choice left on my agenda.

Still wondering who the man was but not really anxious to find out, I spotted Doc Kinsey among that smelly mass of mankind. About then it occurred to me that in no time at all I'd be as stinky and miserable as anybody else in the tank. Time spent in jail is a bit similar to all-male barracks life except there's no topkick to tell you to shower just before the second looie comes for inspection. The only inspection in joyless gaol is conducted by oneself internally. It's called a gut-check.

Doc scared me shitless for a second after I located him because he didn't want to wake up and, for another second there, I thought he wasn't going to. Men die behind bars for reasons besides execution. Doc was no kid.

Then, when I poked a finger into him as if he were the Pillsbury Doughboy and called hoarsely, "Doc, it's Rich," I wished right away I hadn't bothered him. As I said, sleep is a hard-to-find blessing in lockup. One of the troubles with incarceration is the way the institution's officers refuse to acknowledge the fact that most inmates are unlike farmers and usually arise, sober or drunk, later than 5:00 A.M. I wondered later the degree to which that simple difference played a key role in everything that happened. In any case, they'd be bringing around what passed for breakfast on clanging carts before light had even started squeezing through the barred windows. So if a man had gotten drunk and originally planned on being awakened by a jangling clock at, say, 8:00 A.M., he awoke not only with a kingsize hangover in a cell, but lacking three hours of shuteye. As for the other meals; "lunch" was served from 10:30 to noon, and "dinner" — to give cooks like Eddie Po the benefit of the doubt — was brought to us about 4:00 P.M.

Maybe I should write a book that'd become a huge best seller entitled *The REALLY Compulsory Diet Book!* Believe it or not, some smart asses on their first morning in the tank actually manage to wisecrack, "Ah, breakfast in bed!" They're generally allowed to say that about once each.

100

My friend Doc had found a bunk within staggering or crawling distance of the commode—always a wise move, particularly for those in their middle years. Or for that matter, their years of advanced and elderly boozing. I guess Doc Kinsey spent much of his life in one or the other of those age brackets, though I heard a rumor once that he'd served some rather more distinguished time in Nam. The fact that he was lying flat on his back in wholly relative comfort did not mean, however, that Doc had necessarily arrived early at the party. It meant mostly that my remarkable but alcoholic compadre had wished to recline—the word I'm certain he'd have used.

Kinsey wasn't Doc's real name, maybe I mentioned that. He'd confided that to me the last time we met in jail. He wasn't a true medical doctor, either. He'd just liked the silly idea of sounding like he was an expert in sex, maybe in smirking privately to himself whenever a young and uninformed inmate failed to be surprised by what he was called. "A name is a mere appellation, Richard," he said then, "and it describes one no better than the face and form he has had no choice but to display."

Then he'd gone on to explain that the basic and essential "Doc" couldn't conceivably be seen merely by *looking* at him, regardless of where the physical him was at the time. "That which *I* call *me* dwells deep in my busy brain, Richard"—and also, I supposed, inside his chubby little body. He was talking about me, too, I think.

Yet what Doc really meant, I believe, was that being behind bars so many times represented or symbolized the series of downhill tumbles and pratfalls he took that seemed to wound Doc's pride far more than it did most men. I'm not claiming he was any saint, but there was a nice mix of gentility and gentleness to Doc that I found moving. There was a pain that had stayed with and hardened him, too—and that pain combined with his dignity and a comical element that kept bubbling out of him, made dudes in the drunk tank defer to him. I had become a periodic pal because Doc seemed to see potential in me that I couldn't. He wouldn't reveal his life on the outside and he didn't like my idea of us getting together sometime for coffee. But he could be terribly amusing, and I could've used a friend for my civilian and sober days. Apparently, Doc couldn't—or no longer could. It amounted to the same thing.

"Sorry I woke you," I told him. "Just didn't think."

He'd squirmed until his back was propped against the cell wall, a common posture for idle conversation. Something in the way he knuckled his eyes beneath his thick-lensed specs—he was nearsighted as hell—made him suddenly appear younger, like a wise, sardonic boy who'd passed out, come to, and found himself both imprisoned and fiftysomething.

"Yours is not an uncommon state, Richard," he remarked, blinking. "I seem to have been carried off in the cozy arms of Morpheus." He was shorter than I by inches, and I was 'just under six feet tall,' at least that was the cherished lie I'd saved for blind dates on the phone. "Yet if memory remains intact and Alzheimer's continues merely to hover in the distance, you had not arrived when, perchance, I was overcome by ennui."

I grinned and felt better about the first tangible product of my dis-ease. "I only just got here," I said. Uneasily, I played with the idea that the two of us, friends in a way, had both succumbed to . . . whatever was happening. Unwilling to make myself share the floor with the other inmates and the permanent, tinier residents of the tank, I squeezed on to the cot beside Doc.

"Execrable grammar for a gent with literary aspirations," he reproved me, mildly. But he made room. His small, cautious eyes turned to me and his fine brows lifted curiously in unison. "You wouldn't happen to know the hour, would you, my boy—E.S.T.?"

"It's after 1:00 A.M. by now."

Doc revolved his graying head slowly, inclined it in an admission of shared frustration. "I have never grasped the motive behind their removal of our time pieces, Richard." He glanced up from lowered lids. "Is it possible they might be *copying* them in the devout hope of deciphering the secret of how to *use* them?"

He made it sound as if we'd been captured behind somebody's enemy lines, and I laughed at the way his own imagination sketched the picture of a society of stunted jail officials. Them against us. But I no-

103

ticed again the way the men sleeping at our feet were crumpled in abnormal, stony silence, unmoving. They looked quite dead. I wondered out loud, "Why is it always late at night when they get around to arresting us?"

"Alas, your question is couched in superfluity, my boy," Doc replied. Yawning, he stretched his pudgy arms. "In the lockup, Richard . . . it's *always* night." And with that, still sitting up, he fell asleep!

No noise of any sort was emitted by Doc's fairly sizable, reddish nose or his relaxed lips. I hadn't seen him drop off that way before, not ever. Doc Kinsey was given to working out elaborate speeches for the benefit of the judge—more to be amusing than in any hope of leaving without a fine—or spending long hours of the night offering his sage advice to anyone who had the sense to seek it. He was allowed to take the bunk in the tank if he wanted it largely because he gave good counsel and was devoid of bigotry; he said once that he "husbanded" his malice "for targets and for towers worthy of personal attack," never for people. Anxiously, I studied his sleeping face while perspiration gushed from my own. But there was no sweat on his forehead, temples, or cheeks, no sign of discomfort about his peaceful snoozing or that of the other inmates.

Peering around, however, I found cutting through the stench of booze, beer, and wine—of dried spittle, old sweat, and generally unclean carcasses—a whiff

104

of an entirely *different* kind of odor. It was sweeter but with a remote bitterness. Cloying.

It made me want to run, right then—but that was too stupid to consider. I had to combat the immediate reaction I had to the curious scent and overcome it. I had no choice but to be brave—which is the gist of my entire performance in this building of nightmares. I mean that, absolutely: I had no other choice.

Before dawn, sometime, I dozed, fitfully. I'm sure of that because jagged slices of the weird dreams I'd had before awakening yesterday morning—just *yesterday!*—got mixed up with new nightmares. The images climbed up and clung to me like miniature fingers and arms groping up from a reeking, nocturnal quagmire. I saw mind's-eye glimpses of human men who raced in place till their mortal hearts exploded, other men rooted to the floor while tumors grew in their bellies to bloat and deform them all the way down to and including their toes. *I wished it would just change everyone,* Bett, my stepdaughter, wept . . . but her voice was much older than she is now— *and I wish it would get you! And it will, Daddy, it* will— *because it's coming out, it's coming OUUUUT!*

Only yesterday I believed that the dis-ease I had was clueing Rich Stenvall in, *warning* me. But already, that was yesterday. I knew by 1:30 A.M. that I'd blown any opportunities to either save other people or myself and that the dis-ease had *me,* not the other way around. I reminded myself when I

105

woke, sweating like a horse, this was only a jail and a large cell where they locked the rummies away for a while. It was torment, sure, but I'd been here before and nothing terrible was going to happen — not to me or anybody. The only factual element of my early warning system was this: It was warning me to stock up on beer before the liquor stores closed!

I looked up the word "disease" in an encyclopedia, and I believe what I found will surprise you. Disease is a disturbance of normal bodily functions in an organism. If they're talking about either the human body or a big place like the jail as "an organism." Check. It's brought to our attention by symptoms. We had symptoms up the poopchute. People become aware of change in the bodily functions; pain, fever, coughing, shortness of breath, blood loss, lumps, numbness and paralysis, and loss of consciousness. Check! Possible causes were examined, and *that* lay ahead for me; some of them include trauma, inflammation, infection, tumors, and poisoning. Check and double-check!

Disease could be present in the categories of skin lacerations, fractures, bacteria, parasitic attacks, psychological breakdown, and occupational hazard — *bingo, bull's-eye,* head-on *hit,* if being locked up inside an institution with no chance for escape qualified as occupational hazard or psychologically contributory factors!

So I was ready that night to accept the strong possibility that my hunches, my dis-ease and its symptoms, were neurotic and unreal, and I castigated myself one hell of a lot for being so goddamn expensively wrong—but I hadn't any way of knowing what lay ahead.

Not until morning came and it was a new day . . .

2. *Home Is Where the Heart Is*

It wasn't usually Ronnie's mind that knew when Rich wasn't in bed with her. It was more her skin, since she'd always believed that her woman's body was mostly what men noticed about her. If that. Somehow she knew in the flesh of her breasts and belly and buttocks when her husband had not come to bed.

Such as last night, when she somehow knew he'd entered their room quietly—for *him*—and gazed down at her awhile before leaving. In no way had he awakened her, unless, Ronnie realized, she was lying to herself and had chosen not to get up and have a row with him about the fact that he was surely drinking again. But she didn't think that was true.

Their marriage hadn't yet run aground on any of the unforgivable shoals she'd promised herself she would not tolerate in her second marriage. A part of Ronnie knew that it wasn't fair to Rich for her to treat this marriage as though it was connected to her first. It wasn't decent to see Rich simply as Husband, as a continuation of her horrid first marriage. So she sometimes gave Rich more latitude than she'd ever given Pete . . . Even if both men did ultimately embarrass the hell out of her by staring at her like she was an oil painting or a centerfold for a men's magazine. They should change the wedding vows around again. Make them read something like, "I now pronounce you man and skin!"

She woke in the morning with a complete certainty that Rich was in trouble, very possibly in jail. She glanced, with a sense of duty to the gods of practicality, at where he usually lay beside her, incapable of registering even marginal surprise at the unrumpled look of pillow and sheet and just as unable to feel any deep concern for him. That surprised her.

Often, she'd done her best to keep Rich from knowing how worried she was when he was tying one on. But his previous absences had frightened her more than she could have told anyone, and when he'd phoned her sheepishly from the jail, her first reaction of fury—the urge to demand to know how he could *do* that to her—was swiftly replaced by the great need to save him. To get him out of such a place and home where he belonged, where he would be safe, for a while at least, as quickly as she was able. He didn't even know she had memorized the phone numbers of Craig Silverman, the lawyer, and of at least two bail bondsmen. Her instant and frantic desire on such occasions was to make contact with the men of magic who could snatch him from the world of common criminals and perverts without the loss of a single moment; she probably would have helped him escape if she'd known how.

Today she felt both apathetic about her husband and weird, not herself. Perhaps it was because it was so damn *hot* that she wanted to take a quick shower even before fixing breakfast for the kids. Or because she was getting used to Rich's binges at last. Or maybe it was something else.

Like the way the sky looked to Ronnie as she raised one of the window blinds. Looked as if it was trying to hatch something. The way the humidity was so ferocious already that day, the only thing she could really imagine wanting to do was take off her nightgown and go naked, outside, lifting her bare arms and body to the smothering skies and sort of *give in* to nature and whatever it was trying to say.

"What a ridiculous idea," Ronnie said to herself aloud, frowning. Ideas like that weren't like her at all.

But she couldn't make herself leave the bathroom, and the cool water soothing her flesh, the flesh that Richie (and Pete before him) loved looking at, until Bett knocked at the door, wailing that she had to "use the toilet or burst."

It amazed Ronnie to discover she had locked the door behind her. She had no recollection of ever having done that before except the times there were guests in the house.

Instantly, automatically, she wondered how the children would handle it when they realized Daddy hadn't been home last night. She wouldn't lie to them. That wasn't Ronnie's style of rearing kids. How could you expect children to grow up honest if you were dishonest with them?

Toweling down, putting on panties and an old pair of shorts that really needed washing, she decided it wouldn't hurt — wouldn't exactly be dishonest — not to bring up Rich's absence. Little people were often unobservant, and reticent. They might not want to ask about their father and they might not even miss him. Which, in Ronnie Stenvall's book, was the kiss of damnation to any parent and just what Rich had coming.

She reached for her cheap cotton bra and let her hand hover over it — not touching, just letting fingers hang in the air. She always wore a bra, white and functional. There was always a chance that people might stop by, or she might have to go out. Her mother'd taught her that nice ladies wore underwear, period; Mother would've liked it if there was a way to pee without removing a stitch. During Ronnie's marriage to Pete, she'd worn a bra to bed for almost six months, and it wasn't until she was pregnant with Bett that her breasts had felt so heavy she caved in to Pete's rough kidding.

Today she knew she'd be going out — on behalf of Rich — but she simply didn't care about wearing the bra. It was humid, terribly hot. She was a wife and

110

mother, she was well into her thirties . . .

"Let the sons of bitches stare," Ronnie said aloud, more loudly than she'd intended, and went back into the bathroom for the halter her husband had given her. Which husband, she couldn't remember then. But she had never worn it before. Putting it on, she reveled in the feeling of freedom it gave her.

The glance at herself in the mirror was brief but thorough. Reasonably approving.

Markie was still asleep. Getting him up took forever. Ronnie was going to slap him if he didn't sit up *right now*—but he did.

She went to the tiny kitchen feeling weirder than ever. The little bit of sunlight coming in the window over the sink glared, hurt her eyes. *They don't have to have poached eggs every day,* she assured herself. It wasn't worth the trouble that morning. Cereal had vitamins up the ass these days. *What a funny place to put vitamins!* Ronnie thought, slopping sugary golden flakes on the table and not noticing it. "Get your ass in here, Mark Stenvall!" she called. She nearly added, "Your vitamin ass," and remembered the problem of dealing with the children's questions about Rich. Better not borrow his sense of humor.

Neither child brought him up in conversation.

"Daddy stayed out last night, if you're wondering where he is." It was Ronnie who brought him up, late in the meal. "That means he's drunk again," said Bett, looking at her mother. Her eyes were red-rimmed; nearly mean. Waiting for a denial, some

111

reaction, Bett got none. She said, "Good, I'm glad he's gone," then drank most of her milk in one swallow.

"Good," Markie said without raising his head or eyes. Ronnie thought he was merely echoing big sister, but she wasn't sure. He was spooning his food as fast as he could and it occurred to Ronnie that this wasn't the kind of breakfast food Markie liked, it was Bett's favorite. Something in the wind today?

"Look," Bett said, pointing to several golden flakes her mother had spilled. Then she ground them into the tablecloth with the heel of her fist and glanced around. "Know what that makes me?" she asked. She laughed so hard her joke was scarcely intelligible. "A *cereal* killer!"

Ronnie collapsed in laughter, her coffee splashing everywhere.

Markie stood and quietly left the room. Unnoticed.

3. Family Life

My first day back in the slammer went according to Hoyle for a while: it was terrible but strictly by the book. The book of low expectations. For a while it even seemed that nothing had changed, but by noon I discovered this was untrue.

The day began predictably early with the sound of carts rattling along the corridors and my glimpse of a broad Hawaiian face. Eddie Po, perspiration dripping from the blunt tip of his nose, started shoveling food trays into the opening at the door of the drunk tank. I never did find out the nature of Eddie's criminal activity. He was there every time I was arrested, yet he was never sent on to prison. Maybe he wasn't ever convicted of anything, maybe he was just a guy the police enjoyed hassling.

Or maybe Gargan and the other guards liked his cooking, since they always put him to work in the kitchen. "Hey, Eddie," I said while I got stiffly to my feet, "why don't you just get a regular job here?"

"And eat the shit *I* cook?" he answered, grinning. He massaged his big belly, covered by a torn and sleeveless undershirt with so many stains Sherlock Holmes would have easily deduced every stop on the man's journey back to jail. Sweat went on dripping off Eddie's swarthy face and onto the trays he was shoving toward us. "I like Kailani's meals better, Stenvall."

That remark reminded me of the need to call Ronnie — and the unpleasantness of the obligation. Before I had a chance to get morose about it, Doc was chowing down while trying to say something from beside me on the bunk. I asked him to repeat it.

"To think that the author of *The Telltale Heart* and *The Masque of the Red Death* has been reincarnated and failed to take advantage of his second chance," Doc said around a mouthful of fundamentally uni-

113

dentifiable food.

I glanced at the meal on my own tin tray, grimaced, shook my head. "Afraid I don't follow you, Doc."

Doc tilted his head to indicate the Hawaiian cook waddling along to the regular cells. "For shame, Richard," Doc murmured. "Our colleague's *full* name is surely Edgar Allan Po!" He gave me an amiable smile. "You'd best eat your breakfast, Richard. It may prove to be a long day's journey into night."

Someone groaned with the pain of a hangover — I'd recognize the sound anywhere — and I turned my head to see a young white man, maybe twenty-three, sitting up on the floor. When he buried his face in his hands and moaned again, I knew precisely why: he was wishing he wasn't here. And he felt guilty as well as dumb.

"Lou Vick," Doc said quietly, putting a name to the good-looking kid with the weepy eyes. "Married twice, divorced twice, became one of us between mates." He meant alcoholics. Lou wore a tanktop and the yellow inmate pants plus a bandido mustache meant, I felt sure, to make him look both older and tougher. "The standard, sad soap opera, my boy. Wife One would not let him see his little girl when he acquired a new lady-love and stopped making his support payments."

"I see," I grunted. "So any time now Lou will realize that it's not just a drunk charge he faces, right? Judge Neblake does his homework and Lou's afraid

114

he'll find out about the overdue support, then throw away the book on him."

"Perfectly correct," Doc applauded me. "Good to see your capacity for perspicacity has not yet been eroded by demon rum."

"Demon beer," I said, forking into my mouth stuff that might have been scrambled eggs. "If I ever finish that novel I started to write and I wind up back in here, I wonder if that will change things with Neblake. Maybe it's illegal to throw the book away if the drunk at the bench wrote one."

Before Doc had a chance to reply to my feeble quip, young Lou looked around at us and the others in the tank and forced a smile onto his handsome features. "Well, at least they let ya have breakfast in bed," he called.

Doc's gaze met mine. "That's once," he said.

A guard I didn't know, and an old one I did named Gargan—guards don't have first names so far as I can tell—handed out mops when our scheduled "dining" time had expired. All of us except Doc Kinsey began washing down the drunk tank floor, and my friend provided his assistance in the form of advice about areas we might otherwise overlook, waving his pudgy arms grandly. None of us complained about Doc's assumption of marginal authority or about the task we'd been given. None of us might have agreed about many things, but we certainly wanted to kill all the crawlies we could—especially those men, strangers to me, who were stuck with sleeping on the floor.

The only discordant event during the mop-up occurred when I spotted a number of potted plants near a wall of the tank. I started to move them out of the way, wondering if the flowers produced the bitter-sweet smell I'd noticed before drowsing last night.

"Don't." The word came from a man about my size and age, face vaguely eastern European of cast, and it wasn't so much a threat as it was a request that somehow conveyed that a threat would come next if I touched the plants. I shrugged and mopped around them.

So we became a Nuclear Family. That was what Doc and I, and a few others we'd known during our earlier visits, called the populace of the drunk tank. Regulars or not, and most of us were, none of us considered ourselves anything worse than what we were—people with a crummy habit at worst or a disease at best, who were passing through some kind of advanced training camp on our way to maturity. Attitude is almost everything, and we knew we weren't bad asses like some of the dudes in the jail. Some of us suspected that we were quite a bit like slow students, or kids who'd been sick with the sniffles and missed the class that explained how grownups kept from becoming rummies. Any day now we were bound to grow up enough to figure out how to get a handle on this sobriety thing. Frankly, we were probably as far removed from the real "criminal element"

116

as any human beings anywhere.

By standing deep in the corner of the tank, waiting for them to come get me for my phone call, I was able to survey a good part of this floor of the jail. I can't remember how much of this I saw at that time; I didn't even realize certain men were there until after I made my call home.

But I did see Deadlock—we all thought that cell's name should be spelled with a capital D, as in Doom. It was vacant that morning; I knew because the door to the max security isolation cell yawned widely. Even that way, peering at its permeable, permanent night from safely behind the drunk tank bars, I shuddered inside. True, they almost never used it; but its existence was as ominous as if they'd had a mute half-naked giant posted across the way, arms like tree trunks folded across his chest and belly and a bullwhip gripped in one great paw. I can't explain the terror Deadlock held for me, for us, beyond that. Not now.

I can offer an overview of sorts of the various inmates so they'll have some meaning to you when I begin describing the things that happened to them. To everybody.

I guess I'll begin with one of the nicer regulars in the county jail. I recognized him in a cell partway down the line where he was sitting on his bunk with a crayon in his long-fingered hand, busily working on something. His name was Dwight Lakens and they called him "Dee Dee," sometimes "Double D."

He was around six-eight or so and Dee Dee's problems began with that fact in a way, because his height was the first thing you noticed, not his charm. Black of skin, no older than Lou Vick, this kid had dreamed wonderful dreams and, when they turned out to be too high even for him to reach, Dee had crashed right along with them. I'd asked him exactly what went wrong. He'd given me a dynamite smile, then an answer that I thought defined most of what was wrong in our society: "I'm too short," he told me from Olympian heights. "And I couldn't convert to forward."

I saw a salesman named Alyear, nickname "Race," but he wasn't looking my way and I was glad about that.

Another cell housed a couple of professional gamblers I recognized as Lew and Jimmie, no last names please, and a tall towheaded ex-football player named Leighton who liked to beat up on people. Jimmie caught a glimpse of me and nodded curtly before returning to a card game. He was stuck with playing gin with his partner and the two gamblers hated each other.

When my curious gaze fell on a cell across the corridor in which three men had been locked, I don't know whether I was more appalled by the ignorance of the guards who'd stuck them in there together or by the fact that one of the three had his eyes turned on me, that he'd obviously been *waiting* for me to look in his direction. It was as if I'd turned into a stupid little gopher, who'd poked his head out of a hole in the desert to stare at the sunny new morning in hell only to discover that a *snake* was watching him all along.

You ever catch that TV commercial? The one with a bunch of black guys playing hoops on the playground and then speaking in hushed, marveling tones about a legendary basketball player named Lamar Mundayne—or something like that? Every arena of human contact and confrontation, every town and maybe even every block, has a cat like that—athlete, rebel, gang leader, social worker, prize-winning goddamn *pie*-maker—the kind of person whose reputation is so titanic in your own area of interest that you feel they've got to be famous *everywhere*. Good or bad, the man or the woman becomes seared into your memory; images of that dude or that lady get plastered to the back of your memory's eyelids like old-fashioned photographic slides ready to pop into sight along with silhouettes of Abraham Lincoln, Ruby shooting Oswald, and the first girl—or boy—you ever laid.

The snake waiting for me to discover him was Crock. That's all the name I ever knew him by, and it was already more than I wished to know about him. He was a pimp by trade, he had a reputation as a stud who not only broke in his women but positively broke them *period*. The moment he was put behind bars, he instantly became a rutting bisexual. Not the droll British character actor type, or the experimenting rock star kind, not even the pathetically mixed-up kid on the street who needed some way to find money. No. Crock was the kind who appointed his prick both simultaneous god and armed weapon, who'd frighten some dude into holding the living object of his desire while he—

Doc was not the only person who'd insisted to me that Crock was the cruelest white man on earth. I'd seen enough during my previous stopovers to believe him. Not that I ever personally *saw* anything—but I didn't have to. Crock was that kind. He oozed what he was from every pore: When he took a leak in the cell toilet without even thinking to turn his back, or when he lay on his back with one knee bent and his shorts were tented so damned tightly you'd swear it wasn't possible for him to be able to converse, stretch and yawn, or smile—like he was smiling at me then.

And Lester Piercy was the second man in Crock's cell across the corridor. I identified little Lester with a certain near-empathy I could never muster for flagrant gays on the outside, and with a certain chagrin that verged on incipient horror. That might be hard for you to grasp, I realize—if you're the kind of person who isn't terribly independent and who can't understand that being permitted to make one's own choice in the matter of when to have sex and when not to have sex is not something that's the sole ownership of heterosexual women.

Lester Piercy wore a wig and a dress. Not part of

the time, according to what I'd heard; all the time. He was what they used to call a "flaming faggot." Though I don't think we've quite got to the place of setting many of them on fire. He wasn't just gay, Lester. He really wanted to be a woman, and he *believed* he was a woman. According to the snickering storytellers in lockup, he had approached Crock a few years ago about the possibility of working for the pimp as a *lady* "ho." In absolute earnestness, yes. But he hadn't known that Crock had a penchant for introducing his hookers to the trade in the most violent ways and that he specialized in picking up children off the streets. And when Crock had explained his method of operation, Lester'd slapped him smartly in the face and run—narrowly escaping the pimp's wrath.

Why they had put Piercy in with Crock, I couldn't guess. But I feared the worst. Something about little Les—something I believed had nothing to do with being slapped—made the cruel Crock despise him. Many of us were sure Lester was going to be squashed, the way a spider is squashed when someone discovers it in the room where he sleeps.

Even worse, Andre August had been tossed in the cell with Crock and Piercy. August was just as tall as the pimp but broad-shouldered and black. Powerfully constructed, he could've played high school football in Gary but had turned to drugs instead. Like Dee Dee Lakens, August tended to dwell in the past, except for a major difference: "Lakens of the

121

Lakers" was a genuine high school All-Star in his sport. Andre had never gone out to make the team — if he had, his drug test probably would've gotten him kicked out of school. Is that a really important difference, you wonder? Jesus, I think so. Dwight Lakens still liked people. He didn't rip them off unless he didn't have the strength to work out and practice his patented favorite shot; and even when he broke into an occasional house to find eating money, he was careful to wait until the family was out so he wouldn't have to hurt them.

Andre August was an addict. He shared Dee Dee's disappointment in himself but lacked any other passions except his addiction. When Andre stole to have his regular fix, he did whatever was necessary. Right now, he still looked fine. The shakes, pacing, and madness over withdrawal hadn't started yet. I wondered, once they began, what August would make of Crock's supposed yearning for him. I didn't believe August had much of a sexual drive left, and I damned sure didn't think the former would-be footballer was bi. With Lester Piercy peering apprehensively at Crock and then shyly at Andre, an Odd Trio was formed that looked more potentially incendiary to *moi* than anything I'd heard of since the Gaza Strip.

Just about the moment a guard came to escort me to my single phone call, I caught August's big black eye and offered him a wave. It was probably meant to tell him whose side I was on, if things ever got to that. He didn't acknowledge the greeting, of course. Our Nuclear Family is disposed to first pairing off— when that seems individually acceptable—, and then forming isolated groups. Cliques. Since we can't get our hands on anybody in charge, we look sullenly at everyone else and basically set up streetgang-like boundaries—lines that cannot be crossed without trouble. I wasn't—in the customary sense of the word—a druggie, a black, a thief, or a pimp, so it occurred to me, as I followed the guard to the end of the cell block, that there were some ways in which inmate life was not particularly different from the way we'd begun living on the outside.

The phone call was short. But not sweet. It felt all wrong, for some reason. My wife did not sound even remotely apprehensive—about me, or the kids and her. Was this a new way of exhibiting her hurt, or was it just that Ron had deduced where I must be? God knows, it wouldn't have required a prophet's psychic skill. Still, it just didn't quite seem like Ronnie on the other end.

Despite the fact that other men were grumbling as they waited to make their calls, I asked Ron to let me speak with Markie. What happened next was queer: my wife said he'd gone over to her sister's to play with her son, Joey. Yet I *heard* Markie in the background. It was *my home,* and I could picture Ronnie standing with the phone clasped to her ear. I could even *see* my boy asking if that was his daddy calling.

There was only one explanation I could imagine for Ronnie to lie; so, to hurt her a little too, I didn't ask about Bett's whereabouts.

Sighing, Ron informed me that Craig Silverman would get to the jail soon. Finding me gone when she woke up, she'd automatically dialed Craig's number, and he'd said he would arrive before they took me to the City-County Building and then the courtroom. "Thanks," I told her, suddenly awkward and feeling like a teenager making his first date. "I'm sorry and I *love* you"—

But the connection was severed—obligation fulfilled, understanding and affection put on hold. Maybe forever, I thought bitterly.

I relinquished the receiver and then retraced my steps to the cell area in a mood of such bleakness that I started wondering if I wasn't one of those bad guys behind bars, if I wasn't perhaps where I actually belonged. Hawaiian Eddie's duties in the kitchen were over for awhile and he was back in his cell, fiddling with a houseplant of his own. I wondered at the same instant where the flowers were coming from and if Eddie's drooling perspiration would encourage the plant to grow. Race Alyear saw me eyeballing him this time. A wavy-haired, thickset salesman, Race had a reputation for liking little girls more than he had any right to, but he'd never been booked for sexual child abuse. They charged him with inventing too many golden business opportunities, fined him, and let him go. I nodded but didn't

124

return his wave.

I supposed Lew and Jimmie had been caught in another raid. They were slapping down cards the way I imagined duelists of yore threw down gauntlets and the language coming out of their mouths included words I hadn't heard since my prior arrest. Yet they were amusing. Leighton, forty-four or so, also waved when I passed. Fairhaired, rangy, with a crewcut both anachronistic and balding, he had been a promising football prospect in his day but lacked self-discipline — a quality quarterbacks required, I've heard. Since he was a bully even when he was sober, I assumed Leighton was back in the joint for brawling in public. I muttered a few words of salutation. It seemed safer that way.

Like I said, I wasn't courageous when the dying began, I did what I had to do. Drunks aren't usually heroes; many of us wouldn't be alkies if we could be heroes.

Doc told me about two of the others I saw who were not part of the Family. Back in the tank, I let him identify the snappy dresser of thirty-six who'd loftily ignored me when, before the door shut behind me again, our eyes met. Stephen Blackledge was his name, and he was a banker who, according to my pal Doc's reliable computerlike memory, had been caught with his hand — and entire body — in the vault. Neither Blackledge nor I had been given a uniform yet, and it seemed likely to Doc and me that ol' Steve would be OR'd — out on bail on his

125

own recognizance—before sundown. Blackledge's crime was strictly white collar.

The other new guy I asked about was in the tank with us. Al Calderone was short and squat, with a nature so lachrymose that tears leaked from his eyes and streaked the cheeks of his moonface virtually every time I glanced his way. He held a pocket Bible, reading it at arm's length until he felt somebody staring at him; then he'd press it so near his watery eyes that it looked like it was stuck to his button nose.

Doc told me the important things about Al with his own lip curled in scorn and his chubby hands fisted. Calderone had been there a while, since before Doc arrived. Wearing drab, gold-colored seamless trousers and a shirt that scarcely closed around his abundant belly, the man had informed Doc that he himself was "saved."

When I pretended ignorance and asked him from *what*, Doc remarked, "he replied unhesitatingly, 'From Satan.'"

I leaned against the wall, part of my mind replaying Ronnie's comments and her attitude. At least Craig was coming to get me out of there—after we paid both a visit to Judge Neblake and a fine. "Hell, Doc," I murmured, "this place could use a little religion, right?"

"Agreed," Doc answered, bobbing his head. A brow rose. "However, Richard, our Albert appears to have a rather awkward flaw for a gentleman who

126

brandishes his faith as a shield—or sword."

I played straight man. "Which is?"

Doc scarcely lowered his voice in spite of Calderone's bowed presence on the bunk across the tank. I couldn't tell whether he was reading the small Bible in his lap or nodding off. "Mr. Gargan, the esteemed guard, informed me that Albert was found in the act of converting a young sinner to his own faith of preference, and exposed himself." Sighing, Doc shook his big head. "Alas, brother Calderone is not present for that reason . . . *Brother* Richard. Seems the phone company overheard our fully saved little colleague breathing heavily into one of their instruments, and conveying sentiments that aren't even included in the *Song of Solomon.*"

I joined Doc in head shaking and silently reviewed our current crop of losers. A crooked salesperson with a fondness for female children; a young guy trapped in dreams of yesteryear's athletic glory; a Hawaiian mystery man; a gambling duo that detested each other; a crewcut and balding quarterback with a penchant for assaulting other people; an embezzler from the pages of *GQ;* a gay guy in a dress; a dude with an enviable bod who was an addict partly because he hadn't tried organized sports; a white pimp who threw young girls away like snot-filled Kleenex and really preferred men; and a religious zealot with a hankering for little boys. Plus many other unfamiliar losers. Plus Doc and me.

Right that second I was desperate to be out of

there, but knew it was impossible. Sweating and filled with panic I experienced a powerlessness that was more dispiriting than anything I could remember from the past. The plants in the drunk tank made it smell like a whorehouse. I didn't have a dime or anything at all to trade for a frigging cigarette, and my wife wouldn't let my own boy speak with me on the goddamn telephone. I'd sunk to the pits.

Or at least, at the time, it seemed like the pits.

But Doc kidded with me, then lunch arrived and gave me a marginal lift. Noon had finally come and gone on my first day in jail, and my mood improved. Not great but improved.

Then I began to wonder what had happened to my attorney. Craig Silverman was always so prompt. There was no way of knowing that I'd probably never see him again.

Five

1. Enter the Noble Doctor

In my fewer than forty years on this gyroscope, I guess I've met maybe a dozen men whom I could term "elegant." Each was either gay, had learned how to make big bucks, was trying with great perseverance to impress *somebody* — or was Dr. Noble Ellair.

He'd come personally to fetch me, insisting loudly that no one needed to accompany us to his office on the next floor. And that seemed to me either reasonably ballsy on his part or connected to some uninformed assumption that drunks without violent records aren't likely to hit anybody or try to escape.

He was right in my case, of course, the way he usually was. Damn him.

En route to his professional domain, the doctor appeared to be keenly disappointed that no one had mentioned him to me, or so much as described his recent "good works." Ellair used that term in my presence more than once, believe it or not. And as he stood grandly aside to allow me to pass into his office, I had already formed a fairly amazing number of opinions about this elegant guy. Ellair projected the convincing impression that he had absolutely no interest in sexual intercourse. But unlike the addict, Andre August, he hadn't developed that way because he'd been riding a guilty hobby-horse much of his life or used drugs to the extent that his whole system was out of whack.

It seemed that Ellair lacked a sex drive, refrained from drinking anything stronger than table wine, using illegal drugs, or — another wonderment of an idea came up — experiencing any guilt for his deeds. You see, guilt is a steady-state attitude rising from a recognition of error and imperfections — in *my* experience. But Noble Ellair was the type of professional person who'd learned early in life where his passion lay. He'd then headed arrow-like in that direction without permitting a single iota of deviation from his course.

He now seemed to be filled with so much unspent energy that he probably had to *raise* his sights, focusing his tremendous drive on even loftier ambitions. Although I didn't know any priests to speak of, or *to*, it seemed ducksoup easy to picture Dr. Noble Ellair clad in a virginal clerical collar — publicly going by the book, in every instance, but privately setting his sights on nothing short of the Vatican. But . . . not making it.

Much of what I sensed during our initial meeting seemed to have turned out to be right, so I hope you're following me. See, somewhere along Ellair's ever rising lifeline, he was bound to meet far less impressive people; people who'd refuse to let the Ellairs of society have absolutely *everything* their way.

It was entirely possible, I thought as I sat across the desk from him, that a bird like him was smart enough to deal with leadership better than a clown like me. But it was my kind—if we had connections and stayed both cool and sober—who reached the top. You see, the Ellairs of the world couldn't consider compromising on anything except their deepest private yens. These driven intellectual giants were so severe that the king-makers, who were far less impressive, couldn't be sure a Noble Ellair would ever forgive a fuck-up. I realized that might be why we rarely got presidential titans any more—men who obliged the rest of us to wonder what it was that made them great even while we were stuck groveling at their feet.

Noble was the jail's new psychiatrist. I believed from the start that he was a remarkably dedicated man capable of removing anybody's brain in the clinical urge to discover what went wrong. But then, he'd leave it to some dumdum assistant to put the organ back in place without permanently screwing up anything. As we conversed, I didn't have any problem believing that he'd like to help me stop boozing. Being ordinary, however, I preferred that *my* brain be left where it was, dis-ease and all, to having the organ perfectly repaired and then poked, pickled, and put into a jar!

Something else set warning signals sounding throughout my system. Ellair had the credentials and the experience to be somewhere vastly more important and profitable than the goddamn county jail, so I wondered — with growing apprehension — just what he was doing there. And what the hell he wanted with me.

"I have a gift for you, Mr. Stenvall," he began. His eyes were very bright — with knowledge, I guessed, and also raw tension. In spite of the terrible heat I marveled that the man was not perspiring. Nothing at all was on his highly-polished desk except his wiry wrists, so where was the gift he referred to?

In for a penny — or pint — in for a pound, I thought. "Shall I guess?"

Ellair's eyelids slowly closed. It was not a blink; it was an acceptance of my initial reaction and his big brain was recording it. He didn't otherwise move a muscle. "Interesting. You didn't ask 'What is it?' Or" — his eyes burned with a trait that escaped me — " 'Why would you wish to give me a gift, good Doctor?' "

"No, I didn't." I crossed my legs. "Good Doctor."

"Or you might have said, 'Why would the distin-guished Dr. Ellair wish to give something to a drunk he had scarcely met?' " Now I knew the trait was growing irritation. His brows lifted. "Instead, you selected — a pointless quip."

I was both pissed and on guard. "Well then, why *would* Dr. Ellair give something to a crummy alcoholic he's just met?" I kept my voice as level as I could. "Or was that too late for a second chance?" He smiled frig-idly, contemplated me, so I rephrased it: "Why would the elegantly distinguished Dr. Ellair want to give *any* stranger a present?"

His smile warmed up, and he sort of laughed. "Capital, Richard! May I call you that?" Then he ducked down beneath his desk to get something.

I said tonelessly, softly, "If I may call you 'Noble.' "

He froze. Why I wanted to bring him up short like that I really didn't know. But then he began lifting something, the curve of his shoulders keeping it partly hidden. "*This* is my gift—*Mr.* Stenvall." He added the faintest emphasis to my last name and had replaced his dogged smirk. "It is . . . a *goodwill gift.*"

There on top of his uncluttered, gleaming desk he had placed a sizable potted plant not unlike those I'd glimpsed in the cells. It was only starting to flower, but the hues were the most vivid and also the most beautiful I had ever seen.

I let my gaze return to the good doctor and really looked at him for the first time.

He probably wasn't as old as I was, but his hairline was already receding, showing pink scalp. I had the impression that he blushed a lot. He stared fixedly at me and waited for my reaction. His most notable feature was his aquiline, aristocratically thin, blade of a nose with small slits for nostrils. From temple to temple, Ellair's skull was much wider than from the colorless hyphen of a mouth on down. When he aged, he would clearly be bald, belatedly and precociously childlike, yet skeletal too. And I shivered for a moment in a peculiar apprehension of what he would become, recalling sketches I'd seen of aliens alighting from unidentified flying objects. Weirdly, his eyes, except for their brightness, were hard for me to remember.

133

I got the impression of an amazingly brilliant man who was capable of being boyishly impetuous where his innovations were concerned. He was like a mutant child with a head full of inherited, arcane knowledge, messing around in a chem class. And I had a hunch that his pastimes must be connected with his own personal past, his own ambitions and fears.

"Traditional scientists," he began with a lofty note of derision, "hold that plants such as this can't adapt away from the tropical climate. Or, cannot adapt well; certainly not prolifically." He apparently ranked his own approach well ahead of the work done by less advanced thinkers. That really got my guard up! "Mr. Stenvall, this little beauty hails from directly under the dense rain forest of Costa Rica's Caribbean slopes."

I'd done well in geography and recalled that Costa Rica wasn't far from Colombia; could the Noble One have been trying to make a coke deal when he went there originally? After all, his profession was that of a psychiatrist, not a botanist.

"By monitoring the plant's progress carefully during my annual visits to the *meseta central* from December through April, and near the lowland at the Gulf of Nicoya," Ellair continued, "I found ways to encourage their inherently . . . mutable . . . characteristics." He spoke in a rather nasal but otherwise normal tone, and I sensed he listened closely to each of his own words in a kind of self-admiration. "Imagine beauty, wherever one looks."

In the midst of political chaos, I thought. "Could be that

134

banana republics work better if we just leave them the hell alone."

Ellair was pained. "Not everyone who goes to Central America does so to interfere. It was Columbus who began their colonial period, after all."

"But after him," I answered, "came the pirates, the cacao plantations, times of arson, war—fascists, communists, opportunists, all there to check out the natural beauty, I suppose."

Ellair bristled. "The Gulf of Nicoya is in the north, sir. Nowhere near Panama, Colombia, the drug scene. I admired Costa Rica, Stenvall—the towns had names to conjure with—like Alajuela, Cartago, Heredia. The Coronado Bay and the Talamanca Mountains." He hesitated, seemed to be reconsidering me. "But you're an intelligent fellow, aren't you? Your case folder suggests as much." The thin lips turned up faintly. "Intelligent, but an alcoholic with the dream of becoming a novelist."

"I know I'm only a maintenance man," I said, feeling a temple begin to twitch. "But I'm not an idiot, and I'm not Jack the Ripper. What case folder are you talking about?" The possible existence of such a thing made me mad as hell. "And what are *you* doing with it anyway—if it actually exists!"

"Oh, it exists." Ellair's right index finger tapped his desk. Twice. "I daresay there are files concerning you virtually . . . everywhere. Everywhere business is done, and you're a part of it."

Digging deeper in that direction was a paranoia trap. Big Brother was waiting to set it off. I indicated the

135

plant with a nod. "Is this the same 'good will gift' littering our good old drunk tank, Doctor? I wondered where they came from."

"Now you know." A smirk. "Mr. Stenvall, your BP is racing; I'm certain of it. Would you be able to mollify your defensive attitude slightly if you had an opportunity to, ah, leave your drunk tank in a few days?" He stared attentively at me. "And to do so without last night's gauche little loss of self-discipline becoming a part of that permanent record I mentioned?" I found that quite intriguing. "And with *no* fine, *no* suspension of your driving privileges?"

I nearly agreed on the spot to whatever he had in mind. Then I shifted around in the chair across from the shrink, crossing my legs and folding my arms. What in God's name had made me interesting to Dr. Ellair, and what were his real interests—why was he singling me out? For what? I decided to bite the bullet. "My attorney is expected any minute, sir. He's good; he'll get me out." I made a pass at a nonchalant shrug. "I'll be fine without your help, Doctor."

That got to him the way I figured it would but his reaction shocked me. "I wouldn't make book on going home today. I *really* wouldn't!"

His abrupt change of manner and switch to slang made me blink. He stood, quite a bit taller than me and so thin he looked undernourished, cadaverous. Yet he had a distinct flair for command. From within his suit jacket he withdrew a notebook. He turned one page, then another. Softly, he said, "You are scheduled

136

to appear before Judge Isidore Neblake. That old boy is engaged in something of a crusade, whether he wants to be or not. Unofficially, I understand, he's aligned himself with Mothers Against Drunk Drivers. I suppose they were making it a bit hot for His Honor. I believe you've been up before Judge Neblake in the past, Stenvall . . . And he won't like the resisting arrest charge, either."

"I didn't get charged with resisting arrest."

"I suppose that's true. Not" — Ellair's eyes managed a dry, toad-like blink — "up to now. Yet it seems that charge is in the process of being *added,* even as we speak." A smile.

"What's going on?" I felt my heart racing, perspiration dripping into my eyes. I was being railroaded, and I didn't have a clue as to why. "Who do you know, Ellair? What in the hell are you *after?*"

He entered a phrase or sentence with a gold Cross pen that moved over the page smoothly, precisely. He underscored something. He slipped his notebook back into his inner pocket without replying, without uttering a word. He turned his back to me, clasping his hands behind it.

"Okay." I hoped it sounded less open-ended than that. "Obviously, since you mentioned my leaving in a few days, you have something you need me to do for you. For a few days." I stressed that, feebly. I was scared now. "That will guarantee I won't go up before Neblake, right? Or, if I do, he'll let me go, leave it all off my record, agreed? Well, then, tell me what it is you

137

want." My voice broke. "But I'm not gonna be part of any scientific experiment, Ellair! I'm not going to become a guinea pig for you!"

"No, no! Of *course* not!" Facing me, he waggled a long index finger from side to side. He was nearly laughing at my discomfiture. When he reached over the desk to pat my shoulder, I flinched. "Your work guarantees you won't have to see His Honor at all, Mr. Stenvall." His tone was softer. "You give me your work—three or maybe four days of assistance, *unharmed*—and then you return home. With my thanks and"—a delicate wave—"and with my little gift."

I raged with paranoia. "No searches for cancer, no needles? No monkey glands?" I couldn't stop. "And the CIA isn't setting me up or anything?"

"No." He slipped out of his suitcoat, draped it with exaggerated care on a padded hanger lifted from the back of an interior door. He smiled. "Now, then. I do believe that you already understand my reasoning behind the inmate gifts. Or you will, if you'll pause to reason it through. You're too intelligent not to perceive my purposes, I believe."

"Maybe." Actually, I was afraid I did, in general terms. I nodded once.

"Mr. Stenvall, I wish to provide the men with some beauty in their lives. Something alive that needs them, for care. It is elementary psychology, but it has never been applied in this fashion. The inmates require a new focus for their repressed but finer emotions. You see, when they depart this revolting place, they will be taking with them to their rude hovels a beautiful and living object that no floral shop in the entire nation can offer them at any price. I am so informing each of you. You alone will possess something quite exquisitely special to nurture as a replacement for your grubby little self-interests.

I blurted, "What were you doing in Costa Rica?" It wasn't much of a comeback after my wimpy performance, but he'd pissed me off again. And for a few awful moments I thought I'd finally gone too far.

Standing board-straight, Ellair's eyes glared at me. I had never seen such a weird expression. There was no fury, not of the kind I was used to seeing. No impression of a loss of control, either, nothing edged with the suggestion that he might be ready to boil over. If he were to act on the emotions behind those eyes then, I realized, it would be to kill me *coldly,* virtually execute me. "I will not listen to such implications. I will not be addressed in that fashion by a janitorial rummy with a start toward delusions of grandeur that any first-year psychology student could recognize."

"I'm sorry," my lips formed. There was no sound.

"Stenvall, you're not my patient and I don't have to humor *you.* I'm a medical doctor and a graduate research psychiatrist. It's your problem and not mine if you're unaware of such rarefied intellectual pursuits. My interests are farflung, enormous in scope, beyond your ken! Now: I do not have any intention whatever of explaining anything more about myself to the likes of you. Are we *clear?*"

139

That's when I really should have wimped out. Instead, shaking, I rose. "Yes. We're clear." My voice sounded funny to me. "Craig Silverman's a good lawyer. I have every confidence in his ability to protect my rights—and that he'll do so." I swallowed. "I'm an American, Doctor, even if I am a janitorial lush. Get *this* clear: Fuck you."

Then I turned to leave, knowing I'd either collapse on the spot or hit him. I took two steps. "Silverman won't be coming," Ellair called, casually.

I looked back over my shoulder. Ellair was slumped almost lethargically in his leather chair. He wasn't looking me in the eye, and I couldn't tell whether he was hugely delighted about freezing me in place, or about the possibility of calling the guards in to beat me to a pulp. "Why not?"

"A telephone call was made to Mr. Silverman's office a short while ago, notifying him that he wasn't needed—"

"What?" I exploded, spinning toward Ellair.

"—And informing him that you will be working with me. That an error was made by the arresting officers and the charges have been—dropped."

My mind reeled, fury replacing fear and a mixture of relief and incredulity supplanting the anger. "You had them dropped before I came into your office?" A jolt of ire spasmed inside me like lava. "You *knew* you could force me to agree with your plan—you never doubted it for a *moment?* You're *that* manipulative?"

A quick smile. "Let us not explore the question too

closely. That's my suggestion, Mr. Stenvall—a mere suggestion." That was no answer and Ellair still wasn't looking back at me. Then he did, though, with an amazing wry smile. "Now, if it is more important to you to learn if the charges actually *have* been dropped than anything else . . . well, I'm afraid there's just one way you can get the answer to that!"

Right, I dug it, I understood. His threat was adroit, amusing, American Candid. I was still concerned about what he had in mind, but I allowed myself a measure of hope and tentatively lowered one buttock. To the edge of his desk, not his chair. Thus, do we sell ourselves in increments, attempting to stave off that last surrendering of autonomy and . . . anatomy. "I take it you want me to demonstrate something beyond my expertise as a custodian?"

Astonishingly, he broke into a smile that came pretty close to resembling the genuine article. "Look," he said, putting out his hand. "I apologize about the cracks, okay? I need someone out there among the other inmates who is *one* of them, who—"

"But I'm *not*," I stuck in, "one of them *generally*. Please. I'm not one with Crock or Race Alyear, or one with that phony minister Calderone who likes hitting on little boys." I had not accepted his outthrust hand, but it was still waiting.

"Come, let's not split hairs," Ellair murmured. Embarrassed, he turned the waiting hand into a basically bemused gesture of grand apologia. "Let me explain what I have in mind." He gazed steadily at me. "I want

141

you to put on our usual uniform and mingle freely among them. *Freely.* I want you to *observe* them, Mr. Stenvall. *Closely.*" Just once his eyes blinked. "Please be sure to make accurate notes. I also want you to draw imaginative conclusions from your notes, from all that you see and hear."

"I'll need a notebook."

He reached into a drawer, pulled one out, tossed it across the desk to me. "Now, this is important: Whenever it's possible, I'd like you to work the conversation with the men around to the subject of the plants. I want to know their reactions to the good will gift and to me."

I said, "All right," slowly.

Ellair caught my tone, the look in my eye. It had to be clear to him that I suspected his motives. In fact, I was wary of everything about him, although I doubt he knew *that.* "I know you're not the criminal sort, Mr. Stenvall. According to most of the men in my profession, you're afflicted with a disease." Little did he know. "I'm not going to say what I think of that kind of indulgent outlook. Consider my plight. How I've struggled to convince my superiors to go along at least this far with my grand plan."

I asked quickly, "Which is?"

"Nothing sinister. I'm trying to provide decent, humane treatment for the salvageable inmates, as I've implied. It's my hope to transform them, for their own good, into something better." He shrugged. "Clearly, if a pretty, exotic plant succeeds in easing their animosities, reducing their individual and collective hostility,

142

enabling them to find a new focus in their lives"—Ellair virtually blushed—"then I shall be allowed to undertake other good works, eventually moving on to the *permanent* facilities."

I thought it made sense on the surface, but he'd played his mind games with me well enough that I wasn't sure. I didn't know what to say.

He rose, making it clear we were nearing the end of the time he'd allotted to stubborn old me. "Mr. Stenvall, the records of an intelligent third party—particularly if the conclusions he draws from the interviews he conducts are supportive—can only advance the cause, *my* cause. You can see that."

Here, out in the open, was the catch to my task—I was supposed to slant the results of my interviews, if I had to. It didn't bother me that much. Maybe I even expected such a thing. I'd never imagined that scientists wanting to verify a lot of hard work would be above creating a bit of an edge for themselves—vigerish, I think Lew and Jimmie might have termed it. "But I don't see how I can mingle 'freely,' Dr. Ellair," I said. "The bars tend to pose an obstruction to that. Remember?"

Another small burst of enthusiasm shone in his young but strangely sexless eyes at that moment. The eyes said that he knew he had me now. I supposed that he had. "I arranged things like that with Sheriff Bottoms and Chief Officer Shirley Boswell when I first came here," Ellair explained, adding, "in the prayerful hope that somebody just like you would eventually be picked up." One of the annoying habits our Noble physician had was implying he was "letting me in on" something. Just by hesitating in what he was explaining, or by using a certain inflection. "The oldtimers around here—"

"The Family," I added.

"—The Family knows that, from time to time, certain inmates are selected as trusties. They serve as a combination of errand boy and all-purpose assistant to the guards, or other officials. No disrespect meant."

"The term you're hunting for," I said with bitterness, "is fink."

"Okay, all right!" Ellair honked a laugh as if I'd come up with something clever. And funny. "Fink, sure— stool pigeon, okay? A spy, a lowly rat!" He presented me with another goosehonk and displayed two wide rows of snowy horselike teeth that looked like dentures. That shrink had the cleanest, reddest, purest goddamn tongue I've ever noticed, the tongue of a man without a nervous stomach, a drinking or smoking addiction, or that first fraction of guilt. Yet I'd have sworn he wasn't really amused at all and that he was aware of the fact that I wasn't either.

Then he shifted gears suddenly and jabbed me with a shrewd and challenging stare and a threatening index finger, pointed as if it might go off. "But tell me, Mr. Stenvall: Why would the other inmates hold back or think of beating you up if you simply asked them their thoughts about . . . houseplants? Sweet-smelling, feminine, delicately lovely . . . *plants?*"

In spite of myself, I chuckled. I was actually amused.

144

Maybe you Had to Be There, as the saying goes, but his reasoning appeared to be so airtight that I nearly thrust out my hand to shake his. "Damned if I don't see your point," I confessed, reddening a little. I cleared my throat. "Is it as beautiful in Costa Rica as this incredible plant?"

"You've never seen such topography, Richard. That's because of the long rainy season, from May to November." Dr. Ellair beamed his memories as if I might find a way to share them. "The drenched tropical plains on the coast become a central plateau that's temperate, about 3000 feet in altitude, and there are two chains of volcanic mountains that rise to more than 12,000 feet." Even his sober expression was meant to draw me to him, to unite us. "Of course, there's poverty. A severe lack of mineral resources throughout Costa Rica. But their welfare system is the best in the entire region." His eyes virtually patted me on the back. "They've been friendly with our country for many years, Richard. They're not Panama or Colombia."

"Three days of work as the Question Man," I said, "and I go home?"

Briefly, Ellair closed his eyes. "Not an hour more than"—the eyelids batted at me—"five days. *No!*" he corrected himself as though reaching a firm and considered decision. "Four and a *half* days, all right?" That long arm of his was snaking out again. "You keep good notes, work out your own conclusions with no pressure from me, and report your findings—twice a day, say. And find out what their feelings are for me. Got it?

145

Okay?" The smile. "A deal?"

"Not quite," I said. "What about my regular job? I'll have my ass fired if I don't return to work, probably before five o'clock today." Thoughts racing, I worked at putting it the right way and keeping my neck out of all possible nooses. "Could you give my supervisor, Rudy Loomis, a buzz and make some arrangements for me? I'll want to notify my wife, too. We can't afford to lose—"

"I'll make it sound as if you have no other alternative, Richard, except to serve your fellow citizens. Mr. Loomis won't have a clue that you were arrested. And I shall apprise him of the stiff penalties stemming from . . . um . . . discharging a man who is obliged to perform his civic duty." The fingers of his raised hand were working spastically in a passion for me to shake. "As for Mrs. Stenvall, why . . . call her anytime! Remember, you won't have to spend any time behind bars unless you go there to interview someone, or to sleep."

And I knew at that second that I'd have a chance to square things with Ron and the kids, maybe give my wife just enough of the same story this unusual man intended to give Rudy that I might win my way back into her good graces.

"Deal," I agreed with Noble Ellair, and our hands clasped.

Consumed with delight, Ellair got busy locating a jail uniform in my size—a guard named Hawkins who was roughly the size of one of those Costa Rican volcanoes brought it, and I was afraid he'd pop his bulldog eyes out of his skull trying to dope out what the hell was coming down. When he'd draped it over my arm with the air of a fine tailor delivering the goods, I let Ellair steer me toward his office door. Frankly, I felt one hell of a lot more appreciative than I was going to allow the good doctor to see.

Without warning, he spun away to snatch up the potted plant from his desk. "Don't forget your goodwill gift, Richie," he said almost merrily.

"Richard," I corrected him. But I didn't say it until the door was nearly closed behind me.

This might not be all bad, I thought while I jogged back down to the cell floor, ignoring Hawkins' imploring, information-seeking stare. He'd heard and seen enough to know Ellair wanted me running around freely and he was bound to clear the way with the other guards. With the plant in one hand and a nice yellow suit of clothes over my arm, I felt like some kind of horticultural James Bond. There might even be a book in this, I thought.

And I was pretty sure my early warning system had blown a fuse and had been exposed as a fake.

2. The Fine

The man hadn't wanted to keep any secrets from his wife, he wasn't the kind of husband who did that.

He was a young husband with a young wife and he was the kind who *confided* all his secrets to his wife. So

147

they could explore them, adventurously, together.

He'd been married such a relatively short time to such an enthusiastically adventurous woman that almost all the secrets he had were connected with sexual possibilities. Some things worked and some things didn't, but you couldn't know for sure what was impossible unless you tried it.

You could always go back to one of the surefire, familiar methods, and never even regret that you had to strike one of the more inventive positions off the list. That was why you got married, in his viewpoint. There were no regrets, no failures, and no secrets. Except for the one that had taken him downtown early this morning.

He stepped up to the uniformed man behind the ordinary table and reached into his jacket pocket for his billfold. When he had it halfway out, he paused and then drew out his check book instead.

"You wouldn't by any chance be willing to take a check, would you?" he inquired.

Gimlet-eyed, the uniformed officer just looked at him. No wasted motion, no valuable words; no chance.

Mildly flustered, the young husband replaced his check book and produced his billfold. A glance inside made him grimace. Paying the damn speeding fine would leave him short the rest of the week.

But not too short for Stef, he thought happily, turning the citation over in his fingers to be sure of the amount. The asshole bureaucrat in the real policeman's clothes might *shoot* him if he asked for change. No, there was

148

no cause for dismay at the prospect of having to eat lunch at home every day — except for the fact that eating lunch with Stef wasn't very *nutritious!* But what a way to keep in shape!

The husband slipped the money out of his billfold with a new happy thought leaping into his mind: This was actually *justice*, in *action!* It was his wife's fault he'd been speeding to begin with — because Stef had promised to apply herself with all her customary zeal to one of the positions he knew from experience was very *definitely* possible. Therefore, paying the fine for speeding and then keeping it a secret from her and, in effect, going home every day to collect his full money's worth, was only fair. Knowing about it when she *didn't* might even add a *soupçon* of spice — put a little *esprit* in the old corps!

A tall, very skinny man with a peculiarly horsey face had slipped into the cubicle behind the uncharmable desk cop. He had a file folder in one hand, a house plant in the other. The husband felt so buoyed by his own rationalizations while he waited for the make-be-lieve policeman to scribble out a receipt that he couldn't keep from speaking to the newcomer. *Someone* had to bring a bit of sunshine and sociability into a world so officious, so drab!

"That," he told the thin man with the pinched nostrils who glanced blankly at him as he realized he was being addressed, "is one of the *loveliest* plants I've seen in my whole life."

The eyes in the unidentified stranger's face stared

149

unblinkingly at Karl. "Do you really think so?"

"I do," the young husband said, "I really do!" But even while he went on smiling, he tended to regret speaking. The man in the civilian suit had yet to blink and the stare was offputting.

"Here," said the desk cop.

Karl glanced at the receipt. "You should have been a doctor," he quipped, and nearly giggled. Nerves ragged, he turned to leave.

"Were you here to pay a fine?" the tall man inquired.

He nodded.

"For what charge, may I ask?"

"Speeding." The husband shrugged. The questions were put to him so expressionlessly, so deftly, he felt compelled to answer. Who was this odd-looking bird anyway? "I tried to explain to the arresting officer that I'm still on my honeymoon, in a way, and my cupcake was going to add a little icing to our married life. But I guess his cake went flat a long time ago!"

"I see." The skinny guy rested his file folder beside the police officer. His attitude and dignity made him seem impossible to leave. He walked closer to Karl and grimaced. Yet it was a smile. "You're very much in love?"

The young man's eyebrows shot back in surprise. "Well, yeah," he said.

The thin man nodded. "Ah, *I* see. You're very *sexually active*." It wasn't a question but an observation, a startling statement. His lips pursed, spread again in the peculiar smile. "I was going to give this to Emil, but I

150

think it might be more properly bestowed on you — and, of course, your wife."

The desk cop, Emil presumably, did not register any disappointment.

The thin man held out the plant, waited until the young husband responded, then placed it in his hands. Without another comment, he retrieved the file folder from the desk and turned away.

"Well, gosh," said the young husband, peering down at his gift. "Thanks. My wife will certainly be—"

The man walked to the rear of the cubicle, opened a door, and disappeared from view.

"Well, gosh," Karl said in amazement, addressing the cop who was sorting the cash for the speeding fine in the proper partitions of an opened drawer, "that was awfully nice of the guy. Wasn't it? And I didn't really get a chance to thank him." Karl looked at the seated officer almost searchingly. "Sir," he said—"who *was* that man anyway?"

Emil closed the drawer, yawned, swiveled his chair around so he sat facing a typewriter of ancient and unknown origins. He didn't look up. "That was the lone ranger."

Six

1. *Pap for the Masses*

I was explaining to Doc Kinsey what had happened in Dr. Ellair's office when the air conditioning throughout the jail conked out. I know, it's happened to you, it's happened to everybody. It's no big deal; it's just a nuisance. Right?

Wrong—when your temporary address is the county jail, you're marooned. You're stuck on an island in the South Pacific with hundreds of men who don't want to be there, and the temperature is already so high you can hear your brains sizzle. Especially wrong if you're one of the seventy-five prisoners working on a kitchen shift and the temp is unbearable even with the ancient air conditioning system functioning. Or if the men in your cell hate you and none have had a chance to exercise and work off some of that nervous energy.

Whether you're innocent of any crime but know the cards are stacked against you; or you're guilty of crimes they haven't thought up names for, it's no frigging fun having to put your sweaty butt over a toilet seat when

153

dudes who might be perverts are making no pretense of looking away. And when you might as well be as far as the moon from anyone who's capable of loving you, and the only people who seem to like you at all look like they're raging with syphilis, herpes, or AIDS, it's very, very wrong. And since inmates quickly reach a stage where they can't tolerate anything else going wrong in their lives, it's dangerous for any small measure of comfort to be taken away without warning.

The *first* of those things was the air conditioning.

They carried Eddie Po back to his bunk from the kitchen. He wasn't quite unconscious but it didn't take a doctor to see he ought to be carried instead to the infirmary — it merely took giving a damn. Eddie was raving and mumbling in a language I didn't remember hearing before. They left him lying on one of the two racks in that steamroom of a cell; he tore his shirt open trying to get some air into his lungs. His hairy arms drooped to the floor, twitching. Ed was nearly ready for an oblong box, I thought.

" 'Down the Valley of the Shadow, Ride, boldly ride,' " Doc said gently beside me, as if reading my mind.

I found the rest of the poem surge into my thoughts as though I'd read it yesterday. " 'The shade replied — "If you seek for Eldorado!" ' "

Another fellow, the one my age with the eastern European cast to his features, who'd told me "no" when I tried to mop around the houseplants in the tank, did go to the infirmary that afternoon and I never saw the guy again. If *you* don't know what happened to him after that, you're not alone. All I know is that by nightfall Doc Kinsey, Lou Vick, Al Calderone, and I were the only people in the drunk tank. The one bright spot appeared to be that many of the morning's temporary residents began to be processed. Even that, of course, only *seemed* to be a bright spot.

Doc started perspiring profusely for the first time, but he said nothing about it. Angry and potentially violent demands for air conditioning began to echo from one end of the floor to the other. Much of the racket and most of the especially colorful shouting came from lanky, rawboned Clyde Leighton. But over, under, and through the commotion of understandable complaint, I heard the strangely feminine wail of Lester Piercy and the steady monotone — no raising of his voice, no audible curses uttered in any human language — of evil Crock's vowing vengeance.

All Doc said about the absence of minimal relief was: "I don't think the Family can cope with this if it stays off for long." Then he returned to the topic of Noble Ellair's plans for me and what Doc termed my "appointment." He seemed mysteriously absorbed by the arrangement and, propping his well-worn but respectable shoes against the wall of the tank, opined that he didn't like it. "Not anything about it, my boy. Tell me. Did you *see* this hypothetical file of yours?"

"No," I admitted.

"I doubt that it exists at all, Richard. This isn't old Alcatraz." The frown lines above his perpetually red nose deepened. "You and I are drunks, not desperados."

"I don't quite understand what you're saying," I said. Remarkably, boyish Lou, the kid who was behind in his support payments, had fallen asleep sitting up at the foot of the other bunk. Figuring we should keep this confidential, I knelt closer to my wise and chubby friend Doc. It had become the long portion of the afternoon all inmates remember, shadows force themselves between the bars as if grudgingly seeking companionship and lie like slender, tenuous stains on the lane between the long rows of jail cells. "I was suspicious of Ellair's motives, but it still seemed like a good deal to me. *For* me."

"Mayhap I am jealous," Doc said slowly, self-questioningly. "I may have to be here for a considerable period of time. Possibly I am prompting you to look a gift horse in the mouth — and hang the risk of equine halitosis!" He managed a smile, turned confidential. "Ere your own arrival, Richard, I had myself considered Dr. Ellair's presence in our blighted midst with dubiety. You see, when he spoke with me yesterday morning—"

I was surprised. "He had you in for a little chat too?"

"Indeed. I, and many others." A brow lifted. "How else do you imagine a personal presentation of his 'goodwill gifts' could be made?" He gestured toward our inoffensive-looking lineup of plants. "I was conscious, of course, of his psychologist's interest in subtly questioning us."

It was my turn to frown. I wondered why he'd wanted me to be conducting interviews with the other inmates when Ellair had already spoken with those on whom he'd bestowed his presents.

"I myself, alas," Doc continued, "have seeped away most of the nurturing instinct that once was mine. Yet I am not a violent chap, my boy. Tell me: Can you begin to conceive of the procurer, Crock—or the powerfully powerless Andre August—literally taking *care* of their little floral beauties?"

"Not in my wildest dreams," I agreed.

The middle-aged man shifted on his cot. "I've learned Ellair's credentials and they're impressive. Presumably, he found me to be a docile but educated man. He is indescribably over-qualified for service in a county jail, Richard. Then does it strike you as middling strange that he seeks *your* services so badly that he resorts to *blackmailing* you, a guest of the drunk tank? Isn't it possible, at least, that Dr. Ellair may have less than noble ulterior motives up his sleeve?"

It was, but I had no idea what to make of it. "What did you mean by saying you may be here 'for a considerable period of time?' Surely there are no other charges against you besides—well, something connected with booze."

Doc's somewhat W. C. Fieldsian features achieved an expression of dignity that could have surpassed Noble Ellair's any day. "I've insisted on a trial," he intoned.

I was flabbergasted. "Why?" I demanded. "I mean, it's none of my business. But—"

"It's a matter of pride, Richard—and I haven't enjoyed an occasion of suchlike for lo, these many years." The dignity in Doc's face deepened and, along with it, there was a sincerity that I realized I had probably never before seen in my sometime-chum. "You see, old

157

fellow, I'm innocent. I wasn't drunk. I've done nothing to warrant this arrest or imprisonment."

My lips parted wide. I kept from repeating the word "innocent" aloud, from making my astonishment and doubt an audible insult. But I really didn't know what to say to such a declaration.

It became immediately evident that my silence and my dumbly yawning yawp might as well have been laughter, howls of derisive hilarity. Doc, I saw, was angry and hurt. "Damn your dubious eyes, man, what I said happens to be the *truth!*"

"Doc, I'm sorry—"

He removed his feet from the wall and slapped them against the floor. The Bible-reading Al Calderone jumped, glanced at Doc with apprehension spread all over his lunar face; Lou Vick moaned in his sleep. "What is there about people that makes them so cruel, so inclined to doubt? What is its origin?" Doc averted his gaze hoping I might not see tears rising suddenly in his eyes. "Common holdup men who terrify aged clerks or demolish their stores for a self-destructive line of white devil's powder go on work release inside of a year. Rapists who'd make anybody's skin crawl boast of their ghastly crimes, yet all they need to do to be paroled— over and over—is serve some magical fraction of their sentences! Truly, Richard, it's probably easier for a monster who slaughtered a whole family in their beds to persuade an idiot like Noble Ellair of his contrition than for an alcoholic to convince a friend that he's given up the bubbly!" His jaw was grimly set as he glanced back at me. "For the record, I came within a hair's breadth not only of getting looped but of taking my life. My reward for remaining sober — and alive — was my landlady calling the cops!"

"Well," I said quickly, a bit defensively, "couldn't you have demanded a Breathalyzer test to prove you *weren't* drinking?"

Doc sighed ponderously. He seemed to be conjuring an abashed grin. "Alas, my boy, they 'had the goods on me, as the old movie phrase goes. I'd bought enough booze to open a liquor store of my own. I just hadn't *opened* it." He waggled a hand when I tried to inject an apology. "I became irate at the intrusion, sought to throw our city's finest from my quarters. I compounded that mistake by refusing to take the test on the grounds of self-incrimination." A pat at my shoulder. "Don't fret. I want now merely to argue the truth. On behalf of my own tenuously restored self-respect, and a boy you don't know named Andy." Another great sigh. "They'll probably let me out of this place just in time to begin drawing social security, don't you think?"

I didn't pry, though I wanted to know more.

Instead, since Doc appeared to be mollified by my apology, I spent some time reflecting on his comments about the psychiatrist and the task ahead of me. While my friend's reasoning looked sound enough, it seemed he was forgetting the degree to which an educated and egotistical man hungers for an audience — a knowing audience, capable of grasping what he was doing. Ambitious people needed fans until their insecurities were finally overcome and Ellair's offputting ways certainly were bound to deter any easily-tendered praise. I

159

thought he was mainly looking forward to exercising his power over me and reading the complimentary reports he was forcing me to compile. And it probably *was* true that he needed some kind of written record to support the papers he was preparing, or whatever.

It seemed I was right about a lot of that, but I shouldn't have stopped there. I really shouldn't have.

As evening approached, I found that the jail phone was tied up—I'd tried to use it in mid-afternoon, but the horrible heat was causing more of the men to seek contact with their loved ones. So, I couldn't tell Ronnie the good news. Feeling odd about walking around unchaperoned while the guards eyed me suspiciously and the guys behind bars shot out catcalls demanding to know whose ass I was kissing, I decided to begin holding up my end of the bargain with the shrink. Knowing that Dee Dee Lakens, the former basketball player, was friendly and that the banker named Blackledge was charged only with a white collar crime, I selected them for openers.

Safety first was always my motto when I was tossed into the slammer, hard as that might be to believe now.

The 6'8" Lakens was just completing the sign I'd seen him working on earlier in the day. He was trying industriously to hang it over his cell—outside the bars—by reaching between them. Sweat rolled off his affable face in torrents. The crooked Blackledge, his "roomie," wasn't even watching, let alone lending a hand. Dwight Alfonso Lakens had used his crayon to print a message on rolls of toilet paper he must've hoarded, straightened, then ingeniously clipped together. Drawing nearer and ignoring a blast of sound from Dee's radio, I admired the clever use of rips in the cardboard rolls he'd made to sort of hook them up.

The message on the homemade sign read, GOD BLESS THIS CELL. I gave him a hand, from outside, and after he turned down his boom-box, we started to rap.

"Aren't you afraid one of the guards will just tear this down?" I asked.

"Man has t'do somethin' to pass the time," Dee Dee answered. But the "who cares?" shrug in his tone of voice wasn't honest and he knew it. "Ain' nobody gonna mess with it."

I knotted the strip of rag he'd tied to the end of the sign around a bar, as high up as I could reach. The top of each cell reached almost to heaven or thereabouts, but Dwight was so much taller than I was that he had to lower his end, to hang the thing straight. "What about Hawkins?" I asked softly, peering quickly in that big screw's direction and back again. "The Hawk" was hard-working, enormous, and hated cons.

"Shee-it, *no* dude's gonna fuck with God!"

"What about Crock," I asked, keeping my voice even lower, "when he's coming back from the shower?"

"He'd need to come real close to the bars. I might have to cut him." Dee Dee spoke loudly. I figured it for a warning, doubting that Dee had been in long enough to devise a makeshift blade. I doubted a whole lot more that he'd cut anybody, even the pimp. The tall youth grinned, reached through the bars to give me a half-hearted, mid-range five. " 'Sides, we was talkin' 'bout

161

normal dudes!"

"I get your point," I said.

"Thanks for the assist. What you doin' out there, Dick? You cozy up to some big cats since the last time you were in?"

Dick, I thought. That pleased me. It was the name some of his fellow black football players called the Colts' Eric Dickerson. Maybe a Family of sorts did exist, the way Doc and I liked to imagine it. I gave Dee Dee a shortened version of my deal with Ellair and then got out the notebook the man had handed me.

"I can dig an exotic plant like mine," he told me, bobbing his head at a vertical remove that looked like yards to me. "It's pretty. It's cool."

"Does it seem kinda odd for him to go to all that trouble for us?"

Lakens frowned, tried to stuff his huge hands into his yellow pants pocket. Only the long fingers made it. I couldn't tell if he was wondering if I was a spy for the establishment and meant to report any criticisms back to Ellair, or sorting through his own emotions. I wondered how many people knew he had any. "Lots of social workers, they do weird shit sometimes, and *say* they're helpin'. Most times, a shot at a good job, a phone call to the man, or maybe a few dollars, could help more than posies."

I wondered aloud if he thought about keeping the plant after he went home. The question, to my surprise, brought a wan smile. "If the prosecutor and a brother who thinks he's Columbo have their way about it, this ol' baby plant will be fertilizer 'fore *I* go home!"

162

He drooped against the cell door, slumped to within half a foot of my height, looking particularly young and vulnerable. "My auntie had a garden, Dick. Time was when my mama let me visit Auntie Grace and help out with the diggin' and plantin'. It was nice."

"Didn't your mama have a garden?"

"Sheee-it!" Dee cried with a sudden frown. Just as quickly it became a rueful grin. "Mama works nights in a bunch of big ol' office buildings. When *she* gets up, there ain't no time t'mess with no flower gardens!"

"Right." I sighed, decided to alter the topic. Already I was starting to hate my "60 Minutes" gig and I knew I wouldn't tell Ellair anything incriminating that the Family confided in me. "Dee Dee, do you think the doctor might just have something with his goodwill gift idea? D'you think he really wants to help by giving us these plants?" I looked straight into his eyes, albeit at an upward angle.

"You askin' if these plants gonna make Andre stop snortin' coke, or turn Lester Piercy straight?" He emitted a laugh that was more like a raucous bray. "Look, you ain't no outsider, Dick. But you're *workin'* for the man. I ain' no mental genius, but you put down there that I said 'That Ellair, he's a regular St. Nicholas!' He's prob'ly gonna call up ol' Donnie Walsh at the Pacers, n' get me a tryout!" The laugh, a boyish grin, and he sat back on his cot with his arms folded. Shaking his head.

I turned toward Blackledge. He still wore his expensive street clothing even though jail garb awaited him at the foot of his bunk. I figured they might not insist a banker put them on, might even let Blackledge be one of the few inmates permitted a phone. He was standing, too, gazing at nothing much—except away from me—when I mentioned my name. I put my hand between the bars.

"You a trusty, that it?" he murmured. His arm didn't rise to shake hands. He barely glanced my way. "From the drunk tank, right?" His glance was withering.

"That's the size of it." I found the fingers of my other hand squeezing the notebook in lieu of Blackledge's neck.

"So you're out there, free to go where you please. And I am in here." He shook his well-styled head. "The world gets more bizarre by the day."

"That's *not* the size of it," I said. I went closer to him, conscious of the need to get something from him about the damn plants. "If I could go wherever I wanted, Blackledge, I'd go home."

He made a frown that etched an H—for hell, maybe—between his dark brows. He had distinguishing streaks of near-white at the temples, fluffed up in pretty tufts that had to be regularly trimmed to stay fluffy. He wore the obligatory tailored suit, he had these very broad shoulders—from Working Out at the Club, I guessed—and he kept his fingers laced behind his back as though restraining himself and his temper. "I suppose your relative freedom and the misunderstanding that put me in this place is what one can expect from our legal system these days."

I tensed but drew in a breath, telling myself the guy needed somebody to tell off. This was new to him. "Look, Steve, all I need to know is if you like having a nice plant around or not. How it makes you feel about Ellair, the psychiatrist. If you'd—"

"If I'd *what?*" He jumped up to the bars close to me, his face an unhealthy crimson. The other cellmates, Lew and Jimmie, studiously looked away. "My name is 'Blackledge' and I'll thank you to remember that." Rivulets of sweat were making his white collar go limp but everything else about him was tense, abnormally stressed. "It's bad enough I'm supposed to stay in here like an animal without brown-nosing drunks plaguing me with first-year psychology questions!"

He caught me entirely offguard with his attack. I didn't know quite what obscene words to use in rebuttal. I saw Dee retreat to a corner, wanting none of it; Jimmy picked up the deck of greasy cards they used and quietly rose.

Then, before I said a word, Blackledge whirled around. His eyes sank into the scarlet mass of his well-groomed face as he snatched up the potted plant Ellair had given him and brought it to shoulder level. *"This* is what I think of condescending gestures like fucking psychiatrist's gifts!" he spat. Then he slammed the plant against the wall of his cell, missing a ducking Dee Dee Lakens by inches. The detonation sent shards and meaty dirt flying in every direction, and left Steve Blackledge with both arms drooping, panting and oozing high-class sweat. Lew, roughly my age, coolly flicked a flower petal off his shoulder.

"Jus' don't mess with my sign or my radio, man," Dee told the banker, sidling over to retrieve the boom-box and cuddle it to him. He looked positively paternal.

"You don't know how to *spell* that answer, do you, Steve?" I asked sardonically before leaving. I decided to catch Lew and Jimmie later. When things were less hectic. But that would never transpire.

I elected to try phoning Ronnie to tell her what was happening. There was no way Noble Ellair was going to be happy with Steve Blackledge's answers, I thought. But what really bothered me about it was the extent of his over-reaction. The man's hair-trigger behavior was more what I would have expected from Andre August, or Crock. And I still had them to talk with, plus a lot of others.

The air conditioning must be a lot better at the bank, I reflected, dialing the apartment number.

2. *One Man's Ideals, and Idols*

Stepping back into the front of his office from his interior room, pouring sweat now, Noble Ellair recalled something he'd read in Colin Wilson's book about Carl Gustav Jung, *Lord of the Underworld*. When Jung was young, Krafft-Ebbing's comments about a still undeveloped, formative psychiatry — a truly wide-open field of inquiry to any bold and curious youth with the imagination to ask the right questions — "probably evoked an image of a kind of magician — or at least a Professor Frankenstein — exploring the underground passages of the human soul."

Noble felt the same way, even today. Always had. He smiled as he toweled his naked body thoroughly and put his clothes back on.

He continued to see himself as the *right sort* of Frankenstein because he'd had the courage to explore the history of alchemy from a scientist's vantage point, and also because he'd read the scarce works of Friedrich von Schelling concerning Gustav Theodor Fechner, von Schelling's idol.

To some degree, Dr. Noble Ellair had made Fechner his idol also. The significance of that, Ellair knew, was that old Gustav and Friedrich—for that matter, Krafft-Ebbing and Jung, *even* Doctor Frankenstein!—were born much too soon to have the tools of knowledge and of modern science at their disposal which Noble Ellair had available.

Jung had experienced some of the same problems as Ellair at a comparably early point in his brilliant career. Noble knew that. Trying to read, comprehend, and utilize the ideas contained in the essays of the great alchemist Paracelsus, Carl had known he himself was—as Colin Wilson expressed it—"dealing with an alien intellectual tradition." It was Jung's flights of fancy into his theories of archetypes and projections that had provided him with a way of "entering into" the spirit of Paracelsus, the spirit of alchemy, of magic.

But it was Noble Ellair's complete grasp of von Schelling's remarks about Mind sleeping in stone, dreaming in plants, awaking in animals, but becoming conscious in the human being, that had enabled him to enter into the spirit of Gustav Fechner, born April 19, 1801, in Germany—not hundreds of years in the past.

Fechner was the first man to see a way to establish a

psychophysical lab. He'd also striven to unite the un-studied topic of human stimuli and sensation with a study of "the last things," or eschatology. The most neglected field of inquiry left to man, Noble believed. For Ellair, Fechner's *Little Book of Life After Death* had been something of an inspiration.

He took his best brush from a drawer of the desk, went to an inconspicuous mirror in one corner of the office, and carefully stroked his sparse hair. Since boyhood, he'd sensed at some tantalizingly deep level of his brain that man was not destined to *remain* the dominant species on the planet. It was not until the use of illegal drugs spread so far and began making the medical journals that he'd identified clearcut evidence of his belief. Then it was perfectly clear! As man regressed, what von Schelling called "all-mind" was making *its advance.*

Man was starting to *lose* consciousness, the awareness of what he was; he even gave it up voluntarily by falling into a pattern of flagrant indulgence. And while he regressed, the earlier parts of the life-chain, of all-mind, were *progressing;* moving *upward;* achieving a consciousness only man had known hitherto! And, as they awakened, they would eschew the lower dream state completely. Ellair saw this as their right. Pushed to it, Fechner had confessed his belief that there was a form of life even in inanimate creatures.

Noble sat snugly in his chair behind his desk, amused when he remembered the task he had given the tank's latest drunkard. He hoped Stenvall was a decent writer, or at least had a minimal acquaintance with the language. The man was probably incapable of appreciating the opportunity he'd been given. Wilson had quoted William James in his essay "The Energies of Man" saying that in comparison to "what we ought to be, we are only half-awake." James had an inkling of it, but the fellow hadn't possessed the imagination or the brass to take it far enough. James also had written that a man "possesses powers of various sorts which he habitually fails to use. He energises below his maximum, and he behaves below his optimum."

"Ah, but so did you, William," Ellair said softly, settling back in his chair to wait, his fingers entwined behind his long head. "So did you."

Noble Ellair would exceed his optimum.

3. They've Killed Satan!

I told Ronnie the story and then waited to see if she'd buy the big part—how I'd been cold sober all along and how I was attempting to "help out with an important scientific experiment that could benefit a lot of people." My reward, I explained, would be that I alone was getting the inside poop for a book I'd be writing. *The* book, the one that would do it for us.

Then—out of the blue—there was a positively terrible, caromming kind of sound that seemed to shake the whole jail! For a minute I thought it was a divine rebuke for the lousy lies I'd been feeding Ron. In its scary wake, the noise left a vibratory quiver that trembled in the air like something nearly tangible; and a truly frightened Rich Stenvall.

"What was that?" Ronnie whispered in my left ear. "Rich. What was that *noise?*"

A cold gust of air slapped my right cheek. Like the frail, hurtful blow of an aged mother, unforgiving but dying. "I think," I began but had to stop to clear my throat. "I think it was a generator going on." How could I feel so *cold* when I'd been so damn *hot?* Shakily, I glanced behind me. Two other inmates were waiting to use the phone. They had the look of men who'd been asked to identify corpses in the morgue, and had. It was them. "Something — well, someone got the air conditioning going again." I laughed to convince myself. "What a relief."

"Are you all right?" my wife asked. It wasn't more than a murmur, but I knew at once she'd forgiven me, whether or not she'd bought the rotten lies I'd laid on her. "So many strange things are happening here that I think . . . something's wrong. Richie, the air conditioners are going out all over the complex, too. And our star maintenance guy isn't here to take care of it." Her voice shivered like branches of trees close to the sky, and she seemed a continent away from me just then. "Can you say when you're coming home?"

"In just a few days," I replied, my mind analyzing the things she'd just told me, searching for the things she wasn't saying. Ronnie was showing me the kind of understanding that only a certain sort of wife ever allows anyone to see, and I yearned to hold her, tell her the truth but in the right way. "Ron, are —"

"Say hello to Daddy," she said with her mouth turned

170

away from the phone. Small rustling sounds of woman and child . . . their couple of yards of clothing and this telephone line all they had to protect them without me there . . . whispering in the background. Then he had the phone pressed to his ear, and I knew my boy was there even though he didn't utter a sound.

"Markie," I said, projecting a false confidence. "How's my main man?"

"-Addy," he answered, and I guess the phone kept slipping around in his small hand. He echoed Ronnie to say the right things. "When --- you comin' home?"

"Real soon, son!" I exclaimed. Shit, I sounded like a blend of Captain Kangoroo, Mr. Wizard, the Yo-Yo Man, and a scared old Santa Claus. "Hey, I love you!"

"- ---- you too," he replied.

"Buddy, what's wrong over there, what's going on? Tell Daddy, Pal." Rat to daddy, fink for your old man.

"Here's Bett." The announcement was without warning. I imagined Ron getting them in line so I tried to keep the artificial joviality of my tone in place while upgrading the maturity level.

"We need you at *home,* Daddy," Bett said loudly in my ear. She wasn't screaming; she wasn't trying to boss me around. She'd called me "Daddy," her lips were close to the mouthpiece of the phone, and I'd have bet that her eyes were the size of saucers.

"Honey, Bett, what's *happening?*" I asked her. Now I felt cold inside. "Just *tell* me, please, so—"

The connection was broken, the call cut off. There were no sounds of bodies falling to the floor of our apartment, but there was also no dial tone. I didn't know if Bett just passed the phone back to her mother and pulled it out or what. Silence.

Somebody at my back nudged me. He didn't startle me. I didn't hang the phone back up, just gave it to him. Reluctantly. Sweating chilly droplets from the base of my neck to my tailbone.

The idea that my family, my real family, had been disconnected from me — *purposely* disconnected, *knowingly* cut off — was overwhelming. I couldn't be sure about it, but Bett had seemed . . . well, desperate. I stared at the guy taking the phone from my hand as if he were taking away my lifeline to all that was decent and good. I was isolated, along with hundreds of other men, from the only things I could believe in, so I gave the guy a hard nudge back. He was wearing a Citizens Gas uniform, and I didn't know why he'd been arrested unless the gas company had turned into a collective of holdup men during the winter and the cops had finally decided to do something about it. The guy was oily all over with disgusting splotches on his hands and uniform shirt. He whipped around fast when he felt my elbow in his ribs; and we sized each other up, hungry to kill. The other guy waiting to use the phone prudently left.

The guard at the end of the corridor — a Polish kid — rose part way from his chair.

"Fuck you," the man from the gas company growled.

"Fuck *you*," I replied. A dazzling show of originality.

Then both of us froze to stare at the apparition.

He materialized yards from us, eyes wide. He wasn't there for me or for the impatient prick

172

from Citizens Gas specifically, but I saw that he *had* to notify someone and we were right there, clustered around the phone to the outside.

I knew the apparition. Al Calderone, the round-faced religious zealot Doc had described to me as flasher and heavy breather. He was certainly breathing heavy now but this had nothing to do with sex — I'd never seen such fright in a man's expression. He was positively screaming at us with his eyes. Coming right after the talk with Ron and the shocking generator noise, he made me feel simultaneously cold and hot with shock. How Calderone had gotten out there — unless another guard had released him so he could make a phone call — I didn't know.

But then he was yelling, "He's among us! *Satan's among us!*", and I was gawking at every shadow that moved around Al. "He's got *horns* — b-but *something's done killed him!*"

When the squat little shit motioned frantically for me to follow, I broke into a hesitant run between the facing cells and wondered what the fuck was going on. Guys inside cells looked around, called out, "What's wrong, what's happening?" and all I could do was shrug, keep going. The guard automatically shouted for me to halt — maybe he thought I was escaping or something. I wasn't, but I slowed down when I realized Al was doing his best to stay close behind me and the possibility of danger occurred to me.

Lew and Jimmie, who usually didn't give a damn about people, and who hated to get involved, waved their arms. "Over here!" I saw they were gesturing *inside*

173

their own cell. "Stenvall, in here!"

I rushed up against the bars, Al at my heels, sticking his moonhead around my side and pointing. Now the street-smart gamblers in the cell were back against the wall, cringing away from the object they too were pointing at. *Who made me chief problem-solver?* I wondered.

"They killed Satan!" Calderone wheezed — "he's *dead!*" Who did he think Satan was in our motley crew? Al's breath was foul on my cheek. "*Look* at him — *look!*"

Plant-smashing Steve Blackledge had apparently given up and decided to exchange some of his tailored threads for jail garb. The infuriating, recently-hysterical banker wore the faded-gold trousers with his own white silk shirt, which was open down the front. Surprisingly, he wore no T-shirt. A crucifix glittered incongruously amidst his dense graying chest hair — . It hadn't protected him.

Blackledge had fallen forward on his knees with his hands groping for the bars as though he'd *needed* to either break out, grapple with my neck, or pray. I remember experiencing a standard Rich Stenvall kind of guilt: Did we less successful men somehow wish this white-collar son of a bitch dead?

Blackledge's head, the hair expensively styled, was caught between two bars. He was face up and the eyes were open but filming over. Glossy, like transparencies. I felt sick. Then I understood why the pair of substances inexplicably sprouting from his fluffy temples — mushy, cumulus — had seemed like *horns*. To a man like Al Calderone, they made poor Blackledge into the Prince of Evil.

174

But those growths that were squeezing his fine, dead head now — and *suddenly, horrifically forcing his tongue to pop out of his mouth* — grew instead from the banker's ears, not the temples of his head.

And I saw with disgust that the shit was still *growing* . . .

If he'd tried to ask for forgiveness there at the last, the poor bastard's prayers had been turned down. His answer was punishment.

"He came straight from hell and he got sent back, *straight back!*" Al squealed. His eyes were as immense as his logic was small. When I went in to kneel beside Blackledge's body, Calderone performed a crazy little impromptu fox-trot. Of exultation, I guess. "Praise be! I looked Satan right in the eyes, and I didn't even *flinch!*"

I just shook my head, then gingerly reached for the banker's limp wrist to test for a pulse. The guard grabbed me by my shoulder and threw me aside. Turned out it'd taken him so long to get there because he'd stopped to buzz Ellair in his office. And by the time the Noble One arrived, on the run, Al and I were again locked up in the drunk tank — whether or not it was temporary I didn't know.

The staring corpse, weird growths and all, was toted away under a sheet, and Ellair just glanced at me from the corner of his eye as he passed. I wondered if he was avoiding me or if, just temporarily, he'd put his great social experiment on hold.

The scared but animated chatter among the inmates kept me up late that night. But when I slept, I dreamed troubling dreams again, . . . dreams beyond comprehension. I awoke with a jolt as *another* tumultuous explosive sound rocked the entire building. And I shared several stunned, stares of bewilderment and fear with Doc and Lou Vick.

"They's comin' outta the Pit, comin' after *us,"* rotund Calderone claimed, his voice a croon of delivery. Bug-eyed, he rocked back and forth on the squalid floor of the tank. He had a hard-on, unmistakably, and he was absently, sporadically, rubbing it. "You-all killed Satan so the *demons* are free now. *That's* what's happening!" He laughed, the pitch high, nasal. "But they ain't gonna get *me,* 'cause I'm *saved!"*

Truly fed up, Lou went for him. But Doc Kinsey stopped the kid. Minutes after that, it was hotter than I'd ever known a place could become. Al went on muttering to anybody who would listen. "They killed Satan"—just sufficiently under his breath to keep from being attacked again. It occurred to me that a religious man who believed he was saved from his sins should be marginally less vindictive and less inclined to keep slipping into terror.

I had nothing better to do, so I leaned back against the wall and focussed my attention on the quiet and pacifying beauty of our plants. Lou had lined them in a row like so many small, obedient, untroubled kids. They smelled sweet in the shadows.

None of us went back to sleep in that heat, that dungeon, and Doc said that he knew for the first time in his life what they really meant by the old cliché: "It's hotter than hell in here."

When daylight came and the next man died, I began wondering if Al Calderone could be right.

4. Nightmare Madness

This is going to sound crazy as shit, but come the next morning it was almost as if nothing had happened. On the surface, at least, where most human beings keep damn near everything, never facing any fact that can be avoided.

A correction officer I knew from before, Gargan—a potbellied, aging, intentionally cold-eyed fish who was still one of the more *human* guards in my experience—came around after breakfast to let me out. Ellair's orders, I knew. Remarkably, that meant I was also supposed to resume my interviews on his behalf; as if Stephen Blackledge hadn't been eaten alive by some disease that came close to making AIDS resemble chicken pox.

Lou Vick and some new alcoholic loser they'd brought in around three o'clock in the morning shouted some mild catcalls at me. Lou implied that I probably wouldn't be able to sit down again after Doctor Ellair got through with me, but he was grinning when he said it. I think the men were kidding, and not as jealous of my relative freedom as circumstances demanded they pretend to be. Maybe not.

The Noble One's self-serving survey seemed absurd to me now; and while I had no choice about whether to continue it or not, I did fall into step with old Gargan to quietly ask what they'd done with the banker's body. I wanted to know if it was being autopsied and what the results would show.

"How the hell would I know?" Irritably, he turned to lumber back toward the stool waiting for him at the end of the corridor. Gargan had his Tough Screw mask up, and I could dig that. No official of the jail would like the idea of us inmates panicking. "I just came on duty an hour ago."

"Gargan," I called, fast, and caught his arm lightly in my fingertips. "That poor bastard didn't just *die*. C'mon, talk to me. Please. Whatever killed Blackledge could be contagious as hell."

For a second I thought the old Irishman was going to ignore me. But the word "contagious" got through to him. Pausing, he tugged an earlobe that practically drooped to his uniform collar. "I ain't sayin' you're right about that notion, Stenvall. Or wrong, either. But them gamblers who was in with him, they demanded another cell. Can't say I blame them." Gargan shrugged. "But when I told them there wasn't no room anywhere else 'less they wanted to squeeze in with Crock, well, Lew and Jimmie just kept bitchin' anyways. So I had to do something."

From where we stood early morning light was piddling into the closer cells. One of them had contained Steve Blackledge's god-awful corpse. Now, except for a still-dozing Dee Dee Lakens, it was empty. Several drops of sweat turned icy and trickled down my spine. "So where did you *put* them?"

As if covering some second thoughts, the old man

178

scratched his chin where his razor'd missed. "It ain't my fault, Stenvall. I told 'em the only vacant slot was Dead-lock." His lips came together like he might yet change his mind, or spit. "Some more men will go to court this mornin'. That'll open up another cell, so they decided to move." His eyelids worked. "How bad *did* that Bracker fella look?"

"His name was Blackledge," I said, and tried to weigh what I'd just heard. Steve had looked bad enough that two wiseguys had preferred maximum security—a black *hole*—to staying where the poor bastard had died. They'd get no showers that day, they wouldn't be able to see a damned thing in there, yet they'd opted for Dead-lock. "Gargan, why don't you just let your breakfast set-tle first?" I suggested almost gently. "Maybe I'll describe it for you later." *Him,* I corrected myself silently—*him,* as in an ex-human being—not *it*.

I tried putting the recent events on hold mentally, and went about my business asking idiotic questions. At least my assignment kept me from being locked up with all the other spooked men. Because his cell was straight across the corridor from where Steve Black-ledge bought it, I wanted to rap with Andre August next. But Crock and Lester Piercy were in with him, and I preferred to catch the pimp and home-coming queen at the end, the absolute end. It was possible El-lair would have enough data by then that he'd let me skip them.

I'd already rapped with the sleeping Dee Dee Lakens; I had no acquaintance at all with most of the others; and though Lou Vick and Doc were cooperative guys who wouldn't give me a hard time, I was hoping to save them for last—until I had quizzed everybody who was weird or surly and I really needed a break. After wondering fleetingly if this was how Larry King had gotten his start, I elected to swallow my disgust and pick up the interviews with Race Alyear. At least he wasn't violent. Not toward grown males.

Alyear was a thickset guy with the kind of face that most men took to at first sight. Not sexually, I don't mean that; I mean that he appeared to be a man's man: tall and husky; big boned; a sandy mustache decorating his face; and a world-weary self-absorption with which other guys instantly identified. He had reddish coloring that indicated his willingness to tie one on, and little bitty pig eyes that were ready to light up in agreeable humor at the first syllable of the smuttiest and dumbest jokes. Race could run both hamhock paws through his coarse, sandy hair and still keep it looking as if he'd just exited a barbershop. Smiling yet warily businesslike, Race gave the impression that he'd been around the block a few times and hadn't minded it.

He also didn't mind little girls for sex partners. And according to his repulsive legend, he liked to spend his commissions on child porn in general.

There's one more point to cover: He hadn't gotten his nickname of Race because he was a racist—even though three sentences out of his mouth proved that he was—but because of an exceptionally smooth line he'd memorized to use on any and every attractive broad he met. Rumor had it, he delivered the line at top speed.

The goal wasn't that Alyear be especially *successful;* but that his male sales prospects—whom he called "push-overs" and "suckers"—recognize him as one of them. When Race was crude and insulting to the "squeezes," as he called women, the men around responded extremely well to his sales pitch. Besides, ol' Race didn't want to bed *women;* grownup females were much too mature, imposing and, I guess, developed for his perverted tastes.

"Why they's nothin' wrong with Ellair givin' us plants, Stenvall, nothin' at all." Alyear spoke airily, leaning against the bars as if he'd been lounging in his den. The attitude suggested that this was nothing but an inconvenience, a pitstop, this period in the jail; that his next million-dollar deal was waiting right out front. "That Doc Ellair makes me think of a Fuller Brush man of old . . . you follow? He don't make his big pitch right *off*—the minute the prospect opens the door. He just puts a leetle present, a gift, in that sucker's palm." Alyear shot his hand between the bars to grab my hand and poke into my palm painfully. "Right *there,* like a center snappin' the ball to his quarterback. Then—*zap; poweee!*" His arm snaked back into the cell. Race grinned crookedly, in both senses of the word, and his eyes glittered smugly. "Why, she's all set up for the qualifying statement: 'I'll jest step inside a second t'show y'all what *else* you can git, for next to nothing!' That's sexual in-you-ando, y'get me?"

I hoped I didn't get *any* damn thing he had.

"Then, Race, you figure Ellair is actually setting us up for some reason? For what he *really* wants us to

181

buy — is that it? For some ulterior motive?"

I started scribbling down the salesman's answers, using a shorthand technique I made up on the spur of the moment.

"Definitely!" Race exclaimed. He nodded that big head as if it contained all the wisdom of the ages. I didn't mind that, but I minded the way Alyear seemed to see ulterior motives anywhere and everywhere. It wasn't hard to picture how ingratiating, assured, and probably father-like he would seem to a little girl, and I wanted him not to touch me any more. Or anyone else, if it had been up to me. Race inclined his head nearer to the bars, and me, lowering his voice to a conspiratorial drone. "By the way, they's something I'd like t'talk with you about, Stenvall. If you've got another moment."

I said doubtfully, tentatively, "Well . . ." Then I was saved from attempting an evasive answer when we both heard the scream.

"Sweeeet *Jesus!* Oh, *sweet* JESUS!"

I gaped at Race, and he gaped at me. Underlying the screams were whines and shrieks — not loud, but piercing, as if we heard them with our souls and not our ears.

I spun away from Alyear and started down the middle aisle. I didn't know where the original screams had come from, but the whining and garbled shrieks, sounded like they were near Dee Dee Lakens' cell. Glancing behind me, I saw Gargan awkwardly limping in the same direction from his distant guardpost. I was closer, so I covered the distance to Dwight's cell at a

182

sprint. By then, his voice was truly beastlike, awful to hear.

I peered through the bars from just outside the cell, but I couldn't see the kid. Then I spotted him. Dee Dee was climbing the bars, squirming up quickly, his lips working. He knocked down his religious message — by accident, I thought — because he was trying to go as high up as he could get. What was he trying to do?

Then, with his extremely long legs locked round the bars, Dee was letting go, putting out his skinny arms to reach perilously toward the distant ceiling of his cell. I saw he had his precious boom-box clutched in one large hand, but he seemed determined to crawl across the ceiling like a goddamned fly. What his motivations were, I hadn't a clue.

Next he let go of the radio, dropped it from his hand, and turned to watch it fall. I studied his features, tried to detect what was wrong, and all I made out was a combined blankness and private *knowing* — a pained horror that verged just at that second on real madness. I think I called to him, "Dee Dee, be *careful!* —"

But he lost his balance and fell. He did it in the oddest way, curling into a fetal ball enroute. His long limbs were tucked in as if he were getting ready to be born again. Then he landed with the small of his back on his beloved radio.

But the peculiar thing to me was how Dee *kept right on howling.* There was no waver, no interruption, during his drop or when he hit — not until he was tugging himself to a lopsided sitting position where he began bawling his eyes out like a little boy, the tears streaming

183

down his long face. He cupped his crotch, too, held it in those "palm-it/one-bounce/*jam*-it" hands of his, and rocked to and fro, to and fro. I never saw so many tears on a man's face before. But I also saw no growths bursting out of him as they had from Stephen Blackledge, thank God—only some internal pain that had stayed inside the tall kid, and something positively stark in his big black eyes . . . something that knew he was doomed, too.

I began to speak, trying to calm him. But Doc Kinsey's shout broke through poor Dwight Lakens' racking sobs to reach my ears: "*Rich!* Richard, *help* me for God's sake!"

Old Gargan, who'd just begun unlocking Dee's cell door with trembling fingers, glanced at me as I vaulted past him. I was sure that more weird things were happening in the tank. And I feared they were happening to the only friend I had in the freaking hole. The inmate clamor of fear hammered on the bars and in my ears and sweat stung my eyes as I ran, but when I was only a short distance away, I saw that Doc was okay. He was simply calling for my help with another man in the drunk tank.

May God forgive me, I hoped it was Al Calderone. It wasn't.

Young Lou, guilty of wedding unwisely and too often and, I supposed, passing in the same fashion through the educational system, had been given the death sentence for his crimes. I saw that immediately, just as Doc had.

I clutched the bars to the locked tank and tugged at

them, yelling at Gargan to hurry and let me inside. *Someone* had to help.

Lou was racing around in circles, faster than I'd ever seen, the perspiration geysering off him in torrents. I couldn't tell if he was attempting to run away from himself or catch himself, and didn't know what he meant to do if he succeeded; but Vick's all-out run and the unimaginable speed he was generating were bizarre, unnatural, and jolting to watch. Al was off in a corner with his fingers stuffed into his fat mouth to the second knuckles, probably muttering prayers. Doc was trying to get a hold on Lou's furiously pumping arms, but they were too muscular and Kinsey was too old and slow. Lou's heart, I thought, could not *take* much more of that. No one's could. Two or more of the beautiful plants Noble Ellair'd given us were crunched beneath the churning, pounding feet, and the spray of ruined petals gave the scene a weird, ritualistic look.

But now the circles Vick was forming began to narrow. From a sweeping, electrified bolt of impossible dashes, he'd gone to decreasing and wavering loops at a speed that was more human.

And as he finished another swing, then spun brokenly, unknowingly, toward me, I saw shooting out of the boy's straining mouth a spiky growth that looked like a combination of colorless barbed wire and unsprung human intestines. The stuff wobbled in the air and jerked with each terrifying lurch Lou took.

Yet his vivid blue eyes were more alive that second, more alert and clear and *aware*, than any eyes I had ever

185

looked into; and Lou was violently *pointing* at his growth-crammed mouth—*jabbing* with his index finger at it—as if he needed for me to see it, too, and verify that he had not gone mad. I nodded at him . . . Then I heard the sharp crack of bone splintering as Lou's jaw broke.

That was when his legs finally gave out. He crumpled to the drunk tank floor as Irish Gargan rushed up beside me; the guard and Calderone said *Jesus!* together as if they'd rehearsed it; and I saw Lou Vick begin the damndest convulsions anyone has ever seen. Sweet God! His arms, his head, and his back kicked so hard and so fast it was as if the kid was a machine coming apart, as if his batteries were running down. When Doc saw how Vick was batting out his brains on the floor, he tried to make him stop or to cushion the blows with his own arms—and meanwhile, that *stuff* kept uncurling from his mouth. Sausage-like but crisp and spiky, it almost seemed intent on preventing Doc from assisting.

The guard and I were inside the cell a fraction of a second later but it might as well have been a million years, for Lou's sake. He wasn't moving. Like *that*, he was still, his agony ended. At least that's what I prayed.

And yet that fucking *growth* was rising into the air above Lou's busted mouth and dead form. It was *climbing on nothing*, straight up, the way Dee Dee had been shinnying up the bars in his cell—groping for the ceiling, the sky! Then, exactly the way Dee had spread out his arms, the growth suddenly angled out, darting, prodding, doing a frigging bump-and-grind in our

186

faces! Man, it was like a cobra soaring up out of a basket, threatening to *strike;* and I just took root, simply stood and stared at it.

"Get away from that!"

The shout made me jump out of the growing substance's path. Noble Ellair, presumably summoned by the howls of the agonized Lakens, was right behind me. Weirdly, he looked not only authoritative and commanding but nearly angry with us, with me. "*All* of you," he ordered, "get out of the cell! Come on, come on, *move it!*"

We did, including Gargan; and it occurred to me how, in emergencies, we welcome almost anyone who will take charge. How we're like little kids, happily obeying the teacher at the sound of a fire alarm bell — because you can never be sure it isn't a drill.

Despite Ellair's command, however, I stayed in the open doorway for another few beats because I heard him mutter something like, *"Don't hurt it . . ."*

Now something wet and slobbering was at my ear. "They're comin' out *after* you. You better get right with Jesus!" Calderone.

Doc — smiley, warmhearted Doc — shoved Al, hard. Then Gargan made a big show of separating them even though Calderone wasn't hurt and didn't say a word; the guard could deal with guys bickering, *that* he understood.

I turned and ran back toward Dee Dee while I had the chance, ignoring an assault of inmate questions as I passed cell after cell. The racket and the fear were nearly tangible.

I saw Dee Dee's toilet paper roll sign before I saw him. I picked it up, and slipped it into my pocket to save it for him. His radio was already smashed, and we have few things in there as it is.

Gargan had left the door open, so I reluctantly went into the cell. Instantly I discovered the young black man alive and squatting on the floor. He was still holding himself, but he wasn't crying or howling, he was simply staring. For half a second I didn't see that his focus was the pretty plant — *"I can dig it!"* — Ellair had given him. And I wondered what was going on in Dee's brain to produce the expression of mute and hideous terror on his boyish face.

We weren't alone. Half a dozen guards were there, but not the chief jailer (whoever the hell he was), or the sheriff — not any of those people. *Why not?* I wondered, shuddering. Because the notion I had was that the jail had been shut off somehow, sealed away from the outside world — the real world — and I got to wondering also if I'd ever see Ronnie and the kids again. One guard shouted himself redfaced demanding to know why I was out of my cell. I realized that he'd be clubbing me with his stick in another moment — because the poor son of a bitch had to find a way to release his own fear of the unknown. I was relieved to spot Doctor Ellair arriving again. I grabbed the psychiatrist's arm and gazed imploringly at him.

"It's all right," Ellair told the guard. His calm amazed me. "This man is conducting a survey for me; he's an acting trusty."

"We need to talk," I said to Ellair quickly, softly.

"Now."

He frowned, withdrew his arm from my hand. I think he was about to say "No," or "Later." I don't know what I might have done but, before Ellair could reply, Gargan was there, his expression aghast with fright. "Look!" he gasped, and we did.

Moving athletically, gracefully, Dee Dee had stripped to his shorts and then clambered to the top bunk of the cell. He was poised on the edge, his arms out like a six-foot, eight inch condor; his eyes enormous, and for a fleeting moment black as pitch. *"Dick,"* he greeted me with a friendly grin twitching the corners of his mouth. Then he soared off the top bunk, a crane in flight for one microsecond — and dove onto the concrete floor, headfirst.

Dwight didn't move any more.

But under the waistband of his shorts, I saw a steady *rippling* — like running water. Something was inside his smooth brown belly, and it was trying to get out. I did not want to see what that something looked like, so I bolted into the corridor and simply shook.

"We'll have that meeting now, I believe," Noble Ellair said, mildly concerned at best. "Bring your notes, Mr. Stenvall, please. Life goes on."

Does it? I asked him with my astonished eyes.

I did what he said, of course. Even though I thought that bringing up anything connected with his fucking goodwill gifts at a time like that was definitely worse than anything else I'd seen or heard. I wanted to see *him,* even if he was trying to twist it around the other way.

We went up to his office with the Noble One a pace ahead, and it began to seem increasingly unlikely to me that our benefactor had twisted a great many other things around *another* way.

Part Three

Graveyard Flowers

"I have lived with shades, a shade;
I am hung with graveyard flowers."

— Dorothy Parker
"Rainy Night"

Seven

1. Hungry Shadows

"It sure as shit looked a lot bigger, outside."

"That's because *you're* bothered by claustrophobia."

"I'm not bothered by shit! 'Specially not no phobias." It came out "fobies" with Jimmie's pronunciation. "I just don't cotton to no tight-ass places like this." Deeply aggrieved, he got to his feet again, shuffled, sighed. "Sure looked bigger from outside." He edged forward nervously.

"*Will* you stay on your side of the cell!" Lew exclaimed. He tried to shove his partner away but was unable to define Jimmie's shadowed form in the inky blackness. He missed. "You make it worse when you pace all over the place that way. You stay on *your* side, and *I'll* stay on mine!"

"How the hell can I even tell which part of this goddamn cell is mine, when I can't even see my goddamn hand in front of my face?"

"You can tell the part that *isn't* yours when you're *draped* over me like a faggot! It takes out the creases in my uniform."

"I ain't no goddamn faggot, Lew. *You're* the homo in *here*. You're the only guy I ever did know who gave a

193

fuck how his jail clothes looked!"

A sigh. "I have tried to tell you for nearly nine years that appearance is important in our business, that it begins by developing the *habit* of looking nice. How d'you expect us to ever get into any really high-stakes games if the other gents at the table can't *stand* you?"

"Can you go blind in a place like this, Lewie?" There was a note of naked fright in Jimmie's voice. *"Can* you, if'n you can't see nothin' for a long enough time?"

"Your eyes will start adjusting to the light any time now. Then it won't be anywhere near as bad."

"We been in this here hole *hours* now, and I ain't seen any goddamn light at all. How'm I goin to *adjust* to light when there *ain't* any?"

A sigh. "The reason you can't see any light is because you have those shitty little eyes like a mole, and yet you won't purchase any glasses."

"I got glasses!" Jimmie argued. "I *do!*"

"You bought them at a *store*, Jimmie," Lew retorted. "You walked in off the street, ransacked through a bin of cheap spectacles with ordinary *glass;* and when you could make out the sales girl's *tits,* you decided they were perfect." Lew frowned. "Besides, you don't *wear them!*"

"I do *so!*" Jimmie argued. "Don'tcha remember the game with them two black fellers from De-troit, back in April, when you had the full boat 'n' I kep' raisin' and raisin' until there was mebbe a hundred and twenny bucks in the pot?"

"Well, *if* you wear your dime-store spectacles, Jim," Lew said with studiously mustered, cool reason, "where *are* they? Tell me that? If you're an intelligent man who wears his four-ninety-eight spectacles from a department store *bin* to ease his handicap, where *are* they?"

"It's so fucking *hot* in here!" Jimmie moaned. "Yew think we made a mistake askin' Gargan to put us in Deadlock?" Another tremor rippled through his voice. It was scarcely audible, like an earthquake's first tentative rumble. "We been in this place *hours*. When they gonna have another reg'lar cell ready, you think?"

"It's impossible to know exactly how much time has passed," Lew replied. It dawned on him that he'd heard a tone of anxiety in his own voice. He cleared his throat noisily before continuing. "There are no reference points, as they're called, no indications of the hour." He drew in a breath carefully. "Prisoners of war are subjected to"—Lew paused to summon the proper word—"sensory deprivation. Are *we* lesser men?" He waited for his partner to reply, but Jimmie didn't. "They survived their ordeals, and so shall we."

"Lewie?" The voice was quieter and also farther away somehow. It took Lew a second to understand that Jimmie had moved as far off as he could and then lowered himself to his haunches in a corner. "Lewie . . . what if Gargan *forgot* about us?"

"That's ridiculous! That's the silliest, dumbest thing I ever heard in my life!" He heard his heart begin picking up its tempo. Just that moment he felt inclined to take the not-quite-three full steps toward the myopic smaller man, but he didn't know why he felt that way. Smart gamblers kept their feelings under control, made only the moves based on *other* guys' whims, worries, emotions. By the time he knew why he'd wanted to step over next to Jimmie, it was too late. He'd conquered his own feelings again. "How in the world could Gargan forget we were here?"

"Deadlock," Jimmie answered slowly, the way he said things when he was trying to think them through, "it ain't been *used* for a *long time,* Lew. Nobody ever comes near it, 'cause everyone's skeered shitless of it. Lew, we ain't even had no water or food brought to us yet, remember? All this heat, and they ain't even bringin' us *water!*" There was a noticeable lilt of enthusiasm entering Jimmie's voice. It was as if he saw a chance—one horrible, last chance—to score a point on the man who often put him down.

"This is bullshit, James," Lew said. Something twanged deep in his gut.

"Lewie . . . Gargan's old. O-l-l-l-d, Lewie." Jimmie stretched it out like that. "He might get sick 'n just go home. For days. He might even *retire.*" Jimmie stood. Fighting perspiration that dripped into his eyes, down his uniform collar, dampened his shorts. Lew couldn't recall the last time Jimmie'd sounded so pleased—so happy. "Lew. Lewie, Lewis—that ol' Gargan could fucking *die.* If he *did*—"

"Shut up! Just shut your *damn mouth!* And keep it shut!"

"You gettin' hot now too, Lew, hot like me?" Jimmie shuffled forward a toe-length at a time, in baby paces. Lew heard the soft footsteps approach. "You sweatin' out that nice-fittin' uniform? The reason I ask, Lew, is that you're startin' to stink real bad—only it smells more like piss and shit."

"Don't you touch me, goddamn your little rabbit

eyes!" Lew commanded. What in hell was the *matter* with Jimmie—why was he beginning to *enjoy* this . . . this nightmare? Lew backed up an inch, tried to retreat. From his partner, from the special cell of isolation, the fear building up inside, the sensory deprivation; from the life he had lived and the life he had wasted with flops like Jimmie; from the sweat turning his own uniform to clinging, fetid mush; from the chance that Jimmie was right; and from something else he suddenly felt building up inside of him. It was like agonizing, sharp pain, and things tearing. *Let it be a heart attack,* he prayed when he could retreat no more. "They'll come let us out any minute now," he grunted, "they'll take us back to a regular cell, and we'll be okay. Fine."

"If 'n you can see a whole lot better'n me, Lew," Jimmie began, close now, "can you tell me if that's *spiders* I hear movin' over in the corner? Lewie, is that *just* spiders?" His enthusiasm for having made sense and winning a point against Lew turned to total, abject terror so quickly that the palm and fingers he had put out to tease Lew, to taunt and chide him, turned to ice on the larger man's wrist. "And is that just spiders right *there* . . . *behind* you?"

Lew jerked his neck around to look. Light glinting from somewhere made the shadows break up, define themselves against the murky backdrop of Deadlock. The shadows broke into several pieces of various lengths—twisting lengths of creepy black that were all around both of them, *lying* on them suddenly.

At the instant that his much greater pain also broke through, Lew saw that the shadows were only spiders *in part.*

He and Jimmie were casting the rest of the shadows.

2. *Raising Entomogenic Histoplasmosis for Fun and Profit*

With little cartoon question marks fairly leaping from his eyes as well as the top of his balding head, Noble Ellair clasped his hands and leaned across his desk to me.

The shrink's receding hairline, coast-to-coast forehead, and nearly lipless mouth turned his head skulllike as he put his face next to the emergency lamp on his desk. He always kept the expression in his eyes veiled. I decided that if he ever experienced lust for a woman, she'd probably think he was about to diagnose her as anal-repressive.

"What do you think has happened here?" he asked conversationally. "What do you *think* is going wrong?"

"I think that people are dying," I said, "in fact, I know it." Ellair looked rather disappointed by that so I added with a decisive bob of my head, "Hideously."

"I see," he said, and straightened. Frowning in mild disapproval, he stared down at his hands, revolved his thumbs around each other, pursed his lips. "That's rather inadequate, I'd say. Not in the least what I would have expected from a man who has the imagination to be a writer." A brow shot up. He bent forward and thrust himself over the desk at me. "Or were we, perhaps, being somewhat evasive?"

"I think," I started over, "that people are dying hideously in this place — because of your goddamn plants." Then I folded my hands too, rested them on the desk in front of me. His breath was odd. Not bad, just odd. "But I can't figure out how it works." I met his gaze. "Or just what the hell you've done."

"Ah!" Ellair said, mildly pleased. "*Invasion of the Body Snatchers?* That kind of thing, Mr. Stenvall?" He stood, moved behind his chair, rested his hands on top of it, and leaned toward me.

"I said I don't know yet exactly what's going on. What kind of . . . invasion it is." I stopped. I'd begun going too far, too dangerously far, if Ellair *was* dangerous. "I don't know *yet*."

"The jury is still out, then; I see." Ellair performed what he probably would've called "smiling" and the upper part of his body twisted away from me. The head stayed put, the face attentive, intent. "You're attempting to decide whether I am myself a thief of human bodies, born on a distant and doubtlessly unknown planet—unless you've already decided on Mars, of course—or merely a mad professor who has escaped from a late show on television. Come, Mr. Stenvall, which is it? Your fantasies are most intriguing!"

I stalled on giving any answer. The truth was that without clearcut evidence of Noble Ellair being the cause of what was going "wrong" in the jail, any conclusion of mine along those lines would make me look paranoid. Yet I *was* pretty sure his plants were behind it all and even more sure that I didn't want to play mind games with this prick. He was a psychiatrist who knew all the terms and buzzwords, and all the symptoms from neurosis to actual madness. Trying to match wits with the son of a bitch would've been like going one-on-one with Dee Dee Lakens in hoops.

But Dee was dead. No one was ever going to go one-on-one with him again. And I didn't see any choice except playing Ellair's game if I wanted to forestall further deaths—including my own. "Look," I said. "If you brought all these plants here for the reasons you explained to me, and it's some characteristic of the plants that's killing people—but *you didn't know any of this would happen*—well, hell, then you're probably not guilty of anything except poor judgment." Everything I was trying to say was making me nervous as hell. I hated the fact that his laid-back love of logic was putting *me* on the defensive! "If so, well, that's the same sort of bad judgment a drunk displays when he knows he should think about it and instead goes ahead and orders another drink." My heart was racing a little. I unclasped my fingers, drummed them on his desk until I noticed he was looking at them, appraising me. "Probably no worse crime than that, I guess."

He sat down in his chair. In the process, one shoulder seemed accidentally to nudge the battery-operated lamp, beaming it fully into my face. Ellair didn't move it. "Your pardon, your tender forgiveness, touches me deeply," he said sardonically. The heels of his hands were pressed against the desk, then his left index finger suddenly pointed at me. "Go on. Challenge me. Ask any questions you wish to ask."

"All right. Why did you want me to go out and talk to the inmates about your plants? I don't think you leveled with me on that." Sweating, I shifted to get the light out of my eyes. "Did you have anything to do with the air conditioning going off and on—and if so, why? *What killed those guys?*"

"My, you *are* full of interesting suspicions—aren't you?" His eyes flashed some kind of signal, but I didn't know what or how to read it. He'd already read my first batch of notes—untranscribed and unedited—but I wasn't sure what he made of them. Now he used his thumb to riffle through the pages again. He opened his mouth to make another snotty remark.

But I hadn't finished. "Where did you *put* the dead guys, Doctor? What did you do with their *bodies?*"

He shut his mouth, tried not to frown or glare. He didn't answer, either.

"Ellair," I said softly, "have they already been buried?"

He rose. Slowly. "The correct and customary procedures have been observed, Mr. Stenvall." He parted the drapes at his window. It looked like a beautiful day in hell. The windows were barred like everything else in the goddamn joint and that fascinated me for some reason. It made it harder, I thought, to tell the inmates from the officials, the animals from their keepers. But he used an old-fashioned crank to raise the window a couple of grudging little inches; even allowing that much fresh air to piddle into his office was a blessing. "Stenvall, you are that rare prisoner who can communicate effectively. You have the ears of your fellows. Take Race Alyear, for example."

"*You* take him," I snapped. "He's no 'fellow' of mine." I made a lopsided smile without any more warmth than Ellair's. "You know, Doctor, I can never be certain when you're complimenting or insulting me. D'you think that's my fault, or yours?"

He irritated me for reasons other than his reference to Alyear. Apart from the fact that I could scarcely ever find the words to say what I really yearned to say to my wife and children, I'd never bought the goddamn elitist notion that some people could not communicate effectively. It was, I thought, more a case of most ordinary folks thinking badly on their feet; of not realizing they had been used, or attacked, until later; of their being more straightforward, honest, even more polite, than smart-ass types like Doctor Noble Ellair. Most people liked thinking they were engaging in conversation, not seeing how clever or phony they could be.

And it bothered me, too, that men like Noble Ellair enjoyed pretending that a punch in the mouth didn't qualify either as communication or social commentary. It might not be as sophisticated or glib as a satirist's quip, but it conveyed a message, a meaning, exceedingly well. Like the punch I ached to throw at Ellair just then. *Badly*.

"When you have completed a decent working sample of inmate interviews," he continued, taking his seat as if I had asked him nothing more than a few rhetorical questions, "I expect to have the proof to support my program, then take it into other institutions." His smile of pleasure appeared genuine enough. "Richard, the public regards scientists today in a dichotomous fashion previously reserved for the divinity. A love/hate relationship, as it were. So much that is done in science is viewed almost as if the work was being undertaken by a god."

"I think scientists set that up themselves," I said. "That they ask for it by pretending to have all the answers. They love it and eat up that shit like it was Mom's apple pie." I let my lips smile. "No offense, Noble."

"No offense taken," Ellair replied quickly. *Wow*, I thought as he tilted his chair back, *we're buddies now! Mano-a-mano all the way!* "What the public cannot conceivably understand is that there are numerous kinds of scientists today, so many disciplines and subsets of disciplines that something rather strange has happened. I've heard it said that because of educational pressures and the high demands specialization places on men of science, the average biologist knows less about zoology, to take one example, than the average high school biology student knows."

"I can believe that," I gave him, nodding. "There's almost no such thing as a handyman any longer. The guy who comes to repair your furnace seldom has any clue how to replace a light bulb." *Where the fuck was he going with this?*

"I've decided to take you rather more deeply into my confidence," Ellair said. This time he had the common sense not to pause and wait for a smart remark. "To the extent, Richard, of informing you that I'm in the process of conducting . . . an experiment. You see, I'm no stodgy, conservative, timid little organization-man of a scientist. I'm the sort who quests, openly, for the truth."

Goody, I thought.

"It's my belief that there is vast progress to be made by casting aside countless unproven assumptions. By wandering wide-eyed, Richard, into really new, original realms of exploration. By going—"

" 'Where no man's gone before?' " I suggested as in-

203

nocently as possible. And for one scary moment I had no way of knowing how Ellair would take that.

Then I did. *"Exactly!"* he said exultantly, beaming at me along with his damn lamp. "You certainly do have a flair for words, Stenvall—I must say that!"

"Or for television," I added without smiling.

"Well, you are obviously intelligent enough to perceive that we cannot have *panic* in this place. Or the remotest possibility of a riot. People get hurt under such conditions, inmates as well as . . . well, everyone gets hurt at such times."

I tried my own experiment. "That can happen when you try to explore strange, new worlds," I said as offhandedly as possible.

"Quite." But he glanced up from the notes I'd brought him as if suspecting at last that I was having fun at his expense. Then he looked down again, finger pointing. "Lakens, the black . . ."

"I remember him."

"According to your notes Lakens said that I was 'like Santa Claus,' to him. Very good. Alyear, whatever you say about him, responded well enough; he recognized the potential merit of what I'm attempting to do. Two men from very different avenues of life and crime." He looked pleased. "Both approved my goodwill gift."

"Dee Dee was a frustrated basketball star, a case of arrested development—but I've met men whose development was arrested at a lot worse point than his. Race Alyear is *pus* plus *feet!*"

"But neither man failed to appreciate the value of my generosity!" Ellair's brow, rising, asked me to concede the point. To let him have his satisfaction.

"That crooked fucking banker didn't appreciate it," I retorted. I wondered if that might be why Steve Blackledge had been the first to die.

"Survey questions that fail to evoke the projected, anticipated responses are sometimes traceable to the interviewer, Richard—to seemingly meaningless minutiae ranging from the interviewer's facial expression and vocal intonation to the stifling of yawns. Even the deodorant he wears, or any incidence of flatulence."

"Sheesh, doc, I didn't *fart* in his face!" I exploded. Then, what he'd told me started churning in my mind. Was this really the way researchers at the upper levels operated—by putting their clothes on just so and trying to set up their test subjects so they'd give back the answers they wanted? It sounded to me more like those commercials filmed at drug stores and supermarkets, where interviewees are handed free samples and are expected to like the product. I'd already read that today's best-educated shrinks were being hired by corporations in the expectation of "loading" their demographic studies or to win government grants simply to research better deodorants, or fart-free onions!

"It's a matter of how you automatically improved your interview technique as you began to go from inmate to inmate," Ellair told me. He regarded me judiciously. "It isn't possible for a bright, ambitious man like you, or a man like me, *not* to become better at a task as we grow familiar with it. Stenvall, don't you see it?" He beamed. "You, yourself, began phrasing your questions in order to get the desired answers! Not to satisfy me, but because your fear lowered your resistance to helping me and, instinc-

205

tively, you *performed* better! You can't keep from being rational, perfectionistic!"

I shook my head helplessly. "Is that an insult or a compliment?"

"Neither," he answered promptly. Was that the first time he'd given me a direct reply to a question or not? I couldn't remember. "Richard, we *need* your communication skills. Now. *All* of us do. You can see that there must be no panic or rioting."

I blanched. "What are you saying? You expect *me* to calm them down? Is *that* it?" This master of mental obfuscation was confusing the shit out of me. He was also starting to wear me down and make me want to be somewhere else, even the drunk tank. Alkies are what star-gazers call "fixed" people, I read. We get along great in unchanging, no-wave environments and then, when the world turns into something you could positively *surf* on, we try to swallow every drop of wet stuff in sight.

"I can't do it myself," Ellair admitted. "They can't relate to me. I couldn't do it" — his odd smirk flickered — "without the aid of modern chemistry."

Then I figured it out. "You're asking me to get all those men to stay cool. You need me to convince them to chill down, and stay put — and *adjust to whatever happens,* right?" My shirt was sticking to my chest like skin and my heart was suddenly in my mouth. I swallowed, my throat very dry. "That's as *opposed to making a big stink!* To creating so much trouble for you that *you might have to cancel your experiment!* Do I understand you now, Ellair?"

"Well, that isn't the only reason I ask you to quell any disturbances before they get out of hand, obviously," he said. Once more, his hands were braced against the desk. He was carefully, tightly, controlling his facial expressions. "But that's the gist of it."

"Uh-uh," I said flatly, and folded my arms. "No way." Then I lowered them, thinking hard. "At least, not until I know exactly what's happening. Not until you persuade me I'm doing this for everybody, not just for you."

He gave me a blank stare. The wheels were spinning busily. All I could hope for was that I wasn't following his script like some unsuspecting ignorant little Pavlovian pet.

To my surprise, ultimately, he uttered that one word I asked for. *"Fungi."*

"Fungi?" I repeated. "That crap growing from Lou Vick's mouth, from Steve Blackledge's ears. That was . . . a *fungus?*"

Noble Ellair gave me an almost elegant shrug. "Since I did not want any of this, since it's not *my* fault and *I* did not *plan* for this, I can only admit to you that it's the only explanation that seems to fit the facts."

He'd completely thrown me. For a loop. "I don't know what to say. I mean, I don't know enough about . . . *it* . . . to make much of a judgment."

"Fungi, or *eumycetes,*" he said promptly, "are a subdivision of plants that comprises many simpler plants. They reproduce mainly with spores—"

"Spores?" I said, my voice pitched low.

"Oh yes," Ellair said. He pressed his fingertips together. "Slime molds, which are closely related, produce no cell walls in their amoeboid states, while yeasts are absolutely single-celled. Most *true* fungi,

207

however, generate very small filaments, or *hyphae,* that band together in a nearly . . . well, family-like situation, called a *weft.* Then they are known as *mycelium,* or" — Ellair wafted his eyebrows — "or what we call *spawn."*

"You're saying that the guys in here are somehow being tortured and killed by spores?" I asked in a whisper. "By crap called 'spawn?' "

"I'm not saying that," the Noble One said on a note of denial. "I'm saying, for reasons I needn't go into now, that I consider it a definite possibility, one that fits the bill." He went on talking, and I must have heard the man since I remember the words. But I felt sickened — revolted — by his little fact-fitter. "Now then, I mentioned that there was another reason why I wanted you to keep the inmates calm. You'll be able to do so without concern that they'll question your motives or believe that you have somehow become 'my' man."

"How's that?" I mumbled. *Fungi?*

"Even before the last two men died so tragically, I had spoken both with the mayor's and the governor's offices." The shrink allowed himself to look deeply satisfied; proud. "All the prisoners will shortly be moved to another, much safer facility. And *you,* Mr. Stenvall, are going home!"

He surprised me so much I couldn't even answer.

"You'll be able to notify them that their safety was our major concern." His eyes were bright as diamonds and just as hard. "I believe they may look upon my floral gifts in a most positive fashion. Don't you?"

I nodded. The ancient gag-line — *there's a fungus among us* — kept repeating itself in my head. But Ellair

208

wasn't through boggling my mind.

"In any case, I'm calling back all my plants. So it's a moot point." He spoke as if he'd had an interesting, minor afterthought, but the implications of what he was saying shook me further. "All that you and the other men will have left of my fine and humane experiment will be a lingering memory of something that's rather special these days: Real caring; true generosity — from men at the top." He bobbed his skeletal head. "Too bad, but I've decided I just can't risk leaving the plants out there."

I gaped at him. The office spun. Amazingly, I hadn't made a logical connection of any kind between Noble Ellair's gabble about fungi, and his *houseplants!* I felt electrically charged by a paranoia that was tinged with resentful bewilderment. Was I so hopelessly fucking uninformed about flowers that they posed risks to human life that I'd never even heard of? Was Ellair saying that harmless, pretty posies in little pots actually concealed some sort of goddamn murderous fungus?

"You finish up your survey to the best of your ability before you check out," he was saying quietly now, "while I arrange for the guards to fetch the plants." Abruptly and with apparent sincerity, Ellair lurched forward in his chair, struck his desk with his fist. *"Damn,* how miserable it makes me feel to reach this decision! It can't conceivably be *all* of my ill-timed goodwill gifts that are responsible, of course." The man was rueful, truly unhappy, I thought. "I feel like such a damn Indian giver!"

That childish term, and his reference to my "checking out" (as if the jail had been nothing more than a

Marriott that wasn't operated very well) and his doomsday hints related to flowers that Mom would've considered beautiful made the situation absolutely surreal. I turned to the slightly-opened window, tried to drink in the air. Again, I yearned to hit him. Simultaneously, though, I felt, for the first time, a sense of common humanity with the man. Both of us had our precious dreams, ambitions toward accomplishing new and important things. Both of us were victims of our own mistakes and inadequacies, a lack of help or understanding from other human beings. And plain shitty bad luck had conspired to hold both of us back. Incredibly, he was tugging at my heartstrings—but I determined to ignore the feelings and ignore him. "Could you just tell me what's gone wrong, what has happened to everybody?" I asked. "I can probably follow you if you don't get too technical."

His sigh was apologetic. "Of course." He even made an honest effort to keep his usual condescension from his expression while he explained. "You'll recall from your schooling that fungi do not produce their own food but depend upon getting their energy by means of organic, living matter." He squirmed around to get as comfortable as possible across the desk from me. "Before you start thinking how awful that is, bear in mind it is what all animals do—including man."

"I guess that's true."

"It is," he assured me with a nod. "We consume organic matter—vegetables—without a twinge of conscience. But a fungus becomes a parasite when it dines on living matter, according to our superior way of viewing things." The corners of his mouth turned up, turned down. "The fungus as parasite becomes *rusts* or *smuts* but is termed a *saprophyte* when the organic matter it devours is—already *dead.*"

"I think," I said slowly, "I'm more concerned about fungus that causes diseases in man."

" '*Fungi,*' please, when you pluralize it, Richard." He couldn't keep from his pedantic ways. "There are several varieties of fungi which . . . um . . . munch away inside us."

"I see you have a way with words, too," I told him, as I made a face. "I can think of ringworms, myself—and athlete's foot. Am I right?"

"You *are!* Excellent!" His eyes glittered. "*Tinea cruris,* that's the term for the fungal disease that is especially harmful to diabetics. *Thrush* attacks the mouth, the vagina—and lung disease is certainly possible when *aspergillosis* is on the scene! As for ringworm, Stenvall, steroid users are far more susceptible to it than other persons."

He was getting to me. "Christ, Ellair, those diseases are a goddamn far cry from athlete's foot!"

"Yes, because we tend to think of fungi as nuisances at worst." One of his half-smiles. "But I'm not through categorizing them for you. There are the infections of the human lymph nodes, too, called *African histoplasmosis.*" He peered down at his newly clasped hands. "We have underrated their potential for a long, long time, Richard." His eyes leapt up and found mine. "I wouldn't be astonished if it was some of those organisms we find in our deceased inmates, when the autopsies are completed."

"Fungi are so—so *small.*" I blurted. And my limbs jerked in instinctive revulsion. I glanced around Ellair's office as if for some kind of sneak attack.

"You forget that if we don't die in a nuclear holocaust," Ellair murmured, "we will *still* perish, one by one, from cells in our own bodies that cannot be seen with the naked eye. Human kind looks automatically to the immense, the colossal, as the enemy that may strike; it's an evidence of our overweening egos that we prefer believing it requires something of great, visible power to hurt us." His thumbs revolved round each other. "A bullet one-inch long, well placed, murders us. Cancer cells devour us. Even our little human hearts fail us and we die." He glanced at me. "Ever *see* a human heart, Richard? You could carry it in the palm of your hand or pop it into your pocket without noticing the extra weight."

He made me increasingly uneasy, squeamish, but he'd already sold me. I guess he became an authority figure to me in fact with the sequence of speeches. "So some fungus hiding in your plants attacked the men?"

"I should think our specific culprit was the *entomogenic fungi,* Richard," he said ruminatively. "But in a more powerful guise than we're accustomed to in America. By which I mean that fungus that customarily germinates and grows in—*and from*—the bodies of insects."

"Insects?" I asked with horror. *"Bugs?"*

"During the period when I was endeavoring to modify the survival needs of the little beauties I brought from Costa Rica—after all, they had to be able to adjust to a less than tropical climate—I believe that a virulent new strain of the *entomogenic* must have . . . stowed away." He made a sound close to a chuckle, in honor of his cleverness. "Yes," he declared, "that must be it." Then he added with a wink, "And that certainly proves to have been a highly interesting choice!"

"A choice?" I echoed him, startled by his wording. "You're not suggesting that something . . . well . . . volitional occurred? Something *planned?*"

"No, no, no," Ellair answered firmly, "at least, not in the sense that you mean it. Not quite?"

I almost repeated it—*Not quite?*—before realizing I sounded like a fucking parrot. "What does that *mean?*"

Ellair's almost hairless brows rose as he considered his reply, choosing the words carefully. "The Chinese have always known, Richard, that the mind is infinitely more involved with nature than we in the West have been willing to believe. They would understand, as we cannot, that when we are psychologically healthy, amazing things occur, seemingly spontaneously. But when we lack harmony with one another and with out natural environment, things go badly amiss." He tapped his index finger noiselessly on the desk. "Other thoughtful, independent men have observed the signs of—well, of a *mind-aura* dwelling in everything from subatomic life to immense galaxies. It may be, or may have been, dormant . . . insentient . . . up until now. But there was never any pledge from God that it must *stay* so."

"Be more specific," I coaxed him, sweating.

Ellair's expression seemed dreamy. "More than one species of fungus secretes an exceptionally sticky substance it uses for the capture of much *larger* creatures. It evolved remarkably, Stenvall, in Costa Rica." A pause. "It learned how to form a tube and attach itself to the larger host's body." His eyes brightened.

213

"For the purpose of sucking its food any time it pleases."

He was making my flesh crawl, and I rubbed and scratched at myself surreptitiously. But I fought for my sanity, for the natural order in life which, I began to suspect, I'd taken for granted.

"That 'larger' thing it feasts on, Noble," I said. *"We're* pretty big." I laughed nervously. "You're talking about 'larger' in insect terms, right? I mean, spiders come in all sizes. Ants are pretty small—as a rule—so a tarantula is *gigantic* to a little red ant. Right?"

Ellair rose so fast he startled me. He closed the window although I didn't know why . . . maybe what he was telling me was chilling to him, too. "Fifty-thousand species of fungi have been described scientifically, catalogued." He turned to me with concern. "But we know of more than two-hundred and fifty thousand types—and there may well be myriad more. Stenvall, it looks to me as if the pace quickened at some stage of their evolution, and several intriguing varieties of entomogenic beasties have *crossed the line.*"

"What line?" I asked quickly. Heat enveloped me and it was easy to believe I was already being devoured.

Ellair took his time answering. I watched him cross to the door, unlock it—I hadn't noticed he locked it after us—and step aside. Obviously, he meant for me to leave. He was dismissing me. I sensed his gaze, steady as a rock and focused. I also sensed an electric, inner tension about him as I rose to leave and felt inclined to imagine it as excitement—an excitement not wholly unpleasant. *Crossed* what *fucking line?* I wondered.

214

Then we were out in the dimly lit hallway over the cell floor, and I recognized a subtle shift in Noble Ellair's mood, as if he'd controlled and reordered the mood himself.

"Folklore in Central America," Ellair began anew, "has it that the kind of plant I brought to our shores possesses a benign and calming effect — even a tranquilizing one." He laid his hand on my shoulder and I jumped at his touch. "Richard, my motives were one-hundred percent honorable. But you remember the reference I made to the probability that the *entomogenic* has crossed an evolutionary line?"

"Of course," I nodded as his hand urged me forward. With every step, the sounds from below swept upward like a wave. I was going back down there with the other men. "Please explain."

"Richard, I meant the line between parasite," Ellair said quite distinctly, *"and predator."*

3. Eldorado

When he awoke in the long, clean, apparently empty room, Eddie Po believed for several frightening moments that he was dead.

Fear knows no logic. It is the antithesis of logic. As Eddie struggled to twist his big head around for a better look at his sterile surroundings, his terror made him acknowledge that he was a very large man who'd overeaten willfully and hugely nearly all of his life; so it seemed quite reasonable to the Hawaii-born inmate that he'd actually been buried in a room, and not a coffin.

And since Eddie had always tried to believe in an afterlife, the idea that he considered himself dead did not seem to make for any sort of awkward contradictions. He had grown up within sight of the active volcano called Mauna Loa; had matured in the shadow of its four-thousand-foot crater Kilauea; was awed and intimidated by its intermittent shows of deadly power, certain the gods might elect to kill him at any whimsical instant. His family had been so poor that none of its members would even have understood the term "economic deprivation," but they had believed in *mana,* the supernatural abilities granted certain individuals—and with just as much whimsy as the volcano's erupting.

Eddie, in fact, once had an uncle who belonged to the secret *Iniat* society and had been given the magic to defend the family against its enemies. Uncle had been what was known as a *tena agagura,* a sorcerer or shaman, and Uncle had exercised his powers by obtaining eating utensils—or anything the enemy might have put into his mouth—and practicing the oldest variety of magic. He'd planted the spoon or other utensil deep in a skillfully dug hole, along with certain plants known to be poisonous as well as razorish grasses akin to bamboo, then muttered incantations above the sacred stone he placed on top of the mound. Instantly, the family's foe fell very ill, and it became incumbent on him to get the magic spell removed. Because, if he didn't succeed—through earnest apologies and promises—he would die.

The enemy who succeeded in having the spell recalled, however—and Eddie'd been extremely impressed by this fact—never became angry and rarely

216

felt resentful. Instead, if the regret he voiced seemed sincere, he tended to become a new friend of the family! At least until he, too, became insulted or imperiled and it became necessary to locate his own *tena agagura* and continue the cycle.

It was due to those commonplace experiences of his boyhood that Eddie Po had decided to become a cook. When the mainland wasn't bewildering him with its complicated mix of sometimes unreasonable laws, Eddie had worked as a very *good* amateur cook. Most of the time since departing the islands he had worked for fast food restaurants, but he preferred little, out-of-the-way greasyspoons where meals were prepared from scratch. What better place to be sure that the cooking utensils were clean — and that each and every one was *returned* at the close of a meal?

When Eddie had been sprawled out in the drunk tank, sweat draining off his obese body in buckets, he'd tried with all his waning strength to understand what was happening to him. Doc, Rich, the other men had obviously imagined the awful heat in the jail had caused a heart attack. Eddie'd known that wasn't the case for a good reason: He'd already had three mild attacks and this illness wasn't quite like the others. The temperature and humidity were terrible, but he'd grown up at the foot of Mauna Loa, his corpulent body was used to oppressive heat. At first Eddie had thought of an old enemy who belonged to an offshoot cult of *Iniat* and might have made off with a fork or spoon he'd used, but he knew that was unlikely. Eddie counted all the utensils in the jail kitchen and besides, where could an enemy *tena agagura* have dug the proper hole inside a building?

217

Then he'd remembered that part of the spell involved the acquisition of poisonous plants, and the shrink, Ellair, had been somewhere hot named Costa Rica—which for all Eddie knew might have some cultural, magical connection with his people. By a fairly simple process of elimination, he was fairly certain this was the answer to what had made him so terribly ill. And, without question, it was going to kill him and all the other men in the county jail.

Nonetheless, Eddie had said nothing about it. During the many years he lived on the mainland, Eddie'd acquired most of the ways of his fellow Americans—which is to say, those with whom he came into contact—and he was privately quite proud about that. Central to the ways of these people was the machismo ideal that a man would not voluntarily, under any circumstances, make a complete fool of himself. Perhaps he would tolerate it if he was called nasty names reflecting on his or his family's ancestry; perhaps he'd let himself be described as a warthog, an ugly pig who should be roasted with a piece of fruit crammed into his mouth; perhaps he would permit the women he knew to call him a disgusting alcoholic lush . . . But he would have to consider slaughtering and then skinning the man who called him a faggot or, almost as bad, a nerd, wuss, or coward.

So he'd allowed himself to die and, opening his eyes in the afterlife, found himself in a casket, unable to move or, if he wished to explore paradise at all; unable to escape from the ponderous and still sweating mound of himself that had been left lying on some kind of metallic table. But if he was lying on a *table*, he surely wasn't inside his coffin after all!

218

Exerting enormous will power that produced a surge of pain in his mammoth belly, Eddie succeeded in turning his head—just marginally—to one side. A goodwill gift, a beautiful but exotic, foreign house-plant, had been left on the floor of the room. *Is it an infirmary?* he wondered. Seeing the plant renewed his fear, but the dreadful misery in his stomach kept it at a tolerable level. Barely. Through Eddie's jangled mind rushed recollections of the way flowers were placed in mainland funeral homes, of his conviction that the shrink Ellair's Costa Rican plants were filled with evil *agagura,* and the realization that the shrink might *know* they murdered people—might *purposely* have put this plant in the room in order to *finish him off!*

The possibility of that coupled with his inability to sit up or stand made Eddie jerk back his head in fresh alarm and terror. He saw Lou Vick lying dead on another cold table behind him, and Lou was star-ing straight at him!

Eddie wasn't certain how he had known the dead young man was Vick since the only things showing through the folds of vegetable-like growth wrapped around him from head to toe *were* Lou's eyes. The folds looked like cabbage, not moving now; on closer inspection Eddie could glimpse strands of *pinkness* showing through the folds. *He looks like corned beef and cabbage,* Eddie realized, nauseated, conscious that reeking juices were seeping out of the leafy mess—and from his own fat lips.

Muttering a short prayer in a tongue his Uncle would have recognized, feeling more nausea then pain, Eddie thrust his big head up from the coroner's table. The idea was to get *all* of him into a sitting position, if possible, then to throw himself onto the floor and, if he could not walk, to *roll* himself out of the room. The presence of the plant was enough reason for that; the company of Lou Vick's vegetable-stew remains made it worth actually killing himself, if it came to that.

All Eddie managed to do was look down the length of his body just to his stomach which was much too large for him to see any parts of his body below it. His genitals, legs, and feet might as well have been beneath the Kilaeua crater, or in Costa Rica.

He discovered large orange and red splotches covering his chest and belly, each of them raised just slightly from his skin—which appeared to be turning light-green—and, as Eddie watched, *jiggled*. Moved independently as though to a rhythm he could not hear. *Wiggled*.

If Lou Vick was corned beef and cabbage now, or vegetable stew, he had himself become a salad, a movable feast . . . the rest of the *luau*.

What happened to him next felt much like the three heart attacks Eddie'd had in the past and tried to ignore, but worse . . .

It delivered him from the nightmare.

Eight

1. *The Enemy's Image in the Mirror*

Shaken by his remark, I stopped in my tracks. But Ellair announced he would go with me "and personally check out how things were going by now," then gripped my shoulder to guide me toward the stairway down. In near darkness the image of Satan as Temptor, a familiar one in uncountable paintings of centuries ago (as well as in the memory of former little boys with fundamentalist upbringings) inevitably sprang to mind. I had no way of estimating with certainty, then, if the image was fair to Noble Ellair or not, but he had once more enlisted my aid . . . *knowing* when he asked me that I could not say "no" with his promise of my going home the next day ringing in my ears.

I began to think, as we proceeded in virtual lockstep toward the stairs, of what he had said about cells and other living things of puny size with the power to destroy, to expunge from the earth beings of vastly greater proportion; and about lines being crossed between the merely instinctive, naturally parasitical, and the aggressively predatorial.

"Thoughts are *things*," I recalled a great man once saying, and thoughts were little, unseeable, invisible. Too many of them in my time upon the planet had been similarly aggressively predatorial and murderous, had lusted for blood and for the forbidden. I had to admit to more than a few of such thoughts myself, particularly in Noble Ellair's company.

Beneath us, the steady but unintelligible mutter of frightened male voices rose like murmurs from a collective grave. Like me, those men were not yet dead, and it was the ultimately self-serving thoughts forming in their minds that could lead to panic and riot.

"It's unfortunate that you've found yourself in this position, Stenvall," Ellair said softly, but in a brisk businesslike manner. "Yet you can't deny your own excesses brought it on, can you?"

"I could *try* to deny it," I said, bristling. "In fact, I *have*, many times!"

"You may be a truly worthwhile man, at base," Ellair said, in his way a compliment. "It's hard, these days, to remain worthy. And to get at the nitty-gritty of one's own merit or value."

"Why's that?" I asked. Our footsteps seemed insensitively loud, weirdly hollow, to me. It occurred to me then that the jail would be without light that night. Private terrors; jealousies and longings and hatreds; bleak and lonely thoughts in the dark. I was shocked I hadn't realized it.

"I believe that mankind is slipping back, perhaps

222·

away—for good. And I've concluded that the problem is linked to our nervous systems," opined the Noble One. "Benjamin Walker described that system as the 'sub-ego' of the human entity, Stenvall. Because it's at that level where most animals—the lesser kinds, as *we* regard them—live. So if we *are* regressing as a species, our first step backward, logically, would be to the level of *most* animal life."

"What if I don't agree that we're regressing?" I asked. I was trying not to let him hear my labored breathing, but it had been a long day. "What if I said I think we're still progressing—evolving?"

"Oh, come!" he snorted in mild exasperation. His fingers gripped my shoulder, but he was so wrapped up in what he was saying I don't believe he realized I tried to twist away. "One of the sure signs of specie regression would obviously be a loss of individuality, of the sense of personhood which lesser creatures have only been dimly aware of, until now. Think of the men downstairs and you think of a mob, basically—a group, or herd, mind. Walker also wrote that the intelligence that 'dreams' within plants clearly 'exists in the meso-consciousness of elementary protobiological ents like viruses . . . and also fungi, plants, and trees.' Walker added that it manifests in metabolism—in nutrition, growth, even reproduction—even *decay*."

What the fuck was meso-consciousness? I wondered. "I suppose an alcoholic's nutrition leaves something to be desired." Did he have in mind the crazy notion that we were altering the future of an entire race by eating chili and Frostees at Wendy's, or devouring too

223

many Big Macs? I spotted the stairway just ahead of us.

He paused, and this time he echoed me. "An *alcoholic's* nutrition?" he sneered. "I had in mind mostly the crack, cocaine, and heroin addicts' woeful nutritional intake, Richard." He sounded excited as we started down the steps. "If my theory is right, the regression of the whole human race can be identified by a series of drastically altered neurological characteristics—*so* drastic and possibly irreversible that the entomogenic fungus may virtually be *encouraging* such sweeping modifications!" His eyes flashed above the nearly fleshless nose and his nostrils were like microscopic black dots. "Tell me, if you can, what would better serve their own advancement as a small part of the plant kingdom?"

"Noble," I said, carefully choosing my words, "I don't think of the men locked up here as a mob. I can see *more* individuality, *more* 'personhood' in some ways, then I recognize *outside* of the jail. My friend Kinsey; that banker who your plants killed; Dee Dee, with his dream of playing basketball in the NBA . . . even *me*, since you seem to have some need of my abilities. Each of us is, or was, a special, different kind of individual."

"No, they merely *want* different things. Stenvall, they yearn to fit in with some group they fancy to be desirable. If only the affluent." We were trotting down the steps to the first floor by then. I'd started the descent mainly to get his hand off my shoulder. It worked. "Truly *aware* individualism in humankind is constructed of *two* minds, remember—the conscious and the unconscious, the left and right hemispheres of the brain. The unconscious, or mind right, is creative and original, it houses its own longings and fears, its view of *potential* realities. The commissure between the two halves is used to send along information to the other half; what Jung termed the 'individuation process.' When it's *cut,* a person becomes two people. As a creative person, you *must* have observed the similarity today of all music, art, fiction, drama—and the way that each great success is instantly imitated by a host of lesser talents who are solely interested in more money, more power or autonomy—not the full expression of their *own* gifts!"

He had me there. There was nothing I could say to that. But what was he driving at?

"I see the lamentable but unplanned result of my goodwill gifts as part of the evidence for fungal purposefulness, Richard," he said. We were a few steps from the main floor so his words were scarcely audible. "In effect, they may be severing that hemispheric bridge in the brain with their own indulgent, narcotic cooperation. If people can be induced to surrender their individuality to *anything* collective, they immediately become more vulnerable to attack, and modification." He stopped where we were, changing the subject dizzyingly. "I see Crock, the pimp, as a potential troublemaker during the long night ahead of us."

Numb from the strange crap he'd dumped on me— a week ago, I could never have dreamed I'd have such a discussion! — I agreed. I would have anyway, of course.

Just then I needed to think. Independently. My growing awareness that we'd have to make it through a night of total darkness was making me only partly satisfied with the psychiatrist's theories and explanations. Wasn't it convenient for Ellair that the air conditioner had broken down on a steaming day and worse, that the fungal spores could only be released by sudden, positively mercurial heat. It had already been miserably hot in lockup, but the press of hundreds of confined bodies under conditions of acute tension was making it worse by the hour, if not the minute.

We were, I thought, like people marooned in a series of highrises, on so many layered islands. Since Doctor Ellair had been bestowing his flowery presents on all of us and had done so for a period of time before my own incarceration, and since some people had been released and others arrested, there was no way I could estimate how many people had died. For all I knew, there could be dozens of them dropping dead horribly in their homes, where they had taken their plants.

Now nearly a thousand of us were crammed into circumscribed, barred spaces with no chance to leave and nothing to do but wait — wait to see who the Great Unknown might choose next.

Night was fast approaching. Darkness in a great palace of pain and terror. Night and darkness, when the American *Zeitgeist* always *expected* evil . . .

It truly wasn't fair, this time. It sucked a b-i-i-g one. Possibly two hundred or so of the men were society's discards, rejected largely because *they* had rejected the rest of humankind. But whether Noble Ellair and others like him cared to see it that way or not, many hundreds more were just people who had already lost goddamn near everything of importance to them. From ignorance; from an inexperience husbanded through long generations as if it had been cherishable. They'd lost it all to a mainstream we'd be positively overjoyed to return to, if we knew how. There were guys who, like Lou Vick, really couldn't pay what they owed. People whose lifelong, squalid unAmerican frigging poverty *or* uncommunicable fury *or* inability to ask the right questions, *or* to explain their actions, *or* whose races and faces and crude antisocial hungry *cravings* had landed them in The Slammer.

And some of them—this was a point I never got across to Noble and probably never could have—*some of them would never be back!* Some of them—hell's bells, some of *us*—had been finally shocked into awareness and taught our lesson, just as the system was *supposed* to do. Not all of us, maybe not many—but *some* of us would raise *our children better* than *we'd* been reared; work out our vocational or marital or in-law or racial problems; educate ourselves, at last; turn over new leaves and locate the dimly-illumined path to decent, responsible existence as human beings!

This would have been the alternative to the haunted, bug-ridden life of shadows we'd found when we started living in cells as if *we* were the microscopic beings, the parasites and predators.

And I know to this moment that some of us would have made it.

2. *Shake, Rattle, Roll*

Sitting on the edge of his bunk in the deepening darkness should've suited Andre just fine because he'd been a creature of the night for most of the time he could recall. The fact that the memories of those times were becoming shorter every five or six months hadn't escaped him — the way numerous things had since he left Gary, the city of steel mills, behind. Andre was aware of how hard it was to remember the past. For awhile, he'd even imagined that his assorted addictions were turning his young brain old before its time. Then he'd heard somewhere that old folks who got the senility actually recalled the days of their youth extremely well. Unfortunately for Andre, it was the crap happenin' last week or even *yesterday* that was harder than held-in beer piss for him to remember.

For the life of him, Andre could not decide whether that made him worse than old folks, or it meant there was some hope for him. One thing was certain, he'd have much preferred recalling his boyhood to reliving 'most anything that happened to him over the past month. Not because there was anything special about the bad shit comin' down in that period of time, but because there was nothin' nice to remember from any

228

part of his life *'cept* his youth.

Bein' a boy had been spring all year long. Many of the details of it were lost to him now, but Andre remembered the *feel* of it. Didn't matter if it was hot as a muthafucker outside *and* in, because he didn't know anyone who had air conditioning so he didn't crave it. Didn't matter if it was *cold* inside and out, 'cause Mama, she always kep' a roof over their heads and 'cause there was always *runnin'* to do.

Runnin' anywhere, *everywhere*. For errands to keep mama happy, or to get the brothers together for a game of touch. Or runnin' to find Mr. Smoke the dealer, or runnin' from the Man when he come 'round to make a bust. Runnin' from the dean of boys at Roosevelt; runnin' for a touchdown an' jivin' in the end zone — at the intersection of Eison n' Eighth Streets, or even the vacant field over to Cherry Boulevard 'fore they put a shoppin' center right on the lot — an' givin *low* fives, 'n *medium* fives, 'n high an' behine the back an' *upside down* fives! Runnin' from Dandle's Liquor Store after he stuck it up to get walkin' around money — and t'pay Mr. Smoke — or runnin' from Mama, when she come *after* him. It was all one-hundred percent boyhood, one-hundred percent *spring!*

He could not remember, any more than the ol' dudes 'membered last week, the moment when spring turned to winter an' he lost two whole seasons, forever. Or what happened to that big, black, happy kid everyone had said was gonna make All-America an' play in the N.F.L.

Las' thing Andre remembered for sure, apart from the undebated years of glorious spring, was pumpin' iron when he wasn't snortin', puttin' on around a hundred pounds of sheer, hard muscle, then gettin' his ass hauled off to the *real* jail, the *adult* slam, 'stead of juvie. He had tried to get them to look up his record to see he was jes' a *lit-tul* teenage boy. Then they'd tole him he wasn't no kid no more on account of he nearly killed some ol' white man. *"Who?"* he'd begged them, amazed. *"Jes' tell me who!"* Mr. Dandle, they'd said, who ran the liquor store.

But that did not make any *sense.* 'Cause Andre'd always *liked* that ol' man, he had run errands for him n' done *lots* of shit. An' not only that, Mr. Dandle had pretended he didn't know which kid it was who'd hit on him in the past. He'd even allowed Andre to pay him *back* by doin' *more* shit for him! So the idea of Mr. Dandle fingerin' him was so much *shit* — 'cause they'd been no way that ol' man couldn't've told *him* from the other kids, like Shack 'n Ardell 'n "O" 'n Iceboat, when all of them was lit-tul! And there was no *way* the ol' honky muthafucker could *not* have tole those boys from Andre August at the time he got hisself beat up — 'cause Ardell, *he'd* got nearly as tall as that lucky nigger Lakens was, an' Ardell, he weighed jes' about the same. But *Andre,* sheeeit, *Andre* looked like the whole muthafuckin Colt offensive *line* by then!

So this was *ob*viously a mistake. So Andre hadn't said no more, not even to the public defender, a bitch named Curry who wasn't nearly as sweet as any curry Andre had ever tasted, he had jes' waited for Mr.

230

Dandle to wake up 'n *tell* the man it was a mistake.

But Mr. Dandle did not wake up, an' that was when everything got much deeper into the season that was no longer spring for seventeen-year-old Andre August.

First, he'd 'spected to get the chair. A white man was dead 'n they'd said he wasted Mr. Dandle. Truth was, he'd hit him only a little bit harder'n he'd hit the ol' man when Andre was fourteen, but Andre guessed he must've mistakenly hit Mr. Dandle in a bad place, a weak place. Still, if he *had* offed Dandle, that was clearly murder, an' Shack had knowed a cat who cut the *balls* off some fool lawyer and got hisself fried.

Instead, they put Andre back in juvie with all those lit-tul kids. He stayed there until he was eighteen — an' they let him *go!* Even now, there were times when Andre could recall how *amazed* he was when Miz Curry came round 'n tole him to go home. Sure, he had to see the man now and then, 'n what he done was kep' in his file for good, an' Roosevelt didn't want his ass back in *high school,* 'n nobody *he* knew was still there.

But he had seen Iceboat in juvie, too, an' Ice knew some cats now who really knew their way around on the street.

An' while everybody in his Gary neighborhood seemed t'know what he'd done, they also sort-of made a *path* for Andre whenever he come on the street or wanted t'hang out, they showed him *respeck* — and it was almos' as nice as dancin' in the end zone or givin' fives . . . an' the neighborhood cats became his cus-

231

tomers now.

So even if spring was gone and it might never come again; even if his mama passed, right after he come out of juvie n' he had to move to Indy with Ice 'n his well-connected friends; and even if he would never, ever be in the N.F.L. or even make all-state the way that lucky nigger Dee Dee Lakens had . . . it was cool. It was cool for a long, long time that wasn't part of no time Andre August had ever known before.

An' *dark*, too, turnin' darker everyday that he could not remember most details afore them las' few weeks. It wasn't fine t'be a creature of the night no more, 'coz he sat in a cell with *weird* cats like Crock an' the lit-tul cocksucker, name Lester.

Darker tonight *'specially*—'coz Andre could not possibly keep a eye on the muthafuckin' pimp or on Queen Lester with hardly no lights at all burnin', 'specially after it got later that evening. It would be like he was *blind*—but that might be cool, too, 'cept crazy muthafuckers like the white pimp and the lily of the valley in the wig didn't *need* eyes, they used *hands* to get around. Hands was what interested *these* freaks, plus cocks 'n asses 'n mouths. Shuddering, Andre attempted to tuck his large self deeper into himself and eyeballed the pale human shadows only an easy lateral's distance from him. Nobody'd ever got to him in the joint, nobody was gone get his ass *now*, if he stayed ready; alert. Crock was one mean mother but Andre'd seen meaner, *whipped* meaner'n ol' white Crock!

He shivered again, then wondered why, when it

was so fuckin' *hot*. Bein' cold was cool; bein scared was all right too, if *not* cool. Havin' withdrawal tonight—with the pimp and the faggot there, in the dark—was neither cool nor all right. It would mean he was gonna *die* that evening . . .

His shiver turned into a spasm, and Andre embraced himself so tightly with his great arms that the self-administered pain made him aware of another, a *pre-existing* agony within his body. Drugs was bad, he thought with a flicker of humor intended to renew his own courage, but they sure as fuck deadened the pain—or made you think less about any *other* pain!

"I gonna die tonight?" Andre questioned in a whisper intended for the ears of God.

'Coz if Crock *did* it to him—well, Crock'd know for certain to *murder* him, too! Ol' Crock would know if he *didn't*, then Andre August would bust his muthahumpin' *back* when the daylight come!

Spasms sprinted up and down both arms so wildly, so frantically, Andre lifted the powerful limbs to squint and to marvel at them. It was like they was *juiced*, baby, like somethin' both *liquid* and *lumpy* was runnin' back 'n' forth under his skin!

Personal dying hadn't seemed to Andre any kind of remote possibility before. All the other terrible things had—agonizingly sad, painful, and humiliating things. But personal death—*sudden*, beyond muscle or threat, reason or even running—had never touched Andre. He'd been either in Chicago or Detroit when his mama'd died, and he hadn't got back till she was in the ground. Then he'd crammed so much magic

233

powder into his nose and veins that he spent half the night laughingly busting things up and been stuck explaining to Ice where all the product had gone! Now he couldn't *go* to Chicago or Detroit. Now Iceboat hisself had passed—mebbe in the last year, mebbe 'fore that, Andre couldn't remember the details. And now *he* might die tonight, and also *know it when it happened*.

Andre realized for the first time that he had *wanted* to die jes' about since Miss Curry tole him that ol' man Dandle was dead.

He'd never meant to know when it happened.

The white, larger shadow in the same cell with him tilted its head.

"Yo! August!" Crock called to him.

Andre squeezed himself tighter, closed his eyes. He made them pop open when he remembered that wasn't at all safe. *"What?* What you want?"

The whites of his eyes and the glitter of teeth through shadows made Crock resemble a brother for an instant. "What you're feeling, boy," the pimp said—"it's pain. Bad pain, August." He laughed, the sound as raw as a fresh wound. "You been too fucking doped up even to *know* it!"

"Don' you call me boy!" The answer was automatic. Andre frowned. "How you know what *I'm* feelin'?"

"He knows, Andre." The faggot, Lester. His face was averted, his shoulders sagged tiredly, his woman's wig looked askew through the shadows. "Mr. Crock knows about pain."

"Mr. Crock knows *sheeeeit!*" Andre snorted. The

shivering turned to quivering and then to outright shaking as he spoke. He tried to say more, but his teeth were rattling around in his mouth. He settled for as scornful a noise as possible.

"I think you're next, August," Crock said quietly, offhandedly. More white teeth showed. Crouched on the edge of his rack now, he looked ready to get to his feet at any moment. He looked very healthy. Relaxed. Content. "Your number's come up, kid."

Stop it. Andre didn't say it out loud. His legs and feet were beginning to shake too, he could barely remain seated. The flat fish eyes of Crock seemed to see him as clearly in spite of the darkness, as if Crock was *truly* a creature of the night. It was no longer possible for Andre to pretend he wasn't experiencing the worst pain of his life, so he decided he jes' wouldn't say nothing else to nobody again.

"Boy?" The pimp called to him in something a fraction louder than a whisper. How could he be so cool, so content? August hugged his arms to his body and the tangled insides throbbed, pulsed. Crock smiled tenderly at him. "If you . . . *need* me, Andre, I'm here."

3. Comin' Up and Goin' Down

When we stepped out on "my" floor, I suddenly remembered — with fresh horror and more than small concern — the scared and silly gamblers Lew and Jimmie. Gargan said he'd locked them up in Deadlock.

235

Even though they'd been frightened and had actually volunteered, their minds might have turned to mush by now if the distracted and aging guard had neglected to get them out.

"Are you aware," I asked Doctor Ellair, "that the men who were with Stephen Blackledge when he died have probably been kept in Deadlock most of the day?"

"No," the shrink answered. He sounded puzzled. "Is it important to you?"

I didn't especially want to get Gargan in hot water, but I thought it was pretty obvious that the gamblers were sitting in the hot water of their own boiling perspiration. "Think about it a minute; what Deadlock is like," I suggested. The heat I was suffering was starting to make me irritable as hell. "Christ, what is it with you people in charge?" I asked. "Out of sight, out of mind unless the guys under you hold some special significance?" Through the murk I could tell Ellair was starting to understand my point. "It'll be fairly important to *you*, Noble, if those two men die of heat prostration in there. It's got to be a really unsanitary and scorching pisser in that crackerbox!"

Ellair pivoted slowly and summoned Gargan with a waggling index finger. "What are the two men called" (Ellair checked to see if I nodded when he attempted to remember their names) "Lew and Jimmie doing in this county's worst special punishment cell? What did they *do*, Stenvall?"

Bucking and winging and aw-shucksing for all he was worth, Gargan himself explained that both gamblers had preferred the hole to staying at the site of Blackledge's scary demise.

To Ellair's credit, tight-lipped, he snatched the keys from the old Irishman's claw-like hand without waiting for him to stumble through a useless explanation. Then, at a dead run that was more graceful and athletic than I would have expected, Ellair led the way between the cells, with me, and then Gargan, behind him.

At first, the racket was what you might expect. Guards, wardens, highbrow psychiatrists don't run through the institutions they're in charge of, they saunter; inspect; pose and preen. The men bombarded all three of us with questions that there was no time to answer and the two-bit word "cachophony" jumped to mind.

Then I realized that the shouting was dying away, never had been as loud as it normally would've been. It had *seemed* to be deafening because, I thought, there were more people lined up at the bars of the cells than there had been when I first got there. Early weekend arrivals. The new men didn't have a clue to what was going on and could only pick up on what the inmates with longer tenure were doing.

Those who'd been there as long as I, or longer, knew only that men from their own cells, were perishing in a killing heatwave, and that the scarecrow official, who had the right to peer into their most private thoughts, was racing toward Deadlock. For all any of the guys in the cells knew, Ellair was running flatout in a mood of unrestrained fury, meaning to inflict

237

punishment on another man—or on them. Standing and holding tight to the bars, as if to keep the cell doors shut instead of wanting to open them wide, the inmates (some still in street clothes and others in the yellow costume of the jailed unperson) reminded me of Holocaust victims waiting to see what next was in store for them.

Once the inmates in cells within range of Deadlock saw us working to open the massive door, their shouts, gripes, and demands for answers dwindled and became muttered fragments of sentences, unintelligible murmurs of confusion and anxiety. I heard Lester Piercy's incongruous chorine voice guessing that we'd "found out" that Lew and Jimmie "did those awful things," and I marveled at how we humans are constantly trying to pin blame on somebody—anybody—else. Or maybe we believe that once someone or *something* has been identified as the origin of a problem, we think we don't have to cope with it any more and the damned thing will just go away.

It turned out to take more than one key to unlock the nightmarish cell—and, as it turned out, a hell of a lot more dying to make the damned thing growing in that jail even begin to retreat. Now, some cells are built with a single prisoner in mind; bad-ass dudes the prosecution wants to use as witnesses, or pervs like rapists and child abusers who the other men might tear to ribbons—running red ribbons. Some cells, the majority, are constructed for two, four, or more inmates. A few others are practically goddamn dormitories; Delta Tri Truncheon, if you follow me.

But I saw immediately when the door to Deadlock was opened, creaking back like a midnight portal in a haunted-house movie that the hole was made for only one man. A tall midget, maybe. This place was *small*. So small, it made me think of what the old radio comedian Fred Allen once said about Philadelphia hotel rooms—that they were built for hunchbacked mice.

And since Deadlock probably hadn't been used since Quasimodo was a pup, the cell was also prettied-up no more often than every ten years or so—whether it needed it or not. So the stench that assailed me when Ellair, Gargan, and I finally tugged the damn door open was truly outrageous; terrible.

But it reeked for worse than it should from two normal men who'd had to spend most of a day in blazing heat, with none of what the proper people among us euphemistically call "facilities." Glancing inside, I believed for a moment that Lew and Jimmie had known that death was coming and, desiring to make up their longtime childish feud, had enfolded each other in a final embrace.

I took a hurried step backward, fumbled a handkerchief out of my pocket and pressed it to my nose. But that was like putting a zipper on a Frisco quake fissure, and I really needed it over my eyes anyway. Gargan was caught offguard so badly (no pun intended on the "offguard" reference) that he lost his balance and nearly lurched into the hole and against the bodies. Even Noble Ellair was momentarily ashen. Inmates across the passageway between the cells could make out enough through shadows to say a lot of things such as "Jesus Christ" and "God Almighty." This is hard to describe. But away from the marginally cooler or more ventilated air of the larger cellblock as a whole, the goddamned entomogenic fungus had virtually eaten that pair of men alive.

Lew and Jimmie had been invaded, I surmised, by some of the same spores that were showered out when Stephen Blackledge smashed his plant to smithereens. Penetrated by the spores through the pores of their skin. I glanced again at Ellair feeling much the same way Lester'd felt—eager to affix blame—but said nothing. Seeing this horror firsthand surely was making the inventor of the "goodwill gift" concept feel guilty enough, I thought. There was nothing *to* say, really, so I settled for a deep-down forlorn impression made equally of stomach-turning nausea and a tremulous horror of supernatural dread . . . and just *looked*.

In evidence was more of the cactus-like shit "Reverend" Al Calderone had mistaken for horns as it sprouted out of Blackledge and then from poor Lou Vick's tortured mouth and throat. And that was the least of it. Either this fungus was a fucking shape-changer or there were *different varieties* of the killing substance—meaning, I realized but couldn't admit until later, that the fungus was *evolving*.

The sanitation workers for the city weren't due to make their rounds that day and would've refused to do the job anyway; so it was up to Noble, Irish Gargan, and *moi* to haul the dead gamblers out of Deadlock. While we were removing them from the cell in a whimpering sequence of maneuvers that ranged from tentative and revulsed little tugs to the violent yanks of men who could not tolerate for long such a contact with the welded corpses, inmates across the corridor caught and held their breaths. Eeriness that registered under the first layer of our living skin transcended and foreshortened the distance between us and them — the victims-to-be, each and every one of us if nothing was done to stop the dying.

Jimmie and Lew landed on the jail floor out of Deadlock simultaneously and with a plop when without meaning to, we three pallbearers lost our nerve and our grip on them. Gaping down at the bodies, I wondered if we wouldn't lose our grip on sanity next.

The growths from the gamblers' motionless mass had merged, blossomed like gigantic cabbage leaves. Redness filtered through the vegetable foliage as if a mind behind the plants was running tests. Hot-red miniature spiders that looked fat, or bloated, that moved at unbelievable speeds, came squeezing out from under the embracing dead men. They made me think of frightened rats deserting a sinking ship. Jesus, there was so *much* of the pulpy growth, I couldn't tell from what orifices in the guys' anatomies the spores had grown. Hell, there was so much of it, I wasn't positive which end of Lew or Jimmie was up!

Maybe that's what motivated old Gargan to extend a trembling arm and put a shaking finger out, to *tap* one of the enfolding fungal flaps, cautiously and gingerly.

The sonofabitching shit *raised up* from scrawny little

Jimmie's staring face like the wing of a briefly-interrupted creature feeding. Instantly, Gargan hopped away and stood there quivering from head to toe. Fluid drooled from between his lips. Some of it was blood, where he'd bitten his mouth or his tongue.

It was reflex, I told myself as persuasively as possible, *mere reflex that made the damn flap move*.

But a veined root crawled from Jimmie's left nostril and I clearly saw motion. The entomogenic was continuing to sprout, to grow.

It was alive.

"Well," Noble Ellair proclaimed to nobody in particular. "That's it, then."

He swiveled his long neck when he sensed my stunned expression. He peered affably at me and unbelievably, he seemed virtually cheery—and relieved!

"I know this makes your job tougher, Richard," he remarked. His smooth tone was like that of a company president at a board meeting, or a doctor telling his patient the tests were negative—(or maybe that they were positive but all was well since the tests were clear as a bell). I'm a writer so I think strange thoughts, I remembered military commanders speaking of "acceptable losses." Lew and Jimmie had just suffered their biggest lose ever—they lost their lives! "You do see, don't you, that this . . . unfortunate mess *began hours ago?* Thus it's irrelevant to the here-and-now since it is also irrelevant to the other inmates' health." He smiled as he rubbed his palms together briskly. "All you must do is make it clear to the men that this changes nothing."

"It sure as Christ changes things for them!" I snapped, pointing down.

"Tomorrow, Richard," the shrink reminded me, "tomorrow the men will be moved to safety — and you to your own home!"

I nodded at him, unhappy, without confidence, and worried that there was a hole in the Noble One's reasoning that you could drive a truck through.

I wasn't sure the kind of tomorrow we were all used to was going to ever come again. As if to confirm my fears a shriek of piercing terror and warning broke the pause of reflective horror. It came from the cell that held Lester Piercy, Andre August, and Crock, and it sounded as if it might never cease.

4. *Just Watching*

It was far and away the finest show he had seen in years, the most goddamn excitement Crock had been part of since his own career got legs, years before. And it was all LIVE, in glorious technicolor — at least till the sons of bitches *died!* Christ on a crutch, if he'd had any notion jail was going to be so much wonderful fun this time, he'd have simply walked straight up to Bud and the nigger Brownie and that vice broad, Randles, and *clubbed* them with anything handy. Just to get his ticket to the Big Show!

What a difference it was, this time — no longer bearing the burden for creating a little action, incidents that got the juices flowing, the old sap running.

Jesus Christ, all he had to do was just sit back on his rack, diddle with himself a while, then *watch!*

On the outside, assuming you had yourself a long rap sheet, whatever you did for excitement or relief from the pressures of working might be seen, might have some fucking penalty attached to it. Up to a point, that could be fun too. Pickin' your spots, outthinking the cops by varying the ol' game plan slightly from time to time. Locating new blood for the always-thirsty streets by buying leads about the young kids comin' in on planes or in some buddy's car instead of on a train or bus. Stealing the leads, too, cutting down on the competition — except that the majority of pimps he knew were black, and a few of the sons of bitches were damn near as big as Andre August. And you could fink on *them.*

But the kids themselves, well, they almost never offered much challenge no more, almost never gave Crock even as much decent satisfaction as he got with his good right hand. Jesus! they was *odd* these days! They didn't even pretend to like what he did to 'em sexually even when he let on that they'd get a better break if they cooperated (which wasn't true) so there was little chance for him to vent his rage the only way he permitted himself to vent it: As punishment for their low goddamn morals, and for trying to mix business with pleasure. And they didn't object to it when he hooked them on crack or heroin — a necessity of the trade, to bond the little fuckers to him — because that was generally the main reason they'd left the sticks to begin with. Most brats these days had al-

244

ready tried some kind of drug by the time they got to town, anyway; comin' to him was like they'd graduated fucking high school and were entering college!

And the little bastards usually didn't *enjoy* anything he hooked them on either, regardless of how expensive, how pure, it was. Christ on the cross, they stuck the shit in their noses or the needles into their arms like it was some sort of *duty* or fucking *homework*, or it was time they lost their *virginity!*

Or they considered themselves such useless little pussies and pricks that it also was time they died. Maybe they thought of it as a weird sacrifice to some strange damn god made of heavy metal who dwelled in the concrete and asphalt of the city — didn't they know the only god who lived in the streets was a *vampire* and that he'd never have enough of their blood to give them what it was they were looking for?

The way he saw it, life was generally a pretty raw deal, but today's kids — they were just too fucking much to dope out. It seemed to Crock half the time these days that they was heading for hell in a handbasket and askin' him to push it *faster.* Or, maybe, to put an *engine* on the goddamned thing!

So what was happening in the jail this last couple of days really made much more sense, in some ways. Whatever Crock's own feelings were on the subject, he was used to people who did not want to die, people who sure as shooting did not want to die while the other sons of bitches not only survived, but *watched.* Watched, and thought how lucky they were! That was the pleasure in this, the kick of it. Seein'

245

white collar phonies who already had life by the balls strangling to death on their own tongues, and skinny-assed nigger kids gettin' killed by *diving* onto their *heads!* Fuck, he was behind bars like everyone else so nobody'd ever finger him for the deaths. He was free as a bird t'fold his arms, just lean back and watch the show!

And the way Crock had it figured, there wasn't one chance in million that he, himself, was about to die with any of that weird-ass crap growing out of *him!* Hell, every other man-jack in the whole fucking joint might very well get eaten *up* by the shit—infected, poisoned, chewed, swallowed and digested, pissed or vomited or *shat* out—but he would survive, he would make it. He would live through everything that happened to all the other men; and he'd watch the entire, wonderfully exciting show from a goddamn ringside *catbird* seat!

Because he was pure.

He had denied himself so much pleasure and dedicated himself so thoroughly to his work every minute of his miserable existence that he deserved happiness for a while, and he certainly deserved to *live!* He'd controlled each and every whim he'd ever felt germinating in his brain. He'd raped some of the most pitiful excuses for men and women, boys and girls, it had been his misfortune to meet; he'd murdered only in the line of business, never any of the times he had wanted to kill so badly it made his scrotum tighten and his balls ache with longing for release. They either had it coming, or they didn't.

Crock was pure. He had lived his life strictly according to his own code; how many people could make such a claim? Christ, with every drug invented by the fertile imaginations of men available to him any day of the world, he had never so much as *tried* anything that wasn't prescribed. The pushers and the few distributors he knew were ready to swear he was the most honest son of a bitch that ever drew a breath!

He was good, so he would live.

Crock looked at Lester, who'd tucked himself in a corner of the cell. Cowering in fear of everything happening around him, his mascara-dripping lashes batted as he peeked through the bars at the fascinating corpses dragged from Deadlock; Crock smiled tolerantly.

Then he looked at Andre August. *Damn*, he thought, *I'll never have him now.* But Crock figured that at the very least August's death should take awhile and might be even more entertaining than the others. "Bye, Andre," Crock said softly.

Lester saw what Crock was looking at and started to scream.

5. *August Heatwave*

I spun around in a fancy move that could have matched anything in the late Dee Dee's repertoire and immediately identified the source of the newest awful scream.

247

Lester, the woeful little gay who had yearned for the pimp Crock to take him on as a female hooker seemed stuck midway between the next arcing shriek, and whatever was starting to drip out of his long-beaked nose. For about ten seconds I thought he was under attack. Lester looked like he had tried by mistake to sniff in a handful of salt water and found it was battery acid instead.

Yet nothing else seemed to be wrong with him except for his expression—and the way he was crouching on his knees and pointing.

At Andre August.

Whether Lester himself had craved the enormous ex-football player I had no way of knowing. I knew from scuttlebutt in the jail and the way he'd sneaked admiring glances at August that Crock hankered for him, but even that sadistic pimp hadn't had the gall to tell Andre how he felt. Crockie might have had both his heart *and* his back broken! But given the possibility that Crock had *any* emotional interest in Andre, his performance just then was both astonishing and strangely depressing to me.

Because Crock was also eyeballing the one-time athlete but from a casual lounging position on his bunk. His arms were folded, the flat eyes in his horsy face were hooded, and he looked as though he might have been watching an old rerun on TV. That was the coldest sight I ever saw, a match for anything I'd seen pulled by Ellair, at least.

Well, *my* reaction was much stronger. Heartfelt; *gut* felt.

He would never run with the ball or block a man again. He would never hit on anyone for drug money, feel guilt or envy because he'd not made diddly of himself, or even get a kick from snorting or shooting up. All in the world Andre had scheduled for him now was dying, in agony — and in an almost *silent* agony that I found I respected enormously.

First I saw the stuff bursting out of his ears. Churning, fairly *rolling* out of the ears at an identical, matching pace that amazed me, because it looked purposeful, it looked like team play. But when I tore my gaze away from August's ears, I found that had only been the start.

Huge yellowish pustules were beginning to rise out of the innumerable needle punctures — the heroin tracks — along his inner arms and great biceps. Probably that was what had set little Lester off, then drawn the sociopathic Crock's cold, utterly absorbed attention.

Everyone but Crock who was in a position to witness August's dying agonies had fallen still, too, as if Andre was already dead and we were simply paying our horrified respects. And one by one, those inmates who couldn't directly witness this merciless passage from life were lapsing into silence or numbly asking questions (directed mainly to God, I assumed). Their terror stricken faces stared at this tableau from cells all along the corridor, mutely questioning how much longer the dying would take. Till you've observed hundreds of inmates in a jail fall into shocked silence you haven't experienced the capacity of a captive crowd for shared horror. Add to that the relentless humidity. Add to that a pleased smile on the pimp's pallid face, and the shadows starting to thicken in the corridor like corpse stains, bleaknesses prefiguring the end for any or all of us.

I held my ground, watching, realizing each of us needed to be witness for the others. And I knew I had to be detached, to see and record it all.

Presumably Andre was aware of the stuff in him, growing and then forcing its way through his muscled body like a street gang plundering a path through some long-ignored tenement. Now he had thrown his powerful arms out from his body as if he was part gigantic scarecrow and part black Jesus. He seemed hypnotized by the sight of the growths writhing up out of his pores and out of the needle scars running up and down his tree-branch arms . . . those arms he'd once believed the Lord gave him for breaking tackles but that he'd used instead for breaking heads — and as heroin receptacles. Part of me wanted to cry for the loss, to shout at the waste of a remarkable-looking man. But I could merely stare as colorless, twitching, mushroom *things* now drooped from his great limbs like alien fur. It weighted his arms down; it began to sap the energy, the lifeforce, from Andre's anatomy, to drag it all down.

Ellair broke the spell, heading for the cell door when we suddenly realized that the damned burgeoning tissue murdering Andre didn't just grow or hang as it oozed from deep inside his body and out through the needle tracks and deafened ears: It *moved*.

Flapping and fluttering it moved *toward* the rest of the emerging fungal tissue as if it wished to commune, to become a whole entity. And still no sound came from the dying man.

Then, before I could follow, Noble was inside the cell with Andre and the other two, trying to help. As I glimpsed Crock rising idly, noiselessly, from his rack, I reached out—and slammed the cell gate shut! It was probably the bravest thing I ever did, and I'd startled the hell out of myself in the process. Crock, swinging his shark eyes around to see who'd thwarted his bright idea of escape, wouldn't forget who had locked the door on him. But we had enough nightmarish trouble without any human monsters running around loose.

"I wish I had my bag here but it probably wouldn't be much help," Ellair murmured, inclining his head for my benefit. *"Observe*, Richard," he said quite softly.

And I did. Observed, watched uselessly, while the big man sank slowly, conscious and silent still, to the cell floor. His eyes were wide open. They knew. He was kneeling, but he was alive.

"Oh, Jesus," old Gargan said gagging, "it's eatin' him. Jesus, Mary, and Joseph, the sonofabitchin' stuff is *eating* that poor peckerhead!"

I just nodded. Around us the inmate voices poured in a unified, rasping chant—a prayer, perhaps, to forces or powers they had never totally believed in; or to forces they'd never believed in except when they slept and all their dreams were mad.

251

Still August lived. But in spite of the valiant way he struggled to keep his arms raised, the sheer mass and weight of the entomogenic was steadily driving him to the floor. Pale, spiky tendrils jabbing out from his ears assiduously, adamantly, worked their way down his back. Now, quivering, they sent out new sucker-like growths, obscene lips that kissed Andre's spine first, then fastened deeply on, then into it. Noble Ellair inhaled sharply. He reached out to try to pluck or pinch the suckers off. Reaching through the bars of the cell in the desire to help, and I saw that the growths were astonishingly sticky; the suckers stank. And when I succeeded with outstretched arm and hand in prying one away from Andre's red-on-brown flesh, the goddamned thing *attacked me*. It plastered itself against the closest skin it could find—the soft flesh of my inner arm—and I had one fleeting instant when I knew it was trying to get a toe hold, working like a demon to bore through and cling to the muscle!

Terrified beyond description, I fell over backward, dislodging it. Gargan jumped with both his feet on the thing, squashing the horror with every iota of Irish pluck in his soul—but not before I felt sickened and oddly *scorched,* or *burnt.* I knew the pain would've been intolerable all over my body and I was swearing out my fear and disgust until, sprawled on the floor, I heard a single strained sound emanating from the man kneel inside the cell: *Hsst,* Andre said through clenched teeth as if it were a warning. *Hsst . . . Hsst . . .*

Then, suddenly, it ended. With shocking yet merci-

252

ful suddenness.

I saw August throw his bulbous-looking arms into the air above his matted, sweat-drenched head in one brave, bold, last effort to rip hell's skin off his body.

Then he pitched forward on his face without another murmur. All that was left of him was the steady wriggling of the fungi down his spine and the nearly inaudible sound of chewing. Then the pasty, roiling husks cloaking Andre's arms began a *new* attack upon his unprotected belly and between his legs.

Nine

1. The Nice People Who Didn't Move

Mama and Bett didn't like him no more so Markie thought he'd take a little walk. Not outside Home, 'cause that wasn't allowed and wasn't safe. Just around the big building where they lived and 'cause Daddy was back in jail and wasn't there to make sure everybody was all right. He'd check it out for his daddy.

"Home" was a word Markie understood very clearly but couldn't have defined very well if anyone had asked. That was partly 'cause there was Home the Good Way, and Home the Bad Way.

The Good Way was when Daddy was there and he wasn't drinking or nervous like Mama said he got sometimes 'cause he had to work so hard for them and, even better, when Daddy was through working for the day and stayed in the 'partment with Markie and Mom and Bett, and they was all happy.

Home the Bad Way was when his daddy was drinking or his mom thought Dad was *going* to drink, and when Bett his sister was sayin' that *her* father was somebuddy else. That really didn't sound smart, right, or nothing, and it made Markie's head sort of *buzz* inside. Or when she was stealin' stuff from him or when Bett *said* he stole stuff from her—and she was right. The Bad Way was when Mama got real worried over money. And that didn't sound smart either, 'cause everbuddy spent money as fast as they got it, so Markie couldn't see why Mama was worried about it none.

An' Home the Bad Way was when they was all sorts of hatin' each other and thinkin' about themselfs and not Markie, and when grownups cried. 'Cause Markie thought he shouldn't cry no more since he was a Big Four now, so that meant his mom and dad shouldn't cry either. 'Specially his daddy.

There were more ways for Home to be the Bad Way than the Good Way 'n' he was thinkin' about that a lot when it got dark out and he opened the door of the 'partment 'n' let himself out into the hallway, pokin' along with his hands trailing against the wall 'n' then the railing of the stairs as he went down a flight. One more Good Way was that Markie could sometimes think of Home as this whole building, as the whole big 'partment complex! Sometimes his daddy said he was sorry he didn't have enough money so he could buy them a "place of their own," and that generally sounded funny to Markie. He felt real sorry for kids with just one little-bitty house to live in when he, Markie Stenvall, had a great, *big* place to see. He thought that way 'specially when Daddy made him his 'sistant and then took him *all over*, carryin' his daddy's tools for him. That was wonderful, that was *good!* 'Cause Markie got to visit ol' Mrs. Reilly, who'd let him see her statue of a pretty lady she called "the Blessed Mother," who smelled nice and that made Markie want to snuggle with her. He got to visit the *real* pretty lady who told him it was okay to call her "Stef," 'n' she was like a person older than Bett but younger'n Mom, and when Stef gave him big squeezes, he liked that a whole lot. 'Cause of her pillows in front.

He was trailing his fingers along the wall and across the closed doors on the second floor, thinking there was *also* Mrs. Silverberg, who was fatter'n Stef or Mrs. Reilly but real *funny*. 'Cause she had what Daddy called an accident or accent, 'n' some days she let him eat big bites of a kind-of roll that was hard and had a hole in the middle but tasted *neat*, 'cause it was different. Mrs. Silverberg usually had food around and, if she saw him at the door starin' in, she'd say to come in and say, "Eat, *eat!*" 'n' wave her arm like he was her grandson or somethin'.

There was Mr. Swanson and Mr. Cunningham too, and they didden have no wifes like Mrs. Silverberg and Mrs. Reilly didden have no hubbans. Now, Stef, *she* had herself a hubban called Karl—but any time he come home, he didden say nothin' to Markie, he just went into his 'partment 'n' closed the door, then there'd be a lot of *giggling*—just like they was little kids, too! And that was when Daddy'd grab Markie's hand and make him go somewheres elst real quick.

He paused in the hot corridor to scratch at the crown of his head, then to throw himself forward quickly, almost falling down, to pick at a scab on his knee. He'd forgotten about that one but it wassen quite ready yet.

Mom 'n' Dad were funny 'bout a lot of stuff. Like Mama said she liked them two old ladies in the complex okay yet she was always askin' questions. Did Mrs. Reilly talk about her Blessed Mother or try to get Markie to convert? *That* was funny since the only thing Markie knew like that was convertibles, and he wasn't no car—and Mom talked sometimes 'bout *her* mother! Or she'd ask if Mrs. Silverberg ever said anything "bad" 'bout Jesus. 'N' Markie patiently replied that it was Mrs. Reilly who had all them pictures of Jesus 'n' stuff, *not* Mrs. Silverberg, so why would *she* say bad things?

'N' Daddy tole Markie not ever, *ever* to go see Mr. Swanson or Mr. Cunningham 'less he was along, too, but that seemed silly 'cause Dad didden say why not.

As a matter of fact, Dad and Mom both said not to go out into the halls alone at night, period— hat was how they would say things, *"blah-blah, period!"* like they forgot his name was Markie!

Grownup people were funny.

And it was funny, too, the way he could go everywhere in the whole place 'n' not get lost or nothing but also never know *whose* 'partment he was closest to. Smiling 'cause he too got silly sometimes, Markie hopped lopsidedly another few feet while he trailed his fingers along the wall, partly to balance himself now.

And the 'partment door he brushed his hands over next time swung wide.

Hafta tell Daddy it needs the hinges oiled, Markie thought, frozen momentarily by the squeaking noise. The door sort-of shook at the end of the swing, vibrating.

Dark in there. 'Cept for light from the TV 'way over in the corner of the front room.

"H'lo?" he called, but received no reply in Irish, Jewish, or any other kind of accents. There was no answer at all, 'cept for the little-bitty people on the television screen. They were talkin' to themselves, and that always seemed funny to Markie, grownups miles 'n' miles away talkin' to themselves with no one out *here* listening to them. He'd got up for a drink of water a lot of times and seen Mom or Dad asleep while the little-bitty people went on acting with nobody watching. It was like somebuddy outside their Home lookin' through a telescope into their house and like somebuddy was dancin' or singin', and nobody was seeing him. It was spooky; it also seemed sad somehow.

Stephanie Ryder came into view as the little boy's vision adjusted to the interior gloom of the apartment. He wouldn't have knowed it was Stef 'cause she had all her clothes off, but her soft pillows weren't like any of the other ladies' pillows in the building and he'd seen 'em once before when Stef was sort-of dancin' by herself and he just walked in. He'd seen

259

his Mom's pillows without any clothes and they were nice too, but his mama was his mama and this was Mrs. Karl Ryder whose age was more'n Bett's and less'n Mom's.

Why was Stef lyin' on the floor not movin'? She could be sleeping, but she had her eyes open 'n' Markie hadn't seen anybuddy do that. "Hi, Stef!" he called loudly. He gave her his greatest smile, too, and shoved the door against the front room wall till it banged. Pretty Stephanie was naked all over 'n' Markie didn't get to see much of that. Bett, his half-sister, she used to take off all her clothes but she didn't do that no more. He knew now that girls were different 'n' Daddy and him, but he had forgotten just how and took one step into the 'partment to find out again. He said softly—not *too* softly 'cause he had to talk loudern'n the bitty people—"Stef? Don't you know who I am?"

One of the pretty lady's bare arms was at an angle Markie hadn't seen at all before and the side of her face he couldn't make out from the hallway was all red 'n' looked kind-of crunched, like old Bud cans. He froze again yards away, spooked by the actor people talking when they wasn't bein' watched. *That looks like it'd hurt a* whole *lot,* he decided, staring at the cavity in Stef Ryder's face.

But how could she be sleepin' if it hurt? And if it hurt, why wasn't Stef cryin' or something?

Markie let his eyes widen and turn so his gaze could sweep the room. There was a bunch of broken stuff there. There were only three legs on the coffee table now, 'n' magazines were slopped off onto the floor. Pieces of glass lay on the Beaumont Estates carpeting here and there like things had got broke against the walls. Brown liquid stained the carpeting and Markie knew Daddy would *hate* that 'cause some kinds of stain was awful hard to get out.

He glanced back at the funny way Stef had gone to sleep both with her eyes open and her arm crooked and he realized for the first time that Stef was *holdin' on* to something.

The biggest plant Markie had ever seen in all his life.

Not that it was pretty or anything like the ones Mrs. Silverberg always kept on the window ledge in her 'partment or those his mama had tried once or twice to make grow, 'cept she didn't have a green thumb, which Markie privately believed was a good thing. The light was dim in the front room so it was hard to see all the details of the plant the sleeping Stephanie was sort-of holding close to her, but it looked not only very, very big but ugly. Almost like some of the green food Mama tried to make him eat.

He didn't like it in that 'partment any more and thinking of his mother reminded him that he better get back Home before she noticed he was gone. When he'd gone out into the hall, and he began thinking about how Mom didn't like him much any more but that was just 'cause she'd been actin' funny lately, with Dad gone. Markie didn't really believe he wasn't loved any longer, it just felt that way sometimes.

He turned away from the naked dead woman on the floor and hurried to the open door without another thought about her and without noticing that the plant, just like Stephanie Ryder, had *its* eyes open too.

When he stumbled against the solid chunks of a smashed flowerpot he found it funny. 'Cause there was no way in the whole world a little pot like could ever have held a man-sized plant like the one on the floor with Stephanie.

2. The Mechanical Bastard

When I felt finally that I could speak again, when I could trust my voice to speak and my belly to keep down the little I'd had to eat that day, I told Ellair plainly, "We have to have another talk. *Now.*"

At first, even in *those* circumstances—even standing *right outside* the cell where Andre had just perished and Piercy might shake to death if nothing else was done—Ellair kept his damn cool. His long face had one of those "who do you think YOU are?" expressions. But he saw my hands turn into fists, he saw something in my eyes, and I think Ellair knew I had his goddamn answer swinging!

Also, he still wanted my cooperation, needed it, I believed. And that became the only quality he possessed that I continued to admire: Ellair knew just how far he could push people. He had the knack for recognizing with mercurial quickness what was in a man's eyes, tone of voice, his *dick* maybe! Which was possibly why he'd trained his own equine face to reflect so little telltale expression.

He was able to perceive at a glance that I was definitely goddamn ready and eager to share with the inmates every detail I knew concerning his fucking attack plants — but with absolutely none of the excuses Noble had used to clean up his irresponsible activities for my benefit. I'm also sure he was aware that I was anxious to challenge the extent of his innocence (if indeed he had any innocence) right out in the open. To wonder, before the hundreds of terrified men, if there existed even the slightest chance that Noble himself might have anticipated — *or planned* — this kind of vegetable-garden holocaust. If Gargan or any of the guards did release the men, and they believed *anything* along those lines, they'd make mincemeat out of the Noble son of a bitch before he could teach them how to *say* "entomogenic," let alone spell it!

There was a renewed clamor for answers making it impossible to talk out there. It was getting darker by the second as, within each of us, the inborn alarm that nightfall was approaching went off like clanging bells. So I let Ellair lead me past two guard stations and out to an anteroom. I caught a glimpse of the balding, burrhead ex-quarterback Leighton leafing through some girlie magazine. I think he spotted me but he didn't wave. Known as a brawler and an occasional bully, Leighton wrapped himself in machismo like it was a magic protective cloak, but he was usually sociable. I wondered if he had concluded I was strictly looking out for Number One, had sold out, or if he'd been infected. For all I knew, the dumbass had simply come across the centerfold of His Dreams and was just trying *to* come!

Something odd, I realized, was also happening to me. I was really beginning to see what most of the men were actually like as individuals. I thought of Doc and wondered how he was making it in the tank, but that was in the other direction and there wasn't time to go see. But the realization also showed me how swiftly and easily one can develop an institutional mentality in a repressive environment. Sure, it was good that I cared about the other men. Yeah, it was right to develop an affinity with fellow human beings, to see the commonalities of mortal flesh.

But there was also a huge damn hazard to that "common man" line that began by failing to see the differences between us, *and* the differences between good and bad, acceptable and unacceptable, behavior. There is a risk in calling *those* guys over there "them" and *these* people, where we're standing, "us," a risk in becoming somebody else because we need to get along, to avoid confrontation, to belong. Then we risk losing sight of our individual identities, what makes us different, what sets beneficially apart.

I trailed after Ellair wishing that more of the men were nodding and waving in the manner of people in a shared crisis. It was then that I realized that losing sight of our individual worth *began* by abandoning those personal connections every man has, beyond the collective group. Sometimes those old connections were merely sidetracked, and that explained why we guys who served our time in the military or in jail might swear we would keep in touch with the guys left behind but never did. Our sidetracked connections were reactivated once we could be where, and with whom, we truly *wanted* to be.

But what happened if we were kept too long from restoring the disconnected lines, what if the length of time we *could* be "disconnected" *varied* from person to person? What if some of us couldn't stand a week or even a day away *without becoming somebody else?*

What if the newer connections grew stronger, the most recent experiences replaced old memories *entirely?* I don't mean any of this from the standpoint of "institutionalized personalities" as Noble Ellair might mean it. My heart's not bleeding over the warped sons of bitches who should be locked up for good, because a lot of *those* fuckers, if this inner journey to "Ellairland" holds up, are the *real* individuals among us anyway! Those true, bad-ass types *remain* individuals, no matter how often they're shrunk or shocked, because they're totally *selfish*. They influence everyone around them: the guards, their lawyers, everybody they come into contact with! You want to know why? Because *they seem* to have what *all* of us *want!*

But what about people of frail spirit and confidence—those whose human decency was destroyed by the way they grew up, lacking any decent breaks. *One* corker of a mistake and their undeveloped intelligence, untapped talent, any positive attributes were destroyed! But they *can't adapt* to the crummy life laid out for them. So they get locked up without finding a way to explore their personal skills, insights, or intellect in any productive way. They're warped into some antisocial mold making it impossible to *remember* what they learned about themselves: That they could have been their own man or woman and been applauded for it! My theory is that some people, already half-defeated by life but still salvageable can't stand too much time away from the sources of their worth potentials without being permanently separated from the memory of experiences that *shaped* that worth potential! When that happens, as I briefly feared it might be happening to me, the individualism they (or we) possess must ultimately be forever altered into the type of discard that is humankind's greatest enemy.

Don't *tell* me there aren't people like that! Look up your leaders of revolutions, your most controversial geniuses and artists. Look up fucking Hitler, who wrote his book behind bars and laid out a goddamn precise *road map* for what he meant to do with his life—and *to* others—and was still *ignored!* The potential he had was there from the start, and could've gone in other directions. The brain power, energy, and raw knack for influencing his fellow man was in that fucker from the outset! He's a prime *negative* example of what I'm working to put into words, okay? No, I'm not recommending sympathy for evil bastards like him; I'm discussing the *little kid* he has to have once been, however hard that is to picture. And I'm not doing a kneejerk blame-it-on-society bit, either—It's just that sometimes, you see, the loss turns out to be *everybody's* . . .

Those thoughts were in my head as I yearned for Leighton and the other guys to say they were behind me, cheering me on — to say "Hi, Rich," or just "Yo," and not turn paranoid with suspicion. Not band together in bunches of Us, and Them. Not cave in before The Man. I wondered if everything wasn't just over-complicated; if the other side of the Golden Rule, or a definition of it, might simply be saying "Yo" to people. And I wondered what would have happened if a guard let the men out then. Not to the Noble One (I think I know what would have happened to him). Rather to *me* . . .

The anteroom Ellair led me to was where infrequent visitors tried to rap with the men they had come to see. There were cute little steel-meshed windows just about the right size for a tear-streaked face. The guards I glimpsed while Noble and I strode past their stations were anything but expressionless. As we went out to the anteroom their frightened eyes followed us. The message in them was "What about the danger to *us?*" but the Noble One had no answers for them, either.

Ellair and I sat on the rickety visitors benches. The building felt haunted. I continued to hear the spooked men muttering. Hundreds of people were in peril and this buzz of fear was probably being sucked into the ceilings and walls, to be available for psychics to hear for a century. . . .

I had *thought* about it before, but now I realized that saving the men might very well be up to me.

Sounds conceited as hell, sure, but I sensed that whether Ellair was directly and completely culpable, there was a quality within him that was essentially theoretical and experimental. He lived in a detached ivory-tower world of intellectual postulates, entranced by hypothetical causes and effects. In the real world, in an environment demanding action he was useless. I saw that my old "dis-ease" might have given me the opportunity of doing something meaningful at last, but that the cards were so stacked against me that I momentarily yearned to be the simplest of men, a cipher, an inert *rock!* I sat there sweat-stained, starting to reek, and I yearned for nothing more than ten or twelve Buds lined up like naked dancing girls—

I understood some of what Ellair'd laid on me about the drift of people backward toward a safer, dreaming stage; that this could be detected by a loss of personhood, individuality, individual exercise of will. A line from William Blake occurred to me: "I must create my own system or be enslaved by another man's . . ." Now it seemed that we had to battle against slipping back, to become more fully awake than we had ever been before, or it would be plants and fungi that imposed *their* system on us.

Noble got me a cold soda from the vending machine—got one for himself as well. Through the mesh-covered window at his back I got a glimpse outside, the crummy part of town. I realized it was only halfway through rush hour out there, yet there wasn't a car in sight. That shocked me, gave me the balls to put an idea I had directly to the shrink:

268

"Look," I said, point-blank. "I want someone authoritative and knowledgeable in here, someone *experienced*. Noble, where in Jesus' name are the jail officials—a freakin' *cop?*"

"You share my concern about the possibility of a riot, then?" he asked.

"Among other things," I said.

"Well, the guards *are* deputy sheriffs." Dapper, ever controlled, he sipped his drink slowly. "They were left under my command so that the administrators could attend an important conference. In Fort Wayne."

I turned into a decent tax-payer with indignation. *"You're* the only one left to mind the fucking store? A *shrink?"*

Ellair appeared hurt and irked. "Mr. Stenvall, I have ample administrative experience. I also graduated from a state-sponsored, advanced course in penology."

"Why would everybody but you go to—to Fort Wayne?" I demanded.

"I recommended the conference myself. It involves jailer/prisoner relationships, and the keynote speaker recently graduated from a course in the psychology of the institutionalized man."

I stared at him, incredulous with comprehension. "Yours?"

"I taught that course, yes," he admitted.

"Christ, you're like a medical doctor recommending a *surgeon!*" I exclaimed. "I assume you shared your fees?"

"Well—"

"You're saying *you* recommended the out of town conference?" I pursued him. "For this particular time, this *very week?*"

Ellair shrugged. "There are no major holidays in June," he said. He allowed himself a mildly offended frown. "I can't be faulted for an unexpected increase in the temperature, Richard. The others will be back soon, and—"

"I don't want a goddamn weather report!" I shouted, awed by the man's knack for blunting even the most reasonable criticism. "Look, just tell me how a fungus germinates, all right? Help me get a handle on what's going on."

He smiled. "Certainly." He sat slightly forward on the visitor's bench, as if picking up the thread of a lecture. "The fungus's spore is itself a reproductive body. It's released in tropical conditions. Directly into hot, clinging air."

Mentally, a vivid image came to me of Steve Blackledge when the air conditioning went out. The way he had thrown, smashed, and scattered his goodwill plant. The thing was close to him. I wondered if his abruptly violent temper had been caused by it or if his hot fury had contributed to the germinational spread. Having taken their own plants into the same Deadlock cell, Blackledge's cellmates, Lew and Jimmie, had then been infected.

"When the spore lands on the body," Ellair went on, giving me no chance to ask another question then, "it attempts *instant* germination. It is usually a rather

270

flimsy growth filament, called a *hypha,* that—well, drills its way through a vulnerable cite to an optimum location."

Like a mouth, I realized. Like an ear. A puncture mark in the arms.

"In the instance of the small animals it attacks, it may even reach the skeleton," Noble droned on. "Once it successfully penetrates its victim and reaches its target, Richard, the hypha . . . *proliferates.*" I nodded, wished he wouldn't call me that. His lecture style, the absence of any sign of human involvement, made me angrier by the second. "It reaches out; expands. And it procreates, *umm,* geometrically . . . somewhat like fish that grow larger as the size of the bowl becomes greater." He batted his eyelids closed for a fractional instant. "It can even ripen in the bodies of the dead."

I had the urge to bathe, to scratch myself till my skin was bleeding. "So it goes *on* growing, is that right?" I plunged ahead, "until—well, until there's nothing left for it to eat?"

An odd light flickered, glimmered, in the psychiatrist's strange eyes. Then it was gone, like a star twinkling out. "Quite so. But . . ."

"What?" I asked as he stopped speaking. I gripped my soda can so tightly it almost crunched. "But what?"

"Well, Richard," Ellair murmured thoughtfully, then paused to glance out the window at the silent downtown street. Finally, he peered back at me as if I were the only man alive to whom he could confide his innermost thoughts. A smirk came and went. "That isn't quite *all* . . ."

3. It's in the Air

When he first developed the itch, Clyde Leighton imagined it was only nerves. Even cool cats who could have lined up behind any damn center in the Big 10 or the N.F.L. and hurled aerial bombs like Jeff George or Dan Marino (*if* they had really wished to do that) got the fidgets at times. Shit-fire, there'd been enough reason to *be* nervous lately!

He'd started the evening two nights back at the Harem House where he lifted a few at the bar, then ambled over to the stage where he eyeballed the dancers till he picked out one he liked. Leighton coaxed her to his end of the raised platform by showing her the corner of a fifty—her stage name was Flounce, blonde on top with bassooms that would be a goodly double handful—then played Tuck-it. He hid the new fifty dollar bill in her G-string while Flounce crouched before him long enough to let his fingertips investigate if she was blonde all over, then collected the French kiss dancers awarded customers with the good taste to slip decent money down their Gees instead of fives or, far worse, singletons.

Clyde had left the House cockily, shoulders back, reassured that he could still speak the right language in any tongue, and with the intention of coming back to pick up Flounce for the night, at 1:30 A.M. The scribbled note he had slipped into the tangle of wavy hair with the crisp, folded fifty had pledged three more bills like the first. He had gone out to hit the other joints on Pendleton and the Avenue till Flounce got off, sure there'd be more bounce to the ounce with Flounce, almost as certain that she was no natural blonde. Those ol' quarterback fingertips rarely deceived him about the texture of either pigskin or pubic hair, but it was a tricky proposition to be absolutely sure. Young girls who had a really thorough commitment to life these days even dyed *that* hair!

Mebbe, Clyde had reflected, it was time to think about a dye job for what was left of his own yellowish locks. He was getting a bit thin on top, even with the crew. A dab of self-improvement might even prove better than the couple of dabs of pomade he'd employed back at Shortridge High. Just mebbe they'd prove effective enough to let him cut back on Flounce to a twenty, or a twenty and a ten at least. It was good t'show a lady a good time, but whore inflation was murder on a divorced man with the piss-poor fortune t'be workin' in an alley garage at age forty-four. Jesus Aitch, even knowin' where an alley *was,* these days, was like wearin' a tag with your age on it!

He'd blown his fifty by never returning to the House that night at all, and by 1:30 he'd been nervous as a cat a stone's throw from the fucking Pink Panther. Something about him beatin' shit out of a Hoosier fan who called Purdue "P.U." and said the P stood for Puke. He'd never gone to Purdue, but he'd drunk two boilermakers at the KitKat and the ad-

273

vanced age and small size of the old sumbitch who'd pissed Clyde off hadn't been crystal clear when he started hitting him. Shit-fire, anyone piss-poor dumb enough t'speak disrespectfully about Purdue to a quarterback wasn't smart enough to live anyhow! Then, with the guy *dying,* a few nervous twitches in the soles of Clyde's feet were only to be *expected*.

But in no time, the itch bothering Leighton was climbing up into his crotch and he'd done the only thing he could think of doing under the circumstances: Got himself a jackoff magazine and set out to make sure his ol' Jim Brown was still in fighting shape. 'Cause a man who could still get it up was never *too* sick, and 'cause there was nothing better for nerves than sex or loftin' a spiral thirty, forty yards downfield. Commonsense told him there wasn't going to be any football playin' till he got out — no Flounce, either — so that left stroking his very own Jim Brown. The real Jim was the meanest mothering athlete of all time; the only player Leighton had ever heard of who was worth givin' up quarterbacking for.

Good thing Lester isn't in here with me, Clyde thought as he studied the centerfold nude. *This here ain't any fuckin team sport*.

Exposed to the humid air in Leighton's cell, this one-time quarterback's smaller edition of Jim Brown didn't look particularly athletic. He had brown splotches all up and down his uninspired and modest length. The real Jim Brown was probably just fine with his own edition, but Leighton doubted that the great runner would've been any more freaking

274

pleased than *he* was by the reddish, or the yellow-green, spots. Or by how his "Jim Brown" plus the two ace blockers beneath him and the long legs supporting the en-tire backfield of a cat called Clyde Leighton were itching like he'd picked up the *clap*—from head to toe, inside and out!

No, not clap. Herpes. *AIDS!* Definitely unsocial social diseases from the goddamn ancient Greeks or Spartans—unidentifiable fucking *Martian* diseases borne from the fucking *future!*

Leighton took ol' Jim outta sight, out of the starting lineup, and ordered his quarterback digits not to begin scratching *nothing.* 'Cause he'd had bad itches before, plenty of times. It was a matter of either goin' to a doctor or using the greatest self-control known to man—putting one's hands into one's pockets, *keeping* them there, never permitting oneself even the slightest wiggle of the magical quarterback *fingernails* over the offending surface skin.

'Cause if you scratched *anything*—the soles of your feet, between the toes, under your arms—that was the pits, *ha-HA!*—or in your groin between your legs—*if you scratched anything even* one *time* . . .

Leighton stared between the bars of his cell, at nothing. He had an itch behind his left ear. He had an itch just under the tip of his nose, next to the nostril. There was another one behind the right kneecap, it itched in the small of his back, his *rectum itched.*

Where don't I itch? Clyde asked himself.

The answer to that wasn't tolerable, thinkable.

So he was a little nervous. So what? "So what?" he

275

challenged the world at large, aloud. So what? It definitely wasn't . . . what *they* had. Uh-uh, couldn't be; no way. *"So what?"* he asked aloud, belligerently.

He looked at the houseplant steeped in shadow across the cell, the goodwill gift Ellair'd given him.

If you scratched anything even one time, you might keep scratching till you made everything bleed and go on bleeding, and you mightn't ever stop.

The pretty plant looked like it was beginning to droop already.

No that wasn't it.

It had growed a *lot* in the last day and a half, and it had budded.

Now, some of the buds lay on the floor of Leighton's cell. He saw that he'd stepped on a few and accidentally broken them. Smashed them flat. Too bad, 'cause they was almost as pretty as Flounce.

4. *A Very Serious Hazard*

"What do you mean—'that isn't quite all?' " I demanded. I'd raised the soda to my mouth to take a gulp, then stopped. What more could Ellair have in his little lexicon of entomogenic horrors?

"That inmate with the problem in making support payments. White fellow named Vick, I think it was. First name Lou?" He waited for my nod. Instead of giving it to him, I downed the rest of my drink chug-a-lug fashion and simply looked at Ellair. "Remember how he ran in circles at such an incredible pace?"

276

I couldn't forget it. Lou'd run till he couldn't run any longer, and he'd never gained an inch on what was chasing him. "I remember."

"Well," Noble Ellair allowed, "I fear we'll be seeing more of that."

Barely whispering, I asked why.

"Let me cite some recent as well as some *old* history to you. During the fall of 1989, a history professor in Maryland, Mary Kilbourne Matossian, came up with a most intriguing theory. While studying the possible explanations for a period of unexplained hysteria among peasants in France, exactly two-hundred years before Professor Matossian's fascinating work, she discovered a food shortage that forced the common people to subsist largely on bread made from a *specific rye wheat.*"

What was this leading to? "Go on," I said with impatience.

"Earlier historians called the wave of hysteria—the weeping, clamoring peasantry running amok and looting their way across the countryside, brandishing muskets and pitchforks, behaving as if they had lost all self-control—'the great Fear.' "

"That's not what it was?"

Noble rose, carefully depositing his empty can in a nearby waste container. "It seems Matossian has written a book. *Poisons of the Past: Molds, Epidemics, and History.*" He waited for my reaction and got it. My mouth dropped open. "The bread those people were obliged to eat was infected by *ergot*, Richard—which contains the same alkaloid lysergic acid from which

277

LSD is extracted."

LSD. The granddaddy, the godfather, of hallucinogenic drugs.

He drew my empty can from my unprotesting fingers. "Ergot sometimes replaces the grain in rye and other cereal grasses," Ellair said slowly, "and it is . . . *a fungus*. From the genus *Claviceps,* it houses masses of usually dormant mycelia and can be *quite* toxic . . . quite capable of creating, *ummm,* distortions of reality."

I watched him jiggle and bounce the green can in his hand. He looked pretty satisfied with himself.

"Richard, the *French Revolution* may have been *caused* by ordinary people eating *bread!* Isn't that a thought that titillates your imagination, that piques your curiosity?"

I said, "Relevance," and it came out a growl.

He seemed disappointed that I hadn't applauded. "Clear support for my theories about what has happened here, Stenvall — support originating two-hundred years ago. You see, inside of insects these fungi of ours dramatically interfere with the nervous system, can *destroy* the nervous system. The more modest *Claviceps* mycelia — without evidence of intent, volition — made French peasants abandon their homes, plunder, exhibit paranoia. The *entomogenic* seems now to have the same effect on some men that it has on *ants!*" A smile. "It shouldn't astonish us, then, when those who are infected behave . . . rather bizarrely."

His smile lingered a moment too long for me. "You *bastard,*" I said, jumping to my feet — "you unfeeling

278

goddamned mechanical *bastard!*"

I guess he'd known I would have to attack him then because he raised his slender hands gracefully and peremptorily, like a choral conductor prepared to direct Handel. "Strike me, Stenvall," he said, exercising his icy self-control once more, "and you're back behind bars to die with the rest of them!"

I probably looked like the Frankenstein monster, posed for a still shot. Clawing the air, my fingers were inches from his throat. I hadn't planned on striking him; I was going to throttle him. He looked more like a skinny turkey already dressed for Thanksgiving than a man, anyway.

But Ellair had somehow selected the words that stopped me, that not only cut through my outrage but also *hurt* me. He put it on a non-idealistic, personal level.

I think Noble Ellair was more closely attuned to the weak spots in other men than anybody I have ever met. He knew precisely when and where to apply pressure, to turn the screws tighter; what to say in subtle terms that made another human being become as docile and helpless as a newborn infant.

I'd turned away from him then to avoid seeing the quick, smug smirk that would crawl onto his mouth, when the next best thing to dismantling him occurred to me.

I said, over my shoulder, "I demand that the plants be removed, *tonight,* from each cell in this chamber of horrors. Tonight, *not tomorrow.*"

"Go on," he said. Not something trite like "Or?" but

"Go on." Because he knew I wasn't finished and he knew he hadn't agreed to anything yet.

"If you don't get that done, you won't stop me merely by locking me up." I kept my eyes averted, I didn't want to be distracted by his tricky expressions. "I can still yell, pass the word. I can shout out everything I know about your 'goodwill gifts,' and begin the riot *myself*."

He said, "Please continue." Not, "You wouldn't do that." Not threats about having me silenced or exterminated.

"Word will be passed from cell to cell, Noble. And this is no maximum security prison. Somebody, maybe one of the guards, will let one or two men out. If they're not Crock, they'll help the rest to escape. If it *is* Crock, why — he'll kill you."

Ellair was at my shoulder, his breath on the side of my neck. "I agree."

I turned slowly, to look at him. "You agree to what? To what I said about Crock?"

"That, yes; certainly. He's an animal." The shrink's deceitful face was expressionless, but I did make out something related to serenity, and that frightened me.

"This damnable heat wave doesn't seem like it's about to break," he remarked. He placed my empty soda can beside his in the container. The symbolism of that made me uncomfortable, made me think of Doc, the unwaving Leighton. "I agree that the continuing presence of the plants in the cells remains a serious hazard even though I imagine those which carried the fungus have already, *umm,* done their

280

damage. Nevertheless, we can't tolerate the risk—can we?" He brushed with his delicate fingertips at something he saw on my shoulder, smiled intimately.

"I don't get it," I said.

"No, you don't," he murmured, "do you?" He left his fingers on my grimy shoulder. "Richard, whatever you think of me, *I'm* not the adversary—perhaps no man is, *nothing* is. In a broader, a more philosophical sense of which you have been deprived, there may only be the enemy each of us creates in his own thoughts—and sees mirrored occasionally in other people. Some of those people whom we hope are . . . conquerable."

I knocked his slimy hand away from my shoulder. "Damn it, what is it I'm not seeing?" I shouted. I avoided the urge to hit him by stepping back and away, and one foot struck the waste container, made the paired cans clatter in a tinny chorus. "What is it that's making you so fucking smug about agreeing to collect your goddamn plants tonight?"

He took a step toward the interior of the jail. He paused. "First, Stenvall, I expect you to keep your word and help us minimize the chances of a riot tonight—while I'm having my little gifts collected." He raised one brow, questioning, and I nodded. I marveled at the warped mind of a man who could come and go freely in the midst of so many others denied both their liberty and the chance to save themselves, yet remain so cheerful, so unalterably unflustered. "As for appearing smug, you may be misinterpreting my approach to this situation. But it's true that I seem to have thought of something important which you have not."

"Go on," I said tightly.

"Well, it constantly amazes me how people of average intelligence appear to be incapable of confronting the fact of their own mortality." His lips turned up at the corners. "Your fellow visitor to the drunk tank, young Vick, has been deceased for around half the day now. Correct?"

I nodded.

"Though now serving as my aide, my emissary among the inmates . . . *you,* sir, were confined to the drunk tank immediately after your arrival at the jail. True?"

I saw him gesture politely for me to precede him back into the cell area but I didn't budge. Couldn't. I was rooted to the ground at that moment.

"Well, Richard, *that* means you spent several hours in the company of poor Mr. Vick," Ellair finished patiently. He patted my arm, smirked. "—*And* the plant that appears to have *killed* him," he added.

Part Four

No One But the Dead

"My door is grave with oaken strength,
   The cool of linen calms my bed,
And there at night I stretch my length,
   And envy no one but the dead."

—Dorothy Parker
"Recurrence"

Ten

1. Rites — and Wrongs — of Spring

When the interior of county lockup began reminding me of an edifice in which some ancient Druidic ritual might begin at any scary instant, I started to patrol the aisle between the facing cells like a combination of friendly monk and the Answer Man. If I'd had a collection plate and they'd had any money, I could've made a fortune. Of course, I was asking the inmates a lot of questions Noble Ellair wanted me to ask. But that was okay since I knew the answers would be colorful, profane, amusing, and something else:

An outlet, a release. For the men. For me.

It was an opportunity for them to sound off and try to get it off their chests — no ghastly quip intended — to express exactly how they felt about continuing to be locked up — defenseless against an unseen enemy that might decide to kill them horribly, any second.

Since I was on the outside of cells that looked increasingly like cages at a freaking zoo, I was the inmates' only source of explanation and information.

I didn't believe that any riot I incited would solve a thing; merely bring their lives to the brink that much more quickly. So there was a limit to how much information I could impart.

I tell you, I walked between those cells and engaged the other guys in conversation with as much sense of commitment to sociability as I've ever generated! My intention was to do anything in my power to quit imagining that inside my own body — legs, arms, my own *face* and *head,* was a hideous *stirring* . . . an *awakening* of perverted life, *invading* life . . . like cancer cells with brains, an instinct and intention to kill, to *eat* me, inside out.

For the first time, I clearly knew what my fellow inmates had been suffering and that made me feel closer to those we dismiss as "other people," as strangers. Never before had I truly understood those folks getting on in years who collected infirmities instead of clipping coupons and pleaded with their families not to let them die in nursing homes.

You see, the other side of the coin carries their faces, and they leer, and scream: You suffer from the same incurable disease as *we* do, and you also know that you're losing your individuality; you sense that the care and attention you're going to get will be diminished when you're One of Many. Therefore your home — *whatever* it's like, *whoever* is there, even no one at all — is preferable to the *collec-*

286

tive death.

When you are finally powerless enough, you can acknowledge that to yourself, along with the fact that you've *always* just been One of Many. But you don't have to *like* it, do you? And you can also acknowledge that the only kinds of power you ever knew, or ever had, come from love — love acquired, love given. And when everybody who constitutes the "us" is miserably perishing, then getting your *own* share of that priceless commodity of love becomes a competition you're just not up to entering. Solution: You must somehow be where it's *accessible.*

I made it through those evening hours in the thickening darkness by concentrating on what other people like me were saying and telling myself that I was going home in the morning. I helped my mind stay focused by dredging up an occasional thought — after all, my brain was freer of booze than it'd been for a while.

Our terrifying predicament was made worse by a number of factors: we didn't understand what was happening, making it part of the Great Unknown; we couldn't get out of the building, away from the nightmare, even for an hour; and our natural rhythms and routines were being shot to hell.

Biorhythm says we remain mentally and physically healthy by keeping our cycles in shape, in order. There's a rhythm, a measured process, in almost everything our bodies do for us. Pulse; blood pressure; body temperature and metabolism; levels of energy; the manufacture of a huge variety of body ingredients from oxygen and blood sugar to semen! The cycles are linked, they overlap, so the way they function inside each of us says a lot about the personality we show the rest of the world. Get it screwed up and you're up the creek.

The cycle of night and day is one of the real Biggies; it's called "circadian rhythm" and it's recognizable in a great many ways: Manic-depressive conditions respond to a sort of "circannual" rhythm; individual weight tends to shift with the seasons; urine output lowers at night; people even get born or die in harmony with a circadian cycle.

People usually enter this sorry old world some time between midnight and 6:00 A.M., the majority of us being born around 4:00 in the morning.

We also tend—at dawn and dusk—to *leave* it then, too. Talk about your Twilight Zones!

I even read about a *sin* cycle! Every nine years (*not* seven according to some experts) people have an urge to kick off the traces, do what they please . . . break out. And consider the horrendous heat. In 1959, a hospital averaging two heart attack patients a day had twenty cases the day after a solar flare. And there was more sunspot activity in the year of the black death plague than there had been for the previous one-hundred years . . .

As for sleep, no one knows why, but almost one-third of human life is spent sleeping. Everyone passes through different sleeping stages every night—hell, think how hard it is to switch from a day- or night-shift job, think about jet-lag. Seventy-year old folks blew twenty years—if that's a question of waste—sleeping. One weird theory is that we require sleep so our astral body can depart from our *regular* one, and be regenerated with cosmic energy! Well, we weren't getting much of it *that* night. We were prisoners, not only to the jail and Doctor Noble Ellair, but to those oddball forces I'd sensed while I was still at home. Those that activated my "dis-ease."

There isn't any word for sleep in most West African languages, I read. Merely a verb that means "to be half dead."

2. Sin Cycle

Hawkins lugged the strangely-paralyzed corpse of the tall rangy white man out of the cell in a couple of burlap bags taken from the kitchen, then wrestled the remains onto a food cart. His timing was perfect, like always; Hawkins boasted of that every chance he got. Before handling the odious task, he had sent the cell's still-living inmate off on a clean-up detail, and delayed the conveyance of a freshly arriving prisoner so he wouldn't be nosing around and asking questions while Orville was executing his chore. "Executing his chore" was another expression the guard in his late thirties liked saying. "Executing my chores properly, within prompt and acceptable time-lines" was even better, dearer.

But this hadn't been a pleasing chore to execute. At a fairly trim 260 when he had time to use the weight room, Orville Hawkins wasn't small, but neither was the late Clyde Leighton. Then there was the fact that the body stank like none of the bodies Hawkins had hauled around before—like a goddamn rose garden or something. And the fact that the dead S.O.B. tucked into the burlap sacks had died standing up, and *stayed* that way! Godamighty, Orville felt like a fool pushing the cart up the aisle between the cells while he tried to hold the bags tightly around the head, first, and then the feet!

So he bitched about the job all the way to where Noble Ellair had instructed him to put the dead cocksucker, but then shut up after Doctor Ellair himself formally accepted the remains and dismissed Hawkins. A good guard executed his orders just the way they were given to him, as promptly as possible, and moved on to the next task.

But as he was returning to his guard post, muttering as he went, Orville was damned unsure if hauling frozen-looking corpses around and hiding them—instead of leaving them on slabs in the infirmary until Sheriff Bottoms or Chief Officer Boswell got back—was part of his job description. It wasn't the first time a superior'd asked him to keep cold meat under wraps for awhile. Hell, he'd stuck Eddie the cook and the kid Vick out of sight without giv-

290

ing it a second thought, and he still had to put the gamblers, that big buck August, and maybe one or two others in the infirmary. Orville had lost track of how many cocksuckers were dead now.

It was the frozen-looking part—more accurately, the *paralyzed* part, since nobody was freezing to death in *this* heat—that made Hawkins fret. As he thought about it he wondered if there might be more to worry about than he'd imagined when the cocksuckers started dying—he thought of the men as cocksuckers, both because he figured that was what most of them would become sooner or later, and because he loathed with all his heart anyone who was dirt dumb enough to allow himself to reach a point where there was no order in his life, no chores to execute promptly and properly. Orville had seen many inmates go to their maker over the years in an assortment of interesting ways, including a couple he'd devised himself. They'd long since failed to revulse, trouble, or surprise him, and his not necessarily private opinion was that that was just fine and dandy. Saved the taxpayers money and Orville Hawkins saw himself not only as guarding the public's interest, he *also* was a taxpayer.

Now, however, as he propped his feet up on the sheriff's desk—what Bottoms didn't know couldn't hurt the prick—and laced his fingers across his meaty, uniformed stomach, he realized that he *was* somewhat surprised. He wasn't revulsed, although August's and Blackledge's remains had given him momentary pause, just surprised.

Abruptly, almost as if certain chemical connections within the mass of his big body had been severed or rewired, he felt exceedingly troubled, nervous, nauseous even. Disposed to grind his fat butt around in the sheriff's leather chair, shake, and maybe toss his cookies.

Orville applied his mind — kept in a container no larger than his left nut — and will-power to the task of making sense of what was happening. One thing to see a cocksucker scared out of his tree, then dying a hideous death; it was another matter entirely if a jail official was endangered. Especially Orville Hawkins.

Shit, was he getting bent out of shape just because the bastard he'd toted on the meal cart to Noble Ellair's office looked mostly like a goddamn statue? He had to deal with this, *cope* with it . . .

Maybe a call home was in order. He started to drum his cigar-sized fingers on the desk, reflecting on the notion of informing Gargan that he was getting sick as a dog and sticking the Irishman with an extra shift. That old fool was nearing retirement so he'd work around the clock, over weekends and holidays, to keep from risking his pension. He'd keep his old yap shut, too, to avoid the additional risk of Orville Hawkins closing it for him!

He got to his feet, shuffled them two times to get them pointed in the direction he wanted. Cinching his belt, he lumbered toward the door, planning to

292

use the public telephone to call his wife, Jeannine. The Hawk had gotten that cocksucker of a phone to work hours before, but hadn't informed the men yet — especially Ellair's stuckup trust, Spanwell, or whatever the hell his name was. This might be as good a way as any to let the cocksuckers know they could phone out again. He would pretend to be surprised, too — just enough for Stenvale to see he was lying and not be able to do one goddamn thing about it!

Then maybe, just maybe, Hawkins would stop by Gargan's post to tell him he was leaving. Maybe not; he might simply go home. Gargan wouldn't fink on him. So who was to know? He had completely lost sight of the fact that Doctor Ellair remained in his office upstairs. Orville's pea-sized brain wasn't really operating that well.

He paused to take into his fat hands what the shrink gave him in appreciation for having once more executed a chore, properly and promptly. Most of the codes and buzzwords he pretended to live by were fading like carelessly-erased chalk from a blackboard.

Dimly, Hawkins hoped Jeannine wouldn't mind too much when she saw that the house plant he was bringing her looked about as sick as he did.

Maybe it was just the heat.

3. More Wrongs

For as long as I could remember, I had hated being in the dark. In some ways, maybe I was a more typical kid than I realized. Whether it was the way Mom saw conspiracies behind the various unexplained occurrences of the sixties and seventies that triggered my juvenile paranoia, or her sister, my Aunt Evelyn, who liked playing weepy melodies on the piano whenever she visited us, sometimes from 2:00 or 3:00 A.M. till daylight; I grew up believing in a supernatural world. A supernatural *system*, too — by which I mean not just a belief in God, Heaven, and Hell, but in an invisible order of superior life that laid down all the rules.

Very often, when I was in my cups, I invested a lot of effort in trying to dope out those rules and in wondering why Something or Somebody didn't explain them clearly. It wasn't that I objected to the regulations; that mode of thinking at least allows a guy to have certain expectations of cause and effect, reward or punishment. It means there *is* a reason for the crap we endure and for continuing to go on. The problem was that so much of life didn't add up for me when I was a kid; and I figured I and everyone I knew would be a lot happier and better if the ground rules were *completely* clear.

I was a big scaredy-cat at nights. I concocted my own system for getting through the hours to unconsciousness or dawn, whichever came first. I insisted that one light be left on in my bedroom and that the bedroom door be closed, just like the closet door.

Then I grew up, of course. I've never received that ideally-refined list of guidelines, we've already sinned so many times it's probably hopeless, and we tell anyone who thinks to ask that I'm not afraid of the dark any more.

So I was very pleased when Gargan and another guard passed out the flashlights they'd found in the jail cellar. The idea was to provide us with at least a modicum of illumination as the night wore on and the shadows darkened. But it was the flashlights that turned the joint into what seemed a site for arcane rituals of old. It was the look of the long center lane and the spotlighted faces of men, a forest of bars painted across their terrified features, that contributed to the appearance of sacrifices to some occult rite. Besides, the men kept the damn things burning. Sooner or later they'd be groaning that the batteries were worn out and then the night would *really* be black.

There was only one sight that I found encouraging—that was the rolypoly form of rumpled ol' Gargan and the other guard beginning to round up the plants. They weren't exactly exerting themselves getting the job done, which might have meant they had orders not to look desperate or urgent—except I knew it was only because of the Irishman's it'll-be-done-when-it's-done approach to life. And maybe because the men who were locked up were "merely" prisoners.

The synchronicity of the way I yearned to speak with Ronnie at home and a sudden, sharp curiosity about Hawkins, a burly guard who should've been helping out the others but wasn't, caused me to snap the beam of my flashlight up the corridor and to follow it with my eyes.

I glimpsed Hawkins' gross body hulked over the lifeline to the outside world, his lips moving—talking—above the mouthpiece. The phone was working again!

I started off at a sprint, then cut it to walking briskly instead, to prevent a furor of demands to use the phone. I'm genuinely ashamed to confess that I didn't even think of calling for help. My sole desire was to hear my wife's voice again, and the voices of my children; to make sure they were okay, and to make arrangements to get home—as soon as possible. I had no way of knowing whether I'd been infected, germinated . . . but living or dying, I wanted to be where I counted for something. That love connection I was talking about.

Now, I think I made a mistake that many men make in similar situations. The notion of phoning a physician did not enter my thoughts; Doctor Ellair *was* Doctor Ellair and the title toted automatic clout. Call somebody in authority for help? We felt as if we were *surrounded* by men in positions of authority! Would the fucking mayor pay any attention if he got an hysterical phone call from some guy behind bars? But I should have called someone who might have saved a few of us.

Anyway, buttressed by my relative freedom, I hurried eagerly to Hawkins, even offered him a smile meant to say how happy we could be that Ma AT&T's favorite invention was in use again.

Hawkins turned to face me, his eyes black hollows, his blubbery lips trying to smirk. I thought he looked sick as hell, but the only things we inmates knew about Orville were that he loved bowling, worked hard, and beat shit out of people now and then. He gestured with his thumb. *". . . Telephone,"* he mumbled.

"Yes, it is, isn't it?" I said, smiling and stepping past him to pick it up. "I'll just call home, then notify the other—"

A hand nearly the match of one of Andre August's clamped itself to my shoulder and the fingers seemed inclined to become teeth and eat it. I dropped the plastic phone, let it bounce against the wall, and found myself being turned around bodily to confront the big guard.

". . . Jeannine? . . ." Hawkins stammered. He was jabbing a finger toward the floor as if he wanted me to look at something, but the way he was gripping me I couldn't glance down unless I liked the idea of my upper vertebrae being permanently rearranged.

"If you could *hum* some of it," I gasped, aware that his fat thumbs were within choking range, "I

297

might remember it. Is that the one about dreaming of her at twilight or something?"

"*N . . . n . . . n . . . !*" he rasped as I became aware finally that he was infinitely more ill than I'd realized at first. He released me suddenly so I could see what he was pointing at, and I bounced off the wall. "*For . . .* Jeannine!"

Hawkins was pointing at a house plant. One of Noble's gifts. One that had already looked for a weak spot in big ol' Orville and found it. I saw then why he was having so much trouble talking to me, remembered what Doctor Ellair had told me about a vesicular fungus disease called thrush that affected the mouth or the vagina. It hadn't been a coin flip for the entomogenic where Orville was concerned. This thrush was ugly, couldn't sing, and wouldn't be migrating at all unless it was through the big guard's system.

"She'll love it, man," I told him. I patted his arm. "But you might think of stopping by to see Ellair before taking it home to Jeannine." Perhaps Noble could treat it, help the guy, since the germination didn't seem to be fatally advanced. If not, maybe the fungus would leave Orville's bod and attack Noble's! "Let me help you up the stairs—"

"*Nnnnnnno!*" he blurted, and a pus-like substance flecked his thick lips. Snatching up the plant, almost falling in the process, he took a step toward the sheriff's office. Through it, a locked-and-bolted door to the street waited. And Jeannine.

298

"C'mon, Hawk," I tried gently a second time. I reached out to catch his sleeve. "You're not well, man. A few seconds—"

Hawkins wheeled like a nimble buffalo and both his arms swept out, hitting me hard in the chest. ". . . Cocksucker . . ." he mumbled and that was the only word I heard clearly.

"Thanks, but no," I grunted, rebounding once more from the wall.

Then he was thundering into Sheriff Bottom's office and slamming the door after him. I heard him wrestle with the locks and mutter "cocksucker" a few more times as he searched for his keys. I thought about trying to follow him, to flee the jail myself, and I'd have to hurry if I was going to do it. The door to freedom would doubtlessly lock automatically behind him. But in Hawkins' state of mind I'd resemble the last pin standing at the end of an alley. And maybe, just maybe, I felt I had to stay and see things through.

Ronnie didn't say hello, she answered the ring with, "Rich?"

I'm not sure when I was ever as happy as I was that second.

"Hi, baby," I replied in a breath, then changed it to, "Hi, honey" because my Ron hates being called "baby." She's a grown woman. "Are you okay?"

Ronnie asked, "Are *you*?" which is also my wife's style.

"Sure," I said as if I'd had a complete physical

and passed it. I could be macho like my wife, my baby, if I had to be. "Probably." How did *that* slip out? "Nothing okay down here. Nothing at all."

"I've tried and tried to get through, but there was trouble on the line." She'd evaded the need to comment on what I had said and I knew it was because she thought I was just complaining. About the usual nightmare of the lockup.

"Yes, there was," I answered. I noticed for the first time in an hour or more how I'd continued sweating, how hot it was even at night. I also realized I was ravenously hungry. "Listen, honey, you can pick me up in the morning. Okay? Will you come get me?"

"I'll have to borrow Rudy Loomis's truck," she said with a doubtful tone. "They impounded the Omni."

I exploded at that point. "Jesus, Ronnie, men are *dying* down here . . . the jail psychiatrist handed out plants that *kill* people! Ronnie, *I* might be infected! That's not the right word, but—"

"Hi, Daddy."

I gaped at the phone—unprepared to hear those words—and couldn't tell if Ron had handed the phone to Markie, dropped it because I'd yelled at her, or dropped it because of reasons I didn't dare guess.

"Hi, Markie."

"Guess what?"

My heart was pounding in a combination of wonderment and angry frustration. I felt stunned by my little boy's "Guess what?" My life had turned into a claustrophobic horror show that I couldn't describe to my wife, and my son was playing guessing games with me!

I was also charmed to the point of tears by Mark's normality, the good and halfway understandable way of life he symbolized just then with his innocuous question. It represented everything I realized my half-assed writing and wholehearted boozing had put in jeopardy, and everything I saw myself losing.

"What, son?" I asked him, smothering a sigh, keeping the smile that surfaced.

"I went to see Stef 'n' she was lyin' on the floor without no clothes."

My eyelids fluttered shut, I shook my head slowly. "Son, how many times—"

"She wooden answer me, though," the sweetly wondering small voice continued purring in my ear, "like maybe she was asleep, or *something*—and there was this funny thing lyin' next to her too."

Ron was telling him to surrender the phone to Bett. I heard her distinctly saying that, realized she wasn't paying any attention to what Markie said. "What kind of funny thing, son?" I asked. My lips had gone dry for some reason.

"Like a plant, Dad," said Markie. His mouth was so near the mouthpiece of the telephone it was as if he were whispering into my ear, telling secrets as he had some times. "The *biggest* plant I ever seen!"

My heartbeat was no longer indecisive. It was a tiger. "Hey, buddy," I said very carefully, softly, "you didn't see Mr. Ryder—Karl—around Stef's apartment, did you? Stef's husband?"

"No, Daddy," Markie said with that emphasis on honesty he used both in earnestness and in telling me whoppers. He really whispered, then, *mano a mano:* "I saw Stef's big pillows, Dad!"

"Put your mother on again, sports fan," I told him without changing my nonchalant tone of voice. Inside, I'd become a thunderstorm, like the one that hadn't quite occurred above the Beaumont Estates. If Karl knew one of the men who had been released, if he was friends with one of the guards, or had even *visited* the jail in the last couple of days . . .

"One more thing, Dad," my son said.

"No," I interrupted. Firmly. "Not *now,* Markie." If the "plant" lying next to Stephanie Ryder was Karl—if the girl and he were both *dead*—I didn't want Ron and the children to come even a block closer to the jail. So I needed to tell Ronnie to stay home, inside the apartment—to lock the door and keep it locked. Until I got there and figured out what to do. "Son . . . Give your mother the phone."

Incredibly, Markie was still at the other end. "There was a b-broken pot in the livin room," he said doggedly, despite the sniffling sound of tears coming because Markie was defying me, and knew

302

it. And I realized too that I should always bear in mind kids were only adult people who had not gotten where they were going, that I should listen to what they were saying. "I don't think it was big enough for that giant flower to've *had* it, but—"

Then he squealed.

"Give me that phone," Bett's higher, older voice cut in. I thought, helplessly, *Noooo,* and *Put Mom on!* While I screamed inside I heard a tussle, a wrestling match, between two normal kids who intended to have their own way. I heard no sign of Ronnie anywhere in the background.

I called, "Bett!", my fear for them all growing; *"Markie—"* . . . But the fumble/break/*gone* noise of disconnection was followed promptly by the inevitable electronical interrogation of the damned dial tone.

I started to ring our number in the apartment, over and over. I went through an operator who began sounding like Lily Tomlin snorting indignantly into the receiver. But the only thing she and I accomplished was hearing the *Unnn, unnn, unn* of the busy signal.

Just for a moment I switched off my torch and stood perfectly alone in the dark.

4. Gutter Ball

Hawkins really needed to wet his whistle by the

303

time he'd staggered through the humid evening blackness to his 2-year-old Toyota truck. After he'd climbed in and got the motor going, he reached into the glove compartment and came out with what appeared to be a much-stained and smelly, pregnant road map. He peeled the map away, revealed the pint bottle he kept hidden inside it, opened it and took a long drag.

Or believed he did. He hadn't managed to get his swollen lips around the mouth of the bottle and succeeded mostly in turning South and North Dakota into wetter states. He'd already wet his shorts and the crotch of his uniform pants during the period it had taken him to lumber across the parking lot to his pickup, but Orville didn't notice that, either. With a grunt, he carelessly replaced the cap of the bottle, wrapped the reeking road map around the pint as the whiskey dripped on him and the passenger seat, and threw the mess back into the glove compartment.

Unnoticed, the booze continued to pour out and pretty much drench the firing mechanism of the revolver that the Hawk kept concealed beneath a couple of filthy rags. There was never any pot or other illegal drugs inside the little convenience-space—because Orville Hawkins believed in the sanctity of the law along with following orders properly and promptly—unless the drugs were there to plant on somebody. That was the original reason Hawkins had not turned in the revolver he'd found on a suspect years back. But he'd acquired a fondness for it that ranked right up there with bowling and Jeannine, whom he considered his *other* piece.

Jeannine. Fat, aging, willing Jeannine. Serene in knowing that her Orville always came home to her even if it was morning by then, or the next night. *Dependable* Jeannine, how he'd loved and hated and always needed her! Hawkins glanced with affection at the relic of a plant on the floor of the truck, ready to swear he could see her face forming in the nest of ruined greenery. Because of the way the plant had detonated its spores he was sure he detected Jeannine's smile with the missing tooth in front, the other one — an incisor — missing at the side. She'd be crazy about his thoughtful gift; sure he had done something else that he couldn't tell her about, or wouldn't, but that didn't matter. Even when he was two or three days late in arriving home she would never dream of asking where he'd been for fear of the Hawk's fabled knuckle sandwich; all that mattered was the thought.

For some minutes Orville had driven mindlessly in the direction of home, the Toyota slanting back and forth across the center stripe. Now, suffused by appreciation of his own basic goodness, and other things, the guard pulled over to the curb, letting his pick-up idle behind a parked eighteen-wheel flatbed. Dimly, he noticed a number of lengths of steel pipes protruding from the second truck's bed, looking like a gigantic opened pack of cigarettes. His foggy

305

thought had been to open the glove compartment once more, excavate his pint of whiskey, and repay himself for his essential decency with a further pull. Gawd, his mouth was so *dry!*

But when he slewed around and glanced briefly through the space between the bucket seats, he caught sight of his bowling bag and was freshly smitten. Jeannine had bought it for him at Christmas. It had his initials under the carrying strap, and the jet-black ball inside featured holes that had been drilled to the precise measurement of Orville's penis-sized digits. Jeannine had done that for him, too, several years back. He'd never forgotten how hard the cow had tried to measure his fingers without him becoming aware of it. That'd been a night! He remembered how he had gotten her to measure something else, first, and used a method of measurement all his own.

Virtually romantic, damply half erect, Hawkins groped between the Toyota seats to open his bowling bag, to peer tenderly at what it contained. He was clumsy doing it, his fingers trembled as he worked the zipper down—carefully, so it wouldn't catch—then the round, firm globe within was laid bare for his fond inspection.

Covered with cabbage leaves! The bowling ball with the perfectly drilled holes, tailored so efficiently for his use that no other man had ever dared touch it looked *green* now!

The Hawk was incensed, maddened.

Thrusting both hands into the gaping bag, plunging his paws around this toy that he loved he shifted his weight until the tip of his left boot pressed down on the accelerator of the pick-up truck.

The response of his Toyota truck had always pleased Orville. He'd boasted to Bottoms that you only had to goose it to make it go. Now, it roared down the double car length toward the larger truck, taking just enough time for him to see the iron piping pounding its ways toward him and then—as if destiny had arranged it so—ramming through the windshield and into his head.

The Hawk had only sufficient time, though, to cry out a syllable: *"Cock—!"*

5. *Assuming Shape*

Overflowing with concern for Ronnie, Markie, and Bett but also knowing nothing useful could come of worry, I switched on my flashlight and resumed prowling the passageway between the cells. Later now, I found it incredibly eerie to wend my way through the darkness with only my light and occasional, answering beacons from the men behind bars. Their illumination flashed like signal flares, laser-bright, stark. In the path of my single, darting beam their faces seemed to emerge from nothingness, like night creatures caught unaware. They ma-

307

terialized as they were that second—frightened, ill, or scared and lonely—and I saw that they were captive not only to their cells but to their individual instants of fear.

I longed to release them.

Somebody'd said that repair men would arrive by 11:00 A.M. the next day to fix both the generator and air conditioner. Supposedly (remembering what Ellair had told me), that wouldn't matter to any of us. Dying or well, I was to go home—and depending on which of the psychiatrist's slightly conflicting stories was true, the plants would be completely collected that night, *and/or* the inmates would be moved to another jail by morning. *If* either or both of his promises was kept . . .

The shift from humidity-drenched day to a much gloomier, but faintly cooler, night had rendered us all relatively passive. Maybe that was because we *were* night creatures by then, famished and exhausted; or perhaps we found it easier to tolerate the fear of sudden, shocking attack by night, when unknown forces possessed the license to skulk. At least, our terrors were banked, under marginal control. But I also felt sure that if anyone else bought the farm in the next few hours, no one and nothing could Scotch-tape our nerves back together.

I got to spend some time with Doc Kinsey that last night. Unable to think of anything to offer the other guys at that point I spoke briefly with Gargan, who agreed that it was essential to crank up the kitchen and get some food to us, then I went back to the drunk tank for the first time in what felt like many days. The tubby old bird had his legs and feet up on the cot, his back propped against the wall in his customary attempt at being as comfortable as possible, and he greeted me with as much amiability as he had when I'd awakened him in the tank earlier.

"You've had yourself a day, Richard," he offered with one of his covertly shrewd glances. Doc unfolded his arms, put his feet on the floor, motioned me to a seat beside him. "I'd say that I'm all ears except the dispersal of my lard makes that statement a difficult assertion to defend."

"You seem sanguine about matters," I answered and settled in.

One brow ascended. "Bless my soul, was that a two-syllable word I heard?"

"Maybe a badly chosen one," I said. "When you express it as 'sanguinary,' it means —"

" 'Pertaining to bloodshed,' " Doc interjected, smiling ruefully. "Yes, I know."

I briefed him on as much of the ongoing melodrama as I could, including Hawkins' apparent infection and the way he'd left the jail in that condition, and the fact that I wasn't telling the rest of the men everything I had learned. He seemed to understand my reticence immediately and didn't say I was wrong to withhold the worst details; I was troubled by that in a man I regarded as perhaps

309

my most moral acquaintance in the place. It's likely that Doc was more a father-figure to me than a friend; I expected to be chastised the way I might have corrected Markie or Bett. In turn, that reminded me that however high a priority I put on friendship—Doc was neither very close to me as a companion nor a Dad. But he was affable, warmly funny, and never an antisocial tyrant in this stinking place, and so he became a kind of role model to me of what I might someday become.

The combination of jail, Noble Ellair, his exotic plants, and the terrible dying were forcing me to reassess a hundred and one things. I saw that each of us begins summoning the cobweb-strewn cachets out of our psychic closets whenever we find ourselves badly spooked, suddenly broke, seriously inconvenienced. And when we're sick with undiagnosed diseases, we start looking for ways to pass the buck then call it "affection," or "interest." We say a mother is the best friend we'll ever have, speak of man's best friend being his dog, give all the best that we have and half our economic resources to create "friendly" nations; but we're across the country when Mom dies, put our dog euphemistically to "sleep" as an act of what we term "mercy," and we'll go to war with our international "friends" if they show a higher gross annual profit! We'll do anything that occurs to us rather than face up to our shallowness of spirit or doing the tough things we have to do for ourselves.

310

Doc Kinsey startled me by appearing nearly to read my mind. He was fiddling with his thick-lensed glasses. He gave up suddenly, took them off and scrubbed at them with the shirttail of his uniform. "We're prisoners of group thought, my boy," he murmured. "But then, I suppose we *always* are but don't usually know it."

"You're talking about the possibility of a riot?" I said. "Of the men getting so scared they take it out on one another?"

"In a way," he rumbled. He held his flashlight in his fleshy hands but I realized he had yet to turn it on. I could see better now, without the spurty flashes of light confusing my vision, and I saw the weariness in Doc's face and the way it somehow made its own shadows. "I called our little group the Family. Remember?"

"Of course," I said. In the distance I heard the meal carts begin to roll and felt impatient for the ordinary comforts of living, even though I assumed they'd just be giving us cold sandwiches. What my late father called "flat meat."

"Every family has its own identity, its own ways, Richard," Doc essayed. "Even in Nam—"

"You were in Vietnam?"

Doc nodded. "Even there, we had our own little family with its own hopes, plans, faith in one another."

I watched him, studied his solemn, pudgy face, closely. He was getting at something. "You saw

311

members of that Family die."

"When that happened," Doc continued, "our group already had its own character, and that sustained those who didn't die. Our thoughts generate a *force,* a *power,* a *gestalt.* You know the word?" he asked. I nodded. "Noble Ellair knows it. A *gestalt* is made and goes on living because our emotions create . . . well, *patterns.* From whatever stimulates each and every member of the group." Doc peered at me thoughtfully. "In a way, it's the opposite of your precious individualism, my boy. Or the sum total of a number of individuals' beliefs and reactions under the same general stimuli."

"Meaning?" I prodded the wise doughboy.

Doc laughed, not unkindly. "People demand either delight or meaning, don't they? Yet they don't pay a great deal of attention to the cost of the delight, or to how much actual truth exists in the meaning!" He flicked his flashlight's switch to *On,* illuminating several square yards of our environment, switched it off again. "Almost one-thousand years ago, *circa* 1000 A.D. to be specific, one of the first great scientists, an Arab named Abu-Ali al-Husayn ibn-Sina who was known as Avicenna, wrote the *Canon of Medicine.* He said that people create sacred places wherein their emotions and thoughts make a group-field. That field attracts supernatural forces capable of altering the entire environment, the actual, physical *reality* of a place.

"And our negative terror merely makes matters

312

worse?"

Doc heard the food wagons coming, and turned his head to sniff the air. There wasn't much to inhale. "If people were ever genuinely united, *together*"—Doc faced me again—"then, my boy, the group-field could alter everything."

"That's what praying amounts to, isn't it?"

A Kinsey brow rose. "When it isn't exclusively self-serving, when it's sincere. Few of us today understand that the writer meant it when he said, in the Bible, that faith moves mountains. We say it is impossible—not truly understanding. Regrettably, in our time, it seems only the occultists and terrorists possess the capacity for such organized intellectual commitment. Here, tonight, we're united only by fear, and our group thoughts are beyond control." Doc sighed. "So, yes, Richard. We're making matters worse."

He went on, with his usual smiling detachment, to speak of his "Family" in Vietnam and added that the *gestalt* they had created would survive as long as any single member of that group lived.

He added one more thought. One that connected Avicenna's assertions with Doc's experience in Nam—that he never quite discussed with me—and the nightmare he and I shared with everyone else in the jail. Sometimes, Doc claimed, group thought that turned exceptionally negative could effectively lift up and away from the organism and assume *its own form,* its own, *potentially destructive life.* "Imagine

313

its power," he said quietly, almost under his breath, "when it is shaped from the emotions and recollections of men who—before they *became* a group—were already filled with negativity or evil. Imagine what kind of . . . *thing* . . . might be created because of Ellair and the perversion of his pretty goodwill gifts."

I did. And I learned afterward that the Arab scientist whose book of medicine remained a standard text until the Renaissance had evolved the groupfield concept at the close of a century—just as we would be doing soon.

That would be a millennium.

I thought again about Ellair's idea of humanity regressing back into a sleeping state while the rest of life moved *up* a notch on the evolutionary ladder, awakening from a long and troubled sleep.

Was the entomogenic fungus beginning to create its own *gestalt?*

Eleven

1. The Calm Before

I had never personally observed the way getting a little grub could work magic on desperate men. It's said that music has the power to soothe the angry beast (purists insist the word is "breast," but I haven't run into many riled-up breasts) but it couldn't compare to how all of us seemed to improve a bit with some lousy "flat meat sandwiches" under our belts.

Then, so suddenly that it seemed nearly miraculous, Gargan and the guard with the name I couldn't pronounce were no longer loping up and down the aisle gathering in the plants, and I realized with a dizzying feeling of relief that there weren't any more of the damned things left in the cells! I even succeeded for awhile in forgetting that any number of them might have already infected us. Any of us, all of us.

Nevertheless I was buoyed up, as I left the tank to rap with more of the inmates. All of them had

315

been badly frightened, and all of us could use a good night's sleep. Some of them—probably more than you can imagine—were smart enough to figure out that the deadly risks of the present still posed a nightmarish hazard to the immediate future. In that, Ellair's "gifts" could be compared to nuclear weapons. Even if the all-encompassing arms agreements were reached, the atomic bomb could never be *un*invented. The dark and evil peril continued.

I kept my word about minimizing the deadliness of the plants as I moved from cell to cell, still obliged to chat through the bars, of course. And all the guys were sufficiently intelligent to realize that the evening recall of the little potted beauties must have a direct connection to the previous inmate deaths. So I told the guys an uncomplicated story that some of us had not been immune to germs or diseases carried by the imported plants, indeed an unforeseen tragedy, then admitted that I didn't know what "the shrink" would do with all those lovely growing things now. "Destroy them, I assume" was what I said a couple of times—but there was no way I knew that for a fact.

Privately, I wondered if the scientist in the Noble One wouldn't run tests in the hope of salvaging a few, or even attempt merely to kill the fungi in them.

Those inmates I knew, and many of those I didn't, made me feel proud by the way they began to calm down. But Al Calderone, who apparently

316

enjoyed looking forward to the end of the world, didn't seem to believe a word I told him—even, God help me, the true parts—but I reminded myself that the beady-eyed little Psalm-singer couldn't buy *anything* that didn't come from the portions of the New Testament that he'd read. "Reverend" Al made me glad to escape the drunk tank for a while by mumbling to me that "we don't escape God's wrath this easily." I managed a parting shot that tore a smile out of Doc and the new guys in the tank: "The last I heard, Al," I called, "it was Satan who was either coming after us or dying. Most folks don't have so much trouble recognizing the difference between him and God."

I was no longer taking any notes as I moved around and spoke with the inmates I knew and those strangers who motioned me over to their cells. Nobody was willing to show Doctor Ellair any cooperation after everything that happened. I sensed that and passed along the information I felt comfortable releasing, strove to shove the festering fear of what might yet occur (especially to me, if Ellair's offhand comment out in the anteroom proved to be the case) totally *out* of my head. The guy from the gas company, who had been impatient about my call home to Ronnie, was so relieved now that we had a nice chat. He'd been arrested because he had tried to rig it somehow so he'd know where to buy winning lottery tickets. When I asked him if he'd made out, if he had come up with any pay cards that made this worthwhile, he just frowned and shook his head. Then there was Terry Malijnowski, the guard I hadn't met during my previous "visits" to the jail. I just looked up his name in order to get it right for the record. A tall drink of water from Chicago, Terry didn't warm up to the idea of conversing with an inmate till I promised I'd never call him "Ski." Turned out he had a dynamite sense of humor. Terry was a nice kid I think you would have liked. Maybe he'll still show up.

Another man I got to know that night was a sports writer for the local *Times*. A columnist. Recognizing his face from the picture that appeared with his column, I introduced myself, we rapped about writing a while, and he was redfaced when, idly, I posed the question everybody got to sooner or later, as to why he was in the clink. "I was framed by a devoted Colts fan for saying we'd never make the Super Bowl unless we got some really hostile, mobile, agile guys to open up the line," he lied to me, knowing I knew he was lying. Well, I haven't heard why he was locked in with the rest of us that night. Ted Traynor, that was his byline. I mention it because Traynor was a good sports writer and he should be remembered.

I was becoming dreadfully tired by then and longed for the long night to end. Sleeping, I decided, was out of the question and, judging by the fact that most of the inmates were talking loudly, messing with their flashlights, or staring out between the bars made me feel the majority of them agreed with me. Sleeping was something you did as a rule when you were almost sure you were going to wake up in the morning.

I had intentionally stayed away from the cell where Andre August and Steve Blackledge died. It was pretty easy to ignore because of its location, the drone of conversations all around us, and because I just hadn't flicked my flashlight beam in that direction.

When I did, Lester Piercy's narrow, long-nosed face showed white, starkly spotlighted between the bars. Purposely not shining my light toward Crock, I aimed it at the space in front of my feet and followed them to where Lester waited.

I couldn't keep myself from stressing to the ladies-toup-wearing Piercy that the principal danger was over, and I witnessed a record-breaking expression of drained, tearful ease. The guy seemed so damn *vulnerable*, so *delicate*, that I couldn't keep from genuinely feeling for him.

Lester behaved as if he had never heard of radiation or any of the other almost undetectable killers. I couldn't think of a single reason to give him any contrary doubts or facts. He sighed, "Bless you for relieving my poor tortured mind." He spoke theatrically, I thought, but I was never sure about that sort of thing. "You cannot imagine what this has meant to a person in my position." My own hand was gripping one of the cell bars for support—I was

319

zonked—and Lester instinctively reached out to squeeze it. I tensed my fingers but left my hand there. His squeeze was warm, spontaneous. Human. "I only wish to heaven they had removed those terrible plants"—Lester's eyelids blinked the phony lashes, his eyes swept toward the corner of the cell—"rather *sooner.*"

I sensed a clear but enigmatic meaning to what he said. It was a code, a guarded side intended only for my ears. He had scarcely whispered. I had no idea what Lester was talking about.

Laughter rose from the dark cell corner. For a beat, I thought it seemed inexplicable, ghostly. I remembered, however, that another man had been brought into the cell earlier that evening. Just as swiftly I knew he hadn't made the crude, cutting sound.

With care, Lester raised the woman's wig from his head. His hair was fluffy, short-cropped, the color of wheat. He was on the verge of tears and I thought for a moment—maybe because I preferred to believe this—that they were tears of relief, of gratitude.

They weren't. "I was frightened, Richie," Lester said, but he wasn't speaking only to me—you know right away when somebody is actually addressing someone else. "Terrified, and lonely." He drew himself to his full height and turned his crimsoning face toward the source of the harsh, pointed laughter. "But now, I would not *dream* of becoming one of

320

Mr. Crock's ladies! Not for all the tea in China!"

I swiveled the beam of my flashlight toward the corner of the cell, and it centered on Crock as though it had been pulled there.

Perched with cool casualness on a cot, the heels of his hands rested there while his shoulders slumped in an air of relaxed conquest, Crock was staring at me unblinkingly. The light didn't hurt his eyes. Unhurriedly, he shook a long, white cigarette—unfiltered—out of a red and white Pall Mall package. The letters on the pack read "Wherever Particular People Congregate."

"You could've left the cell door open, Stenvall," he told me. Crock's voice was pitched just loudly enough to hear his words but made you strain to hear all he had to say. "I'd be long gone from here."

What he and Piercy were saying wasn't getting through to me quickly, but it was getting through. "He was *scared*, Crock," I said. "He—he *needed someone*." I moved along the face of the cell from bar to bar, trying to get closer to the son of a bitch. "You took advantage of the situation."

"I didn't do one fucking thing, Stenvall," he said with nothing offended or aggrieved in his flat tone. He added, "Well, not *literally*," and chuckled. His amusement devalued whatever most of us imagined to be worth protecting. "I just went on sitting right where I am. Just let nature take its course."

I doubled my fist and struck the bars with the heel of my hand. *"Nature?"* I said. "You aren't even

321

part of it!" They say evil does not exist, or exists only in the way the majority define it. But Crock was a man who saw evil as already existing everywhere and accepted it as a reality he might as well use for a profit. And because evil was a fact to him, that's how he justified ruining the lives of young women, young men, *anybody.* "You aren't outside the rest of humankind, Crock—you're outside of *nature!*"

He rose from his rack smiling. He cupped the Pall Mall in his palm and his hand glowed red, drawing my gaze to it. He walked slowly toward me while Lester Piercy edged away from both of us, and Crock paused only to zip up his fly. I raised the beam of my flashlight to his face, nervously brought it down again to his glowing hand, apprehensively jerked the light so it caught his other hand. A blade might be in that one, I realized.

Crock folded the fingers of his free hand around one of the bars, rested the hand with the cigarette against another bar. I saw for the first time that he had a curling tongue of auburn hair that looked pretty; that his nails were well-groomed. Nothing much was in the eyes but Crock. The strength he possessed came almost entirely from that.

"Tell you what," he said in a man-to-man tone, softly. "You care about Lester. Fine! I'm easy to get along with." He was leading up to something I knew I wouldn't like, but I didn't know what. I lifted the flashlight beam to focus it on his face. His pupils were dilated as he smiled. "Make me an offer and you've got him."

I swore, reached out to squeeze his hand. There was a decent shower of red sparks as Crock's fingers closed around the burning Pall Mall.

He didn't even cry out in pain, didn't swear. While I turned to move away from that cell before I lost every ounce of self-control, Crock just stooped minimally from the shoulders, held the offended hand at the wrist and pressed it between his thighs.

There was something in his eyes now as he watched me leave, but it was still nothing but Crock.

2. *The Race Is On*

I almost ran from that cell—that hole—but it was with a different kind of fear than the fear I had endured that endless week. This was a fear of what was in me, and it had nothing to do with fungus.

An unblendable combination of my own character, the disease that was a product of it, seeing the other men closeup at their absolute worst, and now the sad case that was Lester and the bad case that was Crock, were swinging my emotions back and forth like a pendulum. Between infinite empathy for my fellow human beings and the life-taker that dwelled inside of me.

Blinded both by darkness and a certain vision-scorching glimpse of my mind—maybe my soul—I tried to blame everything on the system. What sort of just commitment to punishment, restraint, and reeducation saw Doc, Eddie Po, young Lou, that woeful team of gamblers named Lew and Jimmie, Leighton, Lester, and me as deserving the identical confinement as Lester's "Mr. Crock?" Couldn't any man who *was* blind perceive the differences?

Yet by the same token it was I alone who would gladly have shot Crock's brains out, had there been a gun in my hand moments ago.

I wandered between the rows of cells, dimly aware that Race Alyear's cell would be the next one in which I was acquainted with an inmate. I doubted he had required comforting. Race seemed to have the sort of ego that made the likelihood of his being deeply, personally scarred improbable. From the other cells came a variety of sounds. A mumble of indignation, of genuine anger. A nearly equal number of muttered prayers, sobs, whispered plans for (I'm just guessing here) escape. The sobs were no longer hopeless, a few were tinged with Piercy-like relief. Most of the men seriously questioned whether they were, in fact, secure now or not. I saw that the uplifting and creative sort of group-thought that Doc and I had discussed was impossible for us. How encompassing, how far-flung the "us" was, I decided to wait to determine until I was free again. Or dead.

One by one, the batteries in the flashlights were

giving out. The high temperature in the joint, however, was not.

I observed with relief that there was no sign of a riot.

Just the abrupt presence of Noble Ellair, falling into stride next to me, seemingly excited.

"By George, Richard!" he said, "I think our calamity has been averted!" Amazingly, he looked downright proud. Yet, by now, that wasn't really terribly surprising. "Before long, they'll all be dropping off."

I didn't think his choice of words was the absolute finest. I tended to think of leprosy whenever I heard the term "dropping off." And, these past few days, of the entomogenic fungus. I wondered if this stork-like son of a bitch was totally unfeeling. I tried to see his face clearly, but without turning on my flashlight it was murky and his features seemed to swim and shift. What kind of *gestalt*, of self-changing creative force, was Ellair's mind-set turning *him* into?

"I don't think there'll be much sleeping tonight," I told him as we walked. He was spraying the beam of his flashlight into the cells as we passed with such abandon that I thought he probably had another carton of batteries in his desk drawer. "No one has fallen asleep yet, to the best of my knowledge."

He stopped walking, turned the Eveready in his hand sharply to the right and I watched the light pool around Race Alyear's sturdy body where it lay, face-down, on his rack. Unmoving. We both stared through the bars in matching immobility and waited for Race to exhibit any sign that he was still alive. Waited for a raspy groan of irritation over being awakened; the tensing of muscles in the back of the neck; a leg to twitch, to bend at the knee.

But I'd seen enough over the past few days to know at first glance that this super salesman with the taste for kiddie porn would not show a sign of life if Ellair and I stood there gaping at him for another thousand years.

Because death, like Alyear, was so *still*, I thought, perspiration leaping to my temples and reminding me that it was long hours to go before morning—informing me that the nightmare wasn't over. And dead things couldn't wait to merge with the rest of nature, the way mold does.

And fungi.

3. The Big C

Ellair fumbled with his keys, getting them out of his pocket, then lost more time working the proper key into the lock of Alyear's cell. I couldn't tell if it really was nerves, real horror slowly dawning on Ellair, or if it was merely another show.

I do believe he knew Alyear was a goner and that we were not alone in that knowledge. As the shrink and I fell still and the cell gate snapped open,

swung wide, the entire cellblock grew as quiet as
. . . as a mausoleum with its one, silent resident.
I'd frozen outside the cubicle for another instant.
But when I entered Hell's newest cell, I could imagine that hundreds of men were squeezing in with
us. It was as if the inmates had collectively achieved
astral travel and projected their shades into that
small space. They held their breaths too as I gazed
down in something worse than apprehension and
saw how Race had partly turned the upper area of
his torso so that his big head was facing the un-
painted wall. Roughly then—as if he momentarily
believed the "entrepreneur" had simply passed out—
Ellair shook Alyear.

I caught my breath. Some automatic reflex in
that stocky body clicked into place like the innards
of a complicated machine, and he *flopped over* on his
back! Perhaps he wanted us to see him. My flashlight was already more or less focused at the facial
level, and I saw. Instantly. I saw how fungus was
positively *rolling out*—from *his eyes*.

My own eyes snapped shut immediately in disgust, in terror, or maybe sympathy. Then I looked
again, and saw the way Race's eyeballs had been
completely *forced out* of their sockets—

And that they were lost, they had *disappeared* from
view inside those wafted, curling growths! Jesus—I
couldn't find his *eyes!*

At last, I did—I finally saw them. Impersonally
detached, flopping, ludicrously cockeyed, like the

gosh-I'm-silly-let's-all-have-FUN eyes of an old-time comedian. They lolled and looked soullessly at me from the juncture where that damned fungus was beginning to *flower*. Gosh, it was *pretty!*

I reeled back on my heels. *Oh, God, how much more will there be?* I prayed. At that second I had this mind's-eye image of the incredible gross stuff just flowing on and on—sort of *tumbling* out of Race's sockets, getting bigger and leafier, surging in massive, cauliflower *balls* toward Noble Ellair, toward *me*—with no hint whatsoever of when the fucking growth period would ever subside. I imagined it endlessly continuing to roil out, *bottomlessly*—starting to fill the cells, one after another! I saw it in my mind churning like a mammoth bowling ball along the lane between the aisles, bumping against jail doors, retreating briefly for a running start—*battering* the doors for its escape, until—

"What the hell is going on in there?"

The yell tore me back to what was real, what was already happening.

And Lord help me, I didn't even blame Ellair when, automatically, he raised his head to shout back at the unidentified man, "It's Race Alyear and he's dead. The fungus—it *blinded him!*"

Blame him or not, that just about did it. Just like that, county lockup became Bedlam. Bowing my head and closing my eyes again like an ostrich who might hide from what was going to happen next, I knew Ellair had blown it.

The ostrich disguise didn't work. *"Christ,"* somebody yelled, "it's *got ME*, now!"

To this moment I don't know if that was for real. I couldn't tell. It might just have been an inmate with jock itch, a neurotic, some stupid joker who thought he saw an opportunity to wise-off in everything.

But the rest of the men took it seriously.

The shrink whipped his flash beam around as he rushed from the cell. I guess he wanted to spear the sumbitch who'd shouted the second time. All he succeeded in doing was effectually putting the entire inmate population at centerstage. One second later I couldn't detect the differences between the frustrated cursing, the tearful moans, and violent grunts—many of the men were trampled by bigger men who wanted to clutch and shake the bars and scream—or the shouts that were partly entreaties for freedom, partly curses in every inflection and accent America has to offer. I wondered how many of the guys were strictly short-timers, some due to be released when daylight came; how many were habitually or menacingly crooked; and what number of them had merely run out of both self-control and any respect for authority simultaneously. I wondered in ways that didn't have words if Race's death by blinding might have opened the eyes of uncounted others to the power of their own numbers. And I sensed that the potentiality of group-thought surely had been achieved, and I halfway expected the roof to rise above the building. For us to be collectively borne away on uncanny winds and form a new antinature to celebrate Noble Ellair's antinatural vision of humanity.

And I even wondered if some of us present *were* physiologically or psychologically different than man had been before—well, since before the Bomb, or God-knew-when!—and if those different men among us were to become catalysts for the last retreat of humanity, the new "meso-consciousness," the next evolutionary advance of the stone . . . the animal . . . the plant.

For a second there, I thought I was correct. Down in the drunk tank Al Calderone's shrill accents razored the air, left it raining the bloodied tatters of poise, reasoned thought. He whipped those inmates close to him into frothing terror with his garbled, misinterpreted citations from the Bible; his hate-filled voice soared like an hyena's howl above the sounds of terror, of men striking their bars with anything handy. Was *this* next, what Christ had preached, what God desired—was *this* the choral cadenza for all the new tomorrows?

I trotted slowly between the cells with Ellair, yelling pleas for quiet, for a recovery of their composure, while the psychiatrist sometimes screamed at them—commanded silence—but otherwise just watched, poking at them with his beam of light like the first draft of a character from *Star Wars*. He seemed to have no idea whatever where to begin

330

and I couldn't tell if he *meant* to help at all. He definitely did *not* go near the scared, jeering faces or outthrust hands and arms groping for him. In fairness, he neither looked as if he'd lost control nor as if he was fearful of them. But then, they were safely locked behind bars from Ellair's standpoint. He knew that they could not reach him. That the bars would hold, would contain the prisoners.

Gargan, youthful Terry Malinowski, and one other guard I didn't know, were carefully stationed along the rows of cells, weapons drawn but arms folded, helpless to do a thing without some command from Doctor Ellair. Occasionally, vibrating *whhaaannggggs* jaggedly pierced the vocal panic as a sort of counterpoint and the inmates whaled at the bars. All were under siege, guards and prisoners alike, each man's most basic or primitive emotions were completely aroused—but the former *could* run, *could* go home. Everyone understood that. Everyone had had enough. And the message coming through each obscene sentence or gesture, every shriek of fright, from every human being who could *not* leave, would've been clear to an idiot: *Give me a chance to live. Or let me die free!*

I spun around then, at just that instant, prepared to enforce the plea by whatever means necessary; to *demand* that Ellair let them out, force him to do it.

But he was *gone*. The son of a bitch had apparently *run away!*

The guards knew it, too. Awaiting orders, they

had been glancing toward Ellair with increasing frequency and urgency. I saw young Terry's face just before the real guts of the midnight massacre were fully exposed.

Several squealing noises penetrated even the rest of tumult and stunned my soul. I thought of baby pigs—little fat porkers undergoing systematic, heartless, and unfeeling butchering. Whirling again and crouching, I sought the source of the squeals. My flashlight beam pinned it—him—down.

Yards from where I stared, Lester and Crock. A Lester who, incredibly, appeared to be even more angry—bitchy fucking *furious*—than he was terrified.

The homosexual and the sometime bi-sexual—innocuous little guy, and the meanest bastard for a hundred miles in any direction—they had entered into a ballet of perfect, ghastly, lunatic dying. I'd never forget it.

Each of them, like Dee Dee Lakens, had suddenly become *personally* aware of his own risks. Each man had become aware that the malignant content of the Costa Rican plants *was still with them*—and that he might die. Like poor Dee Dee each of them had chosen to *climb* toward the top of the cell they shared.

Dee, however, had ascended alone to his end. Crock and Lester seemed, amazingly, to have opted for exactly the same space. Because it grew immediately clear to me that the smaller Lester was fighting the sinister, larger Crock for a frightful place in a madman's sun.

My next thought was one of surprise that terror had come at last to the pimp. Perhaps the wavy-haired Crock had seen some space through which he might crawl, and escape. I don't know, now. But it's more likely that he had considered himself immune, for some insane reason, until the death of *one particular man* must have finally got through to him. *Race Alyear,* I realized.

Race was the most recent to die. Craning my neck to follow the battle between these cellmates, I thought, *Of course.* Race Alyear had regarded other people as "suckers," "squeezes," "pushovers." He'd taken advantage of everybody he met in his illegal business dealings by means of consistently pretending to be what he could *never* be . . . normal . . . decent . . . a nice man. And Race had also gotten off on the forbidden, on his covert desires—kiddie porn; using young females when he thought it was safe to do it—even while he was working hard to convince people he was a man's man, a macho stud who could have his choice of women.

The only way the Alyears and Crocks ever had contact with anybody decent in their lives was by stealing away *their* choices, dirtying them till they believed that only God could tell the difference between victimizer and victim. The only quality Crock had been able to relate to in county lockup, the only attribute that had forced him to face the fact that he was mortal, too, was the one he'd recognized—perhaps on nothing but an unconscious plane—in Race.

Crock had a halfway workable grip on the top bunk, but Lester, after shinnying up the bars, was doing his best to dislodge the pimp! For a moment it seemed amusing to me, hilarious, and I guess I laughed. But those pig-squeal noises were going right on, an accompaniment of sound that was as earnest as hell, while the drag queen began to *slap* at Crockie's hand, then started prying industriously at his fingers! All ol' Crock was doing to defend himself apart from hanging on for dear life was swinging his big, muscular body around in order to kick his feet at the smaller man.

It was during one the procurer's flailing pivots that I noticed the seat of his pants was *filling*.

Applause, I figured, would not be appropriate. I was basically aware that the guard, Terry, had come to unlock the cell, had cursed and run off when he remembered Gargan had the key he needed. I wondered if he might keep going, and I saw then that my first impression about the pimp's plight was wrong: He hadn't shit himself after all. The next time Crock thrashed out at Piercy with his leg, my flashlight was trained on his ass—and I spotted the nature of my mistake.

What was starting to spill out over the waistband of Crock's pants was not human waste. I lowered the beam and perceived that both men had been germinated, and each man was beginning to die. Lester as well as Crock.

This terrible stuff emerging was more watery, than the other growths I had witnessed . . . but it was solid enough to execute the lifelike, writhing circumlocutions that ultimately began to sap Crock's strength and to add weight to the pimp's tailbone. Glancing up and away, I noticed again how damn high the old cells were — and Crock. The floor was made of concrete and nobody would wish, voluntarily, to jump from the ceiling. Inwardly, a distant realization of what the entomogenic must surely do to the nervous system took form, and when I found myself sorry for Crock, I broke off my thoughts and stared down.

Crock let out a definite but wordless cry for help. It tore my attention back to him and to where he was hanging by his fingers above the unsympathetic floor. I don't think he realized he had made a sound. Maybe it wasn't pain, or fear; maybe the evil S.O.B. emitted an *unconscious* plea — a murmur of astonishment that he was vulnerable too, and was not going to get to see life from the catbird seat above the common chaos. If so, that made his values, his code, his attitude toward life and his fellow human beings a sham. A crock.

Hearing the desperate moan, Lester let something of the sensitive man he'd been break through — some strain of compassion or kindliness, an empathetic recollection of what it was to be alone; frightened beyond words; detested. Amazingly, he began attempting to *help* the dangling Crock!

335

"Get *away* from me!" the pimp yelled down. I saw his face and it was crimson with terror, and hatred. "Damn you, you faggot, don't *touch* me!"

Something internal that had nothing to do with fungal growth illumined Lester's pale, long-nosed face. It made his cheeks flush, his eyes bright—and the light blazed up at the hanging man. Incredibly, athletically, he lashed out with one leg, the blow landing full on Crock's ribcage. "I *will* touch you!" he said forthrightly, and brought the leg back. "I'll touch you if I *want,* you big bastard, you bully!" He reached out one finger—the middle one—as if showing it to Crock, taunting him with it.

Then he gave the bigger man another kick, and the tips of Crock's fingers began to peel away from his perch like wallpaper coming loose. Seven, six— one hand couldn't regain its hold no matter how the man grappled for it—five, *four, three*—

He landed, hard, on his ass. It was oddly reminiscent of a silent movie scene, partly because the fall didn't kill Crock, either. I gaped at him in amazement.

The fungus sprouting from his rear end had *vanished!* It took about half a second to grasp the fact that the only place the shit could have gone was *up*. Into his insides. That awareness nearly paralyzed me with fresh horror. It meant that the infecting, living fungus had literally *run away* from the impact of the fall, and furrowed its unseen path toward the man's bowels, his stomach, his liver, his heart.

The beam of my flashlight was squarely focused on Crock and I saw his ribcage begin to swell, to expand. As if he'd swallowed a powerful and gigantic balloon. Crock's belly, too, became swollen, gave him the look of an eight-months-pregnant woman inelegantly squatting on the floor. Crock and his fungus moved into the ninth and last month fast, and I thought it would power its way, splittingly, through his chest, or—if it rose—decapitate him.

It didn't. Instead, he began to bleed. Torrents of it; from his mouth, his nostrils. Lord, he looked so *startled,* so uncomprehending!

But he also looked straight at me, and I thought I read in his agonized eyes as they started to pouch and pook-out a last, condemnatory message that read, quite simply . . . *You're next.*

He went over on his side, then—*thhhwwack!*—as if somebody had clubbed him from the other side. He lay still, prone, blood geysering from places that had been impossible moments ago. Dead.

A grunting sound whipped my head around. Lester came down from the bars in a couple of jumps as gracefully as a ballet dancer. For a second of total revulsion I thought he might run over to caress the contaminated meat in the center of the floor, or try to nurse Crock back to life. I guess that demonstrates how much I think in stereotypes, too.

But Lester was thinking about Number One the way anyone would be who knew that he, too, was a goner. Instead of anything idiotically womanish or

337

romantically fanciful, he started a pained, awkward sprint toward a rusted, lidless toilet in the corner of the cell. Midway there, he crashed to his bony knees with an expression of sickness on his face that made me wish Terry'd get back, unlock the cell, do something to help.

Then little Lester was enroute to the head again, still on his knees, making gagging sounds I can hear in my memory this moment. When he had to stop and sort of prop himself up to keep from collapsing, I witnessed the kind of spiky/horny substance I had seen before. It slipped from the poor man's lips and appeared to lap at the air like an antenna, or a lizard's tongue.

At last, Lester reached the toilet bowl. Still kneeling, he thrust his head forward as if hoping he might be able to vomit out the damned cancer-like growth. Clutching his face with his slender hands, he began jerking his head and neck back and forth—over and over—even succeeding in extruding a foot or so of the squirming substance. Yet it *kept* coming out, it *kept* curling from Lester's mouth as if it might be literally endless.

When he took one hand away from his cheek to grope for the flush handle and began batting feebly at it—when he began making the john flush repeatedly, over and over, till it started overflowing with water and fungal growth—I knew I had to get away from there at once or go permanently insane.

4. Waiting

Ronnie Stenvall would probably have said she hadn't slept a wink since Rich took the Omni out that night and managed to get both him and their only car locked up, but it would not have been an accurate assessment of her recent sleeping habits.

Actually, she had found it hard to doze off. And when she did finally fall asleep, it hadn't done her much good. Each morning of her husband's absence, she had awakened with an impression that she hadn't gotten any rest.

That was a 100 percent accurate assessment of her sleep patterns, and combined with a peculiar sense of disconnection from the details of daily life that had disturbed her ever since this hot weather began, Ronnie was experiencing difficulty in distinguishing between facts and fancy, reality and old, recurring fears—especially tonight, the night before her husband was to come home again.

A part of Ron's problem was worrying about Rich's safety. Part of it involved the children and herself. Because Rich's chum Rudy Loomis had to answer to management and he could excuse Rich's absence from the job only so long. Then the bearded supervisor's position might also be on the line.

For maintenance men job loss was terrifying because an apartment—home itself—was often part of the package. Rudy had needed someone reliable to work under him and had arranged for the younger and brighter Rich to get both a free apartment and half of the utilities as part of his pay-base. So if Rich should be fired the family wound up being homeless.

There was always a lot of turnover among maintenance men, too. A person didn't need the greatest personal history in the world to start out shoveling snow, or tidying-up vacant apartments. Getting hired depended on many factors including being able to hit it off with the supervisor (things that didn't necessarily enter into job hunting for other men) as well as some decent experience at other complexes.

Rudy had recognized a married man with two kids as a plum. He'd figured Rich would know the score and try hard not to mess up. That, Ronnie thought rather sourly, was the *theory*, at least. But her husband Rich was also an alcoholic and a dreamer. He *hadn't* known the score — or if he had, like Ronnie when she married him, he hadn't let it exactly *overwhelm* him!

She'd awakened from a nightmare that was plaguing her for what seemed like days, plus another killer headache, and decided she needed some coffee. Peeking in on Bett and Markie, who stirred but didn't awaken, Ronnie shuffled to the kitchen and began wondering why she was making coffee. She'd never cared for it, believed it made her burp, and rarely drank it if Rich wasn't around.

Now that she thought about it, a lot of things hadn't seemed — well, normal — during this time away from Rich. It was nothing she could quite put her finger on except for craving coffee at midnight, having nightmares — Ronnie seldom recalled dreaming, at all —

And the way this persistent bad dream seemed to be trying to *tell* her something, urge her to *notice* something, or take action. But she couldn't remember a single detail. Just awakening in a tangle of damp sheets with her hair plastered to her head, and a feeling that everything in her life that she gave a damn about might be on the line.

"On the line." Puzzled, turning on the coffee maker, she realized that same expression — the same unexplained warning — had recently crossed her mind.

Damn, the apartment was so *hot!* Irritably, Ronnie opened her housecoat more at the neck, wished suddenly she hadn't put the coffee on. *I wonder what Markie really saw in that girl's apartment,* she thought without quite latching on to the concept. Markie didn't really make things up from whole cloth, but he shouldn't have disobeyed her and his father, he had to *learn* to obey them or —

Where was I? Ronnie asked herself. There'd been a point to what she was thinking about Markie . . . or Bett . . . and it had just wandered right out of her head because of this dreadful, sticky humidity.

Fanning herself with a flap of the opened house-coat, she knew everything would be fine when things were back to normal. When Rich was home again. Contrite enough to be sober for—well, for weeks, at least, unless Rudy had to let him go. Not that he'd have any *right* to fire Richie, who'd said he wasn't really drunk at all, but had been helping . . . someone. Some big shot.

It had been hell going to Rudy's apartment and asking to borrow the company truck. There'd been no other way she could go get Rich but Ronnie couldn't stand Loomis. No, that wasn't exactly right—she *disliked* Rudy, she thought as she noticed that the coffee was nearly ready. She decided to fix one fast cup then go back to bed.

Once when Rich was loaded he'd explained about the empty apartment Rudy sometimes used. She suspected strongly that he blackmailed other women—made them pay their back rent by screwing him up there. Why else would anybody do it with *him?* He had this sneaky look in his eyes, they were shifty and couldn't look directly at a woman until he had first checked out what she was wearing. Begging him for the truck was—

She turned her head and her eyes toward the sound of soft, rhythmic knocking at the apartment door. Past midnight and someone was rapping. Softly. Familiarly.

Ron tugged her housecoat closed and made the long walk from the kitchen to the living room, taking her time about it in the hope that the caller would go away.

The knocking stopped when she was three paces from the door, then began again, and Ronnie told herself she was behaving like a senseless child. She pulled the door open as far as the chain permitted, and looked out into the dimly-lit hallway.

Rudy Loomis didn't look as if he ever washed his shoulder-length hair, or his sixties-style beard which looked wiry and capable of cutting tender flesh. She wondered if he had that same wiry hair everywhere on his body, and the thought brought a smile to her lips. Ronnie wiped it off quickly but not before she realized he had seen it.

"Sorry t'bother you," he said. They were just words. He was probably coming back from the apartment he kept "empty." That was surely against company orders, and she wouldn't hesitate to use it against him if he had to fire Rich. "I tapped real soft, so if you hadn't been up I'd have just gone on."

"Markie was crying. He woke me up." Ron wondered at once why she had told him such a lie. What was there about men that made her tell them anything except the truth? She added pointedly, "I was just going back to bed."

Rudy glanced down at her housecoat, her figure, her naked feet. It took her a moment to catch his glance because his eyebrows were so thick and hairy and his face was in the shadows. "Got a day off tomorrow so Rich is on call. Since I won't see him, I need you to give him a message."

"Okay. Sure." She realized she should invite him in. If Rich was on call tomorrow, that meant Rudy had saved his job—that meant they'd be all right! But she couldn't think how to say it was all right for him to come in, and she still didn't trust anyone so *hairy*. "And, thanks for—for everything, Rudy."

"No problem." He shot a look into the apartment, possibly to see if Markie was up. "Ol' Rich knows the score." Rudy glanced anxiously into Ronnie's eyes. "Hey, you okay?"

"What do you want me to tell Rich?" she asked.

Loomis nodded. He seemed, now, to know the score himself. "Just tell him that it looks like Karl and Stephanie Ryder have skipped. So he needs to get their place cleaned up. He can get one of them new guys—Antonio or the black kid—if he wants." He seemed ready to say something else, then grunted and nodded, took a step back from the door.

"They left?" Ronnie asked in surprise. "Didn't turn in their keys, or anything?" The "anything" was a way of asking how precisely Rudy had used the term "skipped."

Rudy scratched his untrimmed beard, pursed his lips as if trying to solve the mystery. "I'm surprised, too, yeah," he said slowly. "Y'can't figure anybody these days. But the thing *is*—"

"Yes?" Ronnie lifted a brow. She sensed, however,

that she would not be pleased to hear the rest of what Loomis was saying.

"Well, the place smells like a who—like a florist's shop, Ronnie." His face momentarily became an enigmatic hirsute mask. Then he frowned. "And they left these two huge plants—big goddamn things about as long as a piano—just lyin' on the floor." Rudy hesitated. "They're *pretty*, don't get me wrong . . ."

"But?" Ronnie prompted him.

"Well, the thing is," he went on, "those mothers've started *grown'* all over the stuff Stef and Karl left behind, like fucking *kudzu*, that crap they've got down south." Rudy got his face together. "Sorry about the 'f' word."

"I'll tell Rich," Ronnie said, promising. She began pushing the door closed. "I'm sure he'll take care of it."

"Yeah, me too." Rudy gazed down the length of Ronnie's body, and smiled. "G'night."

"Goodnight."

Ron closed the door, checked the chain, leaned briefly against the door. How *odd* that was, about the Ryders. And after the things Markie'd told her and told his father on the phone. Exactly *what* those things had been, she couldn't be positive at such a late date.

But her Rich could handle it.

She passed the entrance to the kitchen, coffee forgotten, fully aware of the view Rudy Loomis had gotten of her and how coarse he was. The "f" word, as he called it, was crude and she disliked it intensely when men couldn't come up with any better an adjective than that.

What she *really* objected to, however, was men like Loomis who referred to things that were unpleasant, unwelcome, or generally objectionable as "mothers." Why did they always seem to lose sight of the fact that mothers were beings who brought life, who *gave* life, who populated the entire *world* with their offspring?

In the morning, Ronnie thought as she slipped out of the housecoat and climbed back into bed, Richie would finally be back where he belonged. Beside that fact nothing else seemed terribly important.

5. *Braindead at the Zoo*

I had to get away from the gruesome dead body of Crock and the horribly dying Lester, and I also *had* to *go home.*

I started to say that *psychologically* I had to do those things. Then I realized that the right word might be "spiritually," not just "psychologically." Because the terrible sights around me weren't simply getting to me now—they'd *arrived,* they'd *gotten* there. Not just into my brain, my memory, but into my soul.

But *going* home—actually *doing* it—ah, *that* was a real psychological challenge! It existed regardless of the strong possibility that I could simply stroll down the aisle, past the inmate phone and the guard posts, slip into the sheriff's office unnoticed by anybody, unlock the door to the street, and leave.

You see, I was still myself enough to want to help Lester, even while I could see he was dying and there were nothing I could do. I was myself enough to see what it would mean if I let myself be dragged down with everyone else in ways that were even worse than the definite possibility that I was infected too, and might soon die.

It would mean that I was too horrified and frightened to be of any use to anybody—even me. It'd mean that all my loud-mouth remarks about believing the things that one individual could achieve were phony; that my dis-ease had finally fouled-out as an early warning signal; and it would mean that I could *never* be special in my own eyes, where it matters.

It'd mean that Noble Ellair and his specially-developed fungi had accomplished the last victory. Whether he had planned for it to replace us, or not—yeah, I still had my doubts about his intentions—the entomogenic was winning, and Doctor Ellair really didn't care that much. He could adapt to it. He could adapt to living in a toilet bowl if they let him study the shit coming down.

So even if I might've taken advantage of the tumult, the frantic activity of the guards who were working at calming down the still-living inmates, the clanging uproar—to cover my own escape . . .

I just couldn't go home yet.

If there was to be any meaning to my life at all after what each of us had experienced, I had to see things through all the way.

And I knew what I *truly* meant to do by the time I'd gone four or five paces away from Piercy, the ghosts of Crock, August, the rest. There was no other possibility, so don't make it sound like I have balls the size of ol' Orville Hawkins' bowling balls. There was merely nothing else I could think to do.

But the farther I went and the more I flicked spears of light into the cells, the more ghastly sights met my eyes. Men running in swift, crazed circles, as if Ellair had told them they'd die in seventy-two hours unless they lost eighty-seven pounds. One guy talking animatedly with another guy, and the listener, nodding politely and apparently tuned-in to what his cellmate was telling him, was covered with *slime* all over his body. I saw one of the regulars in the Family, an old man called "Pop" who survived on Coke—as in Coca-Cola. He was sitting cross-legged on the floor of his cell while he carried on a conversation with some obese fellow who was a stranger to me. The stranger looked extremely dead because of the leafy crap growing out of his nostrils and squirming up his face, but the *bad* part was how Pop was rapping with him in a language I never before heard. I don't think anyone else ever heard it before, either.

So I got to thinking of how this place was like a zoo, now. I remembered an old Fredric Brown story about aliens coming to earth and keeping the last man alive, and I felt a little like that — but then maybe a part of me felt *gooood,* 'cause *they* were behind bars, and *I* was out there!

A radio somewhere — maybe it was the fucking *ghost* of Dee Dee's — began blasting through the shouts and screams and curses with the Top 40; there was a newsman talking about the prize money split among drivers in last month's Indy 500 race, and recordings of the race car motors roaring by, and some dude chanting a rap song, a brief commercial for Bell Telephone; and finally a guy with a familiar weatherman's voice. He reported *something* about "a break in the record-setting temperatures," and I *clungggg* to what that sucker was saying with everything I had, and I couldn't *hear* him, I couldn't *understand* his forecast!

For the duration of the walk I strove not to be lured into peeking into any of the cells. I kept the flashlight turned off unless I wasn't sure of my footing — some guys had torn shit out of everything they had with them, then thrown it out between the bars — and wished I could get Doc out of the tank to go along with me. But I didn't have the keys and, if I'd somehow managed to release that ol' doughboy, I wouldn't know how to deal with Al or any other guys they'd locked up in there. I was also trying to figure out to my own satisfaction exactly what was happening, whether the fungus had begun to germinate in a majority of the men at the same time or if the ceaseless screams and sounds of chaos was nothing more than collective terror.

Or—there was another possibility that came to my mind—if there was a method the damned fungus had evolved, consciously or unconsciously, of *leaving* one dead victim and then *moving* to a living one. Ordinarily, I thought, trying to remember what Ellair had said, the entomogenic would not do that. It could be perfectly content munching on a lifeless body.

But if it was not only conscious but purposeful, if the fungi literally *meant* to take us over, they would want to eliminate as many of the enemy—of us—as they could. Otherwise, surely, we'd begin to catch on, we'd begin to fight back, and—

Fiddling nervously with the flashlight switch, I'd snapped it to the *On* slot, and I stopped walking to stare at what the beam disclosed.

A kid, no older than Lou Vick had been when he died, was in a kneeling posture, propped face forward against the bars. I could see at once that he was dead by the way his arms and hands hung limp, one arm reaching through the bars with a couple of the fingers touching the floor, and relative freedom. Something else was groping between the bars, too. A tendril of fungus. It appeared to be

coming out of the Bible that the kid had been trying to read. His broken flashlight was partly outside
the cell, partly inside.

I sprinted the remaining distance to the drunk
tank and to a friend who by then seemed to me to
live there, and returning was like finding an oasis, a
little like going home.

Why the tank door was open, I've never found
out for sure.

And I suppose no one will ever tell me why my
friend Doc had to die, either—the cosmic reason,
that is.

I stood inside the entrance to the drunk tank feeling . . . whatever it is that you feel when a person
you've sort of loved has died. Gone. Let's not try to
get it clearer than that, or try too hard to define
my feelings. Except for *where* and *how* it was ol' Doc
perished, there isn't much point in describing the
details.

But I began thinking, even then, that whoever
"Doc Kinsey" had actually been, he could have done
almost anything—and probably had. I thought that
he had surely been one of the few who'd had what
is called "charisma," as well as special gifts that also
prevented him from forming the amiable acquaint-
anceships that other men take for granted. The
gifts, the individual intelligence and those things he
alone knew, embarrassed Doc, might even have contributed to making him another drunk. Maybe appearing to be that—"just another lush"—was the one

351

way Doc had discovered for remaining a part of society; maybe he should have been a true and complete outsider, but the absolute inner-focussed selfishness of that had been something he couldn't force himself to accept.

It had taken the viciously common killer that Doctor Noble Ellair brought back with him from the rain forests of Costa Rica to enable my friend to be, at last, one of the boys.

All I cared to see — *more* than *that* by far, God knows — was the fleeting glimpse of the now-familiar substance growing from Doc, so I tore the beam of the Eveready away and sprayed it over the other bodies sprawled on the cell floor, as if I were watering them. I didn't, couldn't, count them; there weren't that many guys in the tank, not as many as it seemed there were — in death. The men were collapsed on and over one another like store window mannequins, arms and legs every which way. I recall that my shaking hand twitched the flashlight around and kept *finding* them, like Doc'd had an impromptu goddamn *open house*. I made out the uniform of a guard, then a second guard — recent arrivals, called in maybe by Gargan or Terry — perhaps meant to let everybody out . . .

I suddenly realized that someone was groaning, and that the sound was coming from the inmate lying at my feet. It took me a second to look down — determine which man was still alive . . . and to groan, too, in misery, in lack of comprehension of any cosmic Plan or Order.

"Reverend" Al was unconscious and moaning as his chubby limbs moved and began forcing his mind toward consciousness. God forgive me, I *studied* the man's exposed face and the other portions of Calderone that were in view, *I raised* one of his arms and then the other, looking for signs of germination. But all I found was a rather small, neat smear of blood at the corner of his mouth. Either one of the dying drunks in there had accidentally thrashed out an arm and hit Al, he'd done it to himself in one of his fervent fits, or somebody had intentionally knocked him out. *Did you spare him because he read a part of your Book, Father?* I wondered, glancing up automatically. *Most of the men are dead or dying, except me—and this man?*

"WITCHID."

It sounded like that, the voice. The one at my back. Behind me, in a dark shadowed area I had imagined to be crowded with the dead. The quasi-human voice. It froze me to the spot. Then it sounded again, *directly* behind me: *"WITCHID."* The voice spoke to my shoulder blades, or between them. I felt cold breath on my neck.

Turning only my head, I observed growths of razor-sharp cactus stuff and wiry things that wriggled. I saw what looked like cauliflower—it looked *edible!*—and every other mushrooming goddamned trick the terrible entomogenic had, except fucking *toadstools*. And all of it stuck out, no matter where I

353

looked, from . . . *it*.

It had laboriously worked itself to one knee, then the other, after seeing me. It had somehow moved, *tottered*, toward me. And I guessed "It" was Doc Kinsey. Yes, I knew it was Doc; I just didn't immediately accept the truth. And he was trying hard — very hard — to speak to me.

I have no idea what keeps us from more readily identifying with the disfigured, the utterly blighted, except for the fact that such horror lets us know *we* could be like that, too, if the worst occurred. It's also true for me that . . . this . . . was no Doc I'd ever known. So I edged back from my sometime-friend with cowardly alacrity and did everything but throw my hands before my face, or make the sign of the cross.

Hero, huh? *Me?*

No way.

"*WIT*-CHID . . . ?"

Uh-uh, I thought; *no*. I remember that I shook my head at him. This zombie reject was every nightmare every child has ever had. And now this walking garden of *death* — dear God, it was *putting out its hand,* wrapped in oozing, white, shit like a fucking *mitten* — and I realized the purpose with a more deeply-felt disgust than anything I'd experienced before.

It wants me to *hold its hand*. It wants *me* to *take that* THING!

But I was saved from the ordeal.

"They're *up!*" Happy voice from the vicinity of my knees. Creature, climbing up. Voice from a shadow clump. Al Calderone, proclaiming the gleeful fulfillment of his prophecy. "Praise the Lord, they're *up* — *they're here!*"

My mouth fell open as Al, like a living but roughly human growth, clung to my leg, stared toward Doc, then looked joyously at me as if he was waiting for me to share his big moment.

Doc fell on Al. The thing that had been my friend fell all *over* the creep.

Did he do it on purpose? Hell, *I* don't know! I just watched that shapeless vegetable garden shift weight slightly, and collapse on top of Calderone like a blobby, lumpish vampire eager to feed.

Al started screaming at once. He writhed around under the weight, kicked out a foot which promptly disappeared into the indistinguishable mass as if sucked into it.

And I was *out of there,* man, I was moving, gasping, running, GONE! I was out in the corridor, swallowing bile and God-knows-what as it rose up in my mouth, getting *away* —

And catching a glimpse of the guard, Gargan, leaning against the wall at his post, untroubled gaze centered on me. Good, grumpy, imperturbable, normal Gargan! I don't recall the time it took to rush the rest of the way up to him but I remember my plans. I can't call them "thoughts," because that sounds like ordered thinking. I only remember that my original course of action was back in the fore-front of my mind as if it had been glued there, like an obsession:

I planned to run straight up the steps to ol' Gargan's right and locate Noble Ellair. Locate, and *dislocate*, him.

Around Gargan, beyond the exhausted old man and through the unlocked sheriff's office, I saw that the door leading to the outside was unbolted. It even looked open slightly; ajar. And I remembered that I'd seen no sign of young Terry or the guard who'd been with him back around the time of Crock's death, since then . . .

Crotchety, exasperating, nearing-retirement Irish Gargan had stayed too—and the old S.O.B. would almost certainly try to prevent me from getting to Ellair.

I slowed down and walked up to him nice and easy. "We're both tired, sir," I said. "We may be sick, very sick. I don't want to hurt you. You don't want to hurt anybody." I drew in a breath. "I'm going . . . upstairs. All right?"

Gargan's eyes were trained on mine. He didn't give me any other answer.

"Look," I said, tried to think. "Ellair caused this. All of it. He's a ghoul. Somebody—well, somebody has to make him pay." My muscles tensed as I took the silence for grudging agreement and cut past the man. "Do the crime and you do the time, isn't that the way it goes?"

I thought I saw Gargan nod.

But his head kept going forward, kept going. Then his entire body went along.

Went face down on the floor. No spasm, no involuntary lolling of the head, no nothing except fungus that strained against the back of his proud uniform blouse, seeking an exit from the old fellow's spine and bloodstream.

"The poor peckerhead," I said shortly, aloud. The term, Gargan's, came to my lips without my consciously seeking it or meaning anything by it. I didn't. I didn't mean anything by the "poor" part, either. Except for the mildest conceivable kind of surprise, I'd drained away most of the emotions that made me human, and all the meaning except one.

I meant to wreak awful violence upon Doctor Noble Ellair.

Before climbing the stairs to find him, I jogged back a few paces to glance at the floor where all the seeds of nightmare—the inception of the night seasons—had been so fertilely planted.

All I could see from where I stopped, using the fading beam of my flashlight, were the drunk tank and those beings that were temporarily locked inside.

I saw what appeared in my dimming light to be dozens of mock swollen tongues waving in the air from the partly-consumed and totally transfigured remains of the alcoholic inmates. Then, from farther down the rows of facing cells—all but indis-

357

cernible through the mesh of late night—other tongues leapt up, noiselessly, to communicate with their kind.

There were a few human sounds that reached my ears, then. The kind no one normal likes to hear. Otherwise, silence. I saw no one moving. No one of my kind.

I took Gargan's gun and began stalking up the steps to the second floor. I listened intently, pausing occasionally, almost certain that the shrink and I were the only ones left.

To my amazement there was the murmur of *other* voices—from the sheriff's office, and the door leading to freedom.

I wouldn't be deterred. Inhaling, holding my breath, I forced my exhausted legs to run the rest of the way. It didn't matter who had shown up from the world outside of the jail because it was too late now.

Noble and I were going to have another little chat.

Twelve

1. Moms Don't Lie

On Doctor Ellair's floor, I decided it was too late for much tiptoeing. I was too damned tired for it anyway. If he stuck his long, horse's head out of his office door, I'd just shoot it off.

There'd been no more sounds from the people entering the jail; worse, there'd been no more sounds from the cells. The place might as well have been a morgue. The majority of the men had died without ever knowing what hit them.

The Noble One was—I like to think—a one of a kind.

He went out a long way to *get* our death sentences for us and bring them back personally.

Then he had run away. Our *glorious* physician was the collector and the conveyor of deadly contagion. He'd caused hundreds of men to die a frightened, hysterical, collective death with less personality or individuality than an ant village experiences when a boot stomps on it.

Shaking from exhaustion and bottled-up outrage, I snapped off the flashlight, stood in front of the office, and raised my hand to Ellair's door.

I touched it and it moved slightly. In the darkness I hadn't seen that the door was ajar. As I tapped it lightly with my fingertips, it swung back silently.

I paused in the entrance, my nerves, the dis-ease, tingling. Ellair's battery-operated lamp was lit, but he wasn't in the room; it was quiet as a tomb. Something about the setup of the place seemed eerie, wrong. Pocketing my flash, I tried to figure out what was going on, what was so disturbing about the office. For some reason, I didn't even wonder where Noble Ellair was.

I stepped inside and halted with my arm outthrust to close the door behind me.

An overpowering, cloyingly sweet, odor permeated the room. Beyond the range of light from the desk lamp there were shadows, thick as molasses; the place made me feel claustrophobic, penned-in, like being inside a microwave oven. I walked to Ellair's desk, thinking I might find a note, a clue as to what he was up to this time.

There I stopped, staring at *another* door beyond the desk, in the far wall. It was almost invisible in the darkness and led to a room I didn't even know existed. That door, too, stood open.

Strength-sapping heat enveloped me, much greater than the temperature in the rest of the jail. And it came from Ellair's secret room along with the overpowering scent, the stink of something vile, like garbage—or like dead flesh decaying in the heat.

Nearly all my passion was leeched away by that mixture of suffocating heat and the effluvium wafted toward me by *eau de mort* . . . the odor of death. I utilized every iota of will power in order to make myself pass through that inner door into what was obviously a hothouse or nursery. Claustrophobic fear almost paralyzed me but I *had* to know—to bear witness.

Reluctantly, I shut the door behind me and turned. I was in a long, narrow room dimly illuminated by a power source ol' Noble appeared to have kept as his own little secret. I hesitated just inside the door, my vision sensitive to even that dim light after hours with only the beam of my flashlight. The heavy humidity and the pervasive smell made the yellowish air seem to swirl around me—it felt like it was trying to adhere to me.

I took a step forward and for a moment had the impression I was *descending*, walking *down* into the place, though there was no actual incline. I couldn't get my bearings, saw no evidence of anyone or anything alive—

Except for Noble Ellair's beautiful plants from Central America, in the full panoply of their variety, scattered haphazardly all over the room. The plants he had *recalled*, I saw with anger—the plants he'd gathered up and said he was going to *destroy!*

After a frantic, sweeping glance, I knew I couldn't be sure which of the wild Indian plants had spent themselves and which ones still contained entomogenic fungal spores . . .

"Ah — *there* you are, Stenvall!"

I couldn't tell whether he had been watering them, genuflecting before them, or what. But there he was at the back of the long room, dozens of plants scattered between us — as unperturbed, nonchalant, and uncaring as ever. But there *was* one difference.

Doctor Noble Ellair was naked.

He appeared to materialize where he stood, like an impoverished scarecrow. But Ellair hadn't eaten crow, I knew that. He never would. If you started, as he did, with an assumption that you were right in everything you said or did, it was hard to be humble and impossible to be wrong. Ever.

"You sound as if you were expecting me," I began.

"Well . . . if *anyone,*" he said. He walked toward me with perfect composure, spring-heeled. Everything about the man was pasty, gaunt, dangling. His eyes riveted into me. "Is it — over?"

I managed a nod, no more.

"Isn't this interesting," he said chattily, "and curious?" He came within a couple of yards before stopping to study my face. "That you, Richard, are the sole survivor?"

"Don't call me that!" I might have shot him then

except I'd put Gargan's gun in my pocket. Also, El-lair's ensemble — or rather, lack thereof — had left me nearly stupefied with surprise. He was as much in control of the situation as if he'd donned a tux. *Ordinary rules don't apply,* I reminded myself. "I can't be sure Calderone is dead. I've survived so far, yeah. Then . . . there's *you.*"

"Calderone, the religious zealot? How symbolic!" He looked taller, nude. "The triumvirate — with yours truly as the father figure, you as the son who spoke for me, and Al as the holy ghost. Lovely!" He clapped his hands and gestured for me to follow him. "Come along, Stenvall. There's something I'd like to show you."

Incredible! He began zigzagging between rows of his beautiful, monstrous plants, confident that I'd follow him. I didn't, not immediately. A part of me was curious to know what he wanted to show me, but I didn't trust myself that near him for another beat or two. The main reason I waited, of course, was that I didn't really *want* to negotiate his floral minefield. Finally I did, exercising caution with every step.

Ellair stopped before five exquisite, ornately painted screens, arranged so that they formed a seven-foot high partition. *What now?* I wondered. "Before proceeding, Mr. Stenvall," he said in his slightly high-pitched voice, "I want you to know that I have a sound philosophical basis for every move I've made. I know what I am doing."

I asked him if his guru was Adolf Hitler but he said it was another German, a 19th century professor named Gustav Fechner, the father of experimental psychology. He talked for awhile about the "germinal work" of his idol, who claimed some sort of psychic power existed in both plants and animals. From that, the Noble One told me, he himself had concluded that there were signs of people starting to "slip back in the chain of life," and he wondered if animals and plants mightn't be advancing. There was something about stimulus and sensation, a law of Professor Fechner's that involved the way certain "forms and proportions" created either pleasing reactions and sensations in humans, or the opposite. At first, I didn't fully understand where Ellair was taking all that—not even when he explained that his idol Gustav had written a study about "last things," including the Last Judgment.

I told him I didn't see the connection those tidbits of science history had with his "goodwill gifts," or his fascination with the notion that Mind "slept" in plants and hadn't awakened until people evolved. The naked shrink rubbed his palms together in anticipation of dropping another bomb or two on me.

"Haven't I said all along, Stenvall, that evidence exists for the development of awareness—of intelligence, of will—in the plant kingdom?" he inquired. "Haven't I adequately suggested that the attack of the entomogenic may prove . . . *purposeful?*"

"You have," I admitted. "But—"

"Richard," Ellair said with upraised index finger, "I predicated my theory on the observation that people today are *unconsciously cooperating* with the growing things that are the undeclared enemy." His flushed face almost glowed with the thrill of full disclosure. "Marijuana, or *Cannabis sativa*, derives from the *hemp plant*. It grows"—Noble flung out his arms in his finest imitation of a scarecrow yet—"almost anywhere!" He bobbed his equine head. "It was the first, in a manner of speaking. Correct?"

I saw where he was headed now and I felt stunned. "Cocaine," I said—

"It *grows, too!*" Ellair finished for me, joyfully. "It derives from the coca *leaf*, does it not? Isn't it all marvelous—the clear purpose, the obvious intent of plant life—when you simply do that which virtually *no man among us* is *doing* any longer, and . . . *think?* Merely *reason* it through?" He danced around a bit, his expression excited. "Now, Richard—we hasten our own doom with *crack*—and with the actual proposition on the part of legislators and others that we *legalize* illegal drugs! That we throw the borders open to our *worst enemy of all*, the *only* enemy to whom we shall lose and never again have *any* chance of ousting!"

I searched for an argument that would stand against his logic and found only one.

The flashlight was in my left hip pocket. The other held my one answer to Noble Ellair. But while it was the oldest argument against reason and against reasoning that I knew of, it had never really provided a very good answer. Just a stall. It was then I decided that whatever I did to punish this horrible excuse for a human being on behalf of all those who'd died in lockup, I wouldn't merely shoot him. I would keep the gun in my pocket. I might have been altered into a gunslinger with the rest, but I wouldn't die with a cliché or a failure drawn and gripped in my own hand.

Such men as Ellair could no longer be just individually expunged, collectively stalled. Each and every one of their kind had to be stopped because we seized the reins in more reasonable and aware ways that kowtowed to no god except the one with a capital G. I figured it was probably okay to deal with them one at a time, for now. But human survival depended on coming up with better ideas, new ones that rejected *any* collective concept to send humankind back into the darkness. It'd taken us at least one-hundred thousand years to get where we were and all *we'd* had to replace was the dinosaur.

"Do you know, Stenvall, what a *fluke* is?"

"Us," I snapped — "if scientists are the ones who are right!"

He smiled coolly. "I refer to *Dicrocoelium dendriticum*. A member of the *trematodes* family of parasites. Its unwilling but nonetheless cooperative host is the ordinary ant."

I nodded, showing I was listening, but started wondering what Ellair had concealed behind the

366

fancy screens.

"It is now, sir, that a *third* party — the brain worm — enters the picture, by exercising a highly interesting form of *mind control*." He saw my brows rise, and so did his index finger. It was like taking Biology 101 with a teacher who'd forgotten to get dressed that day. "Inside the ant's little belly, *Dicrocoelium* — the fluke — encysts a larvae, rather like tadpoles, called *cercaria*."

"Why didn't you just go into one of those sciences," I interrupted, "instead of becoming a shrink?"

His brows rose then but he hesitated, as if deciding whether this was the moment for candor. "I preferred," he replied at last, "to be the brain *behind* the brain worm." I met his gaze while the cold truth of his answer sank in.

"The ant was never the target, Stenvall. Merely a stepping-stone." He tilted his head forward. "Toward — the sheep."

"What sheep?" I demanded.

Ellair grinned. "The *cercaria*, changing their *own cells* to become thin, reedlike, imprison the ant from within and forces the tiny thing to locate the highest stalk of grass within the ant's, *umm*, walking distance. In complete subjugation, the ant then climbs *all* the way to the pinnacle of the grass stalk" — Ellair's grin widened, displayed his delight — "where it waits to be *eaten!* Richard, it even attaches itself to the stalk by its mandibles! Isn't *that* a comprehensive

367

example of mind-control?"

I wiped at the perspiration on my forehead with my sleeve. "If you call me by my first name again," I said, "I'll kill you."

"Come, you haven't heard the *climax* of my story!" Ellair clapped his palms together in sheer, happy exuberance. "Now, the unsuspecting woolly sheep comes along, *devours* the ant—and the so-called 'brain worm' *also* becomes a victim!" He laughed aloud. "Clever *Dicrocoelium* has achieved residence within the sheep and the fluke is, at long last, ready to dine!"

The madman's punchline unnerved me so much that I closed my hand on the ornamental screen to steady myself. It began toppling away at the same second Noble Ellair added, "Consider how wonderfully the fluke's range of possibilities has *increased,* now that its new home is within the much larger and juicier sheep!"

I gaped at what he had wanted me to see, behind the screen, and heard Ellair again—in my mind— saying: *I preferred to be the brain behind the brain worm.*

Rangy Clyde Leighton, the macho man who had been a quarterback once—another guy who rather enjoyed hitting on people but had been friendly enough with me—was the shrink's surprise. Standing, dead, he was seemingly *frozen* in *mid-stride.*

"We ignored too long the marvels of organization within the complex, multicelled things that grow— Mr. Stenvall." Ellair droned on, hypnotic as a brain worm. "Many of their components are capable of *stretching* themselves to one-hundred thousand times their own breadth—or more. They're called 'cable cells' and they often achieve sensory linkups within an animal."

"Shut up," I said.

"Think of *Mimosa pudica,* how it folds in on itself at the slightest touch—brightly, defensively. Of the Venus fly-trap and how explosively it can move to capture a *fly* for its supper."

I tuned him out.

Leighton had gaping holes in him from head to toe, scratch marks everywhere as if he'd clawed at himself repeatedly. Ironically, I guess, one elbow was cocked while the other arm was upraised, the hand open. One leg was slightly bent at the knee. I stared at this eyeless, swiss-cheese corpse and was reminded of wooly mammoths, frozen in the process of digestion forever.

Ellair saw me looking at Leighton. I suppose I reminded him of a guy in a museum looking at a statue. But he also must have realized I was ready to blow. "Among many scientists," he said softly, "there's been discussion of the possibility that entomogenic fungi may have the capacity for possessing the mind of any other creature. Just as the fluke possesses the ant."

"Leighton wasn't a very good person but he was a human being," I said tersely, under my breath. I looked away from Clyde. "Cover him up."

369

"Something happened," Ellair murmured, "right before I began handing out the goodwill gifts. An experimental bomb, possibly a new chemical gas, must have modified the entomogenic—enabled it— them, in reality—to expand their horizons."

"Put the *screen up*," I told him. Sweat came off me in buckets.

"Note the pattern, Mr. Stenvall," he went on. "Originally, the fungus merely killed. Then they appear to have reproduced through, *umm*, substantive ripenings from the men's dying bodies." His eyes glittered in the pink plane of his unnaturally bug-like skull. "And now they can command the mind and nervous system of man, it seems, the way that *Dicrocoelium dendriticum* possesses the ant. They're *all* parasites, but how in God's name—"

"God's name?" The reference to divinity was jarringly wrong from this looney-tunes, this opportunistic nutcase. "Put the fucking screen back!"

"Stenvall, I'm telling you the truth." His apparent sincerity brought my gaze from Clyde Leighton's remains to the scarecrow's face. "The day you were arrested, I received phone calls from a couple of scientists I know—good men—who called to inform me that there were unnatural phenomena being recorded all over the world. The gist of it was that temperatures were expected to soar, go through the ceiling—just as they did." He went on speaking, in terms that made superficial sense, following any move toward confession of his own guilt with a buck-passing connection that drew in anyone helpful to his goals from Costa Rica, to internationally-known meteorologists, to the Almighty. "I had certain . . . expectations . . . once I realized my plants were infected, *yes*—but the amazing evolutionary jump of this fungus in a matter of hours was *not* of my doing."

"Fuck you, then," I snapped, *"I'll* replace the screen!"

And I did. But, I hadn't stopped listening, trying to sort out the truth. Too many unexplained things had happened to blame only Ellair and his plants. "Are you saying that the process which you thought the fungi would follow *changed?* Because of a leak or explosion somewhere that forced temperatures to rise more than anybody expected?"

"Precisely!" he nodded eagerly. "Countless things—not just the entomogenic—were modified in ways completely beyond my control. It's only that I was understandably *willing—*"

I looked at him sharply when his voice trailed off. "Willing to try to *take advantage* of the situation!" I accused him. "So then you decided to . . . to do *what?* Intentionally *breed* the goddamn fungus, train it to force people to do what *you* want—starting right here?" I gestured wildly at the fancy screen. "What was Leighton, then—an experiment to see if the shit can make a dead man *move?*"

He regarded me with false indignation. Then he blinked his eyes and turned, waltzing across the

371

nursery away from me. "Of course I was intrigued by those unusual opportunities, Stenvall. Wouldn't you be?"

"I get it," I said, heading after him. "Now that you have a record of what the entomogenic can do—thanks to *me*—you can threaten the hell out of people!"

He danced farther from me, so gracefully, so cleverly, that he didn't appear to be running away at all. He needed, however, to be doing just that! "I confess it crossed my mind to wonder if the *hyphae* tendrils which choose the perfect nerve ganglia for maximum penetration could be . . . coaxed . . . to—to *animate* a victim. It's intellectually challenging, stimulating." He stopped abruptly and pivoted to face me. I was shocked to see a pink flush all the way from his receding hairline to his bony shoulders. It was the only color on his otherwise dead-white person. His skinny arms opened wide in seeming outrage and defensiveness. "You see me as a sociopath or an egomaniac, don't you? Obsessed by a desire for the plant kingdom to supersede our own?"

I'd halted an arm's length from him. At last, I saw, he was sweating. Fearful of me, maybe. "Aren't you?" I asked simply.

"No, I am not!" His tiny nostrils flared, his eyes shone with intelligence but no humanity. "I don't mind in the least if our kind is replaced by a superior species. But my passions, Richard"—he lofted one brow, mockingly—*"Mister* Stenvall—are those of any inquiring and educated person in this day and age."

"Okay." I grabbed a quick breath, stifled by the smell. "If you don't really want to conquer the world, then you must want to *own* it!"

He beamed at me. For a second I thought he was going to embrace me. "Ultimately, I'm not mad at all. I am—a businessman. I don't *wish* to destroy, I only—"

"Want to make money," I finished his sentence. And Ellair nodded. "Did you see a way for making big bucks in this from the very start?" The nod continued and the smirk returned, *mano a mano.* "But—*how?*"

"I shall whisper two words to you," Ellair answered, taking two steps forward. Nearer to me, he looked content; almost wise. "Pest control," he said conspiratorially.

"Pest control?" The flushed face inches away was excited. I was incredulous.

"Specifically, agricultural pest control, Stenvall." His deepest secret, confidingly conveyed, had stopped me cold—just as he'd known it would. "Remember that I selected a public institution as the site for my work. I behaved with perfect rectitude. As test subjects, I chose the only population without merit, without value. I conducted my experiments responsibly, never wantonly."

"We didn't *volunteer,* damn you!" I yelled at him,

373

enraged.

"Philosophically, the point could be disputed," he said archly. But, he added quickly, "Let that go, all right? My point is that the potential good of the work I've done — not instigated by *me* but by scientists elsewhere — far outweighs the risks and the losses." He lay his thin arms over his narrow, naked chest, reminding me of a poison label on a bottle. "I'm well underway toward the development of a spray that will perform as the first, foolproof biological control of agricultural pests. Richard, it will mean immensely greater food production for us, for the starving millions around the globe."

He'd used my Christian name again. "For *you*, you mean," I shouted. "Your spray will bring you *billions!*" Livid with rage, I brought my arm back to belt the self-serving son of a bitch —

And the screen that primarily concealed Clyde Leighton's towering, stationary body slipped and fell. I didn't turn my head to look but Ellair turned his, his expression a compound of raw guilt and almost superstitious terror.

Which was when I hit him harder than I'd ever struck a man before. The punch's shock ran up my arm to the elbow, then up farther, numbing the shit out of my shoulder.

Ellair went down as though he'd been clubbed.

Down amid his potted plants.

Two or three were smashed by his falling body. Instantly frightened into making a combination of grunts and moans, he threw out a panicky arm and shattered two more goodwill gifts in his anxiety to get to his feet.

The spores came spraying out as if a switch had been thrown. I was shocked by the suddenness of it, terrified by the rain of them.

But I was amazed and awed by the way the torrent of flying fungi had centered their attack on Ellair—amazed, awed, and grateful. Some of the spores were penetrating the accessible apertures of the shrink's body before he could even get to his knees. They didn't come anywhere near me. They went after that which seemed to have attacked them . . .

Swearing I wouldn't stop for anything, I whirled to dash for the exit, hearing in memory the supernatural fear of another man—*They're comin' OUT, they're comin' for you!*—as I darted between the remaining plants.

I did, of course, stop. Look back. But not principally to see Noble Ellair.

As superstitious as the next man, I glanced behind me to try and determine if the screen that had concealed the dead Clyde Leighton had fallen away, or if it had been *pushed* . . . if Leighton had been reanimated.

I saw instead—directly on a line from Clyde's exposed form—Doctor Ellair. Afoot, arms outflung before him, he was staggering after me. I'd known that germination was not immediate, of course, but I'd believed Ellair couldn't or wouldn't rise and follow, not that fast anyway.

Then I saw that the entomogenic was actually working on his skinny anatomy as quickly and hungrily as it had on any of the men — maybe *more quickly* — and realized two more facts with such joy that my relief and happiness were for a moment almost complete: It would take time for the fungi to eat him to death from the inside out, and he'd know better than any of the rest of us had known just what was happening to him.

Wondering if the entomogenic was still evolving and, if so, what new type of monstrosity it would make of Ellair, I began walking briskly toward the door.

After a step or two, I heard stumbling, thrashing sounds to the rear. My heart leaped into my mouth. Despite my own commonsense, in spite of everything Noble had told me about logic, I couldn't shake the haunting impression that the moans and noises of someone lurching in my wake were not those of Ellair alone. At that instant my imagination all too vividly depicted a possible next step in the entomogenic evolution. While the infected shrink was doing his best to dog *my* tracks, maybe something else was stalking *his* . . .

As I wrenched the hothouse door open I realized that Ellair might not be pursuing me at all — but rather trying to enter his office while there was *still time!* It would be precisely *like* that bastard to have an *antidote* hidden somewhere!

When I sensed his presence directly behind me, I

accepted it as absolute fact that I would not give him a chance to live—a chance that he had not given to more decent people.

"Why . . . *you?*" he croaked.

I knew what he meant. He meant, really, why *not* me? Why had *I* been spared—so far.

I didn't turn. "I don't know, Noble," I said. I felt his warm breath on me. "Maybe I was just the logical hero, all right?" I shrugged. "Maybe the answer is simply—*why not?*"

He put his hand on my shoulder. It felt hot and horribly clammy. Glancing down, I noticed that one of his feet was twisted at the ankle. "You haven't . . . won," he managed. I felt cooler air stirring in his office, through the open door. "No one . . . *wins.*" I edged forward, afraid again. But he was still holding on to my shoulder, dragging himself after me. His horse's whinny echoed in my ears. "I will survive. My *work*, my *name* . . . will survive *you.*"

"Wrong!" I was almost out of hell now. "Because I won't mention you when I tell what happened."

"You won't have to!" he said in a rush. Suddenly, he wrapped his long, thin arms around me from behind, then squeezed. I couldn't tear free for a moment, got panicky. Fistulas were forming in his pores already. I heard popping sounds. The skin on his awful arms was watermelon pink. I glanced over my shoulder and saw his face rippling, saw that his bulging eyes were aswarm with the entomogenic. He laughed, shoved his mouth close to me, and I

realized why he was having so much trouble with his speech. Fungi were spewing up from within and forcing his teeth out of their sockets. "Many inmates," he gasped, his gums seeping blood, "have *left . . . already!*"

I swung my elbow back into him with all my might, so swiftly I couldn't tell if it was voluntary or just automatic. I had the satisfaction of hearing Ellair's startled gasp of pain before I was out of his clutches, leaping the rest of the way through the doorway, and slamming the door shut. I hoped it might be thick enough to keep me from hearing the Noble One's last words.

It wasn't. First, there was laughter that was part snort, part giggle. A residue of virulent miasma from the crushed plants sifted through, around the doorframe. "The inmates who left," he rasped, gasping now but willing himself to give me all the bad news in spite of his pain—"they took their gifts . . . *home* with them, *Richard*. They took them . . . *home!*"

"Damn you to hell!" I yelled, and started shoving his desk across the carpeted office toward the door. I had to move it in ferocious spurts and I could never have done it, normally; not without Ellair's added motivation. When I had it positioned so that it barred the door, I knew the monster wouldn't have enough strength left to budge it no matter what.

Then he began *pounding* on the door, heavily, still choking and giggling, and I wasn't sure I'd done enough. I had the impression of having aroused something that had been asleep for all time on the sinside of a forbidden tomb. My emotions unleashed, I cast frantic glances around the office, looking for a weapon if the monster succeeded in pushing the desk aside and breaking through. Finding nothing, I climbed up and sat on the desk. I figured I'd stay there forever if it took that long to be sure the shrink wasn't going to get out.

I was thinking of pulling Gargan's gun out of my pocket when suddenly he stopped battering on the door. Just like *that,* he stopped.

I swear that there was a distinct definite *order*—a sequence—to what I heard next. First, the sound of something segmented—about the size of a man—slithering down the door, into silence. *Then* a footstep . . . a shuffling, scuffing noise . . . and *another* footstep.

"Ellair?" I whispered.

Next came the cloying, deceptive, elusive sweetness of the plants, as if they were uncoiling their hidden, deadly tentacles in readiness to feed—and I had the strong impression of somebody or something *near* the door. Just on the other side. *Listening.*

I was out in the hallway before another moment passed, slamming the office door shut behind me, wobbly as hell but wrestling my flashlight from my hip pocket and trying to catch up with the beam it cast ahead of me. One more second and I was hurrying toward the stairs leading back to the floor of mass extinction, imagining whispers of bleak intent on the pungent air as I took the first step.

The feeling inside of me was that of being hounded by devils, and in my mind was the belief that I would always be.

2. Perdition Call

It's supposedly easier going down a flight of steps than up them. But that's not true when your legs feel as if somebody turned the bones inside them to liquid and then siphoned it off. Your only focus is on trying to keep your body and legs straight and then you *lower* yourself, one step at a time, pawing cautiously with first one foot then another. Your body stiffens into unbendable rods thereby making it far more likely that you *will* slip.

But I was all right while I was descending, partly because I was too frightened of being followed by "something" to stiffen up and also so relieved that there wasn't the slightest sound of pursuit from above and behind me that I sort of relaxed.

That's when they always get you . . . when you least expect it.

I'm not sure if I actually *heard* the explosion or not. I know that sounds ridiculous but I can't help it. I know that the whole, complex apparatus you and I call our "systems"—the entire range of hearing, seeing, smelling, even the sense of *touch* if I can include the first few layers of skin up and down my body and not merely the skin on my fingers — *seemed* to hear something.

But my system felt it, that's what I'm laboring to say. It reacted *totally*, inside my guts and in my mind, as well as what I heard and what I *saw*.

By then, though, I was falling. One moment I was a few steps from the bottom, then there was a sound like a sonic boom. Next, a nearly *blinding* flash of the *purest white light* I ever saw. An *awesome* flareup — the way I'd imagine a nuclear blast would look.

Illumination, but not the light of any truth anybody would want to learn. Today I think of it as a reality bomb and believe my dis-ease was "cured" forever when that unexplainable nova lit up the jail's interior. And I could cry for a long time if I let myself.

Something happened, Ellair had said, *before I handed out my gifts.* Something that instantly speeded up the entomogenic's evolution. "Unnatural phenomena," he claimed; recorded all over the world. Phenomena — modifications of nature — beyond the control of the brain behind the brain worm. But not, I realized, beyond his ability to adapt himself in order to take *advantage* of the situation and turn a fast dollar! I'd resented how Ellair "didn't mind" if humanity was replaced by a different species — even though he'd demonstrated one more time, for all of us, that the one creature on earth more adaptable than man was the cockroach!

Plants, at least, were *pretty*.

Falling the rest of the way downstairs, I struck the side of my head on the wall. I wasn't sure whether I was more dazed by the blow or the realization that my town, at least, had been attacked — more than once — by some powerful, "other-worldly" force. I had been right, back at Beaumont Estates. Swamped by the oddest variety of the dis-ease I'd ever experienced, I had written: "Something's growing out there, and it's EVIL." Something like that.

I told you I could've cried when I saw that my dis-ease was gone because it provided an early-on signal that an opportunity was coming that would enable me to see how best to fit myself into the rest of the world without completely surrendering my own individuality. I'd called the events of the past days, culminating with the flash of brilliant light, a "reality bomb" because, as I lay on the floor just feet from the guard post, I saw that the *real* world was in the process of being blasted to hell. Altered, modified, into something that swallowed up individuality because it was collectively devouring us, *en masse*. Maybe it hadn't won yet, but it had such a good start even a cockroach wouldn't want any part of the planet when it was done. Because it was in the process of *changing* the *nature of reality itself* . . .

Where the hell is ol' Gargan's body? I wondered, turning my head painfully —

And seeing the feet of somebody *walking* toward

me—*quickly!*

For a second, my vision blurred. I fought against it desperately, tried to hurl my body up into a seated position.

Then the voice *called* me—called my *name*, from above—and I reached out with both my hands to grapple with the ankles.

"Richie?!" the voice said disapprovingly, first stepping back, then stooping over me. "Are you all right?"

As my sight cleared I was able to peer up at the silk-clad legs of my wife and then, gradually, see her wonderful face, bending over me with concern. "*Ronnie . . . ?*" I asked. "What are you *doing* here?" She held my bruised head, kissed me, checked my scalp for bleeding, began helping me up. All the while I hoped—*prayed*—this part of reality had remained the same, that *she* was real.

"Rich, it's morning." An American wife, she laughed at my expression of consternation. Behind her—was that *the kids, too?* (*Everythings supposed to be new in spring,* young Bett had promised.) Now Ronnie was pale . . . what had she seen? How much of it? "You asked me to pick you up in the morning. The door was open." Her puzzlement plus a sudden intuition that something was wrong showed in her eyes. "Richie, what is it? Where are the guards?"

My head cleared fast. Ron's question meant she hadn't wandered into the cell area, hadn't seen—the horror. But where *was* Gargan? Markie edged toward me (*The robin mustn't have a calendar*—or perhaps he needed a *new* one now, son) in that shy fashion little boys exhibit, very wisely, about strange places. He would never be in a stranger one.

Early morning sunlight was outlining the small forms of my kids. I wondered, with great hope if that white flash could have been just the rays of the rising sun seen through the windows in the sheriff's office . . . if it might have been that I'd dwelt in the dark so long, merely those first rays of sun had looked to me like a world going nova. I dropped to my knees for a moment to hug the children, to rumple their hair—even if Bett hated it—and tried to formulate an answer to my wife's questions.

Her "what is it?" was the toughest question anybody'd put to me. It's taken me this long, as you can tell, to attempt an answer.

"I don't know where the guards are," I said honestly enough, straightening. Staring hard into Ronnie's eyes I strove with all my might to project into her mind a realization that she would be very, very smart not to pursue the matter. I'd pieced it together that my family must have come downtown in Rudy Loomis' truck, nice and early, expecting there to be miles of red tape involved with my release. Ron had expected uniforms, boredom-inspired rudeness, a chastened husband brought to her from a locked cell by some unfeeling ape of a man—and she'd found no one in the usually busy office. She had seen no faces, only a husband falling down half a flight of steps, and—scariest of all—total silence. More specifically, an absence of sound that was starting to get to me, too.

"C'mon," I said to my threesome, the parts of Rich Stenvall that had been missing. "Let's get out of here."

I had slipped an arm around each of the kids, but Ronnie was too surprised, too disturbed by the incongruity, to budge. "Don't you have to sign something, check out?" she inquired. She was in my path, and the way I had verbalized my desires, my dreams, had filled me with the knowledge that I *could* leave now. Hugging the kids close, I walked straight toward Ron so that it obliged her to move, gave her the choice of either continuing to head in the direction I'd chosen—the sheriff's office and the open door—or just stay there. In a larger sense, my choice of direction amounted to *any-where-in-the-world*, and Ronnie suddenly saw that.

But she added, anyway, "What about your watch and your other things?" as she tagged along.

I almost said, "Fuck 'em," but remembered the kids' presence in time—

At the *same* time I saw from the corner of my eye the cell area—first the drunk tank, then the long line of cells—and a funny thing happened.

My feet began to slow their pace without my brain telling them to do it.

My head, which I had instructed to continue facing forward, was swiveling on my neck, and my eyes, which I'd definitely wanted to see nothing but freedom — the outside world and then home — were photographing facts that were even more shocking than anything else they'd pictured and filed forever in my memory.

The drunk tank gate and the doors of every cell in lockup — *all of them were wide open.*

"Isn't that strange?" Ronnie said softly from in front of me. The kids were looking down there, too, calm and incurious because they did not know what their mother and I had expected.

Ronnie'd thought there would be a great many men locked in cells.

I'd expected to have a final, terrible glimpse of the bodies of hundreds of slaughtered inmates — I'd tried to speed my family past the entrance to the cell area so Ron and the kids wouldn't see them — but there wasn't a single corpse left. Not a body in sight, dead or alive. Not a stain left by the pint-after-pint of blood spilled in that hellhole, and no evidence that the overpoweringly aromatic foreign plants that had taken so many lives had ever been present. It was a spic-and-span lockup. Nearly . . . inviting.

What remained was the unbearable heat and humidity that had enabled the entomogenic to germinate and attack. So I told Ronnie, "Yes, it's strange," then posed a question for her before she could ask about the inmates' absences.

I asked it because I'd broken out in a *new* sweat

386

when I stopped to have my last look, and because I had just realized that I had *not* been miserably hot at the time when my family arrived.

"No, it's not so bad out this morning," Ronnie answered me as her eyes searched mine. I think the first light of comprehension—not of the dying, or Ellair, or the plants, but that of matters gone badly amiss—came into her intelligent eyes then. "I thought it was a bit cooler when I got up. And then, now that you remind me, it was as if the temperature really broke *just after we stepped inside the building!*" She glanced down at the children, concerned. Her expression asked again, *What's wrong?* Aloud, she said simply, to them, "I think it's time we all went home."

"Right!" I said heartily. "I agree!" Ol' Daddy Ho-Ho was back again. "Why don't you guys go ahead, all right?" A sense of what I planned to do then brought the entire, incredible range of horror rushing back. I'd thought I had to go back in there—find out where everybody went—and the threat of the unknown, astoundingly, still had the power to spook the shit out of me. "I'll be right out." I gave Ron a little push, then caught her arm, and her attention: "Get the truck going, then slide over on the passenger seat. Okay?" And she nodded.

I knew it was possible we might want to race away from there like the bats of hell were after us, and my wife wasn't as familiar with the company truck and its idiosyncrasies as I was.

Watching Ronnie, Markie, and Bett walk through that deserted sheriff's office, open the door, and, after brief finger-waggling and uncertain smiles, leave the jail without me was the most truly courageous act I ever performed. It took even more courage than it did when I turned around in that numbing silence and went back into perdition.

3. The Dead Are So Good

The only thing that didn't feel uncomfortably different to me when I headed back into the cell area was the smothering heat. Inside of a few short nights, I'd become accustomed to thinking of the groans and screams, the anguished, shouted prayers, as the norm. Even before the likelihood of horrifying death had occurred to all the men, lockup was always noisy, chaotic. Actually, I doubt there'd ever been a time when there was no moaning or screaming, no desperate and public prayers.

Now I passed between the rows of facing cells in a vacuum of quietude so complete that the atmosphere seemed churchlike. Or funereal. Cell doors open wide were like waiting entrances to private pews. But these mourners were the ghosts themselves, the suddenly unseen objects inside the caskets that had yet to arrive for the services.

I had sufficient light to see. This ordinary daylight enabled me to peer into the cells I passed—or

388

maybe a part of the power had been restored, I couldn't judge. It certainly wasn't bright, but that was appropriate, considering the hundreds who'd perished in such agony. The hand gun I'd kept in my other hip pocket that originally belonged to the dead and missing Gargan had been lost when I fell. But that was all right. It would've proved worthless against phantoms and memories.

An especially bothersome feature of my little stroll toward the other end of the floor was a sight I'd already observed. Up close, it seemed more disturbing: the inmate cells probably hadn't been that clean in decades. Constant turnover and occupancy made it nearly impossible to do anything much to individual cells; we inmates ourselves were responsible for mopping up our messes, and some of the commodes were never, truly, repaired. Lockup also stank; I think I mentioned that.

This early morning in June, it was as if a most fastidious crew had worked around the clock to make everything shipshape.

After what I had been through, I wasn't much of a judge of time and its passage, but I'd have sworn I'd spent two hours or less in Noble Ellair's second floor office and hothouse. But only a small part of the question had to do with how the inmate cells had been cleaned up so rapidly. Two more parts might well be more important:

Why? And—

Who? All the imprisoned men were dead or dying

so far as I'd been able to judge, the on-duty guards along with them, probably. So who or what had gone energetically to work—and with what sort of magical equipment?—to clean each and every cell as if a five-star general was going to do a white-glove inspection?

And what did they do with the *bodies?* Some, maybe, were taken to the infirmary—guys like Blackledge who died early—but what of the rest?

While I was coming into range of the larger cell where, among others, Andre, Lester, and Crock had ended their lives, my mind returned to *Why?* It wasn't hard to devise some likely answers. The best, obviously, was that somebody in authority sought a coverup. The trouble with that was mainly that Ellair had been responsible for his potted plants. Reasoning it through while I kept on the move, it also seemed to me that anyone who had wanted the whole nightmare to appear like nothing but a wild dream would've needed *help, manpower.* So where was he, where were they? I was, so far as I could judge then, the only living thing on the floor.

And I thought that was the case right up to the moment when I spotted *another* door—unlocked, standing wide—several yards ahead of me across the corridor. A door to the one cell I had not imagined would be unlocked again except as a vital part of the official inquiry I fully intended to start, if I ever succeeded in escaping from the building alive.

I stopped walking. At the point when I began seriously doubting that I *was* the only living thing in that high, long, eerily silent room, the arms of panic looked to me like they were offering me the warmest and most welcoming hug a man ever got. I came within an ace of total panic. I imagined I had embarked, literally, on a death march. That I heard muffled drums beating their steady, stately cadence. That poor, ghastly Clyde Leighton stood inside that cell, eyelids up, both arms raised above his head. And that a ripply-faced Doctor Ellair, full of oozing holes, would step coolly from the recesses of the open Deadlock cell to preach an insanely sanctimonious eulogy, in my honor.

Even a moldering Crock-turned-shambling-zombie could not have scared me more than discovering that Deadlock was both open and that its massive door *faced* me, barred me from looking inside—unless I wished to step all the way around it . . .

Very possibly the heavy door did not *really* move, just faintly, as I stared at it. Very possibly.

I don't know why I didn't turn around and go home, right then, when I realized the door to Deadlock was open. Any explanation I gave you would be bullshit.

Instead, once I got it through my head that neither God, nor my conscience, nor any other authority figures, experts, wives, or kids were going to arrive to give me a sign, a clue—hell, a *direct order!*—I just walked nonchalantly and swiftly past the damned door, and stopped. A few feet from the opening. To look inside.

Couldn't see a thing. For two or three seconds, I might as well have been looking into my own closet back home, searching for a new light bulb to replace one that had burned out.

It got different, then. Fast.

Movement — very slight, little more than a twitch — was what enabled my vision to adjust. What narrowed my eyes' focus, let me see through the murky shadows just inside Deadlock, helped my sight penetrate them in order to see at the rear of the cell the *greater* shadows, bulked and hunched and pressed to walls and ceiling.

It was green. Green and verdant. Redness seeped through it in a veining process. Although it did not have any clearcut conformation yet, I made out a surprising number of buds sprinkled throughout the body's mass. They possessed none of the beauty that I associated with most budding plants, probably because their characteristics differed from bud to bud. And because all of them lacked the vivid colors of normal house plants. These buds were, with few exceptions, pale, even pasty — a sort of off-white, or a variety of deep browns verging on black.

The shrink had kept a hothouse or nursery, as I understood the terms. A greenhouse, though kept very hot and built to nurture fragile, exotic plants, was primarily constructed of glass. But I remember that the phenomenon known as "the greenhouse effect" was also considered a misnomer; and I thought

392

about that recent threat of doomsday while I stood at the entrance to Deadlock, felt the reradiation of husbanded sunlight, felt the collective temperatures of many men who no longer lived and yet were not for all times, in all ways, deceased. I also thought of how Doc had said we were making matters worse with our fear. "Imagine the power of thought when it's shaped from the emotions and recollections of men who are already filled with negativity or evil," he'd said. "What kind of a thing could be created because of Ellair's gifts!"

The green mass trembled, shook. Small winged things that could have been insects, fruit flies maybe, rose languidly, from the mass. At roughly the midpoint of the evolving form, a spasm like that of a drawn breath led to more motion near the cell floor, evoked a sound quite like wind astir in branches — or a sigh. The shaking grew agitated, became a violent quaking. Wet and filmy deposits, so overpoweringly sweet to smell that I felt faint, dripped beneath the thing. The drab buds lolled, rolled as if turning to me. And though I believe I caught a glimpse of fine-drawn, miniature lashes and felt strongly that *I* was *seen* — stonily regarded by entities that recognized and yet found *me* very different — I saw no eyes, and I sensed no soul.

But I heard — in my head, not with my ears — a whispering of my name. Distorted, yes, but my name. *"Witchid,"* it called to the cells in my brain, forlornly — as though from a distant system of stars unknown and untracked by humankind. *"Wit-chid . . ."*

It would have taken me several tremendous shoves to accomplish it under ordinary circumstances, but I used both arms and all the terrified strength in my body to slam and lock the Deadlock door in a single, hysterical swing.

I ran. Falling, getting up, looking behind me. I bounced off open cell doors, registered no pain whatever as the bruises were born, ran, caromed off something jutting from the guard post, ripped a sleeve and both the knee of my pants and the right knee of my body, didn't notice. I caught the tail of my shirt on something protruding from the Sheriff's desk and the psychic pain was so dreadful I shrieked at the skies I longed to see outside. I saw that the door to the outside—*the door to the outside!*—remained open, and it was a good thing, because I *was* going to *get out of There* if I left a foot or an arm behind.

I ran five or six steps toward the company truck, identified *Ronnie!* and *Bett!* and *MARKIE!* inside of it, remembered Not To Frighten the Children. I went on running—slower, maybe—across the beautiful sidewalk awash in what appeared to be common (*garden variety?*) sunlight—and Ronnie, *my RONNIE*, had the door open on the driver's side as I had requested it!

"Richie . . . ?"

"Later." Decades, *centuries* later! I knew they were

394

staring at me, but I'd *been* stared at, buddy, I'd *been STARED AT!* I was all thumbs (*green thumbs?*) for a moment, mentally borne back in time to when I had driven trucks and cars without automatic transmissions. "Got to *tell* people," I said through my teeth to nobody in particular, "got to tell *everyone*." Markie—behind the seat—put out a little hand to touch me and I *flinched*, I might even have whimpered something at him.

Then I knew how to drive again, laughed aloud as if I had just stumbled on the special code for eternal life. Triumphal, a Noble Prize-winning *genius*, I slipped the whatchamacallit on the whatever into *D!*

Then, I don't know why, I tilted back my head and looked toward the silent, all but lifeless county jail. Toward the second floor. Toward an office window on that floor.

He was in the window. I don't know how. I don't know who. Inside my mind, I gave him the finger and mashed the accelerator to the floor.

"Richie," Ron said, next to me. *"Honey . . ."*

I didn't answer, merely shook my head. She was going to either ask me more than I could cope with or tell me to watch my speed.

What the hell was a cop going to do to the most sober man in town, give him a *ticket?*

We rode in fast silence for a long time and I began trying to formulate my thoughts, manipulate them into words, tried also to censor myself in advance. For the children. Images kept leaping in front of my eyes—not exactly that, since I knew I'd never, ever do anything again that would place my wife, my kids, in jeopardy—and they kept making me have to start over, mentally. I didn't know where to start, even—not then, not when I was going home. And I certainly didn't see any way that I could make the nightmare understandable to Ronnie without scaring the shit out of the children.

Eventually, all three members of my family gave up asking me questions. They settled for staring— "watching me," that's more accurate—up until I saw our turn half a block ahead. The turn into Beaumont Estates, the final part of the journey home.

"Rudy has today off," my wife informed me. That was all she said, then, except for the rest of it.

I was looking right into her eyes when she completed the message Rudy'd asked her to pass along.

"You're on call."

"Okay," I told her, and reached out to give her a kiss. "Okay!"

I cannot rest, I cannot rest . . .
The dead are all so good!

—Dorothy Parker
"The White Lady"

Acknowledgments

This was originally intended as a parody of the early Stephen King. But as I realized the material was fascinating, it turned serious on me, then grew into a novella. *Night Cry* published one version of it as a year-long serial; before the last installment ran, it was nominated for a World Fantasy Award. That final issue of *Night Cry* (exquisitely edited by Alan Rodgers) was hard to find; many readers never learned how the story ended. For over a year I gave away copies of the Fall '87 issue from my hoarded cache, imagined it was also the end of *The Night Seasons*, and counted myself fortunate. There are few markets for novellas; mine had enjoyed its life. But gifted people such as F. Paul Wilson and Bruce Boston had recommended the yarn for a Science Fiction Writers of America nomination and others wanted to know more about poor Rich Stenvall, his fellow "visitors" to the drunk tank, and the villainous Doctor Noble Ellair.

Several people in the industry, including Jeanne Cavelos and those I cited in the dedication fueled my enthusiasm to flesh out the story. I also wish to acknowledge, as research sources, Patricia Hagan of the Indianapolis *Star*, Lewis Spence's *Encyclopedia of Occultism*, Benjamin Walker's *Man and the Beasts Within*, Colin Wilson's *Lord of the Underworld*, *Science Digest*, *The New American Desk Encyclopedia*, and those people whose personal experiences inside penal institutions played a subtle but integral part in this and their own *Night Seasons*. For those with Rich's or Doc's problems, I recommend reading the anonymous *Alcoholics Anonymous* reprinted by their World Services, Inc., in 1976.